For Jane

SWEET POISON

It is August 1935 and the Duke of Mersham is hosting one of his influential parties, bringing together public figures interested in improving Anglo-German relations. One of his guests is General Sir Alistair Craig VC, who swallows poison in the duke's excellent port and dies just as latecomers Lord Edward Corinth and journalist Verity Browne arrive on the scene. The unlikely pair—the younger son of a duke and a journalist committed to the Communist Party—find common ground as they seek the truth behind the general's murder and discover that everyone present, including the duke himself, had a motive for wanting Sir Alistair out of the way.

SWEET POISON

David Roberts

CHIVERS PRESS
BATH

First published 2001
by
Constable Publishers
This Large Print edition published 2003
by
BBC Audiobooks Ltd
by arrangement with
Constable and Robinson Ltd

ISBN 0 7540 1981 0

Copyright © David Roberts 2001

All rights reserved.

British Library Cataloguing in Publication Data available

Printed and bound in Great Britain by
Antony Rowe Ltd., Chippenham, Wiltshire

Sweet, sweet poison for the age's tooth . . .

Shakespeare, *King John*

If you poison us, do we not die? and if you
wrong us,
shall we not revenge?

Shakespeare, *The Merchant of Venice*

PROLOGUE

The Duke thrust aside his copy of *The Times* in disgust and stared up through the branches of the great copper beech under which he sat. A light wind agitated the leaves and tossed the discarded newspaper into the air so that several sheets lodged among the lower branches. The ancient and noble tree, which the Germans call a blood beech, creaked and groaned. The brittle leaves rustled and whispered. Shafts of white light, like burning arrows, pierced the shadow into which he had taken his deck chair and made him shield his eyes with his hand. August in England is often an unsettled month but this year, 1935, it had been unusually hot. The grass was browned and the river ran slow and sullen, stifled by weed.

The Duke had not been sleeping well, perhaps because of the heat but there were other reasons, and now his eyes closed, unable to withstand the bright sunlight. He drew out of his trouser pocket his red-spotted silk handkerchief and wiped his brow. He had been upset by what he had read in the newspaper and he had shut his eyes in the hope of forgetting but, as was now commonplace, his mind filled with nightmare images of his brother's death all of twenty years ago. They were the more vivid because he had not himself witnessed it. He saw Franklyn, splendid in his uniform, leading his men towards a wood or maybe just a copse, he could not be sure. Then he saw ill-defined figures in grey kneeling around a metal tripod. They seemed to be feeding a long thin muzzle from

1

below as one might milk a cow. His brother was running, waving his revolver in his right hand to urge on the men behind him. He was bare-headed. In these early days of war, steel helmets were not often worn and his cap had been snatched off his head by the wind or by a bullet as he began his charge. He never reached the trees. A few yards short of the wood he fell clumsily as though he had tripped over a furrow or stumbled on a mole hill. On the ground, he made absurd swimming movements before lying still. All about him other men were dropping down with the same gracelessness. At this moment, as was always the way of it, the Duke woke up choking with anxiety, the blood pounding in his head.

He struggled out of his canvas chair cursing and calling for his wife. 'Connie! Connie! Where are you?'

'I'm here, dear. What's the matter?' came her calm, cool voice from across the lawn and the Duke, still stupid with panic and fatigue, half ran towards the woman who alone made his life bearable.

'What is it, my dear?' she said as he came up to her. 'You have upset yourself? Have you been having that dream again?'

The Duke hung his head shamefacedly. 'I was sitting there reading the paper and thinking about the dinner tonight and I must have dozed off.'

'And you started thinking of Frank?'

'Yes, for the first time for a week. I thought I was really free of it but I suppose . . . well, the news from Germany unsettled me.' He gripped his wife's arm so hard it hurt but she made no sign. 'That's why it is so important to get these people talking.

2

Frank cannot, must not, have died in vain. We must . . .'

'I know, Gerald,' said the Duchess gently, stroking his cheek, 'I know. It will all go well tonight; don't worry. Now, why don't you go up to the house and go through the arrangements with Bates and make sure he's clear about the wine.'

'Yes, m'dear,' said the Duke meekly. 'Sorry, old thing. I'm afraid I got myself into a bit of a state.'

The Duke, much calmer now, walked slowly back towards the open French windows through which his wife had come to his rescue. She stood where he had left her, looking at his retreating form with something approaching dismay. She was afraid he was setting too much store by these dinners he had determined to host with the aim of fostering Anglo-German understanding. He had never got over his brother's death in those first few days of the war and the guilt he felt at not himself having fought. He had so wanted to prove himself on the field of battle but his father had forbidden it. He had told his son that his disobedience would kill him. He had tortured himself ever after wondering if he had been a coward not to have defied his father and gone to France. It was this heavy burden, she knew, which made him dread another war with Germany and he considered it his duty to do everything he could to prevent it.

At least the castle was looking at its most delectable for the distinguished guests. It had been built in Elizabethan times by a Swedish princess, one of the Virgin Queen's ladies-in-waiting. The long gravel drive broadened into a graceful sweep outside the great front door made of ancient oak and studded with iron nails. Through the door the

3

visitor entered a hall created in the eighteenth century to replace the somewhat poky original entrance. This new hall, designed by Robert Adam in 1768, was of some considerable size, floored in black and white marble squares and encircled by a magnificent staircase. In the middle of the hall on a table stood a glorious arrangement of summer flowers which scented the whole house. High above, Adam had created a glass dome which matched the airy lightness of the castle to perfection. On the right of the hall there was the dining-room. A Holbein of an unknown man, possibly a relation of the princess who had built the house, hung above an Adam fireplace. Less happily, in the nineteenth century, French windows had been let into a bay for the convenience of those who might wish to step out on to the lawns without the bother of going through the hall. The drawing-room on the other side of the hall had been similarly defaced but there was no doubt that on a summer's day such as this one it was delightful to feel, with the French windows thrown open, a gentle breeze dissipate the stale air of afternoon heat. This was Connie's domain. She did not for one moment consider herself to be the castle's owner; she was merely—if it could ever be considered 'merely'—its chatelaine. Standing on the lawn, she raised her eyes to the castle battlements. They shimmered insubstantial in the early afternoon sun. The castle for all its parapets and embrasures was a confection with the defensive capability of a wedding cake. It pretended to be what it was not. The ancient honey-coloured stone, somnolent in the sun, dreamed not of war but of masques and plays, courtiers and their ladies. It stood, like England itself, unprepared for conflict of any sort—in sleepy forgetfulness of its own history.

CHAPTER ONE

SATURDAY AFTERNOON

Lord Edward Corinth deplored unpunctuality. He pressed down his foot on the accelerator pedal and smiled to himself as he felt the Lagonda Rapier respond. He had only taken delivery of the elegant two-seater three weeks before and he had spent that time lovingly bringing its four-and-a-half-litre six-cylinder engine up to its peak. Now fully run-in, this was his first opportunity of putting it through its paces. The colour of whipped cream, the Lagonda sped along the Great West Road like some latter-day Pegasus. Soon, London was left behind. Sooted houses and modern factories gave way to countryside punctuated by the occasional roadhouse, but Edward had no time or inclination to tarry. He had to reach Mersham Castle by seven thirty at the latest if he didn't want to bring down upon his head the wrath of Gerald, his older brother and Duke of Mersham, and it was already after six. He urged the great car along the empty road, feeling the wind in his face, relishing the beat of the powerful engine. He loved speed and this was equal to anything except flying itself. He had learnt to fly in Africa and the sensation of being at one with the elements, swooping above herds of impala and kudu on the Masai Mara, came vividly back to him. Handling this supreme achievement of modern automobile engineering engendered in him the same ecstasy he had felt swinging above the African plains in his flimsy aeroplane tied together with string—a tiny dot against a vast blue canvas of sky—at one and the same time totally insignificant and a god.

Once he turned the Lagonda on to country roads the going was slower. He glanced at his watch. Damn it, he was going to be *very* late and Gerald would look at him in that special way he had when he was displeased, pulling his moustache and wrinkling his brows. Against his better judgment, Edward had agreed to attend one of his brother's infernal dinners where he would have to make himself pleasant to pompous politicians and stuffy civil servants. It was not his idea of a lively evening and he had at first refused, pointing out that on no account could he let the Cherrypickers down. The Cherrypickers were all friends of his, Old Etonians for the most part like himself, who played cricket against similar clubs all over the south of England. On this occasion they were playing a strong side at Richmond and he had every intention of carrying his bat for his team. However, Gerald had sounded so desperate when he had said he could not come that he had weakened and then given way. The Duke's invitation became even less appealing when he explained why he was begging for his younger brother's presence.

'I know it's not your sort of thing, Ned, and I apologize for inviting you at the last minute like this. The fact of the matter is, I'm in a bit of a hole. I have invited Lord Weaver, the newspaper owner—you know who I mean?'

'I know who you mean,' Edward had replied tartly. 'I may not dine with the nobs on a regular basis like you, Gerald, but I am not a complete ostrich. He owns the *New Gazette*, doesn't he?'

'Yes, and several other papers as well.'

'And why do you need me to entertain him?'

'Well, I don't need you to entertain him, Ned. The thing is, he has a perfectly charming wife and a rather difficult stepdaughter that the wife is insisting on bringing with her. Apparently, she tries not to let her out of her sight.'

'And I'm to be nanny to the poisonous stepdaughter, is that it?'

'Yes. I know it's asking a lot, Ned, but you have to help me.'

'She's called Hermione, isn't she? I have met her a couple of times before.'

'That's wonderful!'

'I said I have met her, Gerald. That doesn't mean I ever want to meet her again. Doesn't she have a young man? I seem to remember seeing her entwined with a nasty piece of work by the name of Charlie Lomax when I bumped into her at the Fellowes' ball.'

'That's right. I invited him at the mother's request but the blighter dropped out an hour ago without a decent excuse. I couldn't think what else to do except telephone you.'

'Thank you, Gerald! That was very well put.'

'Oh, you know what I mean. My acquaintance with bright young things is rather limited. Please, Ned, you must come.'

'Oh well, I suppose so,' said Edward unwillingly. He was fond of his elder brother and loved Connie,

7

his sister-in-law. He guessed she did not have an easy time of it with the Duke, who acted at least ten years older than his real age which was forty-one. 'Mind you, I may have to cut it a bit tight because I can't let the Cherrypickers down.'

'Well, try not to be late, Ned. This dinner is more important than a cricket match.'

'More important than cricket,' exclaimed the young man. 'Pshaw! I say, Gerald . . .' but the Duke had replaced the receiver. He was not enthusiastic about the telephone and associated its use—along with telegrams—with unpleasantness of one sort or another.

Edward persuaded himself that if the Cherrypickers elected to field first and then bat he would knock up a respectable thirty or even forty as opening bat and be on his way to Mersham by four-thirty at the latest. It was not to be. On his day he was a passable spin bowler and a first-class bat. When, after breaking for lunch, he had stood at the crease, resplendent in his white flannels, he had known from the first ball tossed at him that he could do no wrong. That very first ball he had knocked for six and thereafter he never faltered. It was not until, tired but triumphant, he had walked back to the pavilion raising his bat to acknowledge the applause, not out one hundred and five, that he had any idea of how much time had passed. Brushing aside invitations to celebrate a famous victory he had grabbed his clothes, thrown his bag into the back of the Lagonda and raced out of London, part of him still elated by his record-beating innings and part furious with himself for thinking he could combine an afternoon of perfect cricket with a dinner-party at Mersham Castle in

Hampshire, a good two and a half hours away.

Edward was not quite the empty-headed pleasure-seeker his brother supposed him to be. He was intellectually his brother's superior but he liked to disguise his intelligence below a veneer of flippancy. Since coming down from Cambridge he had not found any employment to his taste though he had been tempted by the diplomatic service. He had plenty of money and very little patience so he was not cut out for office work. His restlessness had found an outlet in travel to the most outlandish corners of the world and an addiction to any sport which promised danger. He had an idea, which he had never put into words, that pleasure had to be earned through pain but the life he led, so active but essentially purposeless, did not altogether satisfy him. He knew himself well enough to realize he was looking for something which would test every sinew and brain cell and give his life meaning.

In 1914, when his eldest brother Frank had died trying to take a machine gun emplacement with only courage to set against a murderous hail of bullets, he had still been a schoolboy. He had hardly known his brother, now a dead hero, but he saw the effect his death had on his father and on his other brother Gerald, and he mourned. Though Gerald might not recognize it, Edward had a passionate hatred of war the equal of his own but he did not share Gerald's belief that a new, even more horrible war could be avoided by a series of dinner-parties, however influential the guests.

Edward had asked who, along with the Weavers, was coming to the castle for this particular dinner to drink the Duke's excellent wine and eat his food and talk about how to make a lasting peace in Europe. 'Well, it's not an ordinary dinner-party,' the Duke told him. 'It was the men I wanted but of course, where there are female appendages, I have invited them too. There will be twelve of us altogether. There's Sir Alistair Craig . . .' Craig was an old friend of the family. He had commanded Franklyn's regiment in 1914 when he was already a distinguished soldier—a VC, no less. He had now retired but was said still to wield a lot of influence at Horse Guards. Peter Larmore was also coming with his long-suffering wife. Edward knew him slightly and knew his reputation as a ladies' man. Brilliant but unsound, he was a rising politician—a Conservative—who, it was forecast, would soon be a member of the new Prime Minister's cabinet if he did not blot his copy book.

There was also to be present Cecil Haycraft, Bishop of Worthing, one of the new breed of political bishops who could be seen at the head of protest marches as often as in his cathedral and who enjoyed the sound of his own voice. He made speeches at 'peace rallies'—he was a convinced pacifist—and was beginning to be a familiar voice on the wireless. Even the Duke had heard him though he rarely listened to the wireless except for news bulletins. Finally, a new man in the German embassy, Baron Helmut von Friedberg, who was said to have the ear of the recently appointed German Chancellor Adolf Hitler, had promised to come. He was the Duke's greatest 'catch' and Larmore, who had met Friedberg on several occasions, had used his influence to secure the German's acceptance of the Duke's invitation. Baron von Friedberg was the focus of the dinner

10

and the Duke had high hopes that something useful might be achieved by having the man at his table.

*   *   *

Edward's use as a guest was not confined to his role as Hermione's nursemaid. He had charm. He could, as the Duke put it to himself, 'oil the wheels', fill in any embarrassing pauses in the conversation. As the Duke had said to his wife at breakfast, 'You know, Connie m'dear, that boy must have something. The women like him and yet the men seem not to resent him. In fact, I was talking to Carlisle at the club last week and he said he was one of the ablest men he knew and the bravest. Apparently, Carlisle told me, Ned pulled off an amazing rescue when he was climbing in the Alps last year but he never said a word to me about it. Did he to you?'

'No,' said the Duchess, smiling, 'but then I would not have expected him to. Beneath all that—what shall we call it: braggadocio?—no, not braggadocio—let's say persiflage, your little brother is one of the most modest men I know. He talks and talks, shows off like a peacock in front of the ladies, who love it of course, and yet, as you say, the men see immediately the . . . the iron in his soul. And don't forget he is intelligent.'

'Oh yes, he's clever enough,' said the Duke, massaging honey from Mersham's own apiaries on to his toast. 'He got a first at Cambridge and all that but what I can't understand is he doesn't *do* anything. He rackets around the world trying to break his neck, getting into every scrape, when he

11

could be—well, when he could be in the House or something.'

Connie laughed. 'Can you see Ned surviving one hour in that place? Duffers or crooks—sometimes both—he once described Members of Parliament to me.'

'I just hope he isn't going to be late tonight, that's all,' said the Duke, accepting that he never would understand his brother's lack of interest in what most of the world considered to be important. 'He says he's got to play in some cricket match or other on his way here. I gather that girl of Weaver's—what's her name?'

'Hermione.'

'I gather Hermione is worse than the yellow peril,' he finished morosely, 'and now that cub Lomax has cried off, I'm counting on him to take her off my hands. I don't want anything to distract Weaver from getting to know Friedberg. I think he could really be important to us.'

'When Lady Weaver asked me to invite Mr Lomax,' said Connie, 'she hinted he might make difficulties about coming. Reading between the lines, I guess that Hermione thinks she's in love with him but he is playing hard to get.'

The Duke sighed. 'The young today! They aren't like—'

'Don't start playing the old man, Gerald,' said the Duchess sharply. 'Our generation was just as wilful, especially when they had money like Hermione Weaver. But then the war came and—'

'Perhaps we should just have been honest with Weaver and told him not to bring the gel because without her chap she's going to be bored stiff,' the Duke broke in.

'Well, it's too late now, but don't worry, darling,' said the Duchess comfortably, 'Ned won't let you down. He may cut it fine but he's never late.'

But for once this sensible woman was to be proved wrong.

* * *

Edward looked at his watch again. It had taken him longer than he had expected to negotiate Reading. He considered stopping at a public house to telephone the castle and explain that he was going to be a little late, but that would only delay him still further. No, he would cut across country and make his gorgeous girl fly and be there at least in time for the fish.

He had long ago mastered the spider's web of minor roads, many of them little more than lanes, narrow enough to be sure but passable in a motor car with a little care and which cut half an hour off the journey to Mersham. For several miles he made good time and when he came up a steep slope on to the spine of the Downs, which run deep into Hampshire, he was beginning to feel that he would not be very late after all. The road marched straight ahead of him, whitened by chalk from where the tar had blistered and peeled. He blessed the old Roman road builders who had scorned to circumvent obstacles, preferring simply to pretend they did not exist. He pressed his foot hard on the accelerator pedal and the Lagonda leaped from thirty to forty until the needle on the speedometer wavered above the sixty mark.

Edward experienced for the second time that day the joy of being beyond normal physical restraints. Just as when he felt rather than heard the delicious crack of leather on willow earlier that afternoon, he now felt the electrical charge which comes when nature recognizes a perfect match of mental control over physical power.

Glancing in the mirror, he could see nothing behind him but a cloud of white dust which the Lagonda's wheels were raising from the sun-dried, badly macadamized road. Then he looked ahead. Because of the dust he had put on his leather helmet and goggles and now he took one hand off the wheel to wipe them, for a second not quite believing what had suddenly come into view. The blanched streak of road ahead of him was no longer empty. Although the road had looked quite level, stretching into infinity, he now realized, fatally late in the day, that this had been an illusion. A shallow dip had effectively concealed a wagon piled high with hay, a tottering mountain moving slowly up the gradient towards him pulled by two horses straining against their harnesses. It filled the whole width of the road. The painter Constable, no doubt, would have said, 'Ah, a haywain!' and set up his easel and begun painting. Edward's reaction was rather different. Slamming on the brakes he went into a skid which would have drawn an admiring gasp from an ice-skater. Struggling to control the car he swerved around the wagon before swaying elegantly into a deep dry ditch which ran beside the road. For one moment he was certain the car was going to turn over and crush him but with an angry crack it steadied itself before sinking on its haunches like a broken-down horse. It needed no mechanic to tell him that the axle had broken under the impact.

14

For several moments Edward sat where he was, staring at his gloved hands which were still clenched around the steering wheel. Red drops which he knew must be blood began to stain his ulster. Gingerly, he prised off his goggles and helmet and touched his forehead. He cursed and took his hand away hurriedly. He must have cut his head on the edge of the windshield but he had no memory of doing so. An anxious-looking bewhiskered face appeared beside him.

'You bain't be dead then?' the worried but rubicund face declared. 'I'se feared you was a gonner, leastways you ought t'be.'

'You are quite right,' said Edward gallantly, 'I ought to be dead. I was driving like a lunatic. I hope I did not scare you as much as I scared myself. The truth is, I had no idea there was that dip in the road. I thought I could see miles ahead.'

'Ah,' said the wagoner judiciously, 'I reckons now there be so many o' these here blooming automobiles, begging your pardon, sir, there ought to be a notice. But you're bleeding, sir; are you hurt bad?'

'No, no bones broken, I think.' Edward tried to open the door but it was jammed, so slowly he raised himself out of the driver's seat and clambered out, wincing and hoping he was right about not having broken any bones. He was bruised and he had done something to his knee which made it painful to walk, and no doubt in twenty-four hours he would feel stiff and aching all over. His chest had collided with the steering wheel but fortunately the force of the impact had been cushioned by his heavy ulster. No, he could congratulate himself that his idiocy had not been

15

the death of him. It was to be the first time that evening death had chosen to spare him.

*   *   *

At Mersham Castle the Duke's guests had already repaired to their rooms to rest and bathe before dressing for dinner. It was a pity that none of them was in a mood to appreciate the airy beauty of this magical castellated house. It had something of the feel of a Continental château or maybe an Austrian duke's hunting lodge. Certainly, it was not quite English—light and airy where Norman castles had been dark and claustrophobic. It seemed to float in the evening light as serene as the swans drifting on the river which moated the castle walls. On an August evening as perfect as this one, it was more beautiful than any fairy-tale castle. Lord Tennyson, who knew Mersham well, had, it was said, recalled it in his *Idylls of the King*. No such place could be without a garden where lovers might walk arm in arm and declare to one another everlasting devotion and there were indeed lawns stretching down to the water, also a rather threadbare maze created only a century before in 1830, but the jewel in the crown was an Elizabethan knot garden of intricate design, in August blazing with colour and heady with the scent of roses. Beyond it there was a little woodland called The Pleasury.

It was not love but death upon which General Sir Alistair Craig VC brooded as he stared at himself in the looking-glass; not his own death, though he knew that was crouching at his shoulder like a black cat, but the death of his beloved wife just a year before, friends dead in the war or after

16

it, and the death of the child in his wife's womb so many years ago, the son he was never to clasp in his arms. For some reason he could not begin to explain, he thought too of the funeral of his old and revered chief, Earl Haig, a just and upright man who had saved Britain and the Empire but whose reputation was already being savaged by men who called themselves historians but who, in the eyes of the old soldier, were little better than jackals and not good enough to wipe the Field Marshal's boots. It had been all of seven years ago that he had processed through London with so many other generals, three princes and statesmen from all over the world. From St Columba's Church, Pont Street, they marched bare-headed along the Mall and Whitehall to Westminster Abbey. Crowds lined the route in solemn silence. Many wore poppies, the symbol not just of those millions who had died on the field of battle but of the great work the Field Marshal had done in helping the wounded and dispossessed in the years after the war. It had been an event, a ceremony, which the General would never, nor ever want to, forget. It gave meaning to his own life that this great man, under whom he had served for three cruel years of war, should be so honoured. And now, was this honour to be stripped away like the gold leaf on a pharaoh's coffin? Only last year at Oxford, in a debate in the Union, undergraduates had supported a motion that in no circumstances would they fight for king and country. The report in *The Times* had made his blood run cold when he read it. Pacifism was gnawing away at the nation's manhood. It was a sickness. He, General Craig, had sent men to their deaths, many thousands of men. It had been his

17

duty. Was it now to be said that, in obeying the orders of that great man now lying in honour in Dryburgh Abbey, he had not done well? Was he now to stand accused of . . . of murder? That was no reward for a life's patriotic service.

And what of tonight? Why had he come? Out of respect for the Duke, certainly; he did not altogether agree with the Duke on his attitude to their erstwhile enemy. The General believed, albeit with melancholy bordering on despair, that Britain was enjoying nothing more than a truce in her war with Prussian militarism. He could not believe that anything—talk, diplomacy, treaties, behind-the-scenes-negotiations—anything short of force—naked and brutal—would affect how Hitler behaved. Throughout history, despots had chosen foreign adventures as a way of uniting their people behind them. That way opposition to anything they chose to do could be construed as unpatriotic and be ruthlessly suppressed. The General considered it to be self-evident that the new German Chancellor, like the Kaiser before him, would use mindless xenophobia dressed as patriotism to distract the German people from troubles at home. In his view, the new Germany was worse than the old one—a shabby, disreputable alliance of big business and an army which had convinced itself it had not been defeated in battle but stabbed in the back by its own politicians. But tonight at the Duke's dinner he would play his part in trying to alert his country to the peril he could see looming on the horizon. Maybe there was still something to be done, something only he could do.

General Craig was a solitary man—all the more so since the death of his dear Dolly—and these sorts of social gatherings were even more of a trial to him now, without her, than they had been before. He had little hope of finding a kindred spirit at the Duke's table. There was Larmore who had somehow blackmailed his way into an under-secretaryship at the Foreign Office and that appalling rogue Lord Weaver, the Canadian owner of the *New Gazette*. The General hated journalists, despised the whole pack of them, and he knew a good deal about Weaver through his friend Will Packer who had had business dealings with him back in New Brunswick where Weaver had made his first fortune. Packer had told him that Weaver had come to New Brunswick from Newfoundland, not yet a part of Canada and too impoverished to offer much scope to a man with ideas of making money. Corner Brook, where Weaver had been born, was at the time little more than a village but in New Brunswick, so Packer said, Weaver had spread his wings and turned a few tricks, some at Packer's expense, which had left him very bitter. It made Craig gag to see how high the man had climbed and he was half inclined to spill a few skeletons out of the closet if *Lord* Weaver, as he now styled himself, refused to do the right thing by him. The General curled back his upper lip, revealing long yellow teeth. Fortunately, he was no longer gazing into the looking-glass or he might not have liked what he saw there.

When he had arrived at the castle the Duke had told him that the Bishop of Worthing was already there, but after a strong whisky the General had gone to his room to change without seeing him or any of the other guests. He had never met the Bishop but he was well aware of who he was—a

19

pacifist whose anti-war sermons in 1917 and 1918 had, in his view, gravely damaged the war effort. Worse even than the Bishop, the 'guest of honour'—if such a one could be so called—was to be some German diplomat. He smiled grimly to himself. He was to dine with his enemies; feasting with panthers—hadn't someone thus described such gatherings? It made it worse not being in uniform. He only felt truly comfortable in uniform and among his own kind. In white tie and tails he was just another man to be judged by others on his social talents, in which he knew himself to be deficient: small talk, smiles and jokes. Dolly had often told him he was not a sociable animal but of course, to be fair, the Duke had not invited him to dinner to talk sweet nothings. He was a fighter, always a fighter, and he would hold his corner to the bitter end.

He turned again to the looking-glass and began slowly, unwillingly, to tie his tie. His hands froze on the ribbon. The face in the mirror—was that really his? Why, he could see quite clearly the skull beneath the skin. His hands, flecked with yellow liver freckles, the confetti of old age, dropped from his neck and he looked as though at a stranger: the pale face, the cold sea-water-blue eyes, the sharp nose, the narrow upper lip he was happy to disguise beneath a little brown moustache cut to a bristle every morning for half a century. It was a grim face, he thought, and he wondered for a moment whether, had Dolly lived, it would have still looked so.

His inspection was rudely interrupted by a bayonet stab of violent pain in the stomach. He held his hand to his side. The pain was sharper tonight, perhaps because of the stress he was under, but why prevaricate: in the last few months it was always sharper than it had been the day before. He checked he had with him the little silver snuff box in which he kept his pills. It was there. He contemplated taking one now but decided that that was weakness. They had to be kept for when he was really in pain—later perhaps. He settled his shoulders and stiffened his back. His bearing said 'soldier' as clearly as if the word had been written on his forehead. Well now—he had better get on with it. He had his duty to do, perhaps for the last time, and he had always done his duty.

*   *   *

'I'm not going down—I'm telling you, Mother: I just refuse.' The girl recognized the unpleasant whine in her voice and tried to check herself but really, it was too bad. Her mother had persuaded her to come to Mersham Castle, to what she had known would be the dreariest of dinner-parties, by promising her that among the guests would be Charles Lomax, but she had now been told when it was too late to retreat that Lomax was not to be there after all.

'Bah!' said the girl, her narrow face, not unattractive when she smiled, now disfigured by disappointment. 'I guess his cold won't stop him taking Pamela Finch to Gaston's tonight. What a sell! He swore I meant more to him than . . . Anyway, I need to . . .'

'Now, honey,' said her mother calmly, seated at the little dressing-table vigorously rubbing cream into her face and trying to convince herself the

21

lines under her eyes were no more noticeable than they had been six months ago. 'Maybe it's all for the best. The Duke says his brother—Lord Edward Corinth I think they call him, though why he should have a different name from the Duke's I will never understand—he's going to be at dinner and from what I read in the illustrated papers he is everything a young man ought to be: rich, good-looking, and a duke's brother is *something* after all.'

'Oh, Mother—he's just a younger son,' the girl said, her voice whetted by scorn. 'He's not a duke and never will be. Anyway, I met him at Lady Carey's and he was so stuck up—I quite hated him. He patronized me—treated me like a child. He dared to tell me I was going round with "wrong 'uns" as he quaintly put it and had the cheek to say if I wasn't "deuced careful"'—she mimicked his clipped accent—'I'd get myself into trouble.'

Lady Weaver paused for a moment and looked at her daughter queerly. 'Sound advice I'd say, darling. I like the man already.'

'Oh, Mother, don't be a bore. You would say that. You're so predictable,' and she flounced out of the room.

In the mirror the mother had caught sight of her child's face and she had noticed for the first time that her daughter was in danger of turning into a shrew. She was almost twenty-three but when she scowled, as she was scowling now, she looked older. Why was she so often nervy and irritable? Surely she understood that there were younger, prettier girls being presented at court every year. If she was to marry she would have to make an effort to please. She would have to talk to her about it but this wasn't the moment. Hermione wasn't a fool.

She was just like so many of the younger generation: rootless, pleasure-seeking but essentially unhappy. Spoiled little rich girl, the mother thought ruefully. She needed to find her a good man but where were they? So many had been killed in the war and the new young men—well, they seemed shallow, selfish to her. They liked to assume a 'know-it-all' attitude which she found wearisome. If Hermione was to find a suitable husband—someone a little older, more mature— like Edward Corinth perhaps—she had to learn some winning ways. No wonder the Lomax boy had cancelled. She had seen them together when he had come to collect her from Eaton Place before going on to some dance in Belgrave Square and Hermione had been all over him. She had noticed then, though Hermione did not seem to, that it had embarrassed him. Hermione made it quite plain when she did not like a young man and her snubs were legendary but when she did find a boy wild enough to attract her she couldn't hide her adoration from the poor man, so he usually ran as far and as fast as he could. If only she didn't feel she had to choose men of whom her stepfather would be sure to disapprove. Her mother sighed. She supposed it must be her fault. Wasn't it always a parent's fault if their children turned out—no, she would not say 'bad'—'difficult', that was the word. She had so hoped her daughter would get on with her new father but they had always been like oil and water. Joe had tried. It wasn't his fault. It was the only shadow on her life, which was now so good in so many ways.

She thought with simple pleasure of Joe, Lord Weaver, now closeted with the Duke in the gunroom smoking a cigar, without which he was rarely to be seen, and drinking Scotch whisky, which gave him indigestion. Her husband was what was now being called a press baron. He was immensely wealthy and the owner of two national newspapers, a London evening paper and a large number of North American regional news-sheets much more profitable if less influential than his London stable. Lord Weaver—he had been ennobled by Lloyd George after making a very generous contribution to party funds—had been born and brought up in Newfoundland, in Corner Brook—a one-horse town which he had told her he had got out of as soon as he could. He had not cut his ties with it altogether and when he had made his first money, in New Brunswick, he had financed a paper mill just outside Corner Brook. This had proved a shrewd investment and the town had become almost entirely dependent on woodpulp which was transformed into paper to feed the ever increasing North American newspaper industry. Joe Weaver was now the town's most famous son. He had returned only once, some years before, and endowed a concert hall, a picture gallery and a hospital. He intended to be buried in Corner Brook, so it was important he was remembered in the town as a generous benefactor and a role model for other young men. Until that day, when he returned in his coffin, he had determined he would never go back.

In England, his adopted country, not much was known about how Joe Weaver came to be a millionaire but this did not stop people gossiping. Among the envious and the cynical there were plenty of malicious stories circulating, but no one had ever found any evidence that in his many business dealings as a young man—first in Corner Brook and then in New Brunswick—he had ever been involved in anything illegal. He had taken chances—he admitted as much—done some favours for some fairly undesirable gentlemen, and had, on one occasion at least, almost gone bankrupt but, as he said, no man ever made money without a little luck, a streak of ruthlessness and nerves of steel. It was also said that he had gone through some sort of marriage ceremony in New Brunswick with a woman who had—conveniently perhaps—died in childbirth. Certainly, when he had come to England in 1917 he was a free spirit— rich, unattached, ready to be useful; he had, in short, reinvented himself. In any case, in wartime there weren't the same standards operating in London society which would have kept him out of the houses of the aristocracy before the war.

He quickly became a power in the land, an intimate of the Prime Minister and his cronies; with his newspapers and his money—with which he was generous—he became known as someone who could make or break careers. He was a large man, broad in the shoulders and six foot two, by no means conventionally handsome but with the 'bear' look which some women find attractive, even taking into account his crumpled face which, some unkind observer had remarked, resembled a tennis ball that had been left several days in the rain. He exuded power all the more potent for being kept on a tight rein. He hid his animal energy and ruthless disregard for anyone's interests but his own under a veneer of 'man-of-the-world' sophistication. He insinuated himself into the

Prince of Wales's somewhat raffish circle and he delighted to surround himself with talented young men wholly dependent on him for their livelihood. He was known to be a terrible enemy to any man who tried to double-cross him. He would be quite prepared to wait months or even years before taking his revenge.

He needed about him beautiful women, to make love to—he had the strong sexual drive of the ambitious man—but just as importantly to wear on his arm like jewellery. Even when he first arrived in London he had no difficulty in attracting the type of woman he admired: elegant, intelligent and where possible married to a Member of Parliament. Then something happened which no one could have predicted: he fell in love. He had met Blanche, Lady Marston, in 1918. She was twenty-six, still beautiful but with a small daughter whom Weaver had disliked on sight. Blanche had no husband. He had died—heroically, it was said, though not by his wife—in some terrible battle in France.

It had been with relief that Blanche surrendered to Weaver's dominating personality. Her dead husband had almost destroyed her. Guy Marston, when Blanche had married him, was charming, well connected but not rich. She was naïve, little more than a girl, without sensible parents to advise her. She had married Marston after the briefest of engagements to the delight of their respective friends and relations, but Blanche knew, she might almost have said 'at the altar', that she had made a terrible mistake—how terrible she was to learn that very night. As soon as they were alone in their suite at the Dorchester, where they were to spend the night before crossing the Channel for a month's leisurely honeymoon among the Swiss and Italian lakes, he had sat her down on the bed and been brutally frank with her. She was totally innocent about sex—had only kissed her husband half a dozen times—so she had no idea what was supposed to happen in the bed on which the two of them were now perched fully clothed. She suddenly wondered what on earth she was doing with this complete stranger in a hotel room—the first hotel bedroom she had ever been in—and she was frightened. What she saw in her husband's face did nothing to reassure her. Her mother had considered it unwise to alarm her with any account of the pain and suffering men—English men of the upper classes at least—seemed to delight in inflicting on their wives with the full support of society and the law. Her mother's experience had led her to believe that sex was a cruel joke played on womankind by a God who was unquestionably male, and she pitied her daughter—but not enough to enlighten her as to what fate had in store for her.

Guy Marston made it clear to her in the most graphic terms that his preference was for the male sex and that he had married her as necessary protection from the law. Blanche had never for one moment been aware that men could be attracted to each other sexually so it took her some time and the scathing sarcasm of her husband to understand what he was saying. He then proceeded to rape her so that she could never claim that the marriage had been unconsummated. The attack left her bruised and bleeding and mentally scarred. If this was sex between men and women, then she could only be glad that her husband was not intending to repeat

27

the act. In public, he continued to be the affectionate husband but in private he never lost an opportunity of humiliating her. On one occasion she returned from a shopping expedition to find him in bed with a hotel waiter and she never forgot the smirk on her husband's face when he saw her shock and disgust. Thereafter, she insisted on separate bedrooms. Had war not broken out in 1914, when they had been married almost two years, she might have been driven to murder him but merciful fate relieved her of this necessity. Hermione had been the result of Blanche's sole taste of marital bliss and the baby proved her consolation and joy when so much else made her weep with fear and frustration. Even her husband had been pleased in his own brutish way; to have a wife and a child meant he could scotch any rumours about his sexual preferences. His death on the battlefield renewed her faith in God. Perhaps after all he was not male as she had been led to believe.

Meeting Joe Weaver had been for Blanche the most fortunate of encounters. They had met at a cocktail party—an American invention which the British had taken to with enthusiasm. Neither Blanche nor Weaver normally enjoyed these shouting matches in crowded drawing-rooms but this one, held by a close friend of the Prince of Wales, had seemed unavoidable. Weaver, who was already on good terms with his future King, had felt he had to make an appearance. The friend had placed a beringed hand on his arm and said, 'Joe darling, I've been wanting for months to introduce you to Blanche. I just know you are made for one another. Blanche, this is Joe Weaver. Don't be put off by how ugly he is. He's a lovely man but be warned, he can be dangerous.' She turned to Weaver: 'Joe, this is Lady Marston—Blanche. She is much better than you. In fact, she is the only sincere woman in this room so do not treat her as you do me.' Then with a half-smile she left them together.

The friend had been perspicacious. Though superficially such very different characters from very different backgrounds, they each had something the other desired. From that first moment they were attracted to one another. It was not love, not at the beginning, but mutual need. Blanche had poise, impeccable breeding and a sadness in her eyes which Weaver found intriguing. From their meeting, Blanche saw Weaver in animal terms—half man, half monkey—and he made her laugh. Here was a man who exhibited complete self-confidence. He was not remotely interested in what other men thought of him though he knew they contemptuously used phrases like 'rough diamond' and 'self-made man' to describe him behind his back. He had grown used to being sneered at by nincompoops who had never done a day's work in their lives. Blanche was immediately impressed that he made no attempt to 'show off' in front of her. She had listened so patiently for so many hours to callow young men telling her how wonderful they were that it was a huge relief to find an older, wiser man who asked her about herself and seemed genuinely interested in her answers. They slipped away from the party and had dinner together at the Savoy, despite each being expected elsewhere. Weaver considered himself, with some justification, a shrewd judge of character. As decisive in his personal life as he was in business, he quickly recognized in this sad, sweet-faced woman the wife he could cherish and who would assist him to find his place in British society and discreetly educate him. He knew how to fight dirty, to buy men and influence, but what he wanted was someone to soften his edges; someone who could host his dinner-parties and bring a certain style and elegance to them. He did not want to pretend he was an English gentleman, a breed for which he had something like contempt, but he did want to have an establishment to which no English gentleman would be embarrassed to bring his wife. In Blanche he felt he had found a woman who would be a true helpmeet.

Blanche, in her turn, needed money. Her unlamented husband had left her with nothing but debts and a child to support. It was not easy to keep a small house in Chester Square, a maid and two other servants, dress herself and her child, all on nothing a year. London was awash with widows and though she was not a weak woman she felt in need of a man to give her status and a purpose in life. She had almost despaired of finding one. Joe was different from most of the men she knew. In the first place he was not English and she found his Canadian accent irresistible and delighted to use expressions he used. He called her, in the privacy of their bedroom, honey, sugar pie, his little cookie, and it melted her. She realized she had lived a life without affection so now, when it was so generously offered to her, she found it deeply affecting. Both parties were old enough to understand that their marriage was something of a business arrangement—no cherry blossom and kisses in the

30

moonlight—but to their great surprise they fell in love with one another. When haltingly, the day before they got married, Blanche told him something of what her sex life with her first husband had been—or rather had not been—he had been genuinely horrified. With infinite gentleness—quite unexpected in someone who despised what he termed 'sentimentality'—he showed her what pleasure sex could bring where two people respected each other. It was a miracle to Blanche and her love for Joe—his 'monkeyship' as she called him—became fierce and her loyalty absolute. If only Hermione would marry and leave them to set up her own establishment . . . there was little else necessary to complete their happiness.

'She hates my guts, girlie,' he said to Blanche once, 'and there ain't nothing I can do about it. The sooner she finds a life of her own the happier I shall be, but for your sake, angel, I will stick by her and give her whatever you say she needs. But the day I step up to that altar and the man in the frock says, "Who giveth this woman to be married to this man?" will be the happiest of my life.' Kissing her forehead he added, 'With the glorious exception, of course, of the day you consented to be my wife.'

When she had finished her make-up, Blanche pulled on her robe and went out of her bedroom into the corridor and tapped on the door of her daughter's room opposite. 'Darling, may I come in for a moment?'

She spoke in a low voice, not wishing to draw attention to herself and, not knowing whether Hermione had heard her, she opened the door. At first she could not see what her daughter was doing but then, as she took another pace into the room, the girl heard her and half turned towards the door. Blanche gave a little cry and her hand went to her mouth. It was horrible, unbelievable, and yet she recognized she had known it all along. On Hermione's face there was rage but when she saw her mother's shocked face she smiled and for Blanche this was the worst thing of all.

*　　　*　　　*

'Oh for God's sake, Celia, don't let's discuss it now.'

'But Peter, you promised. Next weekend we would go with Nanny and the children to the seaside: just us. You haven't seen William or Gladys for weeks. They hardly recognize you.'

'God, why did we call that child Gladys? It will hang round her neck like a millstone and when she marries she'll curse us. "I take thee Gladys . . ." I ask you.'

'You know very well why we called her Gladys: so your rich cow of an aunt will leave her all her money.'

Peter Larmore had achieved what he had set out to do, namely make his wife angry and change the subject. He had promised his mistress to take her to Paris for a few days when he had thought his wife was going to a health farm, safely out of the way, but for some reason she had taken it into her head to suggest accompanying the children to Bognor Regis—to the seaside. Bognor of all places! He swore as he tied his tie. 'Damn it, Celia, you'll have to find a new laundry. This shirt is a disgrace and I've hardly got a collar I can wear.'

'Oh, what nonsense, Peter. Come over here and

let me fix it for you.'

Reluctantly he left the looking-glass and went over to the bed where his wife was sitting dressed in a slip and nothing else. He found himself thinking she was still a fine-looking woman. Most men would—probably did—envy him. He had no idea why he went after other women not half as handsome as his own wife and not even as good at . . . at what women were supposed to be good at. He did not know why he found himself so unwilling to say 'sex' even in his head. After all, in the club the men used language which made his hair stand on end, talking about women in the same language they used about their horses—their 'mares'.

He wished he wasn't so damn short of money. He couldn't understand it. He didn't gamble—didn't spend half what some of the other men spent. But women were so expensive and educating the children . . . his slender resources were being drained. As a Member of Parliament he was paid a pittance. He needed this job in the cabinet Stanley Baldwin, the new Prime Minister, had all but promised him—not for the salary but for the influence it would give him, the patronage he would be able to dish out and which *would* bring in money.

Celia thought she saw what was going through his mind and said, 'Oh darling, we haven't got time. The Duke's a stickler for punctuality.'

It took Larmore a moment to understand what she meant and suddenly he found he *did* want his wife—wanted her badly. Without any more words he took her there and then—she in her slip, he in his socks and shirt. While her husband grunted and groaned she clung to him, hiding a tiny smile of relief and satisfaction. She had thought there just might be a woman but surely this proved there was only her . . . only her. The trouble with having a Member of Parliament for a husband was that it gave him any number of reasons for not being with her—and she had just caught a word that silly Jane Garton had said which had upset her. She had gone into Galiere's to buy a hat—a hat she didn't need but she had promised herself a little present to cheer herself up—and as she entered the shop she thought she heard Jane Garton saying something to another woman whom she did not know about—well, about seeing Peter lunching with a woman at the Berkeley. Jane Garton's friend, glancing up and seeing Celia, had poked Jane in the ribs with her elbow and whispered something and both women had smiled and pretended they had not seen her. The cats! They had to have someone to gossip about and Peter was so good-looking, so desirable in every way, it was no surprise they should be gossiping about him. Why should he not be having lunch with a woman friend in the Berkeley? It wasn't a place one would go to for a secret tryst after all. The only odd thing was that when she had casually asked Peter if he would take her to the Berkeley for dinner one evening he said he would like to because he hadn't been there for months. She had been too sensible to question him and now, as she stroked his hair which was getting just a little thin, her suspicions—no, that was too strong a word, her twinges of doubt—were assuaged. They had been married nine years and he still loved her. She was quite certain of it now.

'There, my darling, that was lovely but we really must get dressed now. The gong will be going any

34

minute,' she said.

Larmore disentangled himself from his wife—his shirt and collar now creased and soiled beyond rescue—and in the process almost fell off the bed. He felt rather foolish. Why did he give way whenever he felt the urge? He ought to control himself. He was exasperated with himself, which made him annoyed with his wife. What had she meant: 'lovely'? Was that what it had been— 'lovely'? He had a feeling he was being mothered and he did not like it. He was now quite determined that he would *not* be going to Bognor with his wife and children.

*   *   *

'So why did you say we would come, Cecil, if you hate it so much?'

Honoria Haycraft looked at her husband with a real desire to hear what his answer would be. He was such an honest man; so uninterested in mixing with 'society'. He had often talked angrily of the charity balls and dinners the rich gave to show, as he said sarcastically, 'they cared' about unemployed miners, the homeless, the half-starved: 'They stuff their faces with smoked salmon and caviare and think that in some way they're being Christian when really, of course, they are enjoying having a good time with others of their own class and feeling virtuous into the bargain. We talk about having our cake and eating it but I always think it's a bit much when the cake is taken from the hands of the starving.'

The Bishop's wife would remonstrate with him and he would eventually admit that there were

35

some rich people genuinely concerned to do something for England's great underclass, whose desperate poverty had been exacerbated by the economic 'depression'. He knew the Duke, for one, to be a good man with a strong sense of purpose and responsibility, but he had so often fulminated against the class system which he regarded as unchristian that it was natural his wife should be surprised to find herself at Mersham Castle, the guest of a duke. Yet many of his fellow bishops, and even the Archbishop of Canterbury, had no difficulty in accepting the idea that it was by God's will the duke was in his castle and the poor man at his gate. There was even a hymn about it. He, on the contrary, believed that if he were a Christian he must also be a socialist committed to reforming society and distributing wealth more equitably. It was surely outrageous that 80 per cent of the country's wealth was owned by just 12 per cent of the population. The Bishop was also a pacifist. He believed that wars were fought to benefit the few— the warmongers and the arms dealers—and was convinced that evil could only be defeated by prayer and peaceful resistance. He was a leading figure in a new movement which he hoped would attract support from members of all the political parties: he intended to lead a call for all men of good will to pledge themselves publicly to peace. To pursue his aims he was prepared to go into the lion's den and this was why he had had no hesitation in accepting the invitation to Mersham.

'I decided to accept the Duke's invitation, Honoria,' the Bishop said a little stiffly in answer to his wife, 'because first of all, I believe him to be a genuinely good man trying to do his best to

36

alleviate the conditions of the poor but more importantly because I share his concern that, if we are not careful, we will be dragged into another war with Germany. I intend to enlist him in my Peace Pledge campaign.' He shuddered. 'I promised myself in 1918 that I would do everything I could to prevent such another disaster as almost destroyed this country.'

He saw his wife smiling. 'I know I cannot do much,' he said defensively, 'but that does not excuse me from doing what little I can do. If we all put in our mite, who knows but the balance will be weighted towards peace.'

'I wasn't laughing at you, Cecil,' she said. 'I was just loving you for your Jack-and-the-Beanstalk determination. Giant killer!' Honoria, who had been married to her husband for almost thirty years, kissed him with real feeling. She knew that for all his occasional pomposities and little hypocrisies he was one of the only truly good men she had ever met and that to be married to him was the chief blessing of her life.

'In any case,' the Bishop went on, 'I wanted to meet General Craig. I have it in mind that he is an ogre; that he sent so many young men to their deaths during the war because he was mad or vicious, but I feel it is unjust of me to condemn him without hearing his side of the argument. The new German representative is also, the Duke informed me, coming here to dine tonight and I particularly welcome the chance of telling him that there are many people in Britain today who sympathize with his countrymen's just demands. I am convinced that only if Germany is a full and active member of the League of Nations can we achieve a lasting peace.'

'Oh Cecil darling,' said his wife, alarmed, putting both her hands in his, 'please don't get into any political arguments. You know how bitter they can get and how embarrassing they can be for those of us who don't feel as strongly as you do.'

'Well, you should do—feel strongly, I mean,' said the Bishop vehemently. 'What is a little embarrassment against peace or war?' Then more gently, squeezing his wife's hands, he said, 'Think of our Harry. What is he now? Thirteen? Are we to sit back and see him sacrificed as our fathers' generation sacrificed their sons? It is unthinkable!'

'But, my love—'

'Don't fret, my darling,' said the Bishop, seeing his wife was really upset. 'I mean to listen patiently, not to lecture. If you hear me begin to sermonize you have my full permission to rebuke me.'

* * *

'Look here, Duke,' Lord Weaver was saying, 'we share a common aim, to prevent another European war.' His Canadian twang was a little more evident than usual. He held out his glass and the Duke splashed soda on to whisky. Whenever the Duke wanted to flatter a man into thinking he was of special importance he took him, not into one of the castle's grand public rooms, but into the gunroom. Connie had a little boudoir, or sewing-room as she liked to call it, not that much sewing was ever done there, where she would charm her female guests into believing they were very special to her, but to be alone with the Duke in the gunroom, his holy of holies, was a compliment very few men could resist.

Although the Duke called it his gunroom it was more properly a rod and line room. There *were* guns in cases and some lethal-looking seventeenth-century blunderbusses over the mantelpiece but its walls were covered in fishing rods. There were over a hundred on display in racks and two very ancient rods, alleged to have been used by Izaac Walton himself, in glass display cases. There were no moth-eaten stags' heads staring gloomily from the walls—the Duke had had all these cleared away when he inherited the title and the castle—but there were some magnificent salmon stuffed and mounted, with brass plates below them giving their origin and the history of their capture. The Duke, Weaver knew, had fished all over the world—from barbel in the Zambezi to salmon in Iceland—and Weaver was beginning to think that behind that rather stupid-looking face and the bluff 'good-fellow' air of the country gentleman there might be a true fisher of men. Certainly, he was not the fool his enemies were content to label him.

'I believe we need to give the German people a chance to find their rightful place at the world's conference tables and encourage them to play their part in the League of Nations,' Weaver was saying, rolling his glass between his hands which he did when he was speaking sincerely.

'Yes,' the Duke said eagerly. 'I don't pretend to like this Hitler fellow but we have to deal with the realities and he has the support of the businessmen, "the captains of industry" as your newspapers call them. They believe he is the only man capable of bringing Germany out of recession and into stable, ordered . . . well, not democracy perhaps as we understand it, but at least something like it. Bismarck took Prussia away from parliamentary democracy toward a militaristic society and we know what that led to. That's why we must—we have a duty to—help Germany accept that she is part of the European balance of power.'

Weaver sipped at his whisky and watched the Duke pacing impatiently round the room quite unlike his normal placid self. 'Do you know anything about this Baron Helmut von Friedberg? I don't know much about his background. He's the new—what?—under-secretary at the German embassy here?'

'He's a sort of cousin of mine,' replied the Duke. 'My great-uncle married the daughter of Moritz August von Friedberg, a German princeling and a friend of Bismarck's. This chap, though I have never met him before, is their grandson or great-grandson, I'm not sure which to be honest, and therefore a cousin. But the important thing is that he has direct access to Hitler. Larmore tells me that Hitler does not trust the people at the embassy here and Friedberg has authority to . . . well, to bypass the officials and report back to Hitler direct.'

'Hmmf,' said Weaver. 'Very interesting. He may be very useful to us in getting through to Herr Hitler that we in England wish him well in what he is trying to do in Germany and he does not have to be quite so brutal about it. On the other hand, it makes it very difficult for the Foreign Office. Are they to continue going through the normal diplomatic channels or is that a complete waste of time? This man Friedberg may be all right but the calibre of some of these Nazi new boys swaggering about the world is nothing to write home about, or at least not if you want to write good news.'

'I'm just as worried as you, Joe, about these Nazis but we have to pull their teeth before they can bite by taking away their just cause of complaint—ridiculous demands from France for reparations and so on.'

'What of Larmore?' Weaver said. 'My information is he has some sort of relationship with Friedberg and I gather Baldwin's going to bring him into the cabinet—a new position—military supplies, armaments, that sort of thing. I hear little good of him. He's a womanizer for one thing. If we wanted, the *New Gazette* could blow his career to smithereens.'

'He's not a gentleman,' agreed the Duke, sighing, 'but we have to deal with all sorts nowadays.' Then, thinking Weaver might wonder if he was included among 'all sorts', he hurriedly changed the subject. 'Friedberg should be here in about an hour. He's staying with the Lachberrys at Norham, so you can see he is moving in the highest circles. I gather the Prince of Wales has taken to him. I'm surprised you did not meet him at the Brownlows'. Anyway, I'm determined to make this evening a success. It's important.'

'When is your brother expected?'

The Duke looked at his gold hunter and said, 'Edward? Why, damn it, he ought to be here now.' He rang the bell. When the butler appeared he said, 'Bates, is there any news of Lord Edward?'

'No, your Grace.'

'Where can the boy have got to?' said the Duke to Weaver. 'It is most annoying. We cannot wait dinner for him for ever.'

41

'I expect he'll turn up before long,' said Weaver easily. 'He's probably had a puncture or something.'

'Bates, when Lord Edward does arrive tell him not to dress for dinner but to join us immediately will you?'

'Very good, your Grace,' said Bates, retreating.

'Oh, Bates, inform her Grace that we will not wait dinner for Lord Edward and say that Lord Weaver and I will be in the drawing-room in half an hour.'

When the butler had left the room the Duke said, 'Damn the boy. I wanted him to be here to talk to that stepdaughter of yours. Connie was particularly anxious she had someone of more or less her age to amuse her. Connie said she would be bored to death by all of us old men and no doubt she's right. She says the young man she had counted on to come—Lomax his name is, I believe—bowed out at the last minute. Really, the young men can't be relied upon. If I had been invited to dine . . . oh well, anyway, it can't be helped. I just hope Ned hasn't had an accident. He races around in sports cars and even flies aeroplanes—I'm only surprised he hasn't broken his neck already.'

Weaver's brow was furrowed. 'I say, Duke, as we are alone can I bring you up to date on that matter I had occasion to talk to you about a few weeks ago?' He leant forward confidentially and the Duke could see the bald patch on the top of his head and was reminded of Friar Tuck.

'Of course,' said the Duke. 'Is there something . . . ?'

'I thought you would like to know that the "blackmail" . . . well, it has turned out all right in the end—better than all right, in fact—except for one thing.'

'What's that?' said the Duke.

Lord Weaver bent even closer to the Duke as though he feared someone might be listening at the door and began to explain himself. The Duke was at first intrigued and then disbelieving.

'It's like something out of Shakespeare,' he said at last.

CHAPTER TWO

SATURDAY EVENING

Under other circumstances Edward might have enjoyed his ride. It was peaceful enough lying back against the hay. In the warmth of the summer evening it gave off a sweet smell which reminded him of harvest days in boyhood on Home Farm when he was no different from anyone else, sweating beside lads his own age helping build a haystack or watching unnoticed as the men tinkered with the new threshing machine which was more temperamental even than the farm manager. It was already eight thirty but it was still light. Gradually the frustration he felt at having his plans scuppered by his own folly began to leave him until he was able to contemplate with something approaching equanimity the frosty reception he would receive from the Duke when he finally did arrive at Mersham Castle. He laughed to himself. Here he was sitting beside his agricultural friend behind two handsome carthorses who did not seem to have taken against him for his stupid attempt on the land speed record. Indeed, as Edward stood at the horses' heads before getting up beside the wagoner he was almost certain he detected a satiric glint in the eyes of Myrtle, the left-hand horse. After all, the wagon might roll along the dusty Roman road at three miles an hour but at least it moved, unlike the Lagonda, looking slightly ridiculous in the embrace of a dry ditch.

He quoted to himself as much as he remembered of Lorenzo and Jessica's rhapsody to love on a summer's night in *The Merchant of Venice.* 'In such a night as this, when the sweet wind did gently kiss the trees and they did make no noise, in such a night Troilus methinks mounted the Troyan walls and sighed his soul toward the Grecian tents, where Cressid lay that night. In such a night . . .' How did it go? 'In such a night, did Thisbe fearfully o'ertrip the dew and saw the lion's shadow ere himself, and ran dismayed away.'

It rather pleased him that he could remember so much. 'The Troyan walls,' he mused. They would have been real battlements complete with curtain walls, parapets, corbels, watch towers, bartizans and all the rest of it. Mersham had nothing so warlike. Who of her people would consider withstanding the will of the Virgin Queen, unless it be some rugged Irish kerns who knew no better. Mersham, whose every cubit he knew as well as the palm of his right hand, he loved more than he knew. It was his enchanted childhood playground until he went to school and even then there were long holidays in which to reacquaint himself with each dusty corner. In childhood his rooms—the nursery and his old nanny's rooms—were at the top of the house with only the servants' rooms above them. In winter they could be very cold— the only heating was supplied by inadequate grates. Edward's father had not approved of mollycoddling his children so he had not permitted fires to be lit in the castle between Easter and October. How Nanny had prayed for late Easters as though God might alter the church calendar for her. During the war, the Duke, grieving for his son, took a masochistic pleasure in making himself— and therefore his family—as uncomfortable as possible in solidarity with the soldiers at the front. The old Duke had never been interested in what he ate and by 1915 the food served in the castle was so inadequate the local doctor had been moved to protest that the Duke was endangering his child's health. Thereafter, Edward had been allowed unlimited milk and vegetables but meat was only served on Saturdays and cold on Sundays.

But for all this Edward looked back to those days as a blessed period in his life and when he was in Africa trying to sleep in blistering heat, worried by mosquitoes and sweating pints into the single sheet that covered him, he would summon up images of those winter nights at Mersham when the frost on the *inside* of the windows was as thick as his fingernail.

Behind Edward a mountain of hay threatened a golden avalanche as the cart bumped over each rut in the road and dived into every pot-hole. He pulled at a straw and sucked it pensively. The old carter had said that the nearest public house was four miles back the way he had come and from there he could telephone Mersham for assistance. At this rate it would be an hour before they

45

reached it. He began to wonder if he would even get to the castle that night. Edward and his mercifully unloquacious companion had been trundling over the landscape for three-quarters of an hour without seeing a single soul let alone a motor car when a hooting noise penetrated the creaking and rumbling that gave evidence that the haywain was actually in motion. There was no way of discovering what this hooting signified without bringing the wagon to a halt, which took a full four minutes to achieve. Edward clambered down into the road, his damaged knee making him wince, to see what the matter was.

'Do you think you could move out of the way and let me pass?' The speaker was a black-eyed girl in a beret, which failed to restrain unruly curls. She was alone in a two-seater which Edward, who loved motor cars, was able to identify as the new Morgan four-wheeler.

'I'm afraid that isn't possible,' said Edward, coming round to speak to the girl. 'You can see there are ditches on either side of the road.'

'You're not a local,' said the girl, eyeing him curiously. 'Are you by any chance the owner of that Lagonda I passed nestling in the ditch about three miles back?'

'I am,' said Edward, bowing slightly. 'Like you, I wanted to do the impossible and pass this moving mountain but in my case I was going too fast to stop when I saw it couldn't be done. It is my desire to save you from making the same mistake and adding to the litter in the streets. By the way, could you very kindly turn off the engine for the moment? I can hardly hear myself speak. It's a jolly little car—a Morgan, ain't it?—but noisy.'

'Oh God,' the girl said, clutching her brow. 'This is all I need. I was trying to reach Mersham before dark but I'm hopelessly lost.'

'Mersham,' said Edward hopefully. 'That's where I'm going—or rather where I was going before I had the bad luck to run into this monster. Hey, you're going in absolutely the wrong direction, Miss . . . Miss . . . ?'

'Miss Browne . . . Verity Browne . . .'

'Miss Browne, why don't we turn your car round and I can guide you to Mersham. Are you going to the castle?'

'Not immediately. I am staying at the Mersham Arms. Why, are you?'

'I'm so sorry,' said Edward. 'I should have introduced myself. I'm Edward Corinth and I was expected at the castle in time for dinner. I am now,' he checked his watch, 'two hours late.'

'Edward Corinth? Lord Edward Corinth, the Duke's brother?'

'The very same,' said Edward bowing again. 'Have we met before? If we have, please forgive my—'

'No, no,' said the girl hastily. 'I write for *Country Life* magazine and of course I know your face from . . . oh, you know . . . from the illustrated papers.' She coloured prettily but recovered herself. 'I have an appointment with your sister-in-law, the Duchess, tomorrow, to go over the castle. I am writing a series of articles on castles and the editor particularly wanted to include Mersham and she . . . the Duchess, I mean . . . kindly agreed to see me.'

The girl spoke rapidly, a little over-eager, Edward thought, to provide information about

47

herself.

'Oh, I read *Country Life* but I don't remember seeing—' he said.

'They have not begun to appear yet,' said Verity Browne hurriedly.

By this time they had been joined by the wagon driver who had descended to see what was delaying his passenger.

'I say, my man, think we can swing this little car round so this lady can go back the way she came? I doubt there's enough room to do a three-point turn but let's try.'

'What's that?' said Verity.

'What's what?' said Edward.

'A whatever-you-said-it-was turn.'

'A three-point turn? You know, reverse and then go forward and so on.'

'Oh, I see. I'm sure there is room. Let me try. Now, where is reverse?'

'How long have you had the car?' inquired Edward nervously.

'I picked it up today as a matter of fact and so far I haven't needed to go backwards.'

'Here, let me see what I can do,' said Edward officiously, opening the driver's door. As Verity obediently got out of the car, he was able to get his first proper look at her and he liked what he saw. She was short, not much over five foot he guessed, but her figure was trim and her legs slim and elegant. He suddenly realized she was watching him watching her. He blushed and Verity smiled broadly. Her merry eyes met his in frank enjoyment of his evident appreciation so that he too had to smile.

Hurriedly, he started to lever himself in behind

the wheel but jumped back as fast as his gammy leg allowed him. A black Aberdeen terrier was sitting on the seat and despite its small size it gave every impression that it was capable of defending its mistress's car against all comers. It gave Edward a look of contempt and then, to emphasize its distaste for the intruder, gave three or four little barks.

'Oh, I'm sorry!' said the girl. 'Max, don't be silly and jealous. This kind man is going to help us turn the car round.'

She scooped up the dog in her arms and thrust it at Edward. 'Max, meet Lord Edward Corinth. Lord Edward, this is Max.'

'Delighted,' said Edward beginning to put a hand on the dog's head. He withdrew it quickly as the dog gave a snarl and made an attempt to get out of the girl's clutches.

'I say, I don't think Max likes you. I wonder why. He's usually so nice to people.'

'Yes, well, I'm not sure I like Max. Anyway, please keep a hold on the animal until I have finished.'

'Oh, you don't have to worry. As soon as I have explained to Max you are a friend he will be a pippin. Maxy,' she said, nuzzling the animal, 'this is Mummy's friend and you have to be a good and grateful boy.'

The dog looked unconvinced. 'It's really odd,' said the girl. 'I have never seen him like this before. Of course, he is a bit class conscious and being a working dog I'm not sure he approves of the aristocracy.'

As Edward made his second attempt to get into the Morgan's driving seat, he stumbled a little and

Verity said, 'I say, are you hurt? You've cut your forehead too.'

'I did some damage to myself when I put the kibosh on my car,' said Edward, 'but don't worry, it's nothing serious and it won't affect my driving.'

He found getting the Morgan into reverse gear painful but tried not to show it. After several attempts he managed to face the car in the opposite direction to which it had been travelling without putting it into the ditch. He got out and thanked his companion of the road for the pleasure of his company and tried to slip him half a sovereign.

'Oh no, my lord. There be no call for that. I feels to blame for that fine automobile of yours ending up where it did.'

'No blame to you, Mr . . . I'm so sorry but we met so informally I never got your name.'

'Ben Tranter, your honour,' said the wagoner, passing him his bag, 'I did not think as how—'

'No matter, it was my own silly fault. At least I avoided doing damage to those magnificent animals of yours. I would never have been able to forgive myself if I had harmed Myrtle or Florence.' He turned to Verity. 'Will you allow me?'

'Be my guest, Lord Edward. Together we may yet reach Mersham Castle before break of day.'

With a final wave Edward got into the Morgan— Verity Browne once again in the driving seat, Max curled peaceably at Edward's feet which he tried not to move in case the little dog got irritated—and they set off for Mersham. They passed the Lagonda without stopping to inspect it. Edward knew there was nothing he could do until the morning; then he would get Bates to send someone out to look at it. Half a mile further on there was a bang and the Morgan swerved to one side and came to a sudden halt. Max scrambled up on to Edward's lap and began barking.

'Gosh, what was that?' said Verity, rather shaken.

'Blast it . . . I'm sorry, Miss Browne . . . I did not mean to swear but I do believe we have a puncture. You're not hurt, are you? I am beginning to think that any vehicle I get into is cursed or else there is some conspiracy aimed at stopping us from ever reaching Mersham. I have learnt my lesson. From now on I am keeping to the main roads. Now, let's see if your splendid new car is fitted with a spare tyre.'

In fact there were two spare wheels, so obviously punctures were anticipated by Mr Morgan when he designed his motor car, but it took Edward half an hour to remove the damaged wheel and replace it. He sweated over the jack until he wondered if he would have a heart attack. He got covered in grime and oil—for some reason Mr Morgan had taken upon himself to protect his precious vehicle with pints of the wretched stuff—but in recognition of Miss Browne's presence he kept his language to a moderate damn and blast and then only when the wheel fell on his foot. Max, to his relief, stayed in the car and snored.

Verity, on the other hand, hopped about offering him advice and passing him the occasional spanner. 'I say,' she said, 'it was dashed fortunate for me picking you up like that. I mean, if I had been alone when we ran over that nail I would have had to spend the night in the car or walk miles. Who would think we're in Hampshire? We might be in the middle of the Gobi Desert, except for the cows and the grass and . . . well, you know what I mean.'

It was half-past nine and beginning to get dark when Edward, feeling stiff and tired, restarted the Morgan and they swung on down the road, the headlights illuminating the chalk and stone so it resembled a white ribbon in the gathering gloom. In fifteen minutes they reached the junction with the main road and from there, Edward knew, it was only twenty minutes to the castle.

'Might I suggest, Miss Browne, as it is so late and you have been so kind as to rescue me that, instead of going to the Mersham Arms, we drive straight to the castle. I am sure my brother would never forgive me if I did not offer you a room for the night. We can telephone the hotel and tell them where you are.'

'Oh well, that's very kind,' Verity began, 'but it might be better if—'

'No, I insist, Verity. May I call you Verity? I feel our adventures on the road have brought us closer together than if we had met in the normal way. And you must call me Edward. Well, that's settled then.'

'But I'm just a journalist. I'm not sure the Duke would be—'

Edward was feeling too tired to argue so he merely ignored the girl's protests. 'Right here, and then first left over the cattle grid,' he said. 'I happen to know that Gerald already has a journalist staying at the castle—Lord Weaver. Do you know him?'

'Oh no,' said Verity Browne weakly. 'I don't mix with press barons or whatever they are called.'

'Never mind,' said Edward, 'this is a good

52

opportunity to start. Think what it might do for your career.'

'I don't need that sort of help,' said Verity stiffly.

'No, I'm sorry. That was crass of me. Left here.'

Verity soon found herself on a gravel drive and she gasped as she saw the castle silhouetted in the moonlight. 'Oh, it's so beautiful!' she exclaimed, slowing down. 'It's magic, pure magic. How amazing actually to *live* here.'

'Yes,' agreed Edward, humbled. 'I am fortunate. Of course, I don't live here any more but I come as often as I can and I do regard it as my real home.'

Edward's leg was now very painful but he tried not to show it as he stumbled out of the car and banged on the great door. After a few moments it was opened by the butler.

'Bates, it's me. I had an accident. Oh, and this is Miss Browne. Would you get a bed made up for her? She has been kind enough to give me a lift and I have invited her to stay the night.'

'Good evening, my lord. Good evening, miss. His Grace was concerned that you might have had an automobile accident. I trust that you are not hurt?'

'The Lagonda went off the road about ten miles back, my own silly fault. I'll have to ask you to send out a salvage party in the morning, Bates.'

'You are limping, my lord. Shall I telephone Dr Best?'

'No, in the morning. I bumped my knee, that's all. Just give me a stick, will you?' He indicated an elephant's foot in which umbrellas and walking-sticks were crowded. Bates did as he was asked and then stopped open-mouthed as Edward hobbled inside the house. The chandelier in the hall permitted Bates to see for the first time the state of the young master. His hair and face were messed by oil and dirt and his ulster was smeared and torn.

'His Grace said you were to go straight into the dining-room without changing,' the butler said doubtfully. 'The gentlemen are having their port and cigars, sir, but there is cold ham and salad if you and the lady are—'

At that moment the dining-room door opened and the Duke appeared. 'My dear boy, I thought it must be you,' he said, coming forward agitatedly. 'We have been worried. Have you had an accident? Are you hurt? Bates, tell the Duchess Lord Edward has arrived. Ned, what on earth has happened? You're filthy—'

'Calm down, Gerald. Yes, I did have an accident. Trying to avoid a hay wagon idiotically I went into a ditch and broke the axle but I'm not hurt—just knocked my knee a bit. Say hello to Miss Browne, my guardian angel, who rescued me, don't you know. Miss Browne, the Duke of Mersham.'

'Good evening, Miss Browne. What has my brother been doing to need rescuing?'

Connie opened the drawing-room door with Honoria, Blanche and Celia Larmore just behind. 'Ned, is that you? Goodness me, where have you been? We were becoming alarmed.' Then, seeing her brother-in-law's grimed face and the way he was leaning on his stick, she said anxiously, 'Has there been an accident? Are you hurt?'

'No, Connie, don't be alarmed. I'm not injured—or only my knee. I'm afraid the Lagonda went off the road. It was either that or colliding with a haywain, and this kind lady, Miss Verity Browne, rescued me.'

'Ah, Miss Browne—do come in,' said Connie

54

coming forward. 'We obviously have a lot to be grateful to you for. Ned, give me a kiss. On second thoughts,' she said, backing away, 'I will wait to kiss you until you are cleaned up. Why don't you go and wash off the worst of the . . . whatever it is you are covered with, Ned . . . and then come into the dining-room and tell us your adventures while you eat. Did you say there was cold ham, Bates?'

'Yes, your Grace, and salad—and shall I bring in the claret too, your Grace?'

'Yes, please do, Bates,' said the Duke.

'Miss Browne,' said the Duchess, putting out her hand, 'you have obviously been very kind.' She hesitated. 'You are not by any chance Verity Browne who I was expecting tomorrow?'

'Yes, Duchess, but now I must go and clean up at the hotel.'

'Certainly not!' said the Duchess. 'We would not hear of it, would we, Gerald? You must be our guest. Bates will show you where to wash and then come into the dining-room and have something to eat while we get a room made up for you. We all want to hear what has been happening so we will sit and watch you eat if that does not sound too like the zoo.'

'Talking of animals,' Edward said, 'Miss Browne has with her an Aberdeen terrier.'

'Shall I take it to the kitchen, miss?' inquired Bates. 'Cook will feed the animal and find a place for it to sleep.'

'That's very kind,' said Verity, beaming at the butler. 'I would be grateful if you could feed and water Max—that's his name, by the way—but if the Duchess does not mind, he can sleep in my room. He's very clean and he'll curl up on the floor in the corner and not make any mess.'

'Very good, miss,' said the butler. To Edward's amazement, Bates lifted the dog out of the Morgan and carried it off, the dog making no protest whatsoever.

Ten minutes later everyone forgathered in the dining-room—even Hermione Weaver—anxious to hear Edward's tale and take a good look at the strange girl who had succoured him. Edward, who had had a long and eventful day, was quite happy to leave most of the story-telling to Verity, who seemed quite unawed by the company in which she now found herself; she might regularly have burst in on dinner-parties in ducal mansions for all the effect it appeared to have upon her and yet there was nothing brash or vulgar in her evident pleasure at being the centre of attention. Edward, despite the pain in his leg, enjoyed watching this petite, tousle-haired girl, bright-eyed and pink in the face with excitement, digging into ham and salad while, between mouthfuls, she regaled the assembled company with the story of his brush with death as though she had actually been a witness of the accident. Where Edward might have played down the danger, she exaggerated the damage done to the car and the nearness with which the driver had avoided being seriously injured. Connie kept on glancing at her brother-in-law as if to gauge how much of the story was true, but Edward steadfastly refused to meet her eye. He was in considerable discomfort but he wanted to disguise this from her until the next day. It was unthinkable that he should get Dr Best out of bed, an elderly man on the point of retirement, who in any case would probably be able to do nothing but prescribe rest.

Surprisingly, it was Hermione Weaver who seemed most excited by the new arrivals. It seemed to her mother that, after all, she was not as violently hostile to Edward as she had claimed. When she spoke to him directly it was almost shyly and she seemed even a little jealous that it had been Verity Browne's good fortune to have come across the motorcar accident and not herself. She also seemed abashed that Verity should have a real job. In Hermione's circle not many women had paid jobs. It was unthinkable if you were married, of course, and if you were rich and single as she was, there was so much to do that the idea of spending the day as secretary to some businessman or politician was not attractive. However, Blanche did wonder as she looked at her daughter's animated face if her problems did not stem from sheer boredom. Was she just tired of the empty round of dances, dinner-parties and night-clubs with which she filled her waking hours? Maybe, if Joe could get her a job on one of his papers she might be happier: if Verity Browne could be a journalist why should not Hermione? She decided she would ask her husband when they got to bed that night and see if he thought there was anything in the idea.

The Duke was looking tired and saying very little. It was typical of Ned, he considered, to have an accident driving his motorcar too fast. He was always crashing aeroplanes, motor cars and even boats, and as a result of this accident he had succeeded in breaking up his carefully arranged 'meeting of minds'. It had all been going rather well, too. Ned had arrived just when the men, relaxing over their port and cigars, were at their most suggestible. It was the time when, with the ladies, bless 'em, out of the way, confidences could be made, friendships forged and unlikely alliances built, but Ned bursting in on the scene had destroyed all that. The women were back at the dining-table and the men could no longer speak freely with the easy confidence of gentlemen gathered in sacred harmony. The whole atmosphere had been ruined, the Duke decided. Before they had heard Edward and Verity at the front door, Craig and Friedberg had to their own amazement found common ground in disparaging the performance of the American forces on the Western Front in 1918, conveniently forgetting that without the Americans the war might have dragged on indefinitely. They told stories—no doubt, the Duke thought, apocryphal—illustrating the poor quality of the American infantry officer, and the two men, who had earlier been snapping at each other's heels, had gone so far as to laugh at each other's instances of American ineptitude. That breath of good will was dissipated by the new arrivals. The Duke felt aggrieved but could not say so. As he listened to Verity with half an ear, he reviewed the dinner.

When they sat down there had been some awkwardness about the empty chair but Connie had decided not to clear Edward's place in case he arrived in time for some food. Hermione had in the end behaved herself, to Connie's great relief, and had discussed dress-makers with Celia Larmore quite amiably. She had not even been too rude to Honoria Haycraft when the latter opined that night-clubs were the haunt of the devil. Unwisely perhaps, the Bishop had backed his wife up: 'It's the cocktails which do the harm in my view. They poison the system. All a civilized person needs is a glass or two of dry sherry before dinner.'

'And all that smoking,' went on Honoria, blithely unaware of Hermione's scowl. 'In my day girls did not smoke. It's such a dirty habit.'

'Oh, I don't know,' said the Duke hurriedly. 'I think you are being unfair on the young. We haven't left them much of a world to grow up in, you know. What do you think, Hermione?'

'Don't ask me,' the girl said sullenly. 'I don't feel as if I am one of the "younger generation" anyhow. Ask my stepfather. The *New Gazette* is always doing stuff about "youth". I'm sure he knows all about it.'

There was an awkward silence but the Duke covered it with talk of cricket and the moment passed.

The food had been good and the wine first-rate but the Duke pinned all his hopes on the hour the men would spend over their port once the table had been cleared and the ladies had left to take their coffee in the drawing-room. To grace the occasion he had selected two bottles of his finest port and he was determined, without looking obvious about it, to make it known to his guests just how favoured they were. When Bates had placed the decanter in front of him and offered round the cigars in an oak box which his grandfather had brought back from Cuba in 1883, the Duke dismissed the butler and offered Larmore, the most knowledgeable wine-lover among his guests, a light-hearted challenge. 'Larmore, I remember you telling me you were interested in port so I thought you might like to taste this,' he began, with all the benevolence of one who knows he is going to give his guests a treat they probably don't deserve.

The Duke passed him the decanter and Larmore filled his glass before passing it on. While the others were filling their glasses Larmore was going through an elaborate pantomime, examining the wine as he rolled it in his glass and making curious grunts as he mentally checked off its characteristics. He put the glass to his nose and a strange expression transformed his face. Concentrating fiercely, he drank from his glass. The effect was immediate. The lines of petulance around his rather small mouth vanished and his eyes, which had been narrow and anxious-looking during dinner, shone like those of a dog unexpectedly presented with a particularly juicy beef bone. His whole bearing indicated intense, almost sexual, pleasure. 'By Jove, Duke,' he said at last, 'this is splendid. I don't know I have ever tasted anything finer. Who is the shipper?'

The Duke assumed a look of low cunning. 'If I tell you the shipper, can you tell me the vintage?'

'Very well,' said Larmore.

'Taylor's,' said the Duke.

All eyes were turned on Larmore but he seemed not in the least disconcerted. 'Yes,' he said thoughtfully, 'I thought it was big enough to be the Taylor's—splendidly rich and powerful.' He smelled the port again and then held the glass up to the candlelight. 'As for the vintage, I think it is too mature to be the '12 which really leaves only the 1900 or the 1896. Hmm—the only port I have had which could begin to match this was with the Devonshires last Christmas and that was the '86 Graham's—a regal port but not as good as this—so

I think I am going to go for '96.' He looked at the Duke inquiringly.

'Very well done, Larmore. You have hit the nail on the head. Please, fill your glass.'

There was a murmur of approbation from the General and from Lord Weaver.

'Certainly I couldn't have done that, Larmore—identified the vintage, I mean,' said Weaver admiringly, 'but even I, Duke, can appreciate it's of particular sweetness and strength—the wrong words, I know, but I have always found it difficult to describe the distinctive character of a fine wine, so you'll have to forgive me. You have really done us proud, sir.' Weaver raised his glass towards the Duke and the Duke bowed his head modestly. 'The burgundy we had with the fish, that was Corton Charlemagne, was it not?'

'1921, Louis Latour,' confirmed the Duke.

'And if I may be so vulgar as to inquire,' Weaver continued, 'the claret was . . . ?'

'Château Haut-Brion, 1920,' said the Duke, embarrassed but proud. He did not like to seem to brag but it was well that his guests—even philistines like the Bishop and von Friedberg—should understand the compliment he had paid them.

Once again everyone was silent. Larmore refilled his glass and admired the rich ruby colour which, when he held his glass up to the candle, seemed to flame and flicker. He then lowered his head reverentially as if, the Bishop thought, he was going to pray and inhaled the intoxicating scent of a wine which had been maturing for two generations. Still without speaking, he put his lips to the delicate glass and sipped. The lines of anxiety below his eyes were smoothed and his smile lit up his countenance so that, to the Bishop who was sitting opposite him, he suddenly seemed a much younger man.

General Craig said, 'I don't have your knowledge, Larmore, but even my untutored palate recognizes greatness.' He raised his glass to his lips, his hand shaking so noticeably that the Duke wondered if he were ill. Instead of sipping the wine and savouring its particular character he drank deeply. It seemed to steady him a little, and when he replaced his glass on the table the Duke thought he looked less feverish; quite unconsciously the old man stroked his stomach as though the wine was helping his digestion. 'My doctor tells me I must drink very sparingly but, as I tell him, I have so few pleasures—pleasures of the flesh—left to me that I am loath to give up one of the few I can still enjoy,' Craig said sadly.

The Bishop too claimed to drink very little but the Duke noticed with amusement that he drained his glass quickly and refilled it from the decanter, which was now circulating for the third time. The Duke saw that Friedberg was a little at a loss to know how to enter the conversation about wine without making a fool of himself, and hurriedly moved to include him in the general bonhomie by asking him if port was much drunk in Germany, and was told that it was not. 'We prefer brandy or liqueurs but when I am in England and,' he bowed his head, 'in such distinguished company, I do as the Romans do—that is the phrase, is it not?—and with the greatest of pleasure.' Saying which he tossed down his port as though it was slivovitz, which made the Duke wince. Von Friedberg went on to spoil the mood of quiet contentment around the table by embarking on a long and boring lecture about the superior merits of the wines of Alsace—a part of Germany, he was moved to say with drunken solemnity, whatever the French might like to claim.

The Duke roused himself to bring Friedberg to heel—politely, of course. Rather subtly, he thought, he interrupted Friedberg by asking General Craig if he had any particular memories of other great wines he had drunk. The General said he could not say he remembered tasting wines nobler than those he had drunk this evening—he nodded to the Duke in tribute—but he had drunk wines in some queer places. He launched into a story of finding a case of champagne, almost boiled by the sun, in General Gordon's apartments in Khartoum in 1896. 'It may have been a great year for port,' he said ruefully, 'but not for champagne—at least not in the Sudan. I had always believed General Gordon to have been a teetotaller so what the champagne was doing there in his rooms I have no idea. I brought the wine to Kitchener in his tent and he decreed it would be drunk that night under the stars in memory of the man we had come to rescue. It turned out to be a rather embarrassing occasion. Of course, we had no means of chilling the wine and I got a good deal of chaff for, when the bottles were broached and all we officers—of whom I was the youngest and most junior—had a glass in our hand, and our chief had made a little speech, we all drank only to have to spit out the wine which, as I ought to have guessed, was filthy. Fortunately, the chief thought it was funny. He didn't have much of a sense of humour—great man though he was—but when he did find something funny he would let himself go. On this occasion he roared with laughter, slapped me on the back and said that as a punishment he required me to drink my glass dry, which I did, and was promptly sick. I think perhaps the chief was really celebrating his safe arrival in Khartoum. It had been a most terrible campaign and we were all heartily looking forward to going home. I shall always remember the occasion: the horrible wine, the chief's laughter and my being sick in the sand. It cemented a special relationship all we young officers had with Kitchener, but I have a feeling that poor Gordon's ghost might have been hovering nearby quietly satisfied that we who had come too late to save him had at least come too late to enjoy his wine.'

The Duke smiled and turned to the Bishop. 'I suppose there is no point in soliciting a story from you, is there Cecil? I know you are not a drinker.'

'Well, no, Duke, though I do remember when I was a young curate taking a communion service in place of my vicar, who was away. It was an ill-lit barn of a church in Middlesbrough and it was very hard for the priest to see how many people were intending to take communion. I was dependent on the church warden when he brought up the collection plate telling me the numbers. On this occasion—either I was nervous or he mumbled—but I thought he said thirty-three while in fact he had said twenty-three and of those twenty-three a majority were little old ladies who merely touched the wine with their lips and did not drink it. Imagine my horror when I saw that everyone had taken communion and I had almost a pint left in the chalice. As you know, the wine once it has been consecrated must be consumed, so I had no alternative but to drink it all down. It was not good wine and, like you, General, I felt very sick, but unlike you it was out of the question to give way to it. I think the sidesman seeing me stagger through the end of the sacrament thought I was drunk—as indeed I was—and reported me to the vicar. The latter rebuked me for being a fool and I think it was from that moment that I decided the grape and I were never going to be good friends—but,' and the Bishop refilled his glass for the third time, 'if I may say so, Duke, you are converting me.' He smiled at his little joke. 'This really is quite delicious. Even I can understand that you are paying us a rare compliment, Duke, and I thank you.' He, as Weaver had done, raised his glass to the Duke and smiled benignly.

The Duke wondered if Honoria would reprimand the poor man, as had the vicar all those years ago, when she smelt the wine on her lord's breath that night.

Von Friedberg was still thinking about the General's story of Lord Kitchener and he interrupted Larmore, who wanted to recall for the assembled company the many great wines he had sampled in his life, by asking Craig if Kitchener had been as brave as legend had it.

'Oh yes, brave, stalwart, obstinate, awkward—all these things—a very great soldier in my opinion, second only to my late commander, Field Marshal Earl Haig, God rest his soul, but unlike Haig, Kitchener was not suited to being a politician,' said the General, shaking his head mournfully.

They waited for him to elaborate but it seemed

65

that the General, now deep in his own thoughts, was not going to provide examples of Kitchener's battles with the politicians to prove his point, and the discussion turned to the nature of courage. The Duke, with half an eye on Friedberg, made an eloquent plea for politicians and soldiers to have the moral courage to restrain the 'sabre rattling' of their political leaders.

Von Friedberg looked sour and went into a long tirade about Germany demanding its rightful place at the council tables of Europe. The Bishop chipped in to assure the German that most English people wanted his country to return to its position as a leading power in Europe, and Larmore hurried to agree.

'So, that is what will happen,' said the German sententiously. 'Under the leadership of our great leader, Chancellor Adolf Hitler . . .'

'And is it true you are expanding your army?' asked Weaver, who had been noticeably silent, content to listen to the others and enjoy his port and cigar.

'Certainly,' said Friedberg pugnaciously, 'We need a new model army like your Oliver Cromwell . . .'

'Not *my* Oliver Cromwell,' Weaver muttered but Friedberg did not hear him.

'. . . and we will build aeroplanes and ships so that no one can say to us "You do this, you do that." I may tell you in confidence, we have already . . . But no, the wine speaks, Duke, and makes me wish to be indiscreet.' He simpered knowingly.

The Bishop, his tongue loosened by the wine, said, 'You make my blood run cold, Baron. I fear for all that I hold dear: humanitarianism, brotherly good will between nations and their leaders. These political creeds we see thriving like weeds in an uncared-for garden—they may not in themselves be evil, they may even bring benefits: jobs, food, a steady income and with these, self-respect, but we must recognize that they are imposed by force and rest on a basis of cruelty and fear.'

The Bishop had spoken with so much feeling there was a moment of embarrassment when he ceased speaking. Everyone tried to avoid the German's eye though longing to see how he took the attack. Craig looked at the Duke with burning eyes, a small smile curling the edge of his lips, but he said nothing.

Von Friedberg looked round the table at a ring of troubled faces and realized he had gone too far in his triumphalism. 'Do not worry, my friends,' he said jovially, actually putting a hand on the shoulder of the General, who was sitting next to him. He puffed at his cigar, sending a plume of smoke over his neighbour who coughed and waved his hand in front of his face. The Duke was anxious lest Friedberg would think the General was being rude, but fortunately he was too absorbed in what he wanted to say to notice the waving hand. 'We Germans have no quarrel with the English. We admire your Empire. We admire you . . .' he added mischievously. 'We are all Aryans and should unite against the lesser races,' and he waved his finger at Weaver, perhaps in imitation of his leader.

Weaver grunted but said nothing, for which the Duke was grateful.

'There is room for two empires in the world, surely,' said Larmore nervously.

'Ah, Mr Larmore, you are right.' Friedberg

67

grinned wolfishly. 'Let me repeat, we Aryans must—how do you say it—"stick together"? Communism is the great enemy and our enemies may overwhelm us unless we have our hand on the sword of justice.'

Friedberg smiled, obviously pleased by his grandiloquence and confident that what he had said would reassure his listeners. But the Bishop for one was uneasy.

'I always shiver when I hear anyone talk about swords of justice. If indeed yours is a sword of justice, Baron, I urge you not to draw it from your scabbard.'

'From my scabbard? What is scabbard?' said Friedberg, momentarily puzzled.

'*Die Degenscheide . . .?*' suggested the Duke, tentatively.

'*Ja! die Degenscheide—danke, mein Herzog.* I did not know you spoke German.'

'Only a little,' said the Duke modestly. It was at this point that the conversation turned to what made a good army, and the General and Friedberg unexpectedly found common ground in disparaging Americans. Weaver was just about to put in a mild defence of North American soldiery when they all heard a loud knocking at the door. The Bishop found himself thinking of that ridiculous moment in *Macbeth* when the knocking at the gate disturbs the sleeping castle and the audience want to giggle because they know there will soon be so much blood. Then there was the rattle of bolts, the sound of Bates opening up, followed by the clear, confident cries of the English nobleman returning home.

'Ah!' exclaimed the Duke with irritation. 'That

68

must be my brother. Please forgive me if I leave you for a moment to find out what has happened to make him so late. Sit and enjoy your wine, please, I won't be long.'

For whatever reason, the Duke's guests felt unable to stay put and rose with their host to stroll after him to the door in the dining-room which opened into the hall. Even Friedberg seemed anxious not to be left behind, either alone or with the Bishop, who was rather drunk and feeling melancholy at the bellicosity displayed by the German and by General Craig. The Bishop stumbled to his feet and followed Friedberg, finding himself beside General Craig. 'You were very silent when Friedberg was telling us his vision of a resurrected Germany,' he murmured.

'What is there to say?' said the General shortly. 'It confirms what I already knew—that we will be at war with Germany within ten years. Or rather you will be. I shall be watching from somewhere other.'

The Bishop hardly took in what the General had said to him because at that moment the Duke moved into the hall and they saw through the open door the dirty, dishevelled figures of Lord Edward Corinth and Verity Browne.

'Well,' said the Duke when he had heard Verity's story and tut-tutted over his younger brother's stupidity, 'I suppose I must not grumble. At least you are safe, Ned!'

Everyone had seated themselves or stood around the dining-table with no other thought but to be near enough to Verity and Edward to hear the story they had to tell. When the company had returned to the dining-room after greeting the late arrivals the Duke dropped back wearily into his

69

great carver and made Verity and Edward sit on either side of him. Von Friedberg, who obviously had an eye for a pretty girl, sat himself next to Verity and beside him was Larmore who seemed to be surreptitiously trying to get the German's attention, but Friedberg was intent on charming Verity and would not respond even when Larmore touched him on the sleeve. Beside him sat the General with Hermione Weaver standing at his shoulder, which seemed to be making him uneasy. Perhaps he was thinking that she should not be standing while he was seated or perhaps having her at his elbow made him feel claustrophobic.

On the other side of the table all eyes were on Verity, which she obviously enjoyed. Beside Edward, Weaver listened intently as if she were one of his reporters and next to him the Bishop was feeling the effects of the wine. The latter was attempting to disguise his condition from his wife, who had sat down beside him, by staring across at Verity. Blanche and Connie sat themselves at the end of the table opposite the Duke, Connie only too aware that her husband was not pleased to have women invade that holiest time when the men communed with their port. On the other hand, Edward and Verity's arrival had delighted her. It had given her an excuse for giving up the stilted conversation she was making with Honoria and Celia Larmore, aware out of the corner of her eye that Blanche and Hermione were quarrelling about something in whispers over by the French windows.

'Miss Browne,' said Friedberg gallantly when Verity paused to draw breath, 'you tell us you write for *Country Life*. It is, you must believe me, a pleasure to meet you.' He made her a small bow from his chair. 'I also read the *Country Life*. It is sent to me at my castle in Bavaria.'

Verity looked a little sheepish, perhaps feeling she had made too great claims for herself. 'Oh yes, I am writing some articles for them on life in grand and beautiful houses. The Duchess has very kindly agreed to show me round the castle tomorrow.'

'That is good. It is a very splendid house.' He looked slyly at the Duke. 'They call it a castle but if you wish to see real castles you must visit Germany. Yes,' he said, intoxicated by the wine and the pleasure of having beside him a young and attractive woman instead of these old men who seemed to distrust him, 'you must visit me at Schloss Hertzberg, my family seat.'

He smiled roguishly at Verity which made her want to laugh. He was being so charming but it was all wasted on her. He was quite the chevalier, he thought. He put out his hand as if he might seize Verity's and kiss it. He withdrew it suddenly. He had caught sight of the General's face which seemed to be contorted with an effort not to laugh. He was outraged. How dare this old man who had killed so many of his countrymen laugh at him. He got up and his chair, unbalanced by the suddenness of his movement, fell backwards. For a moment everyone stared at the German but then they became conscious that the General was not laughing. He was making terrible gasping noises and pulling feebly at his necktie. He began to sway from side to side as though he were attempting to release himself from someone's grasp.

'What the deuce . . . ?' exclaimed Larmore.

Edward was the first to understand the situation. He got up and stumbled round the table. He pushed Hermione to one side and tried to loosen the General's tie, but the old man was now twisting and writhing so violently that Edward could not do anything; the General's face was puce with the effort to breathe. With one convulsive jerk he pushed away his chair and fell on to the carpet where he lay twitching like a fish out of water. Edward flopped on to the floor beside him, ignoring an intense spasm of pain which began in his knee and travelled all the way up his spine. He tried to support Craig's head and shoulders but he knew he could do nothing to ease his agony. 'Get me some water, will you,' he called to Hermione, but the girl was too horrified to do anything except shrink backwards, her hand at her throat as though she too were unable to breathe. Connie came rushing up with a glass in her hand but it was too late. As Edward tried to dribble the water into the General's mouth he choked and the water dribbled down his chin. His eyes bulged as though some intense pressure behind them would propel them out of their sockets. The old man arched his back and then gave a long sigh and collapsed into Edward's arms. His lips had turned blue and his mouth was fixed in a grin of agony.

'He's dead,' said Edward unnecessarily, looking up at the frightened faces in a circle above him.

There was a horrified silence before Hermione broke it with a scream. As her mother ran to comfort her, Connie said, 'It was all so sudden. Was it a heart attack?'

Edward looked at her strangely. 'We must ring Dr Best and I'm afraid we must also inform the police. I'm almost certain General Craig has taken poison.'

CHAPTER THREE

SATURDAY NIGHT

'He can't be dead!' the Duke said, clumsily getting on his knees beside his brother.

'I'm afraid he is,' said Edward, trying to sound calm. He heaved himself to his feet. 'Connie, will you take everyone into the drawing-room. We ought not to touch anything until the police get here.'

'Oh, this is too terrible! But poison, whatever do you mean, Ned?' Connie exclaimed. 'He must have had a heart attack or something. How could he have been poisoned?'

'Yes,' said the Duke angrily. 'What do you mean saying he was poisoned? Isn't it enough that the General should have a heart attack here without you . . . without you saying such things?'

'To die here, in our house,' said Connie, her hands to her mouth, unconsciously echoing Lady Macbeth, the Bishop noticed. He suppressed an urge to laugh.

'I mean, it can't be anything he has eaten. We have all eaten the same food,' Connie insisted. She looked round her at her silent guests, who seemed to be considering her words and consulting their insides. The Bishop, remembering his duty, knelt beside the dead man, made the sign of the cross over his face and murmured a prayer.

Lord Weaver, ever the man of action, had rung for Bates. 'I'm sorry, Duke, but Lord Edward is right, we must call the police. Even if it is a heart

73

attack it is better that the police satisfy themselves that it was . . . that it was a natural death.' He looked at Edward. He was quite certain that the General had been poisoned as Edward had said but it was not for him to say so.

The butler came into the room. 'Bates,' said Lord Weaver, 'the General has had a heart attack, we think, and I am afraid he's dead. Could you get something to cover his face—a tablecloth or—'

'I really don't think we should disturb—' began Edward.

'I am not leaving the poor man in this condition without something over his face,' said the Duke fiercely.

'Is there anything else I can do for the poor gentleman?' asked the butler, coming over to where the Duke stood beside the body.

'I am afraid not, Bates,' said the Duke. 'There's nothing anyone can do. I am going to telephone the Chief Constable from my study and I will also ring Dr Best. Connie, take everyone into the drawing-room, would you, and get John to bring brandy. I am afraid this is a terrible shock, terrible. Colonel Philips is a friend of mine and a good man. We don't want a local bobby making a mountain of this.' Then, seeing Celia Larmore looking alarmed, he said, 'I mean, the last thing the General would want is for his death to be some sort of scandal. We owe it to a great soldier that his death should be dignified. What's the time?'

'Five past eleven,' said Edward, consulting his watch. 'Look, Gerald, I really don't think we should touch the body, even to put a cloth over . . .' He could not quite say over 'it' when 'it' had so recently been a living man.

74

The Duke looked thunderously at his brother. 'Do as I say, Bates,' was all he said, however.

'Very good, your Grace,' said the butler with the equanimity associated with that breed.

He bustled out and Connie started shepherding everyone after him. As they walked slowly out of the room Hermione began to weep noisily and had to be comforted by Blanche, but she too was close to tears. It had all been so sudden. One minute the General had been alive and then he was dead. If one wasn't safe seated at a duke's dining-table in an English castle, where could one be safe? It was this realization which was, consciously or unconsciously, going through the minds of everyone present. Death had snuffed out a man's life without warning and without meaning as easily as one might pinch the flame of a candle. It had taken the General less than a minute to die. It could not but put normal day-to-day anxieties in perspective.

Larmore, still white with shock and holding his wife tightly by the arm, pushed his way through the door, keeping well clear of the dead man. 'The Duke's right,' he almost shouted, 'we must do all we can to keep this quiet.'

Von Friedberg, who seemed stunned by the calamity, waved the cigar which he had been smoking before the General had collapsed as though he were a schoolboy requesting permission to leave the room. 'Yes, it is not good for me to be here when the police come. My visit was a secret— how do you say?—informal. I cannot allow it to be known I was here, Duke.'

'I understand, of course, Baron,' said Connie, 'but the Chief Constable is an old friend of ours and you can count on him to be discreet. There is no reason why the newspapers will have to know who was dining with the Duke when this terrible thing happened.'

'The newspapers!' exclaimed Friedberg. 'My name must not appear in the newspapers. The Führer would not be pleased.'

'If I may say so, Baron,' Lord Weaver interjected, 'it might be better if you stayed until the police come so that they can take a statement from you here rather than having to bother you at the embassy.'

'A statement?' said the German. 'But I know nothing. Why do I have to give a statement? In my country there would be no statements.'

'But we have a rule of law in this country,' interjected Verity Browne unexpectedly, 'and——'

'Please, Baron,' said the Duchess. 'If you wish to leave I shall ask Bates to tell your chauffeur to bring round your car immediately.'

'Thank you, Duchess. I apologize if I am—what do you say?—leaving you in the lurches but you and the Duke understand that, although I am here as a private person, I have—'

'Say no more, Baron. We quite understand. Let me see you out. I hope next time we meet, it will be on a happier occasion.'

'No doubt, no doubt,' said the flurried diplomat, briskly shaking hands with his fellow guests. 'That was a very pleasant dinner . . . except . . .'

'Connie, you stay here. I will show the Baron to his car,' said the Duke.

'Well!' said Haycraft when the German had disappeared. 'Just the sort of ally one would wish for in an emergency.'

Edward had not followed the others into the drawing-room. His shock at what had happened was giving way to puzzlement. He sat down once again beside the body. It was not a pleasant sight. The face was contorted in a dreadful snarl, the teeth bared like fangs, the upper lip with its absurd moustache pulled right up. The eyes were glassy and the expression on the face was of great pain. His skin had a bluish tinge, which Edward knew from his reading was consistent with cyanide poisoning. He was quite certain the General had taken poison and he was confident that the poison *was* cyanide. He had never seen a death by cyanide but in Africa he had been present when one of his bearers had been bitten by a snake. The poison had been sucked out of the man's foot by the leader of the party, a white hunter who had much experience of dealing with such emergencies, but Edward had been left looking ineffective and feeling inadequate. He had been prompted by the incident to buy a medical encyclopaedia and read up about poisons and how to administer first aid. He trusted the General was now at peace but the manner of his passing had been unforgivably violent. His eye went down the body and he suddenly saw what he had not previously noticed: the General's right hand was gripping a small silver box. He longed to prise open the dead man's fingers and investigate the box but he knew it would be quite irresponsible to do so.

The first question the police would ask was how the General had been poisoned. It had to have been an accident. Murder was unthinkable but so was suicide. No one in their right mind—though of course, by definition, suicides were presumed not to be in their right minds—no one, surely, would choose to kill themselves at a formal dinner-party, while enjoying a particularly fine port. The port: that made Edward realize he did not even understand how the General had taken the poison. As Connie had pointed out, they had all eaten the same food except Verity and himself, and all the men at least had drunk the same wine. In any case, if it were cyanide, the poison would have taken immediate effect so he had to assume that it was in the port the General had been drinking when he was convulsed. Bates and John the footman had cleared plates and wine glasses as soon as the ladies had left the dining-room so, apart from two tumblers half full of water and the Duke's claret glass which he had retained because it was not quite empty, there were only the port glasses on the table. No, that wasn't quite correct; there were also the two glasses containing claret which Bates had put before Verity and himself to drink with their ham. The General had certainly been drinking port, so which was his glass? There was no port glass in his hand nor on the floor. Edward scanned the table. He assumed the General must have had time to put down his glass before he was convulsed by the burning horror of the cyanide. Although Edward had been sitting opposite him, he had not been looking at him at the crucial moment; his eyes had been on Verity until he heard the General making choking noises. It had all happened so quickly but he was sure he would have noticed if the General had had a glass in his hand when he began to feel the effects of the poison. The unfortunate man had been tearing at his throat, desperate to get air in his lungs, though he must have had tight in the palm of his right hand the little silver box which Edward was itching to examine.

Given then that the General's port glass was still on the table, it ought to have been easy enough to see which it was, but all the men had been clustered so tightly about Verity listening to her tell her story that there was a corresponding jumble of port glasses on the table within reach of the General. Edward counted nine in all. In addition to the Duke and his male guests at dinner, he and Verity had also each been given a glass to lift their spirits and he remembered that Hermione had demanded and been given a glass at the same time. She said if Verity could drink port so could she. Edward remembered the worried look he had seen on Blanche's face, and Honoria Haycraft had pursed her lips in disapproval. Edward decided he must take his own advice and not touch any of the glasses on the table, but there was nothing to prevent him sniffing. He thought he detected a strange acidic smell as he sniffed at one of three glasses nearest to where the General had been sitting but he remembered that hydrocyanic acid is highly volatile and evaporates almost immediately it is exposed to the air.

Bates came in carrying a linen tablecloth which he laid gently over the dead man. 'Thank you, Bates,' Edward said, suddenly feeling very weary. Although he knew it was wrong to have spread the linen on the tortured face he was grateful that it had been done. The General's death agony had left him too exposed. This little shroud would give him the privacy we would all surely crave in death.

'It was poison, wasn't it, my lord?'

'Yes, Bates, I believe it was,' Edward said shortly. 'Is there a key to the dining-room door? I think it should be left locked until the police have seen everything they need. Oh,' he said, looking towards the other end of the room, 'we ought to lock the door into the kitchen too if there is a key to that.'

'There is a key, my lord, which fits both doors. I will go and fetch it from the key cupboard in the pantry. The French windows are open too, my lord. Shall I close them? The key is in the lock.'

'No, that's all right, Bates. I will close them. You go and get the door key.'

The butler hesitated for a moment and Edward said, rather more abruptly than he had intended, 'Out with it, man. Is there something bothering you?'

'I wonder if I might ask you, my lord, to speak to Jeffries?'

'Who is Jeffries?'

'Jeffries is the General's man, my lord—his valet,' he added, seeing that Edward had still not understood.

'By Jove, yes, of course, Bates. He knows what has happened then?'

'He knows that his master has had an attack and died, my lord.' The butler coughed. 'I thought it better not to make any mention of the possibility that the poor gentleman might have been poisoned. He is very much upset, my lord.'

'Of course, he must be. I should have thought of it. It was quite right of you, Bates, not to mention

80

poison until the doctor has examined the General. It's bad enough as it is. We don't want to upset anyone more than they have to be. What about John, though? Have you told him to keep his mouth shut?' said Edward, remembering the footman.

'Yes, my lord. I have taken the liberty of informing the staff of the bare facts of the General's sudden death and I have reminded everyone that the Duke requires complete discretion about anything which happens in this house.'

'Very good. I will wait here until you have brought the key. Then ask Jeffries to come to me in the gunroom.'

While he waited for Bates to return, Edward went over to the French windows. They opened directly on to grass which was dry so there was no way of knowing if anyone had entered or gone out of the windows in the last hour or two. There were no signs of anyone—no suspicious cigar stub or anything like that. In any case, Edward thought, the poison could only have been introduced into the port by the General himself or one of the other guests sitting round the Duke's table. One could not be too careful, however, so Edward closed and locked the windows using his handkerchief. Bates returned as he did so and locked the door through which he had just come and which led to the kitchen. Together, they went out into the hall, securing the dining-room door behind them. In the hall, Edward lit a cigarette; deep in thought, he strolled down the passage to the gunroom.

Jeffries was a wizened little man with a drooping moustache and watery eyes. 'Ah, Jeffries,' said

Edward, 'I'm afraid this is very sad. How long have you been in the General's employment?'

'Twenty-six years, my lord,' said the little man, taking out a large spotted silk handkerchief and dabbing at his eyes. 'My lord, is the General really dead?'

'I'm afraid he is, Jeffries.'

'Can I see him, my lord?'

'I'm afraid that won't be possible until the doctor has examined him.'

'How did he die, sir? Please can you tell me that?'

This put Edward in rather a difficult position. He did not want to lie to the little man and in any case he would have to know the truth very soon.

'I'm afraid the General had some sort of a fit and collapsed while he was drinking his port,' he compromised.

'Ah yes. I was expecting it,' said Jeffries.

'What do you mean?' Edward said, amazed.

'The General has not been well for some months, my lord. He would not say anything much to me but I could see.'

'You could see?' queried Edward.

'He was getting very thin—almost like a skeleton, if you'll excuse me saying so, my lord—and I could see he was often in pain.'

'Had he been to the doctor?'

'He had been to a doctor—Dr Cradel, my lord—but he would say to me that doctors were all fools, my lord, and the last time he went he said he was never going again.'

'When was that, Jeffries?'

'Last week, sir, last Wednesday.'

'Did you know if he was taking anything?'

'Taking anything, my lord?' said the little man, alarmed.

'Medicine—do you know if he was taking any pill or anything like that?'

'The doctor had given him pills, my lord. I think they were just to dull the pain but he said to me that they were no good, sir.'

'Do you know if he was in pain all the time, Jeffries, or did he have attacks?'

'He was in pain all the time, my lord. Even when he was asleep I used to hear him groaning, but I think some times were worse than others.'

'Mmm,' said Edward thoughtfully. 'Well, I am sorry about this, Jeffries. It must be very hard for you.'

'Indeed it is, my lord. Twenty-six years is a good long time.'

'Have you anywhere to go?'

'Now, my lord?'

'Well, not immediately, of course, but presumably after the funeral . . .' Edward wondered how to put it, 'there will be nothing for you to do.'

'Oh yes, my lord. The General was very good. He bought my old mother a house in Hove—that's in Sussex, my lord, on the coast. She has been wanting me to come and live with her for some time. My sister lives with her and I think she would be glad of the company too.'

'I see,' said Edward, suppressing his amazement that anyone as fossilized as Jeffries could possibly have a mother living anywhere, let alone in Hove. 'Well, that's all right, then.' He thought how sad some people's lives were—looking after an old widower and then with nothing left to do but go and look after an old mother. But his view of things was immediately contradicted by Jeffries as if he had read his thoughts.

'I have been very happy, sir, with the General. I was his batman in the war. He was a great man.'

'His wife died a few months ago, didn't she? I met her once or twice when the General came to dinner here. She was a delightful woman. They seemed to be very happy together.'

'Oh yes, sir. It was the saddest day in our lives when Lady Dorothy died.'

Edward was touched that the man identified himself so closely with his master. 'How did she die?' he inquired gently.

'Cancer, my lord, so they said. A year ago it was—almost to the day. The General was very sad. He was never the same again, sir. I thought he would not live very long after . . . after her. He was . . . they were a lovely couple, sir,' said Jeffries patting his eyes with his handkerchief.

It was salutary, Edward thought, to discover that this dry old soldier, who seemed so crusty, so unlovable, had loved so fiercely and had in turn been loved by two people at least. 'As far as you know, Jeffries,' he said at last, 'did the General have any family—brothers or sisters? There were no children, I believe.'

'No, my lord, no children. It was their one great sadness. I think there is a cousin in Edinburgh the General sees . . . saw every now and again but no close relations.'

'I see. Well, you have been most helpful and I am very sorry for you, losing such a good master. You must feel free to stay at Mersham as long as you wish. I am afraid there will almost certainly have to be an inquest before the body can be buried. Do you think you could find out the name and address of the General's cousin or his solicitor—oh, and also his doctor's address? We will need to consult . . . did you say he was called Dr Cradel?'

'Yes, sir. But why does there have to be an inquest?'

Jeffries sounded almost insulted, as if his care of the old man had been called into question.

'Oh,' said Edward vaguely, 'it is usual when death comes rather suddenly, you know.' Then he added, wanting to prepare the man for what might come, 'It is possible that the General might have taken the wrong medicine. I must not say anything which might mislead you. I am, as you know, not a medical man, but the General . . . well, he had some sort of fit and it might just have been his illness but . . . well, it was quite violent.'

'I see, my lord,' said Jeffries but he obviously did not.

Edward patted the man on the back in sympathy and at that moment the Duke burst into the room. 'Oh, there you are, Ned. I have been looking for you.' He eyed Jeffries suspiciously.

'This is Jeffries, General Craig's man, you know.'

'Ah,' said the Duke, distractedly, dismissing Jeffries from his mind.

'Will that be all, my lord?' the little man said, seeing that the Duke wanted to talk to his brother alone.

'Yes, thank you, Jeffries. I will talk to you again tomorrow and I expect the police may want to talk to you. Nothing to be alarmed about,' he added, seeing his face fall. 'They will just want to confirm what you have already told me, I expect.'

Jeffries disappeared and the Duke broke into excited talk. 'I spoke to Philips—got him out of bed, in fact. He's coming round now. He's picking up one of his inspectors on the way. I told him who else was at the castle and he saw at once how important it is to keep the whole thing quiet. He says we are not to touch the body and I said you had locked up the dining-room. I think we can get all this out of the way without the papers reporting anything other than that General Craig was taken ill at dinner and died. By the way, I also rang old Dr Best and he is coming too.'

'Jeffries—the man I have just been talking to, the General's valet—says that the General has been very unwell recently. I don't think you noticed, Gerald, but he has a pill box clasped in his right hand. I think he must have been taking some sort of pill when he died.'

'You mean you don't think it was poison?' said the Duke, his face clearing.

'I don't know what to think,' Edward replied slowly. 'Let's see what the doctor says. That may be him now. Look, Gerald, why don't I join the others in the drawing-room and tell them what is happening while you take the doctor in to see the body, though make sure he doesn't move it before the police arrive. Here's the key to the dining-room.'

Bates came in and said: 'Dr Best is here, your Grace.'

Dr Best was in his seventieth year, silver-haired and slightly stooped but by no means senile. He looked at the Duke with bright black eyes, like a robin's, and there was something birdlike in the way he walked. As Bates helped the doctor off with

86

his coat, the Duke again apologized for getting him out of bed. 'Don't apologize, Duke. What else could you do? The General's dead, is he?'

'Yes. He had some kind of fit when he was drinking his port.' There was a noise of crunching gravel. 'Ah, here's the Chief Constable.'

Colonel Philips was very much the military man—alert, assertive and eager to take charge of the situation. The Duke usually found him tiresomely hearty but on this occasion he welcomed his bluff no-nonsense approach. The Chief Constable shook the hand of the doctor, whom he knew well, and then introduced a tall, lean, grey-haired man smartly attired in a suit and tie despite the lateness of the hour.

'May I introduce Inspector Pride of Scotland Yard, an old friend of mine—or rather, not as old as me but I've known him a very long time—proud to know him, don't you know, what?' Inspector Pride smiled thinly and shook the Duke's hand. 'He happened to be stayin' with me so I thought I'd bring him along. You never know,' the Colonel continued vaguely. 'Sudden death of a distinguished soldier. Need to be seen to have done it all by the book—mustn't miss anything, what?'

The Duke led the way to the dining-room and struggled to turn the key in the lock. 'Don't normally lock this door,' said the Duke apologetically. 'In fact I never knew it had a key.'

'Did *you* lock the door, Duke?' asked Pride. The man, though perfectly polite, had an edge to his voice which implied he was dealing with old fools; this ruffled the Duke's feathers. He wondered just what the relationship was between the Chief Constable and this cold fish of a London policeman. They did not look as if they would be natural friends. 'No, no, it was my brother—my younger brother—Edward who locked the door. He was insistent we left everything untouched for you to examine.'

'Quite right,' said the Chief Constable. 'So Edward's here, is he? Came for dinner?'

'He was supposed to but his car broke down and he only arrived a few minutes ago—just before General Craig . . . before . . . oh, poor man, poor man.'

While they had been talking the Duke had opened the door and they had gone over to the body. Dr Best had gently lifted the cloth off the corpse and revealed the horribly distorted face of the man who had so recently been eating and drinking at the Duke's table. To each of the four men the visible evidence of the great pain the General had suffered in death was shocking and unforgettable. A heart attack could not have left its mark so savagely. Dr Best was the first to speak. 'Duke, the General has died of poisoning. It looks to me like cyanide but the post-mortem will confirm it.'

'That's what my brother said.'

Pride, kneeling beside the dead man, looked up at the Duke. 'Your brother? Is he a doctor?'

'Oh no!' said the Duke. 'But he was sure it was poison.'

'Where is he now?' Pride said, his flat, inexpressive way of speaking making the Duke shiver.

'He is in the drawing-room with my wife and my guests. I really ought to go and see them. They will want to go to their beds.'

Pride said, 'Is everyone here who was at dinner?'

'Everyone except Baron von Friedberg. He insisted on going.'

'Who is Baron von Friedberg?'

The Duke thought there was something insolent about the way the Inspector spoke to him but he felt at a disadvantage, as if he had committed some solecism letting one of his guests be poisoned at his table, so he dared not get on his high horse and tell the man off. The Chief Constable was looking uneasy.

'Von Friedberg is an official at the German embassy,' the Duke said with as much dignity as he could muster. He had taken an instinctive decision not to reveal to Pride the German's importance.

'I see,' said Pride icily. 'No one ought to have left the house before the Chief Constable gave his permission.' The Chief Constable tried to look important but it was evident to the Duke that Pride meant until *he* had given *his* permission.

'I don't suppose you were able to stop him,' said Colonel Philips fruitily, trying to take the sting out of Pride's words.

'No, I wasn't,' said the Duke shortly. 'And I don't think I can keep my other guests out of their beds much longer.' He looked at his watch. 'It's twelve o'clock.'

'Yes, of course,' said the Chief Constable hurriedly. 'Pride, I suggest we have a word with the gentlemen now but let the ladies go to their beds. We can talk to them in the morning.'

Pride looked dubious but since he had no official standing in the house he could only grunt his agreement.

'Duke, may I use your telephone?' Dr Best

inquired. 'I must send for an ambulance to take away the body. I can do the post-mortem tomorrow.'

'Yes, of course,' said the Duke, relieved to have an excuse for leaving the room. 'And I will tell the ladies that they can go to their rooms?'

'Yes,' said Colonel Philips, 'and say to the others, we—I mean Inspector Pride and myself—will come and take brief statements in a few minutes and then they too can go to bed. I don't think there is much we can do until the morning.'

The Duke turned to go. 'What do you think happened?' he said to the doctor, his voice almost breaking. 'I still don't understand. I mean, it wasn't the food. We all had the same food and drank the same wine.'

Dr Best put a sympathetic hand on the Duke's shoulder. 'I'm so sorry, Duke. This must be terrible for you and you need not worry that anything you gave the General caused his death. I cannot be absolutely sure until tomorrow when I do the post-mortem but in my own mind I am sure that the General must have taken poison.'

'That's what Ned said,' reiterated the Duke, puzzled, 'but why should he do it here at dinner?'

'We don't know, Duke,' said Colonel Philips sombrely, 'but we will find out. Perhaps he took the wrong pill.'

'That reminds me,' said the Duke, 'my brother said he had noticed that there was a silver box in the General's hand.'

Inspector Pride knelt again by the corpse and examined the hands of the dead man. He grunted, annoyed to have missed seeing the box when he had first looked at the body. Shaking his head, the

Duke left the two policemen to their gruesome job. He escorted Dr Best into the hall to use the telephone and then braced himself to face his guests. He wondered if ever again he would be able to eat in the dining-room without feeling sick to the stomach. 'What a terrible thing, what a terrible thing,' he muttered to himself. What was he to say to his guests? How could he apologize for involving them in this nightmare?

In the dining-room Pride had prised the pill box out of the General's hand. He had tried not to leave his fingerprints on it by using one of the napkins from the table, but since there could not be any fingerprints on the box except the General's he did not trouble too much. He carefully opened the box and showed it to Colonel Philips. It contained five brownish pills. Pride sniffed at them but the only aroma was a musty smell that he guessed must be the snuff which the box had once contained.

'These will have to go for analysis, of course, but they don't look like cyanide to me,' Pride said.

'Perhaps the General had mistakenly included a cyanide pill along with these indigestion pills or whatever they are and it was pure chance that he took it tonight?'

'Perhaps,' said Pride non-committally. 'Colonel, do you want me to take on this investigation officially or will you have one of your men take charge?'

'Well,' said the Chief Constable, 'I would be very grateful if, since you are here, you could extend your stay with me for a couple of days and tidy all this up. It just happens that of my two best inspectors, one is on leave and the other has a complicated fraud case on his hands. I am sure there is nothing too sinister here—just some bizarre accident—and it is important that the whole thing does not get blown up into a scandal. You know what the press is like—Famous General Poisoned at Duke's Dinner. It would be a gift to them and I gather from the Duke that apart from this German fellow the other guests are people of importance who will want to keep the lid on the whole thing as far as possible. Even if General Craig had died here of a heart attack it would make headlines, but if there is any whiff of . . .'

'I quite understand, Colonel. I think it should not take long to establish what actually happened. I want to talk to the Duke's brother. He seems to have been the first to realize that the General had been poisoned.'

Dr Best came back into the room and agreed to stay by the body until the ambulance arrived. Colonel Philips went out into the hall with Pride where they found the butler, who ushered them into the drawing-room.

'Bates,' said the Colonel, 'will you tell the servants they can go to bed but I shall want to talk to them in the morning. Did the General bring his valet?'

'Yes, sir—Jeffries. Lord Edward was kind enough to talk to him earlier and put his mind at rest.'

'Oh, he did, did he?' said Inspector Pride, who was already beginning to dislike the Duke's younger brother before he had even met him. 'He takes a lot on himself, I must say.'

'I asked him to speak to Jeffries, sir,' said Bates, turning to the Chief Constable as he opened the drawing-room door. 'I hope I did not do wrong but the man was very much upset.'

'No, of course not,' said the Chief Constable soothingly.

As the two men entered the drawing-room they were met by silence. The Duke stepped forward. 'Chief Constable, Inspector Pride, may I introduce you to my guests?'

As Pride stood taking in the scene, Colonel Philips shook the hands of Larmore, Weaver and the Bishop and made soothing noises to the ladies. Edward was sitting in an armchair with his damaged leg propped up on a stool. 'Forgive me if I don't get up, Colonel,' he said, stretching out his hand, 'but I banged my knee earlier today when I was stupid enough to crash my motor car on my way here.'

'Of course,' said Colonel Philips. 'I hope it is nothing serious. I am sure Dr Best will have a look at it after . . . after he is through with poor General Craig. I must explain that Inspector Pride is from Scotland Yard. By good fortune he was staying with me when the Duke telephoned me with the news of the General's death. He has very kindly agreed to stay on a few days longer and establish exactly what happened. My men are very stretched at the moment so I accepted Inspector Pride's offer of assistance with alacrity.' He flashed an avuncular smile at Pride who remained stony-faced.

'But was General Craig poisoned?' asked Weaver.

'It looks like it,' said the Colonel reluctantly, 'but we will know more after the post-mortem.'

'But who . . . how could he have taken poison?' said the Bishop weakly. 'We all ate and drank the same food and wine and none of us—'

'Please, sir,' said Inspector Pride, speaking for the first time, 'there is no point in speculating until we have all the facts. It is late and I know you all want to get to bed. I am going to ask each of you to give me a brief statement of what happened at dinner tonight, then you are quite free to leave.'

'Look,' broke in Larmore in an agitated voice, 'I really have nothing to do with any of this. If my name gets into the papers in connection with this business—'

Colonel Philips looked at him with distaste. 'I'm sure you have no reason to be worried, Mr Larmore, but you will understand that in view of the General's sudden death we do need to take statements from all you gentlemen—just for the record, don't you know.'

'Will there have to be an inquest?' said the politician, sweating visibly.

'There will have to be an inquest but—'

'Oh God,' exclaimed Larmore. 'I can just see the PM's face when he hears I've been mixed up in something like this.'

'Something like what?' said the Duke, going red in the face.

'I'm sorry, Duke. I did not mean to be rude but you can see what I mean.'

The Duke said firmly, 'Inspector, we all want to help you clear up this terrible business as soon as possible and I am sure we are very grateful that you have agreed to look into this horrible accident. We are all conscious of the need for discretion. We owe it to the General that his death should be as dignified as his life. We must let no hint of this poison business get into the press.' He was giving Inspector Pride a warning and the latter did not

94

like it. 'While you were in the dining-room, Colonel,' the Duke went on, 'we discussed how best to keep all this'—he gestured with his hands—'out of the newspapers, and Lord Weaver has offered to handle all that side of things. I think we can be sure that with his assistance even the newspapers he does not control . . .' he smiled gratefully at the tycoon, who gave him a little bow of acknowledgement, '. . . that even his competitors will treat the death of General Craig as the sad but natural death of a great man and make no mention of . . . of anything else.'

Edward said, 'Jeffries, his man, spoke to me earlier. He told me, Inspector, that the General had been unwell for some tune.'

'There we are then,' said the Duke fatuously.

Inspector Pride made no comment. Colonel Philips said, 'Is there a room we might use, Duke, to talk to each one of you separately? It shouldn't take very long.'

Predictably, Colonel Philips and Inspector Pride heard the same story from the Duke and his guests: the sudden arrival of Edward and Verity, the return to the dining-room, listening to the girl's account of Edward's accident with the Lagonda and the Morgan's subsequent puncture, the port being circulated, Friedberg getting up and knocking over his chair believing he was being mocked, the realization that the General was not laughing but choking to death. Only Edward had anything to add—what he had learnt from Jeffries of his master's poor health and his own belief that the General had taken cyanide. He mentioned the pill box he had seen in the General's hand and Colonel Philips told him that they had retrieved it and the

95

contents would be sent for analysis to the Yard along with all the port glasses and the decanter itself.

'Why do you think it was cyanide?' said Inspector Pride coldly.

'I have read about poisons,' Edward explained. 'When you are in Africa you are often a long way from medical help so it is sensible to have some working knowledge of remedies for snake bites and so on.'

'But surely you are unlikely to be poisoned by cyanide in Africa?' said Pride.

'No, but I am a naturally curious fellow so I did not close my book when I had read all there was to read on snake bites. I read on. Is that suspicious, Inspector?'

'No, the Inspector was just interested, that is all,' said the Colonel hurriedly. 'Now, is there anything else you can add, Lord Edward, before we let you go to your bed?' he went on jovially.

'Not really,' said Edward, 'but . . .'

'Yes?' prompted the Colonel.

'Well, it is just that I remember reading that Frederick the Great always carried around with him cyanide pills in case he was captured by the enemy.' Colonel Philips looked puzzled and Inspector Pride suddenly yawned. 'Oh, sorry, I just wondered if officers during the war might also have carried around poison to use in the last resort. I cannot see the General as a man who would allow himself to be captured and imprisoned, somehow.'

'An interesting idea,' said the Colonel politely. 'We will bear it in mind. Ah! I think I can hear Dr Best. Pride, would you ask him to step in here for a moment and look at Lord Edward's leg?'

Pride looked mutinous but did as he was bid. The doctor, who was himself clearly very tired, prescribed bed for Edward and for all of them and said he would come and see the patient in the morning. It was one fifteen before Edward, having splashed his face with cold water from the tin basin in the corner of his room, stumbled into bed. It had been a long day. He had played cricket like a god, survived an automobile accident, been rescued by a girl with a black Aberdeen terrier and seen a man die horribly of poisoning. The pain in his knee was acute and sleep, when it did come, was uneasy, punctuated by bad dreams.

CHAPTER FOUR

SUNDAY AND MONDAY MORNING

Sunday morning and Edward's knee was so swollen he could not get out of bed; he had to ring the bell and ask for a cup of tea to be brought to him. John, the footman, returned with a silver tray bearing scrambled eggs and bacon, tea, toast and marmalade. Edward glanced at the newspaper but, of course, there was no mention of the General's death. Connie came to visit him, her white silk pyjamas showing beneath her white silk dressing-gown. If he had ever thought about it, he probably would not have guessed she wore silk pyjamas in bed—it was almost racy, he considered. With her hair down she looked much younger than her thirty-seven years and Edward found himself thinking that his brother had done very well for himself. He had always liked his sister-in-law. She had stood by him when the Duke scolded him for his rackety life-style and was all in all, he thought, a thoroughly good sort. However, he now realized that she was also a woman and, as if she read his thoughts, she pulled her robe tightly about her.

After she had commiserated with him about his leg, he asked, 'What's happening downstairs? Do you know?'

'Bates tells me Joe Weaver is up and dressed, having breakfast. He wants to go up to London before lunch to prepare for the announcement of General Craig's death. Blanche and Hermione are going after lunch with Peter and Celia Larmore. The Bishop went to early church with Gerald and they have not come back yet. Does that answer your question?'

'Very good, very clear, Connie,' said Edward, putting his hand on hers. 'You make a first-rate witness.' Seeing her face cloud, he cursed himself. 'It's awful for you and Gerald. I'm so sorry,' he said gently.

'Yes, it is horrid. I feel so sad for that lonely old man.'

'The General? How do you know he was lonely?'

'Oh, I don't know. There was something in his eyes and his tie was not quite straight, did you notice?'

'No, I didn't. You think a wife would not have allowed him to come downstairs with his tie crooked?'

'I do. I think he was devoted to his wife and when she died—it must have been a year ago—he was beside himself with grief but in a typically English way hid it behind that terrible stiff upper lip you men seem to think necessary.'

'And that was hidden behind that ridiculous little moustache,' said Edward. 'It reminded me of his arch-enemy's moustache.'

'Adolf Hitler's, you mean?' said the Duchess.

'Yes,' said Edward, 'and that brings me to Gerald. I hope he is not too distressed by the mucking up of his little conference.'

'I think he is, poor old boy,' said the Duchess sadly. 'He has not said anything to me yet but I know it will all come out in due course. It is so important to him, Ned, that we don't get dragged into another war with Germany.'

'It is important to all of us.' Edward almost said something about his fears for the future but then checked himself and said instead, 'The police? When will they invade us?'

'Bates says that Inspector Pride will be here about ten o'clock and some of his people are coming down from Scotland Yard to do scientific tests of some kind. I don't know exactly what. I suppose the wine and so on,' she said vaguely.

'And what about my little guardian angel?'

'Verity Browne? Oh, she's been sweet. She said it was quite the wrong time to go round the castle with me and she had a slice of toast and went back to London—with her dog—such a dear little thing. I think I might get myself a dog.'

Edward was taken aback. 'You mean she has gone back to London without saying goodbye to me? I wanted to thank her.'

'Well,' said Connie reasonably, 'she could hardly come and see you in bed. I think it was very tactful of her. I expect she felt in the way.'

'But won't the police want to see her?'

99

'I don't see why. What can she tell them that you and I can't?'

Edward brooded. He somehow felt rather disappointed that the bright little thing and her thug of a dog had gone out of his life without his giving permission.

The Duchess had been watching him amusedly. 'Tut, Ned! Not used to girls running out on you? If you want a girl, then I get the feeling that Hermione Weaver was rather smitten by you last night.'

Edward shuddered. 'Oh God, not that little harpy, please.'

'Now, don't be unkind. That child is just very unhappy, though why I don't know. She has a nice mother and a rich stepfather. Anyway, you be kind to her. You could do a lot worse, you know. She is going to be very rich one day.'

'Oh no, Connie. You are joking, I know, but not Hermione, not in a million years. I know something about the girl and I promise you she's mad, bad and dangerous to know. I exaggerate, but no— Hermione is not for me.'

The Duchess was rather pleased than otherwise at her brother-in-law's unexpected display of good sense but she tried not to show it. There *was* something unstable about Hermione and she sensed the girl would make serious trouble for someone, assuming she hadn't already. 'Well, I must go and dress. You stay where you are, at least until Dr Best has been to see you.'

A weary Dr Best called in to look at Edward's knee at eleven o'clock. He gave the patient some anti-inflammatory pills and told him to rest. 'Looks like it's you who needs the rest,' said Edward sympathetically.

The doctor smiled wryly. 'Yes, you're right. I am too old to be up all night working on dead bodies.'

'What did you discover?' said Edward eagerly. 'Oh, I am sorry, I ought not to harass you. I expect it's all confidential until the inquest.'

'It is,' the doctor replied, 'but in confidence I don't mind admitting to you that the General was definitely poisoned.'

'Cyanide?'

'Yes.'

'I thought so,' said Edward, unable to suppress a note of triumph. 'But how did it happen?'

'God knows,' said the doctor. 'That's not my problem, I am glad to say.'

'Either he or someone else at the table must have broken a capsule of cyanide into his port sometime after I arrived—but how, and why? I mean, no one in their right mind would commit suicide at the end of a very good and very public dinner.'

'But of course suicides are usually said to be of unsound mind,' said the doctor.

'Unsound to the point of wanting to make an exhibition of one's own death? I can only imagine doing that if one was trying to make some point—to hurt someone or show someone up.'

'And since the General did not know any of his fellow guests, that doesn't make any sense.'

'No,' agreed Edward, 'and in any case I have never heard of anyone committing suicide at a party. You are right—it just doesn't make sense.'

'There is something else which I suppose it doesn't matter me telling you, but please keep it to yourself until after the inquest—the General had stomach cancer. Hawthorn, who did the post-mortem, with me more or less just there as an observer, says that he can only have had a few months or even weeks left to live.'

'I thought so,' said Edward, pulling himself into a sitting position. 'Jeffries—that's his man, you know—Jeffries told me he had been going to the doctor and the last time he went he came away cursing all doctors and saying he was finished with the lot of them. Presumably the doctor must have told him he could do nothing more for him.'

'So the pills he had in his hand . . . ?'

'I bet you anything you like they will prove to be painkillers.'

'So,' said the doctor, 'he took a cyanide pill by mistake for a painkiller?'

'I think it is the most likely explanation. He may have been contemplating taking cyanide if the cancer pain became too much for him to bear, but not, one imagines, at the Duke's table. He was a very private man and would never have exposed his bodily weakness to strangers. However, assuming he had a cyanide pill—left over from the war perhaps—he mistakenly put it in with the pain relievers. Then, while drinking the port, he felt bad pain, fumbled for his pill box and . . .'

Edward and the doctor looked at each other in silence as they played over in their minds the awfulness of what had occurred.

Dr Best said, 'At the end of the meal, after too much and unaccustomed rich food and wine coupled with tiredness—that might well be the time when he would get attacks of pain if he were ill.'

'Of course, I had not met General Craig for

several years before last night but I was shocked at how gaunt he was when I saw him. There was something fevered about his face and his eyes were protruding, I thought. I expect I am imagining it, after the event as it were, but still it does seem plausible. Poor man—all one can say is that if he died unexpectedly he was saved some of the fear and foreboding either of dying of the cancer or committing suicide.'

'But the agony of his death!' said the old doctor, shaking his head. 'You saw his face, Lord Edward. Cyanide poisoning is a terrible way of dying.'

'Will you tell Inspector Pride our theory? I can't,' said Edward. 'He has made it quite clear he doesn't like me. I think he thinks I'm an interfering young idiot with more money than sense.'

'Well,' said the doctor getting up to go, 'if it is any comfort, I think you have a very good mind and you see a lot further than most people.'

'Thank you, Dr Best. That is very kind of you. I might have to ask you to repeat your remarks to my brother, who thinks otherwise,' he said, smiling.

Throughout the day Edward played host to a stream of visitors. Hermione, in particular, was embarrassingly attentive and it was a relief when her mother came to say that her maid had finished packing and they were leaving. 'Please come and see us,' the girl begged.

'Oh yes, please do,' echoed her mother, happy that for once Hermione's attention had been captured by a young man of whom she could approve.

Inspector Pride did not ask to see Edward—rather to his chagrin—presumably content with the brief statement he had taken the night before.

103

Edward spent the afternoon reading and dozing, trying not to devote too much time to futile speculation as to why General Craig chose to die when he did, in the way he did.

The following day, Monday, Edward's knee was less swollen and he decided he must get out of bed and go down to breakfast if he wasn't to die of boredom. Being trapped in his bedroom for more than a day was torture to him. He had no valet to help him dress—he had given Fenton a week off to go and paddle in the sea at Bournemouth—so John the footman helped him manoeuvre himself into his trousers. As they were engaged in this tricky operation, Edward thought to ask him if, as he was helping Bates serve Verity and himself cold ham, he had seen anything which, now he looked back, might indicate that the General was contemplating suicide. It was not really the done thing to question the servants, especially in his brother's house, but he had known John for many years—almost as long as he had known Bates—and he felt he could talk to the man informally without putting him in an awkward position.

'Nothing at all, my lord,' said the footman.

'And during dinner, before we erupted on to the scene, everything was normal? I mean, I know you were concentrating on serving the food but you didn't notice anything strange?'

'No, my lord,' John said. 'Of course, I have been thinking things over, especially since the Inspector—'

'Oh, Inspector Pride has talked to you?'

'Yes, my lord, he has talked to all the servants. Cook was very upset.'

'Why?'

'She took it, my lord, that the Inspector was accusing her of poisoning the General.'

'But that's absurd. The poison can only have been in the wine. When the General died he was not eating, he was drinking his port.'

'Yes, but Inspector Pride has, if I may say so, my lord, a somewhat unfortunate manner.'

'Ah yes, I see what you mean. Is she all right now?'

'Yes sir. The Duchess took her in hand and was good enough to speak to us all and reassure us that none of us was under any shadow of suspicion. It was very good of her Grace and took a great weight off Mr Bates's mind.'

'Bates! Why should Bates be worried?'

'The Inspector was very insistent inquiring about the port, my lord—who decanted it and how it was served.'

'But that is ridiculous. There could be nothing amiss with the port in the decanter. We all drank that. The General must have had the poison in his glass.'

'Yes, my lord.'

Edward was silent as he pushed his left leg into the trouser, trying not to wince as his knee protested. When that was accomplished and he was pulling on a shabby cardigan which he thought he might be excused for wearing given his status as an invalid, he said, 'So you noticed nothing in the behaviour of the General or any of the other guests at dinner—before I arrived, I mean—that you thought odd in any way?'

John considered for a minute. 'I thought, if I may say so, my lord, that the Duke was having a little difficulty with the conversation.'

'How do you mean exactly?'

'Well, my lord, it's not for me to say and I only presume to do so since you ask me, but I had the feeling that there were some long silences—I mean, as though the guests were not quite at ease. Please understand, my lord, I speak in confidence. As you say, my lord, Mr Bates and myself were busy with the food and the wine so I may well be mistaken.'

'That's very interesting, John. Did you tell Inspector Pride that this was your impression?'

'Certainly not, my lord. It would not have been proper.'

Edward considered. 'I expect you are right, John. The Duke particularly wanted to bring together gentlemen with very different views of the world and no doubt, since they did not have much in common, there was little in the way of small talk.'

'The foreign gentleman spoke most of the time, my lord, and Mr Bates and myself commented that what he was saying did not seem to please . . . But I beg your pardon, my lord, Mr Bates would think I was being forward in presuming to say so much.'

'That's quite all right, John. I promise you that what you say will go no further. Such a terrible thing—it is natural that we should try and establish why and how the poor gentleman took his life.'

'Indeed, my lord—nothing like it has ever happened at the castle and we are all most shocked.'

*   *   *

Lord Edward Corinth stopped to steady himself as

106

he was about to descend the great staircase. He had a stick in his right hand and he grasped the banister with the other. John had offered to assist him but Edward had told him not to fuss and that he could manage on his own, but the stairs were precipitous and he had no wish to go head over heels down them and break his neck. While he got his balance he looked at the portrait of his father which hung there, magnificently framed in gold piecrust. It was one of John Singer Sargent's masterpieces. Either the painter or the Duke—almost certainly the latter—had chosen the hall below where he was now standing as the backdrop. The Duke was costumed, somewhat incongruously, in full hunting dress: tightly fitting shiny black boots, jodhpurs, coloured waistcoat, black cravat and black topcoat trimmed with some type of fur. It looked to Edward as though his father had been so impatient to get out of the house and out of the painter's presence that Sargent had only been able to catch him for a few moments at the front door before he went on out to his beloved horses and hounds, and yet, in other ways, it was very studied. Both painter and subject had been making a point but perhaps not the same point. Edward smiled wryly: certainly Sargent had captured the man's arrogance. The Duke was standing feet apart, his right hand in the pocket of his jodhpurs, the other holding a hunting crop so that the whip curled along his leg, proclaiming his status not just as master of foxhounds but as monarch of all he surveyed. His youngest son's eyes were drawn inexorably to his father's face, deathly pale beneath a black silk top hat.

It was a face which combined weakness and

strength of purpose in equal measure: the beaklike nose above thin red lips, the small eyes black like lumps of coal. A memory so vivid it made him clutch his forehead came to Edward out of nowhere. He was six years old. It had snowed heavily during the night and in the morning he had stolen out, unsupervised for once, to build a snowman. He had soon tired of it. The labour was much greater than he had bargained for. Suddenly, just as he was about to give up, his father had arrived dressed much as in the Sargent portrait. Seeing his son defeated and on the point of bursting into tears he had lifted him up and swung him over his head as easily as though he had been his hunting crop and called him 'a jolly little man'. Then together they had completed building the snowman, his father finding an old trilby for the snowman's head, a cigar stump for where his mouth should be, and three shiny black coals, one for a nose and two for cold beady eyes. Edward had been enchanted and had looked at his father in a new light, as a magic man. Only gradually did he come to appreciate that this half-hour with his father, playing in the snow, was to be unique. For months and then years afterwards he waited for his father to come and play with him again but he waited in vain. His father, except for that one time, made no sign that he knew his youngest son existed. Edward held no grudge against him. The Duke was a god, and gods, he knew from his studies, were capricious. He treasured this single moment of communion with the father he had feared but never known. Even now he occasionally dreamed of it.

Then there had been the war which they now

called the Great War and the death of Edward's eldest brother Franklyn almost as soon as he reached France. Franklyn, or Frank as he was known in the family, had joined a smart regiment in 1912 and welcomed the war, seeing it as a path to glory—a way of earning his father's respect—or so his mother had told Edward many years later. He had seen himself leading a cavalry charge on his favourite mare, Star, named for the white mark on her face, but had discovered almost immediately that there were to be no cavalry charges in this horrible new kind of war. Instead, on 23 August 1914, at Obourg, north-east of Mons, he led his men—many from the towns and villages close to home, some he had known all his life—at a group of grey-clad soldiers on the edge of a wood. Waving his revolver in the air as though it was a magic wand, he had died moments later, shot through the head, one of the first British officers to be killed.

The Duke, his mother told Edward shortly before she herself died in 1922, had never shed a tear for his dead son, but for all that, he had been wounded to the heart. He had refused to permit his second son, Gerald, who had just left Eton, to join the army, and father and son had quarrelled bitterly but the father had prevailed. Edward, six years younger than Gerald and still at prep school, had known nothing of this. He had worshipped Frank from afar and had been enormously proud when just before he left for France he had come down to the school, dressed in his uniform, and had taken him and three of his friends to eat scones and jam in the Cockpit, the tea-room in the high street. Then, only a few weeks later, the headmaster had called him into his study and gravely broken the news to him that his brother was dead—that he had died a hero's death. Edward had been unable to understand it. How could his brother, so strong, so solidly there one moment, be not there the next? His friends treated him almost with awe, patting his back and making embarrassed attempts to console him in the English way. 'I say, bad show, Ned, what rotten luck.'

Edward had seen Frank so rarely during his childhood it was a year before he could take in that he would never see him again and that he wasn't just away somewhere, to return unexpectedly and ruffle his hair and present him with a puppy or a Hornby train-set before disappearing again. By this time death was a familiar visitor in the families of all his school companions and his loss was no longer special except to him. His brother was a name to be read out by the headmaster on Sundays along with the other fallen heroes—young men who had been educated to die for king and emperor and had dutifully done so. Now, twenty years later, he could hardly remember what his brother had looked like. There was no portrait of him as there was of their father, and the photographs, however hard Edward looked at them, conveyed nothing; they showed a good-looking young man, virtually featureless, with whom he could hardly associate the dashing, hero figure of his childhood, let alone the reality behind that image. It was a puzzle. Edward liked puzzles but not of this kind with no clues and no witnesses prepared to talk. Neither his mother nor his brother would do more than echo the conventional tributes and it would have been cruel, Edward knew, to have pressed them further. Those dead

110

young men were beyond comment or criticism. They were saints to be prayed for. The Old Duke had considered publishing a book of remembrance, as had the parents of other young officers who had died on the field of battle, but he never got round to it. Maybe there was nothing speakable to say.

Frank had seemed very grown up to Edward when he went off to war but in fact, he could now appreciate, his brother had been little more than a boy, ignorant of life and of the world, and there was the tragedy. It was a burden that fell very heavily on those left behind. Edward turned from the portrait and hopped slowly down the stairs. His father had died in 1920, a shadow of the man Sargent had painted, his mind and body twisted by two strokes, a dribbling incontinent wreck. Gerald was now Duke of Mersham and gathered round his dinner-table men whom his father would have abominated had he ever deigned to notice them: stockbrokers, newspaper editors, politicians and worse. The new Duke saw it as his mission to help prevent another European war and if that meant mixing with men like Lord Weaver, Larmore and Baron von Friedberg then he would do it. What did any of that matter if they could be used to keep the peace? But now, Edward thought grimly, death had entered even into the Duke's own castle and sat at his table and eaten his food and drunk his wine.

As Edward entered the dining-room the Duke, who was munching toast and honey and reading *The Times*, looked up at him in surprise. 'Ned, my boy—are you up? Connie said Dr Best had told you to stay in bed for at least forty-eight hours.'

'Oh well, Gerald,' said Edward, helping himself to scrambled egg and sausages from the silver chafing dishes on the sideboard, 'I got bored. My knee is feeling better so I thought I would come down. Is there anything in the paper?'

He did not need to say what he meant by 'anything'.

'There is a long obituary of General Craig. Wonderful how fast these blighters work, eh?'

'How do you mean, Gerald?'

'Well, Colonel Philips thought it best to put out a brief statement to the *Morning Post* and *The Times* about the General having died rather than let rumours get out about . . . well, about how he died, and here is a long screed about his career and what not. It takes me a day to write a letter and God knows how long it would take me to write something like this, if indeed I could,' he added meditatively.

'Ah well, you see, obituaries of distinguished men past their first flush of youth are written in advance of their death so that they can be printed as soon as news of their demise is received.'

The Duke digested this and seemed to find it shocking. 'You mean, people write things about other people *assuming* they are going to die?'

'We all have to die, Gerald.'

An awful thought occurred to the Duke. 'They haven't written stuff about me, have they, Ned?'

'Oh, I shouldn't think so,' said his brother soothingly, 'after all, what have you done?'

The Duke did not know quite how to take this but then saw that his brother was joking and guffawed. 'Really, Ned,' he said, 'I don't know.'

'Throw me over the *Morning Post* if you are not reading it, will you, Gerald,' said Edward, digging into his eggs.

General Craig's obituary in the *Morning Post* was very full and for the most part flattering. Educated at Wellington College, he had made something of a reputation as a young subaltern on Kitchener's staff in the Sudan in 1896 and had distinguished himself at the battle of Omdurman. It was there he won his Victoria Cross, one of the first to be awarded. Kitchener was passing a pile of 'dead' dervishes after the battle when one of them sprang up and charged with his spear, ignoring pistol shots from Kitchener's entourage. He was about to strike when Craig, throwing himself between the dervish and Kitchener, took the spear in his shoulder and still managed to kill the dervish. However, there was the suggestion of a stain on Craig's record in the Sudan. The anonymous obituarist alluded in a couple of lines to accusations that Craig had killed wounded prisoners on Kitchener's orders, an allegation, the obituarist added, which was denied by Kitchener and Craig and never substantiated.

Craig had been wounded again in 1900 at Spion Kop in South Africa during the Boer War, and at the outbreak of the Great War in 1914 was Major-General Sir Alistair Craig VC. He was on Sir John French's staff and along with a hundred thousand professional soldiers—the British Expeditionary Force—he fought at Mons, on the Marne and at the first battle of Ypres. There was no question, Edward saw with admiration and envy, but that Craig had been a man of exceptional physical courage and an experienced and successful soldier. However, for some reason the General had not ended the war with all the honours and titles one might have expected. He became a full general but not a field marshal and most surprisingly of all he

113

was never given a peerage. What, Edward wondered, had gone wrong for him? The obituarist did not speculate.

Edward folded the newspaper and was about to toss it aside and ask to see *The Times*'s obituary when his eye caught a headline on page three. It read: 'General Sir Alistair Craig's death caused by poison: allegation in the *Daily Worker*.' There followed a summary of a report in the latter journal, a newspaper whose existence the *Morning Post* normally refused to acknowledge, which gave an accurate account of the General's death from cyanide poisoning at Mersham Castle. Edward went white and bit his lip. His brother would be horrified that any newspaper, let alone the organ of the Communist Party, should be describing in such detail how one of his guests at dinner died. The gutter press would leap on the story. The Duke's peace-making dinner-parties would be made mock of or there would be suggestions of backroom conspiracies. It didn't bear thinking about but of course that was just what needed to be done.

He was about to say something to his brother when the Duke gave a howl of anger. He thrust his copy of *The Times* at Edward, stabbing his finger at a story half-way down page two. He was unable to utter, such was his anguish. With a heavy heart Edward took the paper and looked at the offending item. It, too, was an account of the General's demise quoting the *Daily Worker*. Edward might have expected *The Times* to have added words of disbelief; after all, *Times* readers did not normally expect accurate reporting from employees of the *Daily Worker*. The fact that they did not express doubts about the accuracy of the story suggested

114

that they had already checked that it was true.

At last the Duke was able to speak. 'Who has done this? One of the servants, the police? I asked everyone for discretion.'

'I am afraid, Gerald, that it is more likely to be one of your guests.'

'What? You mean one of the women?' The Duke spoke with absolute scorn of that lesser breed of mortals. 'Hermione Weaver, I suppose? Why did Connie insist on having that awful girl in our house? Connie!' he shouted, getting up and going to the door. The Duchess was an early riser and was already in the garden doing something to the hollyhocks with Andrew, the head gardener.

'Yes, dear, what is it?' Edward heard Connie calling. She was used to the Duke's rages. They were unpleasant when they occurred but usually quickly over. On this occasion, however, Edward was inclined to believe that the Duke would not be easily mollified. He valued privacy above almost everything and the idea that he and important guests of his should be held up to public scrutiny was unbearable. Of course, the Duke was aware that at the inquest some account of the General's death would be reported but he had been confident that he could use his influence to keep it to a minimum. But here was a list of guests given with the implication that one or all of them had poisoned General Craig. It was outrageous, it was . . .

Edward was tortured by another thought. The Duke had forgotten it but there had been a journalist present when the General had died, and she had not been a guest proper so may well have considered she had no duty of silence, in fact just the opposite. Edward could quite see that with 'a scoop' handed to her—almost literally on a plate, along with cold ham and salad—she would be mad to do anything but use it. Verity, for of course it was of her he was thinking, had left very early Sunday morning without saying goodbye. It all fitted. The only thing that puzzled him was why she had gone to the *Daily Worker*. *Country Life* would not have been suitable, he realized, but why not the *News Chronicle* or the *Daily Express*? She would have avoided the *New Gazette* as this was owned by Lord Weaver but that still left her lots of choice. She hardly looked like a foot soldier in the class war but that meant nothing. Nowadays it was quite impossible to predict the political views of anyone, even someone one knew well, and he did not know Verity at all except as a black-bereted, tousle-haired young flibbertigibbet completely lacking a sense of direction.

Oh God, he thought, he was in for the high jump. He had inadvertently introduced a spy into the heart of his brother's castle—a spy who had already done incalculable damage. How could his brother invite other important men into his house now? How could any visitor be confident his conversation would not appear in next day's newspapers? No one would dare to accept his invitations except the vulgarly curious and the sensation seekers.

Connie came into the house, her arms full of roses. 'What is it, Gerald? You look as if you are about to have a heart attack. Do sit down.'

As the Duke seemed incapable of speech, Edward quickly told her what was the matter and added sheepishly that he feared the author of all

116

their troubles was the girl he had invited into the castle, Verity Browne.

'Oh no!' exclaimed the Duchess. 'She seemed such a nice girl—one of us. Surely, *Country Life* is quite respectable?'

'Oh, it is,' Edward agreed, 'but we have only her word that she was working for *Country Life*. When she rang you, Connie, to make an appointment to see the castle, did you ask for any references?'

'Of course not! What an idea! She wasn't asking for a job.'

'I'm not blaming you, Connie. I am just saying we don't know she was speaking the truth.'

'I should jolly well hope you are not blaming me, Ned,' she said heatedly. 'If people tell me something I believe them.'

The Duke had now regained enough composure to talk. 'I shall ring up Colonel Philips straight away and have the girl—what do you say her name was? Browne?—arrested.'

'Oh, don't be absurd, Gerald. How can one have anyone arrested? She has done nothing illegal—assuming it is her and not Hermione Weaver or Inspector Pride himself. You have just got to keep quiet and appear to be what you are: the host at a dinner-party where one of the guests has had a terrible accident. It is not your fault and no one will dare say it is.'

Connie's good sense calmed her husband and relieved Edward. Connie was right, he thought: it was annoying, but news of the way the General had died was bound to have got out. There were too many people involved. Still, he felt he ought to do something. 'Look, Gerald,' he said, 'I am frightfully sorry about all this. It is my fault that girl stayed the night here and I apologize but I had no idea—'

The Duke waved his hand. 'I know, Ned,' he said. 'It isn't your fault. It is just damn bad luck. Why did that poor man have to choose my dining-table at which to end his life?'

The Duke's question was rhetorical but Edward thought it was worth asking. He decided he could not stay at the castle a day longer. He would go up to London and see if he could get a line on Verity Browne. He was angry and disappointed with her. She had seemed so frank and open, it was unpleasant to find she had been lying to him. What good it would do talking to Verity, even if he could find her, he did not know but at least it was something to do.

'Connie,' he said, 'I'm just going to run up to town. The inquest won't be until after the weekend and I will be back by then.'

'But are you well enough? Your leg . . . ?'

'I'll go in the train. Fenton is back from his seaside jaunt today and he can look after me.'

In other circumstances Connie would have fiercely opposed his going before his knee was back to normal but she now was too concerned with her husband to worry about her brother-in-law. Gerald was looking a very bad colour. She rang the bell for Bates. When the butler appeared she asked him to telephone Dr Best. 'Bates, the Duke has had rather a shock and I want to be sure he is not . . . his blood pressure . . .'

For a moment she looked close to tears and Edward got up with the help of his stick and limped over to put an arm round her. 'There, there, Connie,' he said. 'Everything will be all right.'

'Oh, will it, Ned? The General dying like that . . .

118

I wonder if anything will be all right again.'

CHAPTER FIVE

MONDAY AFTERNOON AND EVENING

Edward took the eleven thirty-two and got into Waterloo at one o'clock. He took a cab to his rooms in Albany, where he found Fenton polishing the silver.

'Good afternoon, my lord,' said Fenton. 'Mr Bates telephoned to say that you were to be expected so I have taken the liberty of making up a cold collation for your luncheon.'

'Thank you, Fenton. How was your holiday?'

'Very pleasant, thank you, my lord. The weather was clement and I was able to do a little painting.'

Edward nodded respectfully. Fenton was a more than competent portraitist and landscape painter.

'Well, you must let me see what you have done, Fenton. By the way, did Bates say anything to you about the Lagonda?'

'Yes, my lord. He informed me that the car was successfully towed to Mersham where the smith was able to repair the axle. However, there is other damage to the vehicle so Randolph, the Duke's chauffeur, is driving it up to London where the garage can work on it. I hope that your leg is better, my lord.'

'Thank you, Fenton. It is much better. I expect Bates gave you a full account of the unfortunate business at Mersham.'

'He did, my lord. General Craig's death is a sad

119

loss to the country, if I may say so, my lord. He was a great soldier and from what I read in the newspapers I would anticipate that the day will come when we will need soldiers like Sir Alistair.'

'I fear you may be right, Fenton. Bates told you that the General was poisoned?' Edward said, filling his mouth with cold chicken.

'Yes, my lord—a terrible thing. Was it some sort of accident?'

'I really do not know, Fenton. I suppose it must have been. What else could it have been? Fenton, could you get me today's *Daily Worker*?'

'The *Daily Worker*, my lord?'

'Yes, Bates didn't tell you? A detailed account of the General's death, which as you can imagine the Duke was hoping to keep as quiet as possible, appeared in that estimable newspaper, and this—I suppose we must call it a scoop—was reprinted in more respectable organs such as *The Times*.' Fenton registered the heavy irony with which his master spoke and gathered that he was taking the disaster personally.

'It may not be easy to find the newspaper so late in the day, my lord, but if you wish it I will walk down to Piccadilly. There is a paper seller there which stocks the more esoteric journals.'

'Yes, please do. I want to get to the bottom of how they got their story. I believe it was through a young woman of the name of Verity Browne who rescued me when my car went off the road and who had, coincidentally, an appointment to be shown round the castle so she could write an article on great houses for *Country Life*.'

'And you think, my lord, that she was not telling the truth?'

'I think she was not telling the truth,' Edward confirmed, wiping his mouth on his napkin and reaching for his glass of champagne. 'I certainly intend to find out.'

While Fenton went in search of the *Daily Worker*, Edward telephoned a friend of his. The Revd 'Tommie' Fox had been up at Trinity with him and they had both been keen oarsmen. Tommie had taken to religion and ended up a curate in Kilburn. He had roped in many of his Cambridge friends to support the boys' club he ran, and Edward had once or twice been down to box at the club and afterwards talk about life in Kenya, flying and other enthusiasms. The boys were a mixed lot—a few villains but for the most part good lads fighting against a system which deprived them of education and decent jobs and therefore the money to marry and start families. Tommie had been worried by the appeal the Fascists had for many of the boys. The previous September there had been a Fascist march in London and he had been horrified to see several of his lads taking part.

Tommie's own sympathies were predictably on the left of the political spectrum and Edward thought he might have come across Verity Browne if she regularly wrote for the *Daily Worker*. 'Yes, of course I know Verity,' said Tommie when the preliminary 'how-are-yous' had been completed and Edward had stated his business. 'Her father is the lawyer fellow, Donald Browne—Browne with an "e". Isn't he a KC? No, now I come to think of it he refused to take silk on principle. He's certainly a good barrister and highly valued for his commitment to left-wing causes. He represented the trades union—the boiler makers—against the government last year. You must have heard of him.'

Edward had heard of Donald Browne. As Tommie had said, he was an able lawyer, rich enough, he had heard, to bankroll the *Daily Worker* and prepared to take up what he considered worthy causes free of charge. Browne was a common enough name, even with the 'e' at the end of it, which Edward had not known about never having seen Verity's name written down, so there was no reason for him to have made the connection. Verity must have seen the General's death as a golden opportunity to take a dig at the military and at the upper classes. The girl had jumped to the conclusion that the Duke's dinner-party was a conspiracy—which it was not—no doubt having been involved in so many herself, he thought bitterly. Edward hit his forehead in frustration.

'How do you think I could meet her, Tommie?' he said into the telephone. 'Casually, I mean.'

'Why, have you got "a thing" for her, old man?'

'Not quite, Tommie, but I would like to exchange a few words with her without too much of a fuss it that's possible. To tell the truth she has been a little bit naughty.'

'That sounds like Verity,' said Tommie. 'Well, look, I have been invited to a party tonight and she is more than likely to be there. I wasn't actually planning to go. It really isn't my cup of tea—lots of girls in spectacles discussing the joys of Communism and monkey glands.'

'Monkey glands?'

'Yes, they're the new way of keeping young. Gosh, Ned, you really are behind the times!'

Edward rather resented being patronized by his unworldly friend—or at least the friend he considered to have a utopian view of the world which he was too cynical to share. Tommie gave him the address of the house where the party was being held and assured him he had no need of an invitation—'It's not that sort of affair, Ned. In Chelsea we don't have all your stuffy rules about how you should behave which you have in Eaton Square. We are quite informal, and that reminds me, don't come dressed like the frog footman. In Bohemia, we rather espouse the tweed jacket and leather patches, corduroys and knitted ties.'

Edward shuddered.

*　　　*　　　*

'Sorry, say that again?'

The noise was deafening. Edward thought the spotty girl with unwashed hair had asked him if he were sleepy and in fact he did feel rather tired. His knee was still hurting and he was beginning to wish he had not come. The party was in an artist's studio, a barn of a place off the King's Road, packed with mostly young people but with a fair sprinkling of middle-aged women wearing too much make-up. He had not met the artist yet—his host—but he was sure, looking at the pictures piled against the walls or hanging from the picture rail, that he would not like him. Most of them seemed to feature stick-like men, a lot of green paint and some orange suns.

'Not sleepy, CP,' the spotty girl was saying. 'Are you a member of the Party or just a fellow traveller?'

'Neither, I'm afraid,' he admitted. 'I am a member of the despised aristocracy but we are not

123

a political party yet.'

The spotty girl looked at him suspiciously, her head at an angle. 'Are you really an aristocrat? I suppose that's why you are so well dressed . . . and so good-looking,' she added after a moment.

Edward was irritated. He had asked Fenton to put out his oldest suit and a particularly noxious tie he had been given by a girl with whom he had once believed himself to be in love, and he was quite convinced he looked, if not Bohemian, at least scruffy. He had to admit however, looking round the room, that compared with most of the other men, he was well dressed. There appeared to be a mistaken impression among the artistic fraternity that long hair, cravats and dandruff were in some way attractive. When he turned back from his scrutiny he found that the spotty girl had vanished into the crowd and had been replaced by a young man in what looked like a silk smoking-jacket, smoking a cigarette through along ivory-coloured holder.

'Terrible stuff this, don't you think?' he said to Edward, indicating the paintings on the wall.

'They are rather dire, aren't they?' said Edward, feeling he might have more in common with the young man than he had first supposed. 'I don't even know the name of the artist, mine host, don't you know.'

'Adrian Hassel,' said the young man. 'He tries hard but he just can't seem to do it. But tell me why you are here? I'm sure I have never seen you before and if you will forgive me for saying so you do rather stand out in the crowd.'

'I'm a friend of Tommie Fox. He invited me but I really came to see if I could meet Verity Browne.'

124

'Verity!' exclaimed the young man. 'Ah, that explains it. She has some very smart friends. You did say you are a friend of hers?'

'Well, an acquaintance,' said Edward, not wishing to be caught out in an untruth.

'An acquaintance, of course. If you were a friend of hers you would not have to come here to meet her. Wait a moment, I am sure I've seen her. Ah yes, there she is, talking to the man with the beard. Verity!' he shouted and his oddly high voice pierced the din effortlessly.

Verity looked up, began to smile and then saw Edward. She blushed deeply and turned as if to look for an escape, but the young man had taken her by the arm and conducted her across the floor. 'I gather this gentleman—I am afraid we have not been properly introduced so I don't have his name—is an acquaintance of yours. Perhaps you will be good enough to do the honours.'

'What . . . oh yes. Adrian, this is Lord Edward Corinth. Lord Edward, this is Adrian Hassel, your host.'

'Adrian Hassel . . . oh dear,' said Edward. 'You must think me very rude and stupid. I apologize.'

'What is he apologizing for?' said Verity.

'He has nothing to apologize for,' said Hassel gracefully. 'I said the pictures on the wall were hopelessly bad and he agreed with me, that is all.'

Verity giggled. 'Adrian, you are an idiot. You deserve whatever you get.'

'I do, don't I,' said the young man. 'And now I am going to leave the lord and his lady together. That would be the tactful thing to do, would it not?'

Verity punched him in the shoulder, spilling a

125

little of the wine in her glass. 'Yes, go, Adrian, and good riddance.'

She turned to Edward, forestalling him. 'I know you must think me the most awful beast. I expect if I were a man you would call me out or something but you must admit it was a perfectly wonderful scoop. All the others were terribly jealous. It's the first time anything we have written in the *DW* has been used by the proper papers—I mean the capitalist press,' she corrected herself. 'I can't see it did anyone any harm and it did me so much good. It will all come out at the inquest in any case and . . .' She stopped, seeing his expression. 'You are really angry, aren't you? I'm so sorry. Perhaps it was rather a shabby trick.'

'Look here,' said Edward suddenly, 'why not come and have dinner with me? I would like to talk and I can't hear myself think in this place. What about the Savoy? Or will it be betraying your principles to spend the evening with a representative of the capitalist classes in the heart of Mammon?'

Edward was not sure why he had asked the girl to eat with him—he had certainly not meant to— nor why he was quite so concerned that she might refuse. Verity looked at him for a moment consideringly, then she said, 'I'm not dressed for the Savoy.'

'You look very nice to me,' said Edward. She was wearing a short green dress—maybe doing honour to the artist whose favourite colour this was—a feather boa and two long ropes of what pretended to be pearls.

'No,' she said, 'not the Savoy.'

Taking this to be a 'yes' to having dinner with

126

him, he said, 'All right then, not the Savoy. We'll go to Gennaro's.'

'Wait there a minute,' Verity commanded. Edward watched her go over to Adrian Hassel and say something in his ear. He looked at Edward curiously but obviously gave his permission for she bounced back and said, 'I'll just rescue my hat and coat.'

Thirty minutes later the taxi dropped them in New Compton Street and Edward ushered Verity into the mirrored rooms. The head waiter greeted Edward like an old friend and presented Verity with a rose, its stalk wrapped in silver paper. 'You are very busy tonight, Freddy,' said Edward. 'Can you find us a quiet table?'

'Certainly, milord,' said Freddy, bowing. He clicked his fingers and a waiter rushed up to do his bidding. Freddy mumbled something and they were led to an alcove where a table was erected for them, covered with a white tablecloth and laid with 'silver' all in a couple of minutes. Two chairs were brought and the waiter politely held one of them while Verity settled herself. With nothing being said, a bottle of Perrier Jouet was opened with a pop, two glasses filled and the bottle put to rest in an ice-bucket.

'Freddy pretends he is Italian,' said Edward when they were settled, 'but I know for a fact he was born in Bermondsey.'

They had hardly spoken in the taxicab and now he felt he was prattling. He had the feeling that Verity was regretting having said she would come with him.

'Look,' she said suddenly, 'let's get one thing straight. If you think you can impress me with all

127

this . . .' she waved her arms, '. . . with all this flummery, all this "yes-my-lord, no-my-lord" stuff, you have another think coming. I agreed to come with you simply because I feel maybe I do owe you some sort of apology for—you know—doing what I did, but that's all.'

'Yes, of course,' said Edward hastily. He was rather annoyed to find himself being lectured when he had intended to do all the lecturing himself. After all, as she had admitted, he was the wounded party, but there was something so honest and gutsy about her bad temper that he could not be angry for long. The waiter arrived to take their order but Edward waved him away. 'No, it's all right,' said Verity, 'I know what I would like—fritto misto and then fillet of sole.'

'And I'll have the minestrone and the scaloppine al marsala,' said Edward, 'and a bottle of Orvieto.'

'I hope you don't mean to get me drunk and then seduce me,' said Verity, smiling as if she now rather regretted having been sharp with him.

'No,' said Edward, 'I merely wanted to talk to you about the General's death. By the way, you never did write for *Country Life*, did you?'

'No. I am afraid I lied and I will write to the Duchess and apologize. I suppose there is no point in writing to the Duke, is there?'

'No, I'm afraid not.'

'My original idea was to write a series of articles for the *DW* on how the rich live. That was why I wanted to see round the castle, but of course the General dying like that—well, you see, it was an opportunity I could not possibly miss. I did not feel I owed anyone silence. No one had asked me to keep it quiet and if they had I would not have agreed.'

'Have the police been to see you yet?'

'No, do you think they will want to?'

'I expect so. You were a witness.'

'Mm—I suppose I was, though I did not really see anything you didn't see.'

'You know he was murdered?' said Edward. He had no idea that he was going to say what he said until he said it, but having said it he realized it was something he had known since he first knelt awkwardly beside the dying man trying to loosen his tie. He had known it when he was telling himself that it was all a terrible accident and he had known that Gerald had known it and that was one of the reasons he was so upset by Verity's story in the *Daily Worker*.

'I wondered if you thought so too,' said Verity calmly. 'I don't know that there is any evidence but I am sure you are right. I was certain, from the word go, that the warmongering old man would not have committed suicide. If he ever did, he would never kill himself in front of a load of bigwigs.'

Edward said, 'Well, I thought it might have been an accident. He might have considered killing himself because, according to his man Jeffries, he was ill, and Dr Best confirmed it. He was dying of stomach cancer and he had only a very few months to live. He might perhaps have preferred to choose his own day for dying.'

'I see,' said Verity thoughtfully. 'He certainly looked unwell. He was very thin and there was, unless I am imagining it, a feverishness about him. I mean, there was something almost like hysteria in the way he was talking about the war. Or is that nonsense?'

'No, I don't think it is nonsense. I tried to persuade myself that, if he was carrying a cyanide capsule and it got in the silver snuff box he was using to keep his painkillers in, he could have taken the cyanide capsule and put it in his glass instead of the painkiller. He was ill, he may have been in pain, he was tired and maybe a little drunk. He *could* have made a mistake.'

'But you don't think he did?'

'No. He wasn't the sort of man to make mistakes. He was, according to Jeffries, a very tidy man. I looked in his room before I left the castle and before Jeffries had packed away his things. It was almost as though he had not been there. The bed was unslept in, of course. There was his watch and a tiny clock on the bedside table. The only book he had with him was the Bible. There was a photograph of his wife—on the dressing-table; nothing much else. A lifetime soldiering means he was used to travelling light. Each item of clothing or shaving tackle would have its very particular place in his one small suitcase.'

'His wife was dead?'

'Yes, Jeffries said he was quite alone in the world except for some cousin.' He hesitated. 'Tell me, why should you care if the old boy was murdered? Surely he was just the sort of . . . what did you call him—warmonger?—you must really dislike.'

'I don't deny it. In theory,' said Verity seriously, 'if I had read about his death in the paper I would not have cared. I might have said, "Oh well, one less warmonger," but it is different if you have been there. And he died so horribly. I keep on thinking it might have been my father. My father is—'

'Yes, Tommie told me.'

130

'Well, he's had death threats, you know. He—the General, I mean—had no one to care if he lived or died, and if I believe in anything I believe in justice. That's what being a Communist means. If he was killed we ought to see the murderer brought to justice.'

She stopped, quite breathless with passion. Edward was impressed. She looked like a little firebrand, her bosom heaving and her cheeks red, her eyes bright as fireworks. 'So you think a Communist Party member and a scion of the aristocracy ought to combine forces to bring a murderer to book?'

'Don't scoff,' Verity said angrily. 'And don't be bloody patronizing.'

'I'm sorry,' said Edward, a little shocked by her swearing at him. 'I did not mean to scoff. I just wondered what on earth we could do.'

'Don't be feeble,' she answered, still on her high horse. 'To begin with, how easy would it be for the General to have mistaken one of his painkillers for a cyanide capsule?'

'Yes, I asked Dr Best that. He said it was possible—anything is possible—but the pills were a very different shape from the capsule which was probably not round but like a tiny tube. What's more, it was probably made of a kind of glass— though they haven't found any fragment of it yet— and would have to be broken into the wine or bitten in the mouth.'

'We are sure it was in the port then?'

'Yes. Apparently if he had bitten on it there would have been clear burn marks in the mouth and on the teeth but if he swallowed the poison in the port it would not have started . . . you know . . .

killing him . . . until it was in his stomach.'

'Ugh! How horrible!' Verity exclaimed and Edward was surprised how tough she could be in some ways and how sensitive in others.

'It definitely was in the port then,' Verity said, forking up a mouthful of fried squid.

'Cyanide evaporates in the air, so if it wasn't in his mouth it had to have been in liquid and you saw him take a sip of port just before he started choking.'

'Right, so if he was poisoned . . .'

'It had to have been by someone round that dining-room table,' said Edward finishing her thought. 'A distinctly unpleasant conclusion.'

Edward leaned back in his chair and the hovering waiter refilled his champagne glass. 'We really have no evidence that it was murder. What could any of the people at dinner have against him, and if one of them had a secret reason for killing him why would they do it in so public a place when they might so easily be seen?'

Verity leaned forward eagerly. 'No, don't you see? I agree it must have been an opportunistic killing but what safer place to murder a man than at a semi-official dinner surrounded by guests all with important positions in society. The murderer would be able to count on the police being under pressure to find it all to have been a terrible accident.'

'You really think the police would hush up . . . murder?'

'Yes, I do. Can you imagine Colonel Philips, the Chief Constable, realizing he had to find a cabinet minister or a bishop a murderer? He would run a mile.'

'Of course, the irony is that the murderer obviously did not know the General was dying anyway,' Edward said.

'So we can assume then that the murderer did not know the General well enough to know that he was very ill?'

'That's right. According to Jeffries he had no close friends and he had told no no one, not even Jeffries, how ill he was.'

'But the murderer might have known him well years ago.'

'He was a sort of family friend. We had known him for ages. He was a friend of my father's but we certainly did not know him intimately. I don't suppose anyone did.' Edward bit his lip thoughtfully. 'So you think if we were looking for a motive for murder we might have to look back in the General's career? Let's see, what do we think happened on Saturday night?'

'I think,' said Verity, pushing away her empty plate, 'that the murderer had been waiting all through dinner for an opportunity to poison General Craig's wine but no opportunity arose. Then just as the murderer was giving up hope, we arrived. Everyone crowded into the hall to see us. The murderer lingered behind and broke the capsule in the General's port and pop goes the weasel.'

'But how could he—the murderer, I mean—be sure that the General would sit down in the same place he had been sitting in?'

'I suppose he risked it. Did everyone leave their port on the table or were some people holding their glass in the hall?'

'I don't know, Verity, but we could find out. We

would have to go very carefully because we haven't a shred of evidence for thinking that the General really was murdered. We just have our hunches and they carry no weight with anyone, least of all, I suspect, with Inspector Pride. Still, I can see it might make a great story for you if we can prove something—another scoop in fact.'

'That's not my motive,' said Verity stiffly. I told you, I believe in justice and I don't see why he should die unavenged.'

'Golly, you sound like one of the Furies. You remember, they were—'

'I know who the Furies were,' said Verity icily. 'I think I can live with you being an aristocratic ass but if you're going to "little woman" me through all this I shall throw something at you.'

'"Through all this"?' said Edward, suddenly feeling rather pleased. 'Are we a team then? Holmes and Watson?'

'I suppose so,' Verity said, grinning, 'but don't try and tell me I'm Watson. Anyway, aren't you worried about annoying your brother even more?'

'I think the worst has happened as far as Gerald is concerned. Anyway, if we are discreet enough in our Sherlock Holmesing he will never know.'

'You will keep me quiet?'

'I don't think anyone could do that. I just meant it might look pretty absurd for us to look as though we were trying to do the police's job. Our qualifications for sleuthing are precisely zero.'

Verity said, not looking up from her fish, 'I think I did you an injustice. Gosh, this sole is good!'

'How do you mean—"an injustice"?'

'Well, to be honest, I didn't think you had it in you. I took you for a typical wet fish of decayed

aristocracy,'—she indicated her half-eaten sole—
'brainless, useless and asking to be guillotined as
soon as we come to power. You don't mind me
speaking frankly?'

'Not at all,' said Edward. 'And I thought you
were just a typical talentless would-be artist or
writer or something with a rich father prepared to
subsidize absurd political opinions which you did
not begin to understand and a liar to boot.'

They stared at each other, surprised by the
venom of their remarks. Edward was the first to
recover. 'I apologize. I didn't think anything of the
sort. I think I liked you from the moment you
hooted your horn at me on the haywain.'

'Well, let's get one thing straight,' said Verity,
only partly mollified, 'I don't particularly like you
and Max doesn't like you at all and he's a good
judge of men, but I am willing to suspend judgment
on the wet fish issue.'

'Right,' said Edward. 'I don't like Max much
either but I'm quite prepared to be partners in
crime detection on that basis if you are.' He got up
from his chair and put out his hand, attracting
some curious glances from other diners. Verity also
stood up and they solemnly shook hands.

When they had sat down again, Verity said, 'I
expect it does seem rather ridiculous, me and
Daddy being Communists when he drives a Rolls-
Royce and I have a generous allowance. My excuse
is the money allows me to spend my time working
for the cause instead of working just to have
enough to eat, like some of us. I know the
comrades think we . . . Daddy and me . . . are not
. . . are not serious, but so what?' She shrugged.
'Daddy and I are quite sincere. Of course, we could

give away all our money and be poor but it is much more sensible to use the money and our brains to further the cause. It is not as if we believe that everyone has to be poor. We believe that everyone ought to have a good standard of living—that's what we have to work for. In any case, the really important thing is to unite to destroy the Fascists. No one seems to realize that the Fascists are going to make a war, if they don't kill us all first using Oswald Mosley's crew to do it. Have you read Marx and Lenin?' Before he could answer, she said hurriedly, 'Still, don't let's get into politics now.'

'I would just say,' said Edward, 'that I heartily agree with you—about the Fascists being a threat to peace, I mean—but I vigorously rebut the idea that you have to join the Communist Party to oppose Fascism. The old warmonger as you call him—unkindly, I think—hated Fascists as much as you, even if he also hated Communists. Like you, Verity, I believe in justice and I think that is what gives us common ground. Now, let's work out a plan of campaign. I think the first thing that Sherlock Holmes might have done is to make a list of suspects.'

Verity looked at him with something like respect. By the time they were served coffee, the champagne and the Orvieto had been finished and Edward was making notes on the back of the menu.

Verity had insisted he list everyone who had been at the dinner, 'that subservient butler, of course, and the footman and ourselves'.

'Did you murder the General?'

'No, and I don't suppose you did either,' she allowed, 'but we must not start assuming things. I know: allow space beside each name for

136

opportunity and motive.'

'We all had opportunity,' Edward objected, 'that's why we put their names on the list in the first place. And no one has a motive.'

'No,' said Verity, 'be accurate. We do not *know* if anyone had a motive, which is quite different.'

'All right, let's go through the list,' said Edward. 'I can't see what possible motive Bates or John would have. They have both been at Mersham for years—Bates has been there for ever—and it is quite inconceivable that they would murder one of the Duke's guests.'

'Does Bates have a first name?'

'Presumably,' said Edward, 'but it would be more than my life was worth to use it. And before you ask, I do know John's surname. It's Cross.'

'We can assume Jeffries is in the clear?'

'You mean he might have put the cyanide capsule in the General's pill box and hoped he would take it sometime in mistake for his painkillers?'

'Yes, but I agree, he has no possible motive unless it turns out he inherits a large sum of money from his master. You can check that,' said Verity bossily. 'I suppose the Duke doesn't have a motive?' she added, a little embarrassed.

'No, of course not. Wait a moment though, Frank—that's our older brother who died in the war—he was under General Craig's command. The fact he died so uselessly could be said to be a motive.'

'Oh, I—'

Edward steam-rollered on, determined to bring the case against his brother out in the open so it could be considered and dismissed once and for all.

'Gerald might have been waiting all these years to take his revenge on the man who ordered his brother to his death.' He paused and looked Verity in the eye. 'You'll say I am prejudiced but I don't believe it for a moment. For one thing, the dinner was just too important to him to muck it up; for another thing—you saw his face when he saw Craig dying. I just could not begin to suspect him.' Edward had tried to be objective but suddenly his voice broke. 'I'm afraid this has hit him very hard. The one thing he lives for is to use his influence to make peace between Germany and England. Now that work cannot go ahead—at least, not until this is all cleared up.'

Verity was silent for a moment or two, wanting to comfort him but not sure what to say. Finally, deciding he would hate her to go all gooey, she said, 'I agree, I don't suspect the Duke even though I think he is mistaken in thinking he can achieve anything with these dinners. There is nothing to be gained by talking to Fascists. They just think you are weak. Our only hope is in the leadership of the Soviet Union.' She was very earnest. 'Only in Russia is there true freedom.'

'Have you been to the Soviet Union?' Edward asked mildly.

'No, but I hope to go at the end of the year. There's a conference in Moscow and I may be chosen as a delegate.'

'So you don't know for sure that the Soviet Union is the paradise on earth you think it is?'

'Plenty of people I trust have been. I *have* been to Germany and I can tell you that enough terrible things are happening there to convince you that I am telling the truth. We are going to have to stop

138

the Fascists by force one day; it's the only thing they understand.'

'That's a depressing thought but I don't disagree.'

'Maybe, but it is better to face reality even if it is depressing than hide your head in the sand.'

'Why try and convince me; aren't I the class enemy? Anyway, I told you, I think you are right.'

'It is very disconcerting when you agree with me,' said Verity, laughing.

'It won't happen again,' said Edward, with his rather crooked smile. 'But let's get back to our murderer, if there is one.'

'I feel sure there is. All my female intuition is screaming warnings.'

'Golly, do CP members have such bourgeois things as female intuition?'

'Very funny. I think Larmore is my chief suspect. He's rotten to the core—a typical right-wing, corrupt capitalist.'

'Wait a minute, Verity, if we are going to sleuth together you are going to have to put your political prejudices aside. The moment you start stereotyping people you cease to see them as human beings.'

'*Touché*!' Verity said. 'All right then, I think Larmore needs investigation.'

'The German—what's his name? Friedberg—he needs looking at too, but to be honest, I can't see him murdering a distinguished British general within days of being here on government business.'

'No, and the Bishop—he's a good man. He's a great friend of Tommie's, did you know? They do good works together.'

'So who does that leave?'

'Well, there's Lord Weaver, a capitalist if ever there was one.'

'Yes,' agreed Edward, 'and therefore a natural ally of the General's, surely. Would he, even if he wanted to murder someone, choose to do it at the Duke's table in front of his wife and stepdaughter?'

'Probably not,' Verity agreed reluctantly. 'Don't forget Hermione,' she said, cheering up. 'She was leaning over him as he drank his port and she seemed the most shocked of all of us by what happened. Still, I don't see how she could have put poison in the General's glass without anyone seeing.'

'And remember, she was not in the dining-room when the men were drinking their port. She came in with the other ladies when we arrived.'

'Yes, and surely if she had poisoned the port she would have known what to expect and would have been less shocked than the rest of us?' said Verity.

'Hard to say. She might have done it on a whim and then been horrified by what she had done. Still, it does seem unlikely, and unlikely that she would have been clever enough to have dropped the capsule in the General's glass without anyone noticing.'

'More to the point,' said Verity, 'what possible motive could she have? I can't see how her path and the General's could have ever crossed.'

Edward and Verity looked at each other in dismay. At last Edward said, 'It looks as if we're barking up the wrong tree. There seems to be no reason why anyone who could have murdered the General would have wanted to.'

'So have we argued ourselves out of investigating?'

Edward said, 'Not quite, but no one must know that we are investigating. We would be a laughing-stock if people suspected it and possibly alarm the murderer should he exist.'

'Well, I vote we have a casual conversation with each of the possibles and then reconsider. For instance, there would be no problem about talking to the Bishop. We could easily find an excuse. We could say we are interested in his Peace Pledge Union.'

'What's that?' asked Edward.

'Oh, haven't you heard? Everyone from whatever party is going to be urged to join together to promise not to go to war and try and persuade governments to pledge themselves to peace too.'

'Would you join it?' inquired Edward interestedly.

'Of course not,' said Verity scornfully. 'Haven't you been listening? We are going to have to fight the Fascists one day and this sort of wishy-washy Utopianism just weakens people's resolve.'

Edward was impressed. 'And you could accept Friedberg's invitation to go out to dinner with him,' he said slowly.

Verity blushed. 'Ugh! I hated that man on sight but yes, I suppose he did seem to like me.'

'More than that, I'd say,' said Edward, annoyed with himself for minding.

'I could do a bit of vamping, I suppose.'

'You are very good at it. Think how you charmed all of us.'

Verity flushed again, this time in anger. She did feel guilty at tricking the Duchess but she did not want Edward criticizing her. 'You make me sound a scheming bitch,' she said.

141

Edward, shocked at her language, realized that what he had meant as a rather clumsy joke had given offence. 'I am sorry, Verity. Please forgive me. I did not mean to imply . . . It would be too dangerous anyway. Just because we don't like Nazis, we should not underestimate them. They are not fools.'

'Oh, stow it,' she said crossly. 'We'll think how to get to Weaver. We need some excuse to talk to him.'

'I know,' said Edward. 'That ghastly girl Hermione seems to have got a crush on me for no good reason. I could be really underhand and get to know her and then her father. Kill two birds with one stone—oops, sorry!'

'That's more like it,' said Verity. 'If you are as underhand and skulduggerous as me then I won't feel so bad!'

'Done,' said Edward, paying the bill. 'Now, let's leave it at that for the moment. Telephone me if you can arrange for us to see the Bishop without arousing suspicion.'

'Yes, and I will try to get an invitation to go out with the horrible German. God, I will have some explaining to do if the comrades ever find out.'

'No, I don't think you ought to; I think it would be too dangerous. If anyone ought to talk to Friedberg it should be me.'

As dangerous as involving yourself with Hermione Weaver?'

'I will risk it with Hermione,' Edward said grimly.

As the waiter helped them into their coats Edward glimpsed himself and the girl in the mirrored wall: Verity solemn, determined, her

142

seriousness betrayed only by the red feather in her little hat which she wore on the side of her head; he, lean and tanned with the glossy look of a young man-about-town who has never had to worry where his next dinner was coming from. He thought they made an enigmatic couple. What had they got in common—the young lordling and the intense, politically aware young woman? She had guts—he had to admit—and a gaiety of spirit which belied her gloomy prognostications. In a world where women in politics were often thought absurd and 'unfeminine', he found her a refreshing alternative to the silly, languid girls whom he met at balls and in country houses and whose conversation was restricted to horses and dogs or the next party.

Verity held out her hand to him. 'No need to get me a taxi. I live close enough to walk and the fresh air will do me good, and before you ask, I would rather walk alone.' She softened her admonition with a smile. 'Thank you for dinner. I will telephone you in a day or two to report progress, if any.'

'How do you know my number?'

'For one thing, you gave me your card when we first met behind that hay wagon. I knew I had an idiot to deal with when you gave me your address and telephone number within seconds of meeting.'

'And the second thing?' said Edward crossly.

'The second thing? Oh, well, I suppose Tommie Fox has it, hasn't he?'

He watched her disappear into the crowd, for Soho was only just beginning to wake up for the night's pleasures, and he half-hailed a cab before telling himself if Verity could walk, so could he. The Albany was only fifteen minutes away. Then he clicked his fingers in annoyance. He had never got her to give him *her* address or telephone number. What sort of sleuth did that make him? Feeling rather a chump he turned towards Piccadilly. His knee hardly hurt him and he thought after all he might be up to a little dancing. He would ring Hermione.

CHAPTER SIX

TUESDAY EVENING

Edward felt a bit of a cad. Hermione was obviously besotted with him and when he had rung to suggest an evening at the Four Hundred she had responded with embarrassing enthusiasm. 'But not the Four Hundred. That's frightfully old-fashioned now. The place to go is the Cocoanut Grove—you know, in Regent Street.' Hermione sounded brittle and over-eager but, as he reminded himself, the telephone strangled the voice so maybe it was just her excitement.

Edward's worst fears were realized at ten o'clock that evening after dinner at the Savoy, when he escorted Hermione to the Cocoanut Grove, a jungle in more ways than one. They descended a narrow staircase, a fire hazard if ever he had seen one, to a gigantic dance room got up like some film producer's vision of King Kong's natural habitat. Pillars sprouted green fronds and the walls were adorned with fanciful paintings of tropical islands, volcanoes and palm trees. In one corner of the room there was a large glass tank filled with water in which a few depressed-looking fish swum round and round as if they knew they ought not to be there. The dance floor was already crowded with men in evening dress and women in exotic gowns, silk and chiffon, and much jewellery. It was everything that Edward hated. The temperature was already in the high seventies and the band, performing from inside what appeared to be a log cabin, were sweating visibly.

'Oh, how priceless,' said Hermione as they were led to a small table near the aquarium. 'See, that one looks exactly like Charlie Lomax.' She pointed to a flat fish covered in black and white spots.

'You don't like that character any more? Your mother thinks you are in love with him.'

'With Charlie Lomax?' said Hermione in mock amazement. 'He can be quite amusing, I suppose, but just lately he has been a terrible bore.'

The waiter brought champagne and Edward, very uncomfortable on his little gilt chair, said, 'Shall we dance, Hermione?'

'Yes, let's, darling,' said the girl, getting up with alacrity. Edward was beginning to feel that he might have done better to have kept his relationship with Hermione quite formal. He had thought, when talking about it to Verity, it might be easier to ask the girl if she had killed General Craig as they chatted gaily in some pleasant night spot but he had not visualized the full horror of the Cocoanut Grove. Even alcohol in considerable quantities did not seem to be lifting his leaden spirits, and to add to his gloom his knee had begun to hurt. He had put himself in what he recognized to be a false position in regard to Hermione. It was rather shabby making this girl believe he cared about her when really he was aching to be rid of her. He tried to ignore the way she hung on his arm as they danced and how she buried her head on his shoulder whenever the music allowed. Fortunately, at this early hour of the evening the music was lively if rather noisy.

'Miss Weaver,' said a voice behind Edward.

'Oh hello, Captain Gordon,' said Hermione, a little nervously Edward thought. 'Edward, this is Captain Gordon who manages the Cocoanut Grove. Captain Gordon, this is Lord Edward Corinth.'

The Captain looked rather taken aback. 'Lord Edward—I am delighted to see you here. I hope you are enjoying yourself.' He turned back to Hermione. 'Miss Weaver, there's a friend of yours coming in later. He wanted me to tell you because apparently you have something for him.'

'A friend? Oh yes, thank you,' said Hermione vaguely, not asking who the friend was who was so eager to speak to her. Captain Gordon seemed to take the hint because he slipped away without further comment.

'Gosh, did you see how impressed he was that you were my partner, Edward?' said Hermione, pink-faced but triumphant. 'He can't try anything on with you beside me.'

'What might he want to "try on"?' he inquired.

'I don't know but they are all such crooks,' she said distractedly.

They ordered some Chinese food to pick at. They were not hungry but Hermione said the club was famous for its oriental dishes, which seemed rather odd to Edward given its jungle theme. They danced again, drank more champagne, but still

Edward could not bring himself to raise the subject of General Craig's death. It did not seem appropriate somehow and in any case the noise of the band and the dancing couples was too great for sensible conversation. Edward cursed himself for not having asked his question while they were at the Savoy but then he had felt constrained by good manners not to make it too obvious why he had invited her out. If he immediately embarked on his 'investigation' before they had begun to get to know each other she would almost certainly have clammed up or even stormed out of the restaurant. He understood now why Sherlock Holmes had, for the most part, restricted his inquisitions to his consulting rooms. On his own territory he could perhaps have spoken with more authority than in a beastly, showy night-club.

He looked around him for a way of escape but saw none. The women at neighbouring tables looked cheap and he wondered how many of them were 'professionals'. The men were pasty-faced monkeys jumping across the dance floor, throwing their partners about in some desperate imitation of gaiety. Whoa! he warned himself. He must not let his mood spoil the evening for his partner but he was too late.

'You're not enjoying this, are you?' Hermione suddenly demanded.

'Oh no, please, of course I am enjoying myself,' he said hastily. 'Let's dance again. Isn't this a rumba?'

'No, look, the cabaret is starting. The singer they have got is all the rage. Afterwards, then we'll go. I'm not sure I like this place as much as I thought either.'

She was right. Captain Gordon was climbing on to the little stage in front of the log cabin. He almost slipped and fell and Edward guessed his genial host had been drinking. When he had settled himself he announced that they were privileged to have with them tonight the American singing star—'the toast of Broadway'—Amy Pageant. Edward had never heard of her and the polite applause suggested that neither had anyone else, but when she came forward out of the log cabin and began to sing Cole Porter and Gershwin he was bowled over. She had a low husky voice which spoke of regret and lost love in a way which appealed to him in his melancholy. She was also very beautiful. The lights had been dimmed and the singer was encircled by a ring of white light which followed her as she moved around the tiny stage so that her oval face above naked shoulders, ivory in the spotlight, drew every eye.

She sang 'The Man I Love' as if she were at confession but what reduced Edward to pulp was her rendering of 'How's Your Romance?' from Cole Porter's *Gay Divorce*, a show he had seen three times when it had been on in London a couple of years before. He was transfixed by the singer's honesty which seemed to make each song sound as if she was making it up as she went along in order to give voice to her own thoughts. He hardly noticed that Hermione was trying to get his attention. 'Let's go,' she was muttering. 'Come on, I want to go.'

'In a moment, wait a moment,' he mumbled, pushing her hand away. Nothing would distract him from gazing at Amy Pageant. Her lustrous black eyes seemed to search him out in the darkness. He knew it was nonsense, but he was bewitched. Hermione was getting more and more agitated and began to pull at his arm so that even through his pleasure he was becoming annoyed. Really, the girl was very tiresome. Why couldn't she let him alone to concentrate on this astonishing woman? When the singer finished Edward stood up and applauded vigorously, not something he had ever done before in a night-club. He normally hated making a spectacle of himself but on this occasion he was too excited to worry what anyone else thought.

As couples began to return to the dance floor, many throwing him amused glances as they did so, he turned to apologize to Hermione only to find that she had vanished. He wondered if she had gone to 'powder her nose' but when after ten minutes she had not come back he strolled across the room and asked one of the waiters where the ladies' cloakroom was. He was directed towards the corner of the room. He pushed through a swing door and walked down a dimly lit corridor. When he arrived at the end of it he found a door marked 'Powder Room'. He was rather at a loss to know what to do. He could not barge in to see if she were there and risk causing a scandal, or could he? After a minute or two when no one went in or came out he knocked and called Hermione's name. There was no answer so he opened the door a crack and peered in. The room was quite empty but the furniture was scattered about as if there had been a tussle.

Edward returned to the dance room mystified and a little alarmed, hoping to see that Hermione had returned to their table, but not only was she not there but two strangers were sitting where they

149

had sat. He was going to remonstrate with them but then thought better of it and went off to find Captain Gordon. That gentleman he ran to earth in a little office just off the dance room. He was drinking whisky and looked as though he had been doing so for some time. He was not pleased to see Edward but, perhaps remembering that he was the brother of a duke and might be good for attracting high-class clientele, tried to put on a welcoming smile.

'Whisky, Lord Edward?' he slurred, waving an almost empty bottle at him.

'No, thank you. I say, have you seen the girl I was with? She seems to have disappeared.' He felt every kind of ass admitting as much but what else could he do?

'Miss Weaver? I thought I saw her with Mr Lomax during the cabaret. Maybe she has left you in the lurch,' he said insolently.

'Maybe,' Edward said, trying to remain civil. 'Can we find out?'

Captain Gordon smiled derisively and spoke into a telephone which seemed to connect with the front door. He said, 'Caspar, will you come down to my office, please.' He turned to Edward. 'You may have noticed Caspar as you came in. He's our doorman and "chucker-out".'

Edward had. He was a gorilla of a man with a face like a cauliflower.

'Ah, Caspar,' said the Captain as the doorman arrived, huge in the tiny office, 'Lord Edward Corinth wonders if you have seen his lady friend leave without him.'

'Yus, sur,' said the gorilla. 'She got into a taxi along with Mr Lomax. She gave me a note, sur, for the gentleman.' He dipped his ham of a hand into his pocket and came out with a crumpled piece of paper. Edward grabbed it. In smudged, childish handwriting Hermione had written, 'Sorry. Have to go. See you, H.'

'She gave you this as she left the club?' Edward demanded.

'Yus, sur.'

'So why did you not give it to me earlier?'

'She only juss give it me,' Caspar said, aggrieved. 'Anyways, she said to give it you when you asked.'

'I see,' said Edward who certainly did not see. 'Well, thank you.' He gave the man half a crown. It really was a bit thick being left by a girl like this even if she was as unstable as Hermione Weaver.

'Deuced bad luck—losing the gel like that,' said Captain Gordon, a touch of derision audible beneath his unexceptionable words. 'Like the club?' he inquired fatuously as Edward stood silent.

Edward roused himself to answer with an effort. 'Very nice, a jungle in every way.' As he turned to leave the place, he added, 'Amy Pageant—she's something special. Where did you find her?'

'She's good, isn't she? Too good for us really, but she's doing a favour for the owner—or the other way round, I'm not sure which.'

'And who is he?' said Edward casually.

'Shouldn't really tell you, I suppose, but seeing you're a friend of the family in a manner of speaking I expect it's all right: Lord Weaver—he owns the Cocoanut Grove.'

CHAPTER SEVEN

SATURDAY

Verity was too busy at the *Daily Worker* for a couple of days to pursue investigations into the death of General Craig, which in any case, she was inclined to think, were going to be a waste of time. She did not believe that the old man had died by accident but when it came down to it, how was she, a paid-up member of the Communist Party and therefore an object of suspicion to the police and most respectable middle-class Englishmen, going to prove it? She had no faith in the efficacy of Lord Edward Corinth, a sprig of a ducal house and by definition—at least by *her* definition—of no use to man or dog.

On Wednesday morning she found herself by chance very close to Tommie Fox's parish church in Kilburn. She liked Tommie—a thoroughly good man by any standards—but normally they argued so fiercely about politics as to make close friendship an impossibility. Tommie was not a Communist. He called himself a Christian Socialist and he believed that at bottom all men were good. He considered it was his duty, as he put it, 'to mobilize ordinary men and women for peace'. To Verity this was daft, and she told him so.

Running him to earth in the church hall she found the man of God wielding a paint brush against a huge sheet of card on which he was inscribing a slogan.

'Is this for Saturday's march through London?'

asked Verity, craning her neck to read what he was painting. ' "Christian Socialists for Peace",' she read aloud. 'Rubbish! Men aren't peaceable by nature, not even Socialist Christians. For God's sake, Tommie, surely history teaches us *that* if nothing else. Tribal warfare has always existed and always will. Tribes will attempt to dominate other tribes to distract their own people from dwelling on their woes and fighting among themselves. If you can blame someone else for the rotten time you are having you won't blame the government. Simple. Look at the Christian Church: it has been responsible for more tribal conflict than any other movement. Didn't Christ say something like "I bring not peace but a sword"?'

'That's very cynical, Verity,' said Tommie, giving her a kiss on the cheek, 'and please don't use God's name as a swear word. I have asked you before. I believe it is precisely your type of cheap cynicism which leads to war. If you expect the worst of people that's what you'll get. Bishop Haycraft is absolutely right in calling for everyone of all political and religious creeds to join together to march for peace. It's going to be the most democratic movement of all time.' Tommie waved his hands in the air in excitement. 'We'll show all those tired, corrupt politicians that they have to listen to the people for once. How I hate men like that horrible Peter Larmore, but even he believes that we should extend the hand of brotherhood to Germany and right her wrongs.'

'Larmore? What's he got to do with anything?'

'You didn't hear him on the wireless last night calling for Britain to play the honest broker between France and Germany? I did. It was inspirational. I must admit I had him down as simply another of those corrupt cronies of Baldwin's but it looks as if I was wrong and proves my point that even the least promising among us has some good in him—or her,' he added meaningly. 'The next thing, we will hear Baldwin saying he is going to lead the only fight worth fighting: the fight for European peace.'

'Stop preaching at me, Tommie, will you? Let me think—Haycraft? He was at the dinner at the Duke's when that poor old man was killed.'

'The warmonger General, you mean? The Bishop told me all about that. I can't say I am too sad about it even if I'm not being very Christian. The man was notorious for his hatred of all things German. If he had had his way we would have invaded Germany as soon as they started talking about altering the terms of the Versailles treaty.'

'So will Haycraft be on this march for peace on Saturday?'

'He certainly will,' said Tommie warmly. 'He's one of its leaders. What about you? I gather the Communists have not made their mind up if they will take part. Still waiting for instructions from Moscow, no doubt.'

'Oh, do put a sock in it, Tommie,' said Verity crossly. 'Of course the Communist Party will be represented. We are the party for peace, in case you have forgotten it.'

'Well, see you at Speakers' Corner then,' said Tommie mildly, going back to making his banner.

*   *   *

That Saturday, the first in September, was as warm

as any day in August and there was a carnival atmosphere in the crowd which began to gather at the top of Park Lane as early as nine o'clock. There was much laughter and greeting of friends. Banners and slogan-bearing posters attached to makeshift boards and poles were compared: 'Peace with Honour', 'Disarm for Peace', 'Pledged to Peace'. Most of those who were to march saw themselves as liberals but they represented a broad spectrum of opinion only excluding the far right and the far left. The Communist Party had to Verity's disappointment and puzzlement decided Party members should have no part in bourgeois protest movements, but she and a few like-minded CP members decided to risk censure and march.

At eleven thirty, after several bracing speeches, the crowd gradually sorted itself into ranks and followed their leaders into Park Lane under the escort of a small force of Metropolitan Police officers. Verity walked with friends and fellow activists towards the rear of the parade. Tommie was near the front with Cecil Haycraft and three other bishops who were not afraid to take a stance on what many people felt was a political issue but Haycraft believed was a moral imperative. Their object was the Prime Minister's residence in Downing Street where the leaders of the march would hand in a petition demanding international disarmament. It took almost three hours for the slow-moving procession to reach its destination. The marchers brought Piccadilly to a standstill, despite the best efforts of the police, before turning right into St James's Street where old men in their clubs looked out of the windows, their moustaches twitching with indignation and apprehension. Was

155

this the revolution, they wondered? But this was not a march against poverty and unemployment: the economy was picking up at last, at least in the south of England, and these marchers posed no threat to the representatives of capitalism or even to the landed aristocracy slumbering in their leather armchairs.

At Downing Street the petition was handed in, more speeches were made and then the march began to break down into small groups of friends and allies unwilling to go home immediately. Some stood about on street corners, others packed Lyons and ABC tea-rooms. Verity found herself near Tommie who invited her to come along with him and a few others to the Star and Garter just over Westminster Bridge. 'I worked in a boys' club near there when I was first a curate and I used to have a pint there afterwards to congratulate myself on surviving.' He laughed but Verity suddenly realized what a good man Tommie was. He made fun of himself—a do-gooder trying to alleviate some of the worst effects of poverty but constantly seeing his achievements washed away by the sheer scale of the problem. When she said something to him about admiring his work, he said, 'Oh, chuck it, Verity. I don't know if I do any good. Maybe I ought not to try and make the intolerable tolerable.'

'How do you mean?'

'Well, some of the suffering I have witnessed among the poor in slums literally in sight of the Houses of Parliament would make your hair curl. And yet, you know, they might be in the heart of Africa for all most MPs care. I think it is the indifference of the well-to-do rather than the ingratitude of the people we try to help which hurts the most.'

'But surely,' said Verity weakly, 'the Salvation Army . . .'

'Oh yes, the Sally Army do wonderful work and there are other good people like Dr Barnardo's but it's all a drop in the ocean. We really need a complete change to our system.'

'That's what I tell you,' said Verity indignantly. 'The political system is rotten to the core.'

'I know,' said Tommy levelly, 'but I'm not sure your people would make it any better.'

'My people . . . ?' began Verity when a voice said, 'It's Miss Browne, isn't it?'

The Bishop of Worthing, Cecil Haycraft, was at her side. 'Oh yes, hello, Bishop, I didn't think you would recognize me.'

'Of course I recognize you. I may be a happily married bishop but I still notice attractive girls. I hope that's not a sin.'

To her annoyance Verity blushed. She hoped he wasn't going to be tiresome but it did give her an opportunity for some subtle questioning. However, before she could begin he said, 'Still writing for *Country Life*?'

Tommie guffawed and Verity blushed again. 'I am afraid I have to confess that I never did write for *Country Life*. I occasionally write for the *Daily Worker*.'

'I had a feeling you might not be exactly what you seemed,' the Bishop said unmoved.

'How do you mean: "what I seemed"?'

'Fluffy, empty-headed, garrulous . . .' Haycraft answered without hesitation. 'By the way, are you D. F. Browne's daughter?'

She nodded. 'Are you a friend of his?'

'No, not really,' the Bishop replied. 'We come across each other on committees of one sort and another. Do you consider yourself to be a Communist?'

'I am a fully paid-up member of the Party,' said Verity stoutly, not wanting there to be any further excuse for the Bishop to think she was 'something she was not'.

By this time they had reached the pub Tommie knew and they all filed through the frosted glass doors and went to the bar—dirty-looking and ringed with the marks of wet beer mugs. Verity saw that the Bishop was determined to seem quite at home in a public house though she had a feeling that in his heart of hearts he would have preferred not to be there.

'What'll you have, Cecil?' said Tommie chummily. Obviously, off duty the Bishop liked to be 'one of the boys'.

'Pint, please, Tommie, but hey, let me do this.'

'No,' said Tommie, 'this is my round. Even on my salary I can afford a pint of beer now and again or else life's not worth living. Verity, a lemonade?'

'No, a pint, please, Tommie.' Why would these men—these good men—patronize her all the time, she asked herself? She was just as politically effective as any of them and probably a lot more ruthless. If only she didn't blush so easily.

'Tell me, Bishop—' she began.

'Cecil, please, Verity. I hate formality except on formal occasions.'

Verity wasn't quite sure she was ready yet to call the Bishop 'Cecil'. She was used—and indeed, despite being a Communist, happy—to call men of her father's age 'sir'. She ploughed on: 'What do you make of this new spirit of German nationalism? My father says it is Prussian imperialism with added savagery.'

'I agree with him. It is frightening and I detest the Nazis' emphasis on racial pride and "pure Nordic birth", but I do not despair of teaching Mr Hitler the error of his ways. If the League of Nations is united in telling Germany that it just won't do kicking up such a fuss in the world when they can get everything they want by reasonable discussion—'

'Everything they want?' broke in Tommie, returning with a tin tray on which stood three frothing tankards. 'I should hope not "everything", Cecil. I saw the BUF march through the East End and it made my stomach turn over, I can tell you.'

'Oh,' said the Bishop, 'no need to worry. Mosley's a *buff*oon.' He laughed heartily at his feeble pun. Behind him three toughs who had been listening got up from their stools and came over. One of them tapped the Bishop on the shoulder.

'I hope, mister, I did not hear you aright. Wus you sayin' things against our leader?'

'Look,' said Tommie unwisely, 'will you clear off? We are having a private conversation.'

'Youse a clerical gentleman?' said one of the other toughs, seeing his white collar partly hidden under his jersey and tweed jacket.

'That's nothing to do with you,' said Tommie, sitting himself down. 'Clear off, you're not wanted here.'

'Not until you say Sir Oswald Mosley is a good fellow.'

'I shall say nothing of the sort. He is, as my

159

friend said a moment ago, a buffoon.'

Without further ado one of the toughs seized Tommie by the arm and tried to propel him across the room. The other two looked at Verity and the Bishop threateningly and Verity, on an impulse, threw her beer in the face of one of them—she hadn't really wanted to drink it anyhow. As the poor man she had assaulted tried, cursing vigorously, to wipe the beer out of his eyes, she got up and crossed over to help Tommie. But Tommie did not need any help; he had boxed for his school and for Cambridge and he dispatched his assailant with a blow to the jaw of considerable force, knocking him to the ground. The other two toughs, who had been about to join the fray, now looked worried.

'Hey,' one of them said, 'what did you want to go and do that for?'

Tommie, really angry, was an impressive sight. He squared up to the two of them and said, 'I say Mosley is a buffoon. Want to make anything of it?'

The Bishop was looking rather nervous: 'Look, I say, Tommie, that's enough. Here, you men— here's half a sovereign. Take your friend off and let's hear no more of this.'

The publican, who had been pretending not to see what was happening, took courage and came over and added his voice to the Bishop's. 'Clear off, will you—attacking my customers—I won't have it. Now beat it or I'll call the rozzers.'

The three members of the British Union of Fascists, seeing they were facing overwhelming odds, departed muttering oaths, the man Tommie had knocked to the floor distinctly unsteady on his feet. Tommie was triumphant. 'Another pint,

160

Verity? Your tankard is empty but I can't say you wasted your first.'

'No,' said Verity, feeling a little weak now the adrenalin was on the ebb. 'I think I'll have a ginger beer shandy.'

The Bishop said, 'Well done, Tommie. You are a useful man to have around in a scrap but I'm glad it's over. I had a horrid feeling Miss Browne here might be reporting "Bishop in bar-room brawl" in a moment. We can't give her too many scoops, can we?'

Verity was silent. The Bishop was making it clear that he had known all along that she was behind the story in the *Daily Worker* of the General's murder.

At last she said, 'Bishop, I wanted to ask you— do you think that General Craig killed himself accidentally?'

'Don't you?' he countered.

'Well, it seemed to me and to Lord Edward that it was quite unlikely that he would have confused the capsule of cyanide with his painkillers. For one thing they're a different shape. The morphine pills are small and round while the cyanide capsule was probably glass and oblong and rather larger.'

'I see,' said Haycraft. 'I did not know that.'

'Yes, and while the pill—the painkiller, I mean— need only be swallowed, the capsule would have to be broken into the liquid or between the teeth.'

'In other words, it would have to be done deliberately?'

'Yes. You didn't see anything, I suppose?'

'Did I see anyone murder the General? No, I did not. If I had done of course I would have mentioned it to the police,' he added with a touch

161

of sarcasm.

'Yes, of course,' said Verity. 'I'm sorry. I did not mean to be rude. Anyway, why should anyone want to kill the old man? You know he was mortally ill with stomach cancer?'

'No, I did not,' said the Bishop. 'Poor man. When you say mortally ill . . . ?'

'His doctor had given him only a few weeks to live—at least that's what Dr Best says.'

'Hmf,' said the Bishop. 'A terminal case of life exhaustion,' he added slowly, and Verity had no idea if he intended some sort of joke or if it was meant seriously.

Changing the subject, Verity said, 'Might I ask you something, Bishop? Do you think churchmen like yourself have a special duty to speak out on issues such as disarmament or just the duty of any ordinary citizen in a democracy to make their voice heard?'

'It's an interesting question,' said the Bishop, visibly relaxing now the conversation had shifted to more abstract questions of morality. 'Many people would say that a churchman has no right to make any comment on political issues and that he should remain above the hurly-burly in case he is seen to become the member of one particular political party or grouping. I am inclined to think that that is a risk worth taking. I do think a churchman has a special duty to act up to his principles even if he should alienate some of his flock in so doing. Christ was not afraid of being controversial and giving offence when he wanted to make moral statements.'

'So you think *private* morality is a contradiction in terms?'

'Well, yes, I do. Morality only has substance in actions and it's hard to keep most actions private—as a churchman one may actually have a duty to make them public.'

'I see,' said Verity. 'That's very interesting. It seems to me to be close to the Communist philosophy of collective responsibility for political action.' She suddenly had a bright idea: 'I say, if my paper, the *Daily Worker*, asked you to write an article on political morality would you consider it?'

The Bishop looked dubious. 'I would consider it but I would have to be certain that it did not appear as if I were supporting the Communist Party.'

'Of course,' said Verity excitedly. 'I say, Bishop—Cecil—you're a very good sport; not the stuffy clergyman we expect a C of E bishop to be.'

'And you, Verity Browne, are, if I may say so, a clever, persuasive and attractive young woman. You should go right to the top of the tree in your profession. But take an old man's advice: don't be tempted to take one risk too many.'

'You're not an old man,' said Verity, and gave him a quick kiss on the cheek which startled her almost as much as it startled Bishop Haycraft.

CHAPTER EIGHT

VERITY'S MONDAY

'You did what?' said Edward, frankly appalled. 'You embroiled the Bishop in a bar-room fight, asked him if he had murdered General Craig, and then invited him to write for your beastly rag?'

'I thought you would be pleased,' said Verity. 'I have been following up leads. You have been doing nothing but taking women out to disorderly houses. I wish I had pointed out to Tommie that his punching that Fascist on the chin proved my point about tribal warfare,' she added meditatively. 'Oh well, perhaps better not.'

It was eight o'clock and Edward was sitting up in bed eating his lightly boiled egg, toast and marmalade when the telephone had rung. It was Verity. Without pausing to inquire after his knee, she regaled him with the whole story of her day's adventure. Edward had to admit she appeared to have been a more successful sleuth than he, and it rather got up his nose.

'Yes, and I haven't finished yet.' Verity's voice came over tinny and shrill through the instrument. 'Guess what?'

'I can't,' said Edward wearily. 'You've been invited to write for *The Times*.'

'Gosh,' said Verity admiringly, 'that's jolly clever of you. As a matter of fact not *The Times* but the *New Gazette*.'

'Lord Weaver's paper?' said Edward, sitting up in astonishment.

'Well, practically. Apparently he was so impressed with my enterprise in getting that scoop, he wants to meet me.'

'When?'

'This afternoon at two in his office.'

'And you think he is going to offer you a job?'

'Yes—well, what else can it be?'

'I expect,' Edward said with heavy irony, 'rather than offer you a job he is going to shut you up.

164

Don't you realize he controls the whole press except for rags like yours which no one takes seriously except a few cranks and no one reads except a few other cranks.'

Verity, swallowing her annoyance at this put-down, said, 'They all used my story about the General's death. Anyway, how could Weaver stop me from digging the dirt? He can't control the *whole* press. Surely the *New Gazette*'s competitors would be delighted to print what he refuses to.'

'Oh, you innocent young thing,' said Edward patronizingly. 'I grant you that if we are talking about some story about a horse which may or may not win the Derby, or the inside story of Lady Snooty's affair with Lord X, or even new fashions from Paris, there's real competition for the big story, but when it comes to politics they work as a cabal. If the PM tells them not to print some story, they don't, and when I say *they* I mean *all* of the proprietors. They all want their peerages or at least their private dinners at Number Ten. It just wouldn't be playing the game otherwise. And if some rogue paper like your precious *Daily Worker* gets hold of something they shouldn't, they will all gang up and suppress it.'

'How?'

'Rubbish it—make fun of it—deny it—blackmail—do whatever they need to do. It's a rough world out there, kiddo, and don't you forget it.'

'Oh, you men,' said Verity scornfully, 'always so scared of getting into a bit of trouble. Well, even if you are right, I will at least have a chance of asking him if he saw anything suspicious when General Craig died. After all, that's bound to be the subject

165

on the agenda.'

Edward was silent for so long Verity said, 'Are you still there?'

'Yes,' he said, 'I'm still here. I'm just thinking. There are some questions I'd like to ask Lord Weaver myself but I can't discuss them with you over the phone. Would you have time to meet for lunch today?'

'Not really,' she retorted but, relenting, said, 'There's a pub in Fleet Street, the Goat and Grapes, do you know it?' Edward said he did. 'Well, let's meet there for a drink—at twelve thirty, say.'

'All right,' Edward said, aware that this girl he had dismissed at first meeting as a little piece of fluff had once again taken charge.

'Oh, and don't be late,' she added. 'It's all right for the idle rich but some of us have to work for world revolution. I expect you are still in bed, aren't you?'

'No,' lied Edward, 'I've been up for hours,' but Verity had already rung off.

*   *   *

Through a haze of tobacco smoke, Edward saw Verity waving to him from a corner. The Goat and Grapes was a favourite haunt of Fleet Street journalists and was packed as usual at this time of day—or rather at this and all times of the day the licensing laws permitted. As the only lady in the room, with the exception of a slatternly woman behind the bar, one might have expected Verity to have been the object of male admiration but this was not the case. She had been ignored at the bar and every one of the male clientele had offered not chivalric aid but studied indifference at her plight. As far as they were concerned she did not exist. Predictably, she was seething with indignation. 'Do you know,' she said, before he was even seated, 'they would not serve me at the bar. I almost exploded but I didn't want to be thrown out till you arrived. And not one of these "gentlemen",' she gestured scornfully at the men around, 'stood up for me. I'm fuming.'

'Oh gosh, yes, I suppose they see this as a gentlemen's club—members only and all that sort of thing. I'm afraid you are trespassing.'

'Well, it's all bunkum.'

'Why don't we go elsewhere?'

'I haven't got the time. Just get me something ladylike—a gin and lime or something—and then let's swap notes.'

Edward came back from the dingy bar weaving between tables and stools, his hands in the air as if in surrender, bearing a pint for himself and gin for Verity. Verity went over everything she had learned from Cecil Haycraft but in the end it did not seem to amount to very much. She listened intently as he in turn told her about his evening in the Cocoanut Grove.

'And you think there is something fishy about the club? You're not just pipped at being left in the lurch by Hermione?'

'Please, Verity,' Edward expostulated, 'think better of me than that. Hermione is a little monster but I'm still worried that someone is using her for their own ends—Charlie Lomax for one.'

'Could it be dope?'

'I think it might be but I have no proof. In fact

we still have no proof of anything at all. There is one other thing though—two things really. The egregious Captain Gordon, the club's genial host, volunteered the information that the club belonged to Lord Weaver. That's why I wanted to talk to you before you saw him.'

'Golly, why on earth would he want to own a place like that? I mean, if it got out that he owned the club it would do his reputation no good at all.'

'Quite, and it makes no business sense. It doesn't chime in with his other business interests.'

'Unless he is making money from dope and the club is just a front?'

'Yes, that had crossed my mind but it seems so unlikely. He's rich enough as it is and he would lose everything if he were ever revealed to be a dope pedlar. No, I think the answer could be a woman. The cabaret was this stunning American girl who could sing like an angel. In fact, she was much too good to be entertaining a few deadbeats and jackasses in a tinpot West End club.'

'So?' said Verity. 'Maybe this girl you were so smitten with was not as good as you thought.'

'Oh, I imagined she sang Cole Porter like . . . like a smoky-voiced angel, did I?'

'Maybe,' said Verity, annoyed with herself for caring one way or the other.

Edward said calmly, 'Anyway, I think the explanation of her appearing in Weaver's club is that she is his mistress. Captain Gordon almost said as much.'

'Gracious!' Verity exclaimed. She was silent for a moment. 'I don't see how I can ask him that—if he has a mistress singing in a night-club.'

'Of course not, but you will be listening to what

he does say with a different ear. He might say something which would mean nothing to you unless you knew about the club.'

'What was the girl's name again? Oh, and describe her to me properly.'

'She is called Amy Pageant. She is much taller than you, about five foot ten, black—no, brown hair—it was difficult to tell. She was under quite bright lights but they alter colour so much. She had a wide mouth, big eyes and—'

'Yes, yes,' said Verity sulkily. 'I get the picture.'

'You're not jealous, surely?' Edward teased.

'I am certainly not jealous. There is nothing to be jealous about, but no girl likes having some other girl described with lip-smacking relish by the man she is having a drink with.'

'I thought we might have gone to the club tonight so you can see her for yourself.'

'Sorry, no can do,' said Verity firmly. 'There's a lecture at the Parton Street bookshop I said I'd go to.'

'Is that that poetry bookshop in Bloomsbury?'

'Yes,' said Verity, surprised. 'Do you know it?'

'I once knew a girl who took me there. She thought she was an intellectual.'

'Well, you can come if you want to, I suppose, and then I can tell you how I got on with Weaver. It's at six thirty.'

'That gives us plenty of time to have dinner after and then go on to the Cocoanut Grove.'

'No can do, I told you. After the lecture we are all going out together.'

'Who's "we"? Oh, I'm sorry. It's none of my business.'

'Cripes, look at the time,' said Verity. 'I've got to

go. See you tonight.'

She pushed her way out—a diminutive figure in black—almost tipping a paunchy man in tweeds into his pint as she did so. He looked up angrily and Verity smiled sweetly and went on out—a sparrow among crows, Edward caught himself thinking.

*   *   *

Verity shot up to the top floor in a gleaming metal cage under the direction of a uniformed attendant—an ex-soldier by his bearing—who clanged open the doors when the elevator finally came to rest with all the élan of a lion tamer baring his chest to the lion. On her way up Verity had briefly glimpsed through the elevator grille a world of toil, men hurrying from one room to another with harassed expressions on their faces; the shrill sound of telephones ringing and typewriters clacking provided appropriate musical background though, beneath it all, there was the suggestion of thunder rumbling. In the basement somewhere, a great beast snored.

However, this was all a world away from the floor on to which she was now deposited. Here there was light, space and quiet. If there was an air of urgency in the hurried walk of a crisply dressed secretary it was suppressed and sank into the great Persian carpets that lay upon the floors. Through the huge plate-glass windows of this spanking new building, the Weaver Building no less, Verity glimpsed a breath-taking panorama of London. Here, on the tenth floor, lived God, it all seemed to proclaim—if there was a god of newsprint. Verity

170

had no time to absorb more than a fleeting impression of this brave new world before she was ushered by a young woman, immaculately coiffured and dressed in what seemed to Verity to be the height of fashion, into an outer office where several other young women were click-clicking away at typewriters. Her escort knocked at another door and she was shown into a spacious office which she took at first for Lord Weaver's own sanctum. She was soon disabused. A woman of unguessable age and magisterial proportions topped by iron-grey hair sculpted into some kind of a bun rose from a substantial desk to greet her with a wintry smile.

'Miss Browne? I am Miss Barnstable. We spoke on the telephone. The Chairman will see you immediately.'

Miss Barnstable seemed rather to resent the fact that Verity was not going to have to cool her heels for several hours before getting to meet the great man, as was usually the lot of lesser mortals, and at the same time impressed and curious as to why this little girl—almost a child—should command her master's interest.

Verity nodded, and Miss Barnstable knocked on the door which separated her from her lord and waited for the abrupt 'Come!' before turning the door handle. Lord Weaver was revealed rising from behind a vast mahogany desk. Outlined against a great expanse of window, he was undiminished. He appeared to Verity to be big enough in every sense not to be dwarfed by his surroundings but she was still inclined to laugh. She understood the theatre of it: she and all Lord Weaver's visitors were to be put in their place by the press lord's rich yet austere surroundings.

'My dear Miss Browne, or may I call you Verity?' He took the cigar out of his mouth and thrust forth his hand. 'Miss Barnstable, will you bring Miss Browne some—tea? Coffee?'

'No, nothing, thank you, Lord Weaver,' she said.

There had been so much going on when she had met him at Mersham Castle and she had been so flurried by breaking into a dinner-party of distinguished men—hard as she tried to disguise it—that she had not appreciated how physically formidable he was. A great bear of a man with a small head and that extraordinary round face lined with deep creases and crevices, like a turnip, she thought irreverently. His bright penetrating eyes beneath bushy eyebrows bored through her leaving her feeling naked, but it was not an unpleasant feeling. He was, she thought, one of those men whom stupid people called ugly but who were in fact supremely attractive to women they chose to fascinate. Thinking about it afterwards, she decided that where the handsome man so often put himself in competition with the beauty of the woman, a man like Weaver delighted in being something of a monster and instinctively divined the vulnerability that lay behind the mask of even the professional beauty.

'Please sit down, won't you?' He showed Verity to a big leather armchair which almost swallowed her up and sat himself down in one opposite her. 'It is so kind of you to spare me the time, Verity, particularly as I felt I could not very easily explain over the telephone why I desired to meet once again.'

'I imagined it was to reprimand me for reporting General Craig's death in the *Daily Worker*,' said

172

Verity disingenuously.

Lord Weaver smiled. 'I understand your father is D. F. Browne?'

'Yes, that is correct.'

'A remarkable man. We know each other slightly, of course. This is a small world and though we deplore each other's principles I certainly admire his willingness to back his opinions with his pocketbook.'

'You mean that the *Daily Worker* will never make a profit?'

'Well, yes, I do, but for a man like your father who despises the profit motive, that may be a good thing.'

'I don't think my father will ever have to square his conscience for making money from his beliefs. He is one of the few truly principled men I have ever met.'

'And you, Verity, may I ask if you consider yourself to be principled?'

'I do, yes, Lord Weaver. As a member of the Communist Party and as a journalist, I regard it as my duty to reveal the corruption endemic in the capitalist system.'

'And what was there corrupt at Mersham Castle? The only person there when General Craig died we know to have been lying is yourself.'

Verity blushed but refused to lose her temper. 'I admit to having employed a mild subterfuge to gain entrance to the castle. I had the idea of showing how irrelevant is the life led by the Duke of Mersham to the situation this country finds itself in.'

'And when you found yourself a witness to a suicide or horrible accident you did not hesitate to use it to further your career.'

'I have no need to apologize to you. I have and had no personal animosity towards either the Duke or the Duchess. It is true I was, involuntarily, their guest but that cannot excuse me from reporting the truth. I am not a friend of theirs nor did they think I was. It happened I found myself a witness to the violent death of a man who I believe was in a small way responsible for the deaths of many young men on the Western Front. I reported that death—all information which as you are aware will or certainly ought to become public knowledge at the inquest. I may as well say I intend to continue to report on General Craig if I turn up anything of interest in my investigations.' She took a deep breath. 'I may add, Lord Weaver, that I am not convinced that the General did die by accident or even by his own hand. Have you considered he might have been murdered?'

Weaver was taken aback. 'Why do you say that?'

'Well, it's not easy to mistake a cyanide capsule for a small round pill.'

'You mean his morphine tablets?'

'Yes. I am told that the cyanide capsule was probably glass which has either to be broken into liquid or in the mouth and it would have been a different size and shape from his other pills. The General took the cyanide when he drank his port. If it were an accident, the General must have been drunker or less in control of himself than he appeared.'

'I assumed he committed suicide,' said Lord Weaver heavily.

'In front of all of you, at the Duke's table? I don't think so. He was a private man. In any case,

174

he knew he had only a few weeks to live.'

'What do you mean?'

'He had cancer.'

'I see,' said Weaver. 'I did not know that. Do the police know this?'

'I am sure they do, but I am not in Inspector Pride's confidence.'

Lord Weaver said, 'I still think you are wrong about it not being suicide. You see, he had a strong reason to kill himself—at least I guess he would think so. In fact, I went to the castle to try and reassure him he had nothing to worry about but before I could talk to him the poor man was dead.'

'I'm sorry, I don't understand. Why might he have killed himself?'

Lord Weaver was silent for a moment then he said, 'Did you read our obituary of the General?' Verity nodded. 'It was anonymous, of course, but perhaps I could introduce you to the gentleman who wrote it. I am afraid at my insistence he was obliged to leave out certain events in the General's life.' He went to his desk and pressed a bell.

'Yes, sir,' said Miss Barnstable through the intercom.

'Ask Mr Godber and Mr Archer to come to my office, please.' Verity stiffened. Godber was the editor of the *New Gazette* and she did not fool herself that he would welcome being taken from his desk to meet her. Weaver turned back to Verity. 'Would it be unreasonable of me to ask you to regard any information I give you in this room as confidential?'

Verity looked dubious. 'I was intending to write something about the General as a typical representative of the duffers who caused so much

175

unnecessary carnage during the war so I do not think I can give you that assurance, Lord Weaver.'

'I understand. Well, can we say that before you publish anything you inform me? I don't think it would be fair on my Mr Archer if you used any information he had dug up without at least warning him that that was what you intended.'

'Of course. And if there is any particular story which Mr Archer confides in me I can give you my word that I would not use it without his permission.'

'That's all right then. Ah! Here is the estimable Mr Archer now and Mr Godber too. Jim, Reg, come and sit down over here. I would like you to meet Miss Browne, Miss Verity Browne. She writes for the *Daily Worker*.' The young man, James Archer, looked rather put out and Reginald Godber scowled. 'You have no reason to look like that, Reg. Miss Browne is a friend of mine. I want you, Jim, to tell her what you have found out about General Craig's military career. It's all right, Reg. Miss Browne is quite trustworthy and she has promised not to use anything we tell her of our little scoop without our permission.'

The editor, a large harassed-looking man with thin lips and a watery eye, opened his mouth to say something but thought better of it. He was clearly exasperated with his proprietor and resented his interference in what was an editorial matter but knew he risked dismissal if he protested. Verity got the feeling that Weaver was using her to tease his editor and show him who was boss, and she did not much like it. She had no desire to become a pawn in some labyrinthine game of office politics.

'Miss Browne,' said the editor, shaking her hand

without warmth. 'I read your report in the *Daily Worker* of how the General died. Congratulations.'

James Archer also shook her hand but said nothing. He was a tall thin man, perhaps thirty years of age although he might have been taken for forty. His thick-lensed spectacles through which he peered at the world, thin untidy hair flapping across his scalp, flannels and tweed jacket—the latter badly stained and patched at the elbows with leather—made him an unlikely journalist but Lord Weaver quickly explained that he was not a journalist in the ordinary sense.

'Verity, Jim here is an historian with a particular interest in the recent conflict. He is writing a book on the Western Front and while he is doing so is good enough to write the occasional article or obituary for us. I wonder, Jim, if you could tell Miss Browne what you told me about the General?'

'Yes, sir. As you will know, miss, General Craig had a distinguished military career. He was much liked by Lord Kitchener and by Earl Haig. It would hardly have been possible to have had two more influential friends. He was brave, enterprising and utterly reliable but for all this he never got to the very top of the tree. I did some research in the archives, talked to a few people, and I discovered why. He had, unfortunately, a sadistic streak which even Kitchener who was not noted for his kindliness had reason to reprimand him for. After Omdurman there were eyewitness accounts of a massacre of some fifty unarmed tribesmen who Captain Craig, as he then was, believed had been behind an assassination attempt on General Kitchener. That he did save Kitchener's life is indisputable and he justly deserved his Victoria

177

Cross but the whole thing was stained by the killing which followed. Moreover, the witnesses speak of Craig making them do unspeakable things—defiling themselves—before he ordered them to be shot. Fortunately for Craig, Kitchener hushed it all up and the eyewitnesses were silenced.'

'If it was all hushed up, how do you know about it then?'

'I have been given special privileges to examine papers stored at the War Office and there I uncovered the witness statements signed and sealed. I think I am the only person alive who has seen them.'

'And you think,' said Verity, 'that he found out you had knowledge of these . . . allegations and killed himself rather than see them in print?'

Weaver said, 'Not if these had been the only accusations of cruelty or worse to be made against him. He would have been more likely to sue for libel. Anyway, the incident occurred, if it did occur, a long time ago and to natives, so that I doubt the public would have been particularly shocked or even interested. No, there is something else. Tell her, Jim.'

'Well, miss, I went on digging and came across a similar set of allegations much more recently—in April 1918 in fact. There had been some desperate fighting on the Western Front. The British were driven from Messines which had been gained at huge cost only a few months before. The Germans used gas to deadly effect. The British were also intending to use gas but, ironically, the officers in charge of the attack were caught by a German gas attack before they could use their gas shells. Bethune was just about to fall to the Germans,

178

refugees clogged the roads. It was chaos.

'For six days the Allies defended lines behind the River Lys. Haig ordered that every position had to be held to the last man. On 15th April the British evacuated the Passchendaele Ridge won five months before at a terrible cost and on the 20th, south of Ypres, the Germans fired nine million rounds of mustard gas, phosgene and diphenylchlorarsine, a total of two thousand tons of poison gas. Eight thousand British troops were poisoned. This was total war. No weapon was too horrible to use and the British considered their enemy to be less than human.

'Well, the tide was just starting to turn against the Germans—American troops were beginning to reach the front line in strength for the first time. About fifty German soldiers from one of their gas battalions were captured. General Craig, who unlike many generals spent a considerable time near the front and was well aware of the horror his troops had suffered from the gas attacks, instead of directing the prisoners to be shipped back to the prison camps behind the line, ordered that they should be shot out of hand. Of course people protested but he was adamant. Said they were murderers not soldiers and there were enough officers under his command who felt the same way for the order to be carried out.

'It is difficult for us today to put ourselves in Craig's shoes: we need to remember that this was a period of absolute exhaustion, chaotic communications and the fiercest fighting of the whole war. The time had long passed when the enemy might be considered honourable soldiers worthy of respect. Gas had changed all that.

Anyway, what was fifty men being shot to death compared with the thousands dying every day, many choking their lives away in terrible agony? Unfortunately for Craig, one American officer recently arrived at the front and not yet inured to the barbarities of war made an official report on the incident to General Pershing, who in turn took the matter up with Haig.

'Well, to cut a long story short, Haig protected his man as Kitchener had done years before but it remained a shadow on the General's career, and though he reached high rank and was knighted he was never showered with the honours and responsibilities he might have expected.'

There was silence in that light, peaceful room as Verity absorbed what she had heard. She could only guess at what it must have been like in that murderous inferno of April 1918. She felt only pity and horror.

At last Weaver spoke. 'That is why people as disparate as the Duke of Mersham, Cecil Haycraft and myself are so determined to do everything we can to avert another war with Germany. And yet,' he added gloomily, 'I am beginning to doubt whether it will be possible to avoid another blood bath—not next year, nor the year after but sometime in the next decade, I fear. My correspondent in Berlin tells me that Germany has built up in secret a formidable air force in defiance of Versailles and Locarno and I am informed Hitler may soon announce conscription.'

'So you believe the General might have committed suicide to avoid having his reputation destroyed by this story?'

'Yes, I do,' said Lord Weaver. 'He was a proud

man and his reputation as a soldier was, I guess, the only thing which mattered to him. I wanted to discuss the allegations with him on neutral ground—give him the chance of defending himself—but, as I say, before I could do so, he had killed himself. And what's more I think he did it in front of me as some sort of revenge.'

'Well,' said Verity, quite shaken by what she had heard, 'I am flattered you should have let me in on this but I don't understand why.'

'I want you to write for me at the *New Gazette*. In my experience trust breeds trust and I have trusted you. Despite what I said earlier, I have been impressed by your initiative and your evident truthfulness and I would like you to work with Jim here to write a series of articles on the horror of war using General Craig's case as the lynch pin—what war can do to destroy decent men. I feel I must continue trying to tell people what war is like even if in the end we cannot avoid it. In 1914 young men queued to join the army as if they were going to a party; if there is to be a next time, the new army will need to be built on surer foundations.'

Verity said, 'You would employ me—a Communist—to write on your paper?'

'I would employ Miss Verity Browne because whatever label she likes to put on herself I think she believes in doing what is right. Am I correct?'

'I believe in justice—social justice and natural justice. I am not a pacifist but I do think General Craig was little better than a state-sponsored murderer. However, that does not mean I believe he deserved to die in the way he did.'

'You mean suicide?'

'If you press me, Lord Weaver, I would have to

say I still rather doubt that he did commit suicide.'

'You think Craig died by accident?'

'Or murder.'

The editor said, 'Oh, come, Miss Browne, that's absurd. You can't really believe that one of the Duke of Mersham s distinguished guests murdered this great public servant at the Duke's own dining-table? It's preposterous.'

Weaver pursed his lips. 'Well, you may be right, Reg. Miss Browne may be barking up the wrong tree but'—he turned to Verity—'I don't mind risking making a fool of myself. I have done it before and will do it again. I will help you in your investigations in any way I can. I for one have nothing to hide.' Verity thought this to be a rash boast but she kept her mouth firmly closed. 'You see, Reg, Miss Browne is a journalist with what I might call a nose for getting to the bottom of a story,' Weaver continued.

The editor looked unconvinced. 'I'm afraid it all sounds a little far-fetched to me, Miss Browne. Now, if you will excuse me, Lord Weaver, I must get back to my desk.' He managed to show impatience with the interruption to his working day without sounding too impolite.

When Godber and Archer had gone Weaver got to his feet to indicate to Verity that she too was dismissed. 'Think about my offer, Verity. I must have an answer by the end of next week otherwise Jim will go it alone.' There was just the hint of a threat in his voice. 'My paper has room for many voices from all parts of the political spectrum. I would like to add a young voice from the left to balance the greybeards. Goodbye now.'

As Verity went down again in the elevator she

heard more distinctly than ever the boom of thunder in the basement. The elevator operator, hearing it also, said, 'That's the presses rolling for the evening paper. It always make me think of the sound of the guns along the front—silly, I know. That's all over now, isn't it, miss?'

*   *   *

When Verity got back to the office she found two large policemen on the door. The *Daily Worker* liked to cock a snook at the authorities but it remained strictly within the law. As far as she knew, it had never even been sued for libel so she immediately guessed that it was she who had brought the forces of law and order to the newspaper and that the editor, Morris Block, would not like it.

The door into the editor's office was frosted glass and through it she could see the tousle-headed editor gesticulating at a thin figure in a heavy black overcoat. As she tried to slip unobtrusively behind her desk, the editor's secretary called her imperiously: 'There you are at last, Verity. Where have you been? Everyone's been looking for you and I can tell you Mr Block is not pleased.'

Without waiting for any response, she knocked on the glass door and Verity quailed as she heard Block shout, 'What is it, woman? Oh, she is, is she? Well, send her in.'

Verity took a hold of herself, raised her chin and marched in. Damn it, she had given the paper its only scoop this century and she was not going to apologize for it to Morris Block or anyone else.

Block was red in the face and had obviously been shouting. There was sweat on his brow and a vein in his neck was pulsing. The policeman, on the other hand, was as cold as winter.

'Ah, Verity, it's you at last. This is Inspector Pride. He wants to ask you some questions about . . . about your report. He thinks—'

'Please, Mr Block, perhaps you would allow me?'

'Yes, of course. I—'

'Is there anywhere private I could speak to Miss Browne?'

'Only here.' The editor was the only employee of the *Daily Worker* to have his own office.

'Alone,' said Inspector Pride, with meaning.

'Oh, yes, of course. I'll . . . I'll leave you to it. And Verity, mind you—' 'Yes, thank you, Mr Block,' said the policeman, holding open the door.

When the editor had closed the door behind him, Pride sat himself behind Block's desk and gestured to Verity to sit in the chair in front of it. He pretended to scrutinize the mass of paper— galley proofs, bills, lots of these, and printed articles and books—on the editor's desk. Then he said, 'I can't think why, Miss Browne, but your editor doesn't seem very pleased with you despite your little scoop. That's what you call it: a "scoop", isn't it?' He said 'scoop' with a depth of contempt which made Verity tingle with anger but she controlled herself and said nothing, letting what she hoped was an insouciant smile play on her lips.

'You think it funny, Miss Browne, to go into a man's house—and not any house but the house of one of England's most distinguished men—be treated with every kindness and then betray the trust placed in you? You think that something to smile about? You think your little sneers and smears—the suggestion that a great soldier was murdered . . .'

'I've never said that,' she broke in indignantly.

Pride ignored her: '. . . when you know it not to be true? Do you not think that a . . . a girl like you ought to know better?'

'A girl like me, Inspector? What does that mean?'

'A rich, middle-class girl with a flat in Knightsbridge, educated at the best schools—that's what I mean,' he said viciously.

'I see you have gone to the trouble of finding out all about me, Inspector. Should I be flattered?'

Verity was now very angry—in part, at least, because she had said something of the same sort to herself.

'Don't be impertinent!'

She sat silent and sullen until, at last, Pride spoke again.

'How unlikely are the alliances we find in public life today,' he said with an attempt at the conversational. 'A man like your father who ought to be working for his country and he allies himself with Reds, and his daughter—what did he make of her? It seems he made her despise what respectable people might call "morality"—I suppose you know about morality, do you, Miss Browne?'

Verity suddenly became very calm. How dare he bring her father into this? She was being baited. But why? It must be that Inspector Pride was nervous. Why else should he be insulting her in this way? He wanted—not to find out the truth—but to frighten her so she would slink away and cry in a corner. If the police were so anxious to keep General Craig's death quiet, did not that mean they believed there was something to hide?

She must have smiled because suddenly the policeman was standing above her. She had never seen anyone actually spit with rage before and she was now interested, in a scientific way, to see that it really was something which happened.

'I warn you, Miss Browne, if you do not desist from making allegations about some of the most distinguished men in public life—and I have said the same to your editor—you will get into very serious trouble. You are not to approach any person who was in the Duke's house on the day of the General's death and you are not to involve any member of the Duke's family in your . . . in your "journalistic activities". Do you understand me, Miss Browne? I mean what I say. I have very wide powers to close down this newspaper and I will not hesitate to use them if I need to.'

Verity got up and in doing so made the Inspector back away. 'This is still a free country, Inspector, and you shall not intimidate me. You think it is people like me who are a danger to . . . to your "respectable" people. But it is not me, it is you and the people like you. You think I am just a girl to be frightened but I am not so easily frightened. I am a Communist and I am proud of it. You can harass me as much as you like but . . . but . . .'

Suddenly, to her consternation, she found tears welling up in her eyes so she opened the door and left without saying another word furious with herself for showing anything like weakness before the policeman. She vowed that she was going to

186

take no notice whatever of anything the man had said to her and that she would say nothing to Edward of her ordeal. He was too decent not to be angry on her behalf and he would probably go and do something silly. No, her victory must be that Inspector Pride was ignored. That is what he would hate the most.

CHAPTER NINE

EDWARD'S MONDAY

After Verity had left him in the pub to go and see Lord Weaver, Edward found himself at a loose end. Thinking about Weaver made him think about Hermione. He decided he would swallow his pride and go round to Eaton Place to see if she was there and, if she were, whether she had any explanation for her behaviour of the previous Tuesday. He had telephoned the house two or three times but on each occasion he had got no further than a servant who had informed him that Miss Weaver was out. He had had to content himself with leaving messages which had not been returned. It seemed to him pretty clear that Hermione had got over her crush on him. He hailed a cab and had soon left the hustle and bustle of Fleet Street for the genteel tranquillity of that area between Hyde Park Corner and Elizabeth Street where the very rich lived. Their substantial houses presented a cold front to the stranger. Windows were curtained or even shuttered and there were no open front doors to facilitate gossip, the life blood of any neighbourhood and what made living in shabbier London boroughs tolerable and even to be preferred to the icy respectability of SW1.

Deposited on the doorstep of Lord Weaver's mansion, even Edward was momentarily daunted by its air of not welcoming casual visitors. There were shutters on the windows and he noticed the servants had forgotten to water the geraniums in the window boxes. It almost seemed as though the house was in mourning, but that could not be true if Lord Weaver was working a normal day at the *New Gazette*. Telling himself not to be a fool, he rang the electric bell. A superior-looking manservant answered the door and Edward handed him his card. 'Would you inquire if Miss Weaver can see me? She's not expecting me, but as I was passing I thought I would see if she was at home.'

Edward was a little annoyed with himself. He sounded as if he were apologizing. However, it was said.

The servant read the card carefully and was obviously reassured. He unbent a little and directed at Edward a wintry smile. 'My lord, I am afraid Miss Weaver is not at home. Would you wish me to see if Lady Weaver is engaged?'

Edward was just about to say that he had no wish to disturb Lady Weaver when he heard her voice in the hall. 'Who is it, Wilkins?'

The butler stood back, opening the door wide. 'It is Lord Edward Corinth, my lady.'

'Lord Edward, is that really you? Please do come in. Were you looking for Hermione? I am afraid she is not here.'

'Oh, I'm sorry, Lady Weaver. I apologize for

disturbing you. I was just passing and I thought I would see if Hermione was here. We parted rather abruptly after . . . after I had taken her to the Savoy last week and I had no opportunity of . . .'

'Do come in, Lord Edward. I wanted to talk to you in any case and if you have five minutes . . .'

Seated in the drawing-room on an ornate but uncomfortable gilt sofa, Edward, who had refused an offer of refreshment, said, 'I say, Lady Weaver . . .'

Speaking at the same time, her voice high with nervous energy, Blanche said, 'I'm so worried . . .'

They apologized, laughed a little, and the atmosphere lightened. 'Please go on, Lady Weaver.'

'"Blanche", please, Lord Edward. I need to talk to you about Hermione and I cannot do so with you calling me Lady Weaver.'

'Blanche, then,' said Edward smiling. He liked this woman. Underneath a rather fey, almost distrait manner he sensed a sensible, sensitive soul whom he would like to help if he could. How she had ended up with a child as tiresome as Hermione he really could not think.

'You say, Lord Edward—'

'Edward, please,' he interjected, smiling.

'You say, Edward, that you and Hermione parted abruptly last Tuesday. Can you tell me what happened, or would that be breaking confidences?'

'No, I don't think so. We had dinner at the Savoy and then we went on, at your daughter's request, to the Cocoanut Grove. Do you know it?'

'I have never heard of it. It's a night-club? Like the Four Hundred?'

'Yes. Hermione said it was all the rage at the

189

moment so that was where I took her. Anyway, we had hardly got there—I think we had had one dance—when she was agitating to go. I had not particularly wanted to come so that was all right by me. To tell the truth it was rather a gruesome place with a sort of jungle décor and the champagne was disgusting so I was quite ready to depart. However, at that moment the cabaret started and I must confess I was very taken with the girl who came on to sing. I believe she was called Amy Pageant.' Edward tried to see if Lady Weaver had ever heard the name before but if she had she disguised it.

'This girl sang Cole Porter and Gershwin better than . . . well, better than anyone I have heard—at least, this side of the Atlantic. I was bowled over, I have to admit, and I did not take my eyes off her until she had taken her bow. Then, when I looked round for Hermione, she had vanished. I went to find her of course and eventually the doorman gave me a pencilled note from her saying she was sorry but she had had to go. The doorman said she had left in a taxi with Charlie Lomax.'

'I see,' said Blanche thoughtfully. 'That was very rude of her. I don't know what has come over her recently. At Mersham Castle both I and Lord Weaver got the impression that she was . . . well, please forgive me for being frank . . . that she was very . . . she was all over you. I don't suppose you even noticed. Joe and I were so pleased. You see— I know I can speak in complete confidence to you—she has got into rather a bad crowd. I mean, she is not a child any more. There's nothing really I can do except—you know—keep an eye on her. This young man, Charles Lomax, I thought maybe he had thrown her over but . . .'

Edward felt he was behaving shabbily, discussing Hermione behind her back, but he certainly did not consider her to be a friend and she had behaved badly to him. 'Now you mention it, Lady Weaver, Blanche, I remember her in the club being a bit on edge. The manager chappie, Captain Gordon he called himself, came up to her while we were dancing and told her "a friend" was coming in later and wanted to see her. He meant Lomax but no name was mentioned. Hermione acted as though she didn't want me to know who her "friend" was.

'Shortly after, as I say, Hermione said she did not like the place after all and wanted to leave but just then the cabaret started and I told her I wanted to stay until it finished. I blame myself; perhaps if I had taken her away when she asked me to she might never have met Lomax. When I think back, I get the feeling that she half wanted to meet him and half didn't. Do you think he has some sort of hold over her?'

'You mean like drugs?'

'Well, yes, I suppose I do,' said Edward awkwardly.

'I think he must have. Oh God, Edward, I'm so worried. I have been worried about her for a long time. She has never got on with her stepfather and she seemed to be drifting into a thoroughly bad set almost as if she wanted to annoy him. Then, when your brother invited us to Mersham, she insisted I ask the Duke to invite Mr Lomax. I suppose I should just have said no and not brought her with me but, to be honest, I wanted to keep her under my eye and I thought if she mingled with good people . . . I thought . . . oh, I don't know what I thought. If I am being really truthful, when I heard you were coming, I thought she might . . . I thought you and she . . .'

Edward coloured. 'And I did not turn up until late.'

'Yes, but you must have noticed how, when you did come, she was so pleased to see you. I was delighted.'

'Why do you think she so wanted Lomax to be at the castle? Was she in love with him or was it that he had promised to bring her . . . you know—what she needed?'

'I don't know. She had been very nervous and irritable and I thought that was because Mr Lomax seemed to be avoiding her. Then . . . may I speak in complete confidence, Edward? I haven't even told Joe this and I tell him everything.'

'Of course, you have my word.'

'Well, I went into her room at Mersham while she was dressing for dinner. She did not hear me come in and I . . . when she turned I saw . . . Oh, I can't say it!' Blanche buried her face in her hands.

'She was injecting herself?' said Edward gently.

Blanche nodded, avoiding his eye.

'When we were dancing at the night-club she put her head on my shoulder and I saw her arm and I could not help seeing . . . the marks. And you think she was counting on Lomax being unable to resist an invitation to Mersham Castle and if he came he would supply her with the dope she wanted?'

'Yes. For some reason he must have been avoiding her, otherwise, I suppose, she would have met him at the night-club you mentioned—the Cocoanut Grove—or some other place like that. Oh God! What is there to do? When I caught her . . . when I saw her . . . she said such terrible things to me.'

Edward put a hand on her shoulder. 'Please, Blanche, don't give way. She may not have gone too far. She seemed quite normal at Gerald's dinner after all.'

'Oh yes, but then she would if she had taken what she needed beforehand, but when we got back to London she . . . I ought to have talked to her about it but I was afraid . . . I ought to . . . And then she wouldn't stay here. She said it was too dead. She went back to her flat.'

'Her flat?' said Edward surprised. 'I didn't know she had a flat. On Tuesday I picked her up from here.'

'Yes, she has a flat in Beauchamp Place. Joe bought it for her on her twenty-first. To begin with she didn't live there very much but . . .'

Edward could imagine that Weaver had tried everything to get Hermione out of his house and the flat was a carrot to get her to stand on her own feet.

'So how is she now?'

'That's just why I am so anxious—I don't know. She telephoned on Wednesday, the day after you saw her, to say she was going to stay at her flat. I was out when she called and she left a message with Wilkins. I tried to ring her several times but there was never any answer. So on Friday and then again on Saturday I went round to Beauchamp Place and rang the doorbell and knocked but there was no answer.'

'She doesn't have a servant?'

'No. She said a maid would "queer her pitch", whatever that means. I think she was afraid that if she had a servant she would be spied on and I

193

would be told what she was up to.'

'I see. Do you have a key to her flat?'

'Well, yes, I do. Hermione doesn't know I have one and she would kill me if she found out I had been prying on her.'

'You didn't use it then, when you went round on Saturday?'

'I didn't dare.'

'Did you try ringing Mr Lomax?'

'Yes. I got his number out of the telephone book but there was no answer. The operator said he had been cut off. I don't know why.'

'Look, Blanche, I think you have reason to be worried. Give me the key to Hermione's flat and I will go and see if . . . if there is anything wrong.'

'But if she finds you . . .'

'Don't worry. I won't say I have been talking to you. If she catches me I will just say I am a bit of an amateur burglar and she can be as rude to me as she likes, but in any case I won't go in until I am sure she is not there.'

'Bless you, Edward. I don't know how to thank you. I just daren't ask Joe. He would charge round like a bull in a china shop and she would probably never speak to either of us again.'

*　　　*　　　*

Hermione's flat in Beauchamp Place was on the top floor. Getting no reply to his knocking, Edward unlocked the door and went in. There was no one and no sign of anyone having been there lately. There was no food on the table or in the little larder. The windows were closed and the rooms—a bedroom and a living-room along with a tiny

194

kitchen and bathroom—were stuffy and dirty-smelling—neglected. This was clearly not a place for which the owner had any affection. There was a telephone book beside the telephone and he looked up Lomax's number. He dialled but there was only a buzzing tone. The book gave an address in Fulham and he decided he would not sleep easy until he had gone round and made sure Hermione was not . . . was not held prisoner there or something worse. He felt he owed it to Blanche to find Hermione whatever the trouble it caused him. If he had looked after her and taken her away from that awful night-club maybe she might not have run off. Now he hardly dared think what she might have run off to.

When the cab dropped him at the house in Fulham the first thing he noticed was that the tiny garden in front of the house was little better than a rubbish tip. Here was another neglectful owner. Empty bottles, a broken dustbin, the twisted wheel of a bicycle cluttered the path up to the front door. Before opening the iron gate and going up to the door he stepped back across the street and gazed at the house. There was something desolate and even hostile about it. All the windows were blinded either by shabby-looking curtains or by what looked like blankets. It was a respectable street in an area convenient for Mr Lomax's social life in Belgravia but the house itself looked as though it were hiding something nasty. As he stood there summoning up the energy to bang on the door, an elderly woman stepped out of the house at whose garden gate he was standing. In contrast to Mr Lomax's residence, this little house was smart as two pins. The garden was ablaze with colour and the front door had been newly painted a startling electric blue.

'You'll not find anyone up there,' she said, nodding towards the house opposite. 'They go to bed goodness knows how late. I'm woken up in the night often enough with shouting and screaming and they never stir till three or four in the afternoon. It's a disgrace to the neighbourhood, if you ask me. I've threatened to have the police on them but he just laughs.'

'He?'

'Mr Lomax, his name is. A bad 'un if ever I saw one.'

'He has parties?'

'Parties!' The elderly lady raised her voice in disgust. 'Orgies, I would call them. You're not one of them?'

'No,' said Edward, 'I'm not one of them, but I rather think he may have one of my friends in there and I intend to get her out.'

'Oh my! Are you a policeman?'

'Not a policeman, Mrs . . .'

'Mrs Watson.'

'Mrs Watson, no, I am not a policeman.' He raised his hat to her and without more ado crossed the narrow street, pushed open the gate, which resisted his efforts with much creaking and groaning, and hammered on the front door.

There was no answer. He knocked again and there was still no answer. He was about to go away defeated when he thought he might as well walk round the back of the house. The knowledge that at least one pair of eyes was watching his every move from behind net curtains made the hairs on the back of his head prickle. If Mrs Watson decided to call the police then he had not much time. He was both highly reluctant to pursue his search for Hermione and at the same time eager to get it over with and find out what sordid little secrets this unpleasant-looking house might be guarding. The last thing he wanted was to be arrested for attempted burglary, but somehow he did not feel he could hold his head up if he went back to Lady Weaver with the tame news that he had knocked and there had been no answer so he had come away.

If the front garden of the house was disfigured with garbage, which it was, it would have won a best-kept-lawn award when compared with the back. Here the litter was ankle deep. A drain had overflowed and a stream of green slime had coagulated on the stone path, turning it into a potentially lethal skating rink. There was a nauseating stink from a pile of rubbish in one corner of the pocket-sized space which could not truly be called a back garden. Holding his handkerchief to his nose, Edward approached it and put the toe of his shoe against it. He recoiled quickly as a family of rats lurched across his feet. They had been feeding on the corpse of what might once have been a cat.

Turning to look at the back of the house, he noticed that though most of the windows were tightly closed and curtained one on the first floor was broken. He sighed. Here was a means of entry but it meant shinning up the drainpipe and that meant the trousers of his suit would certainly be ruined. Still, there was nothing to be done about it. He took off his hat and jacket and hung them carefully over the spout of a rusting watering-can.

It was chilly and he shivered in his shirt-sleeves. He considered removing his tie but compromised by tucking the end of it between the buttons of his shirt as he had seen office workers do in New York. His shoes were strong walking shoes made for him at Lobb's, not ideal for climbing up drainpipes but in this filth it was unthinkable that he should remove them.

His ascent began well. The drainpipe was slippery but he got a grip quite easily on the clammy metal. Edward Corinth was one of those fortunate young men who, though never seeming to take much exercise, remain fit. It had been three months since he had returned from South Africa but he still had the muscles he had hardened climbing in the Drakensbergs. His tailor had remarked on how he would have to allow for them as he measured him for this very suit, the trousers of which he was now ruining. When he reached the broken window he was triumphant, but pride almost came before a fall. In recent years no one had spent one penny on the upkeep of the structure and the drainpipe had only been pretending to be firmly fixed to the wall of the house. It now revealed that its suitability as a ladder was illusory as it began to come away from the wall as easily as Edward might have peeled a banana. He clutched at the broken window, cutting himself as he did so on some jagged glass. He succeeded in heaving himself up so that his head was just above the window ledge. It was too dark to see more than that it was a bedroom of sorts. Certainly there was a heap of what might be bedclothes in one corner. He made a further effort and, sweating profusely, found a purchase for his right foot in the damaged brickwork. He fumbled for the window catch and found it, only to discover that the window swung outwards, and as it did so he once again almost fell on to the stone paving below. He caught himself in time and rolled his body over the sill, ripping his trousers. Panting hard, he found his feet in a small dank room which smelled of drains, or worse. He assumed the house must be empty: he had made such a noise getting in that he would have disturbed anyone who was awake and woken all but the deepest sleeper.

But he was wrong. The house was not empty. As he prepared to go out of the bedroom door to explore what lay beyond, the pile of bedclothes moved. A snorting sound like that made by a bulldog startled him. He wanted urgently to empty his bladder. He told himself to get a grip on his nerves and stop being a yellow-livered coward. He stepped over to the snuffling, moving blankets and pulled back the corner of the top one.

He had found Hermione. She was hardly recognizable. Her dress, the same one she had been wearing at the Cocoanut Grove, was torn and smeared with what looked like excrement. But it was her face which gave him the greatest shock. It was very red and the flesh was swollen, particularly around her eyes which were closed. He gently raised one of her eyelids. The eyeball had rolled upwards giving her a blind look which was quite shocking. Her hair was matted and she was getting her breath only with great difficulty. It was this snorting which had first alerted him that the pile of rags hid a living thing. Cursing, he ran down the stairs two steps at a time. He found a telephone in the hallway but it was not working. He opened the front door, breathing the fresh air with huge relief. He ran across the road to the electric-blue door and hammered on it, blistering the paintwork. Mrs Watson opened the door to him, white as a sheet.

'What's the matter?' she cried, a hand at her throat. 'Is some-one dead?'

'I have found my friend but she is very ill. I must use your telephone.'

'I am afraid I don't have one,' Mrs Watson said apologetically. 'Wait, my next-door neighbour does.' In her slippers she ran outside and up the garden path of the next-door house. Her neighbour must have been disturbed by the commotion because she opened her door immediately.

'Please—may I use your telephone? It's an emergency,' said Edward who had followed close on the old woman's heels.

The lady seemed too amazed to say anything but indicated the instrument sitting on the hall table. He dialled 999 and summoned an ambulance. He hesitated for a moment and then rang Whitehall 1212 and asked to speak to Inspector Pride. Luck was with him; the Inspector was just on his way out. There was a minute's wait while Edward drummed his fingers on the table and the two women stared at him. Then he heard the Inspector's dry voice: 'Yes, what is it?'

Inspector Pride listened silently to Edward's story. 'I'll come at once,' he said when he had finished.

Edward mumbled his thanks to the two women and returned to the house and to Hermione. Bravely, Mrs Watson came after him. She cried out when she saw Hermione. Between them, they tried to make the girl a little more comfortable but

Edward was frightened of doing more harm than good by moving her. He went back down the stairs to listen for the ambulance. Then it struck him that there might be others in this ghastly house. He looked into a filthy kitchen and then went upstairs again. Mrs Watson was crouched beside Hermione murmuring comfort and stroking her hand. Edward walked out into the passage and opened another door. There was a second bedroom and a bathroom. Both were empty but there were signs that someone had used the rooms quite recently. He noticed a safety razor in a pool of soapy water on the washbasin in the bathroom and several used syringes. He went downstairs again and as he did so noticed a door which he had overlooked when he had been downstairs before. He opened it. It was a lavatory and sitting upon the lavatory bowl was a young man in evening dress. He had not taken off his coat or trousers and Edward guessed that he had gone into the lavatory to hide though the smell suggested that, deliberately or not, his bowels had opened. One thing was quite evident, Charlie Lomax would never need to sell dope again because a knife through his chest skewered him to the wall.

There was a sound of bells clanging as an ambulance and a police car arrived at the same time.

CHAPTER TEN

MONDAY EVENING

'How absolutely frightful,' said Verity, pale of face. 'Will she live?'

'Touch and go,' Edward answered. 'Someone pumped her full of heroin and it will be a couple of days, apparently, before the doctors know.'

'And her poor mother?'

'She's taken it hard, of course—won't move from her bedside. Weaver's been good too. He doesn't pretend he got on with his stepdaughter but he definitely loves his wife and anything which hurts her, hurts him.'

'That's what makes it so odd about your girlfriend.'

'What girlfriend?'

'Amy Pageant. You had her down as Weaver's mistress and every other capitalist tycoon I'm sure has a score of mistresses, but somehow—and I expect I'm being naïve—I don't think Weaver would have one.'

'You asked him?' inquired Edward ironically.

'Of course not, fool, but he treated me like a real person not like a power-hungry sex maniac. I mean, he patronized me but then all men do patronize women—'

'I've never patronized you.'

'You bloody well have and do,' said Verity hotly.

Edward was a little taken aback by her language but even more so by the notion that he could ever be accused of patronizing anyone. 'Look here, my

202

dear—' he began.

'There you are,' she chipped in triumphantly.

'Where?' he said, shaking his head in bewilderment.

'Calling me "my dear", idiot. I'm not your dear. Anyway, what was I saying? Oh yes, I remember. I was saying Weaver patronized me but he seemed willing to admit I might be able to do my job, which was more than either the editor or the historian believed. He didn't try that magnetic sexual power stuff on me.'

'What's wrong with "my dear"?'

'Oh, for God's sake, do shut up and concentrate. And before you say it, I am not using my so-called feminine intuition or Freudian rubbish for that matter. I'm just saying he looks as though he's one of the few men I know who genuinely loves his wife. Now, if it had been that awful Larmore man—'

'You've never read Freud,' said Edward.

'There you go again—patronizing me,' exclaimed Verity in exasperation. 'Of course I have not read Freud but no need to assume it!'

'Oh God, sorry. I apologize. But yes, you are right about Larmore. I agree, he is definitely a cad. I spoke to one or two friends who move in political circles and they all say he is absolutely untrustworthy. I thought I would go and see him after I've been back to the club.'

'You mean the Cocoanut Jungle or whatever it's called? Can I come too? You can't go to a night-club on your own, you know. You would stick out like a sore thumb.'

'Yes, I would like that,' he said, careful not to sound patronizing.

203

'Hasn't Inspector Pride closed it down by now?'

'No. I told him what I suspected and that I thought the dope came from there, but he says there's no evidence and he can't do anything until there is.'

'And does Lord Weaver know that his stepdaughter might have got her dope from a night-club he owns?'

'I don't know. I don't think so. Obviously I did not tell him and I don't think Inspector Pride has.'

There was suddenly a great deal of hushing and Edward saw that a tall, thin man with bad acne and a scraggy beard was on his feet introducing a poet to the little audience. The bookshop was a well-known meeting place for left-wing intellectuals and Edward felt himself to be out of place. He had the feeling that card-carrying Communists and 'fellow travellers' would probably lynch him at the end of the reading. If they did he would probably let them: he was exhausted by the events of the afternoon. By the time Hermione was in hospital and he had been interviewed by Inspector Pride, who could hardly contain his disapproval of Edward's unauthorized entry into a house not his own, it was five thirty and the last thing he wanted to do was to listen to young things spout poetry in Bloomsbury. On the other hand he did not feel like resting: he wanted to discuss things with Verity and make some sense of what had happened to Hermione.

When he saw the poet rising to his feet, acknowledging the applause with a pleased look on his face, he realized that underlying his decision not to obey his first instinct and skip this rendezvous was something else: an instinct that Verity's interest in poetry was not entirely intellectual. The man with acne had given way to a Greek god, or that was the way it seemed to Edward. He was six feet of brawn, tall, broad-shouldered, with a noble head, strong chin and corn-yellow hair which flopped becomingly over his blue eyes. He wore grey flannels, an open-neck Airtex shirt, sleeves rolled to the elbow as though he could not wait to get down to some hard manual work. A tweed jacket was lying where he had tossed it over the back of a chair. Edward disliked him before he had even opened his mouth. He disliked him even more when he did. He had a resonant deep baritone with a pronounced Welsh lilt and Edward immediately put him down as a member of a male-voice choir, a combination of musicians for which he had always had an aversion. Worst of all, when Edward began to listen, he had to admit that the man was spouting some rather good verse, among some exhortatory dross. Certainly, everyone around him seemed to think so. The little Parton Street bookshop was crammed with people leaning against shelves, peering around piles of George Meredith and H.G. Wells. Edward himself was leaning against modern poetry by people whose names, when he examined the dust covers, were unknown to him: someone called Auden was the only one he had heard of. Auden dug into his left buttock and, as he moved to make himself more comfortable, a pile of slim volumes by one David Griffiths-Jones slipped away on to the floor with a slap of protest just as the poet was lamenting, in sonnet form, the death of a dear friend. 'Ssh!' said Verity fiercely.

'Sorry,' he whispered back. 'What's his name?'

'David Griffiths-Jones; I told you, for God's

sake!' she whispered back but so loudly that a man in a black felt hat and a Crombie, leaning against Virginia Woolf's *Orlando*, shushed her. She then listened in seeming rapture as the poet proclaimed:

'When I utter *Stalin* I mean good.
When I utter *Stalin* I mean courage.
I mean eyes shining.
I mean ceaseless activity.

'When I utter *Stalin* I mean yes,
Whenever you call me I am there;
You are my present, my yesterday,
You are my tomorrow.'

When the poet had finished, Verity, along with most of those present, applauded vigorously. The favoured versifier bowed gracefully and accepted the applause with a modest shake of his head. The man with acne got on his hind legs again and said how grateful they all were; what a success the poet had been in Boston and New York and how pleased they were that he had agreed to sign copies of his book. It appeared that most of these were now languishing on the floor owing to Edward having leaned upon them too heavily. He and Verity hurriedly began to scoop them up, Verity all the time complaining at his clumsiness so that he began to wish he had not come after all. He had felt tired and listless when he returned from his burglarious afternoon but had been unable to rest. He felt worse now. The shock of finding poor Hermione close to death and a man murdered, even if the latter would not be missed, was only now beginning to take its toll on him. He wanted Verity to tell him he had acted with decision and vigour but, though she had been very shocked to hear about Hermione, she had not seemed to think *he* might be in need of any comfort.

While he had been half listening to David Griffiths-Jones, it had suddenly occurred to him that Verity might report the attack on Hermione Weaver and the murder of Charles Lomax in the *Daily Worker*, another scoop for that publication, usefully, no doubt, demonstrating how wealth did not bring happiness. But how could he ask Verity not to use what he had told her? They were partners of a sort and he had to trust her, but the truth was he did not altogether trust her. He was attracted to her but he knew her to be capable of subterfuge, and she was incontestably possessed of a ruthless streak which he admired unless he was to be one of its victims—a toad beneath her harrow? He did not quite know what the phrase meant but it seemed to express what he felt now as he saw the poet kissing her on the lips.

Well, of course, a girl as pretty and outgoing as Verity was going to have close friends, lovers even, Edward told himself, and he had no reason to object if she allowed herself to be kissed by Greek gods. After all, he doubted she even considered him to be a friend and certainly there was no question of him being anything more. Why would a girl with strong left-wing principles find anything appealing about a member of the despised upper classes? He continued to flagellate himself until Verity released herself from the poet's embrace and turned to him. 'Oh, David, this is a friend of mine, Edward Corinth.'

He glowed: she *did* consider him a friend and

she had not embarrassed him by using his ridiculous title.

'Lord Edward!' said the poet genially, spoiling it all. 'I thought it was you when I was reading just now and you tipped all my books on the floor. Don't you remember? We were at Cambridge together.'

'Hello, jolly good, were we?' Edward said vacuously.

'Of course we were. You were at Trinity and I was at Queens. We both rowed a bit,' he added, speaking to Verity.

'Golly,' said Edward. 'Yes of course! How rude of me. You got a blue, didn't you?'

'Oh yes, but who cares. Fancy seeing you here! Somehow I would not have put you down as a member of the Party.'

'Oh yes, I came with Verity.'

'Stupid! David means the CP. He's not a member of the Party, David. He's just hanging around because we are investigating a murder.'

'Gosh! That's great,' said David oddly. 'Look, I've got to sign some books.' He gestured deprecatingly at a little table piled with his books and guarded by a cross-looking woman in spectacles, no doubt an employee of the bookshop who wanted the poet to begin earning his keep. 'But why not let's all go and have a meal after?'

David drifted away to be surrounded by adoring fans. 'How well do you know that man?' said Edward suspiciously.

'Well enough,' said Verity haughtily, 'though I don't know what it has to do with you.'

'Are you coming with me to the Cocoanut Grove this evening or not?'

'Yes, but there's lots of time. We can't get there till ten at the earliest. We have plenty of time to have a bite to eat with David first.'

'Oh, do we have to?'

'What's got into you, Edward? Don't you like David? I thought it was rather rude of you to pretend that you did not recognize him.'

'I didn't at first,' said Edward in an injured tone, 'but then I did.'

'But you don't like him,' Verity persisted.

'No, if you want to know, I didn't and still don't. He's all a bit too good to be true, for one thing.'

'Oh, that's nonsense.' She looked at him, suddenly interested. 'I do believe you are jealous!'

'Now you are being silly,' he said. 'What is there to be jealous about?'

'That's not very polite either. It was me who ought to have said that. Anyway, like it or lump it, he's a friend, so either be polite or leave us. It's up to you.'

'No, I'll stay,' said Edward meekly.

It was only with some difficulty that Griffiths-Jones shed his admirers and it was eight thirty before he, Edward and Verity settled themselves in a Greek restaurant in Fitzroy Street where the poet made himself very much at home. The owner and his wife and daughter welcomed David as a long-lost son and fawned over him. Edward was amused to see how he put on a great show of modesty while all the time encouraging the flattery. It seemed unfair that Verity should shout at him for being patronizing but not seem to mind David's careless put-downs and veiled sneers. He reprimanded her for going on the Peace March which apparently had been against the Party's policy. He praised her piece in the *Daily Worker* but criticized it for not being hard-hitting enough.

'You know, my dear,'—Verity seemed not to notice 'my dear' when it came from David—'you have a talent for sniffing out capitalist conspiracy but you must be careful not to become enamoured of the very corruption we have to root out. The world has to be changed,' he added with slightly sinister intensity.

This seemed to Edward to be aimed at himself, and Verity had the grace to look embarrassed. David sailed on quite unconcerned to speak of his work for the cause. He had been to Moscow, it appeared, and he expanded on the joys of five-year plans, workers' communes, collective farms and the honour done to him when he had an audience with the great leader himself. Verity was entranced. He had been to Spain where he said there was a very good chance of seeing the first elected Communist Party government. Verity's eyes shone and Edward got more and more depressed. In an odd way, Griffiths-Jones reminded him of a Catholic convert so in love with the Pope and the Papacy he had abnegated his normal critical faculties.

'When I first read *Kapital*,'—it was fashionable to omit the definite article and pronounce the word '*Kapital*' in as German an accent as one could manage—'it came as a revelation.' David consciously or unconsciously used religious terminology. 'I realized that individualism resulted in tyranny and that the people needed to be liberated. How was that to be done? Their strength had to be forged into one voice, one will.'

He went on to talk about the division of labour, the classless society, superstructure and

210

substructure, empowering the unions. 'We must trust Uncle Joe,' he repeated like a mantra.

Edward's attention had wandered during David's dissertation on Marxism and the eventual overthrow of capitalism by the proletariat so he did not register that he had finally ended his tirade until he heard Verity giving the poet a detailed account of General Craig's death at Mersham Castle.

David seemed uninterested in how the General had died and if he had been killed or had committed suicide or, indeed, if it had all been a terrible accident. His attitude seemed to be that it hardly mattered how an enemy of the people died and Verity ought not to trouble herself with such bourgeois trivialities. However, he was interested in Mersham Castle: who had been at dinner with the Duke, what had been discussed and the purpose of the dinners. Edward felt uneasy when Verity repeated what he had told her about the Duke's design to do all that he could to prevent another war. There was nothing in it that any ordinary person could possibly object to but he still thought that it almost amounted to an act of betrayal discussing it with Griffiths-Jones.

David was particularly interested in the Bishop's presence at the dinner, but whether he approved of Haycraft or disapproved Edward was unable to say. When they got on to Peter Larmore and Friedberg, David really came to life. Verity, half ashamed, said that the German had seemed to take to her and had actually invited her to the embassy; rather to Edward's surprise and certainly to Verity's, David urged her to telephone him and take him up on his invitation. The idea seemed to be that she had a

211

unique opportunity of getting inside the enemy camp and spying out the land. He added, 'We believe the Germans have some kind of hold over Larmore. If you can find out what it is, it would be very useful.'

'Useful in what way?' chipped in Edward. 'You mean you would expose him in the press if, say, you found out he was selling secret information to the Germans?'

'Possibly,' said David, unperturbed by the tone of Edward's voice. 'Would you think that was wrong?'

Edward was stumped. He could not say that Larmore did not deserve to be exposed if he was guilty of spying or selling secret material to a potential enemy but he hated the idea of the Communist Party using such a scandal for its own dubious ends. Fortunately, David had not waited for Edward to answer. 'Anyway,' he was saying, 'it is more likely we would do nothing. Better know your enemy's weakness and let it destroy what it feeds on in its own time.'

Edward was thoroughly exasperated by this time. He found it almost impossible to sit calmly and listen to the man and to witness the effect it was having on Verity; he was also puzzled why David was prepared to speak so frankly in front of one whom he certainly regarded as a class enemy and possibly, though of course unjustifiably, as a rival for Verity's affections. Just as Edward was about to get up from the table and leave David and Verity together, the poet anticipated him. He rose from the table like Poseidon arising out of the ocean, shook Edward warmly by the hand, kissed Verity on the lips—an act of deliberate provocation,

Edward was sure—and vanished, leaving Edward to pick up the bill.

Edward was not sure where to start in his disapproval of David Griffiths-Jones. Not even a husband would kiss his wife on the lips in a crowded restaurant, not even a cad would send a girl to seduce his enemy. Pimping, that was what it amounted to, he thought, encouraging Verity to go and see Friedberg, and only a man of inordinate vanity would tell a girl she was consorting with the class enemy when actually eating in a restaurant at his expense. It was a tribute to Edward's common sense that not one syllable of what he was thinking did he allow to escape him. He knew instinctively that any criticism he might make of Griffiths-Jones, however mildly expressed, would have her down on him like a ton of bricks. Instead, he asked her if she would mind accompanying him to the Albany so he could change. Verity was already dressed for the evening's entertainment, but he had not cared to turn up at a poetry reading in a left-wing bookshop at six o'clock in white tie and tails. He had known he would be enough of a fish out of water without doing that. Verity graciously consented to go. To visit, unchaperoned, a young man's apartment was not something many well-brought-up girls would agree to do but Edward now had evidence enough that Verity was not a conventional girl; she had liberated herself from the rules of propriety laid down by society for the guidance of young women as part of her politics. He was developing a strong curiosity about her upbringing and would have liked to meet her father, the well-known barrister who, he gathered, found no contradiction in being a Rolls-Royce-owning member of the Communist

213

Party. But, he reminded himself, at present Verity had not even told him where she lived let alone invited him to meet her parent.

When they arrived at the Albany they found Fenton cleaning the silver. 'Fenton,' said Edward, 'this is Miss Browne. Could you look after her while I change? Get her a drink and so forth.'

'Very good, my lord,' said Fenton. He looked inquiringly at Verity.

'No, nothing, thank you.' She did not sit down in the armchair Fenton drew up for her but toured the room looking at the pictures and the mantelpiece littered with invitations to weddings, balls and cricket matches. She stared for some time at a portrait on the wall above the mantelpiece of a fine-looking woman with a humorous mouth and a striking resemblance to Edward.

'Who is that, Fenton?'

'His lordship's maternal grandmother, miss, Lady Manners.' Verity came up close to the painting and tried to decipher the artist's signature. Fenton said, 'The artist is the American painter, James McNeill Whistler, miss. Lady Manners was an American, from Boston, his lordship informs me though I understand the portrait was painted in London.'

'I see,' said Verity, rather overwhelmed by so much information. 'May I ask how long you have been with Lord Edward?'

'Seven years in September, miss,' replied Fenton.

'And you like it?'

'His lordship is a most considerate employer,' replied Fenton haughtily, making it clear from the tone of his voice that he regarded Verity's question as impertinent.

Verity, still inspired by Griffiths-Jones' diatribe against the upper classes, unfortunately insisted. 'But surely, working as a valet—'

Fenton, in an unprecedented revolt against his social obligations, refused to hear anything more that Verity might say on the subject of his employment despite her being his master's guest and given into his charge, and said, 'It is a privilege, as a gentleman's personal gentleman, to serve his lordship. Now, if you will excuse me, miss, I must attend to my duties.' Without waiting for her permission he went out of the drawing-room, shutting the door behind him so quietly it was more emphatic than if he had slammed it.

Edward reappeared. 'Where's Fenton?'

'He said he had to attend to his duties.'

'You haven't been annoying him, have you, Verity?'

'Not at all. I merely asked him how long he had worked for you and if he enjoyed it.'

'Oh lord,' said Edward in mock alarm. 'You've been spouting Marxism at him, I know. I'm afraid Fenton is not a suitable candidate for conversion to your way of thinking. If you think I am hidebound, Fenton makes me look a Bolshevik. Oh well, I expect he will forgive you one day. Now let's go, we've got work to do.'

*   *   *

Captain Gordon was not in the club, at least so said his friend Caspar, the chucker-out, who looked at Edward as if he wanted to start the chucking-out process forthwith. This was a bit of a blow because,

215

if Edward had anything approaching a plan, it was to try to get Captain Gordon to incriminate himself, the owner of the club or anyone else he chose. Edward was certain the club was just a front for a drugs ring and that Charlie Lomax and, perhaps just by the accident of being in his company, Hermione had fallen foul of some very unpleasant villains. He had no idea how this might be proved but he felt he owed it to Hermione and to her mother to try to do so. He had no faith that Inspector Pride would be able to penetrate this twilight world where society and the underworld met and did business.

There was also the nagging suspicion that somehow the Cocoanut Grove was tied up with General Craig's death. Edward had convinced himself and, he believed, Verity that the General had been murdered but, despite their joint efforts, they were no further on with proving that it was murder than they had been a week ago, let alone discovering the murderer. Inspector Pride had told Edward that the inquest, at which he might have to give evidence, was fixed for the following Friday and Edward felt, for no very good reason, that if he did not turn up any solid evidence by then, he never would.

He and Verity danced together and he was surprised by what a good dancer she was. He considered asking her if the comrades regarded ballroom dancing as bourgeois depravity, but thought better of it. Verity had not been in a good mood when they were shown to their table but the band was good and the rhythm of the music, the champagne which had appeared on their table without Edward having ordered it, and the dim

216

'jungle' lighting—all greens and reds—had seemed to soothe her.

The cabaret was announced by Captain Gordon's stand-in, a nervous young man who was singularly lacking in Captain Gordon's suavity. Once again, Amy Pageant sang her smoky, moody songs and once again Edward was entranced. She smiled at him, obviously recognizing him from his previous visit, and when she had finished the set he applauded vigorously. Verity could not quite see what all the fuss was about and told him so. Edward summoned a waiter and asked him to take his card backstage and give it to Miss Pageant. He scribbled a note on the back of the card asking her if she would do them the honour of having a drink at their table. Ten minutes later she appeared and listened to Edward's encomiums with polite attention for several minutes before breaking in.'

'You were here with that poor girl Hermione Weaver the night she disappeared, weren't you?'

'Yes, I was,' said Edward, suddenly serious again.

'Is it true that she was . . . abducted?'

'Well, all we know for certain is that she left the club with Charles Lomax who was later found dead.'

'Murdered?' said the girl, her hand to her mouth.

'I'm afraid so. He was stabbed.'

'And Hermione? What happened to her?'

'She's in hospital. I am afraid it looks as if the person who killed Lomax pumped her full of drugs and if she had not been found when she was she would be dead.'

'Why would anyone want to kill Hermione? She's Lord Weaver's daughter, isn't she?'

'His stepdaughter, yes. I don't know why they tried to kill Hermione but I would guess they did not want her telling the police who had killed Lomax. Did you know him at all? I know he came to the club quite a lot.'

'Oh yes,' said Amy, shivering slightly. 'I knew him.'

Edward instinctively acquitted her of any involvement in the death of Lomax or the drugging of Hermione Weaver. There was something so genuine in the horror he heard behind her simple 'I knew him.'

'He tried to sell me drugs,' she said starkly, 'and when I wouldn't bite he threatened me and said he knew who I was and . . . and well, he tried to blackmail me.'

'Did you tell this to the police?'

'No. The police came to the club but they never asked to talk to me and somehow I didn't feel like going to them. You see, Lord Edward, the club belongs to a friend of mine and I would not want to do anything to cause trouble for him.'

'Lord Weaver, you mean?' said Verity.

'Yes,' said Amy, turning to Verity for the first time. 'How did you know?'

'Captain Gordon told me,' said Edward.

'That's another thing,' said Amy, 'the Captain didn't turn up tonight. He hardly ever misses being here but . . . I probably oughtn't to be telling you all this. This is my first break since coming to London and I don't want to get fired.'

'Have you seen Lord Weaver recently?'

'No, he's been so upset about Hermione I wouldn't want to worry him.'

'Look,' said Edward coming to a decision, 'I

218

think you may be in danger. The people here—Captain Gordon anyway—know you are a friend of Lord Weaver's. You have seen what happened to Hermione. What if they try something on you?'

'Oh no, I'm all right. Whoever attacked Mr Lomax and Hermione wouldn't be interested in me. I'm just the cabaret.'

'May I ask you where you live?' said Edward.

'I've got a flat in Poland Street. Why?'

'I think you ought to move until all this is cleared up. I've just got a feeling.'

'Oh no. Anyway, where would I go?'

'Verity would put you up for a few days,' said Edward cheerfully.

Verity gave him a look which he ignored. 'Yes,' she said. 'Come and stay with me.'

'No, honestly, it's very kind of you but there's no need to worry. Now I've got to go or people will start to notice.'

Amy stood up and Edward also rose from his seat. 'You have got my card?'

'Yes,' she said.

'Well, ring me any time, day or night, if you need me. If I'm not there you can leave a message with my valet, Fenton.'

'All right and . . . thank you,' she said and kissed him lightly on the cheek before departing.

'Thanks for offering me as a hotel,' Verity said drily as he sat down.

'Oh, I knew you wouldn't mind,' Edward answered, his thoughts still with the lovely girl who had just kissed him. 'Golly, she's really something, isn't she?'

'If you say so,' Verity replied but Edward did not hear her. 'Don't forget who she belongs to,' she went on maliciously.

'Eh? What? Oh no, I can't believe . . . he's just a friend of hers.'

'A friend who brings her over from America and gives her a job in the club he just happens to own? Please, Edward, I know you are besotted but there's no need to leave all your brain in—'

'I say,' said Edward indignantly. 'I'm not besotted. I just happen to think she's a lovely girl. Anyone would agree.'

'Anyone in trousers.'

They bickered for a few minutes and then decided they would learn nothing else in the Cocoanut Grove. The young man standing in for Captain Gordon said he had no idea where that gentleman was and he knew nothing about anything, and Edward was inclined to believe him. The chucker-out looked at them balefully as they left.

'Taxi, sir?' he inquired satirically. Edward chose to ignore him and walked away from the club with Verity, still complaining, on his arm. It had begun to rain.

CHAPTER ELEVEN

TUESDAY

Edward woke the following morning feeling as if he had swallowed a rug. The champagne at the Cocoanut Grove must have been worse than he had suspected. He felt anxious, irritated, frustrated. Wherever he looked he saw things he did not like

220

and people he suspected of being other than what they seemed. Those, like Verity, who were demonstrably what they claimed to be were at odds with him. Verity and he had had 'words' after leaving the night-club—he could not remember about what precisely—and she had gone off in a huff leaving him to curse womankind in general and female members of the Communist Party in particular.

He thought he would go down to Pall Mall for a swim and maybe a game of squash—his knee was no longer causing him pain. He needed to clear his head and decide whether or not to give up this rather pointless investigation into General Craig's death—a man with terminal cancer whose appointment with death had been brought forward by only a few weeks. And yet . . . there was something niggling at the back of his mind. Something bothered him. In that black and gloomy place he called his subconscious—he *had* read Freud and found what he had to say about fathers interesting if not totally convincing—suspicion stirred.

Fenton, surprised to find his master up before eight, provided him with black coffee and orange juice. He offered to bring the Lagonda to the door but Edward told him snappishly not to be a fool; he was not so decrepit that he could not walk from Piccadilly to Pall Mall without resorting to the internal combustion engine. No sooner were the words out of his mouth than he regretted taking out his frustrations on his valet who could not bite back. 'I'm sorry, Fenton. Fact is, I've put a lot of work into thinking about this murder of poor General Craig—I call it murder without a shred of proof—and every time I begin to think I'm getting somewhere I find I've just slammed my head into a brick wall. By the way, should Miss Amy Pageant telephone when I'm not to hand will you do your best to do whatever she asks and, of course, get hold of me as soon as possible.'

'Yes, sir, and if Miss Browne rings?'

'Oh tell her . . . tell her whatever you like.'

'Very good, sir,' said Fenton, sounding as though he meant it.

*   *   *

Edward greeted several friends before seeing Peter Larmore sitting on a bench morosely watching a game of squash. The little black ball was being beaten into a puddle of warm rubber by two youngsters—the splat, pat, splat as the ball hit the walls sounding like so much heavy rain. 'Don't look so depressed, Larmore,' Edward said, sitting down beside him. 'Neither of us is as young as these two fellows but it doesn't mean we can't hit the ball about a bit.'

'Oh hello, Corinth,' said Larmore unenthusiastically. 'I wasn't thinking about that—though, now you mention it, I am feeling about a decade older than when I saw you at Mersham. The truth is,'—he looked round to check no one was eavesdropping—'I was just nerving myself to go down and join Celia at Bognor. Keep what I say under your hat, won't you, but I feel I really must tell someone: the Larmore millions—God, how I wish they were millions—have finally gone. I owe everyone. I put everything I had and a good deal I didn't have on a nag called First Front in the three

222

o'clock at Goodwood and lost the lot. First Front! It was so far behind the winner it came first in the next race.'

'Well,' said Edward, 'if I can—'

'No! No, thank you. It is very good of you but I owe too much to add to my crimes by touching you.'

'Can't you cut down on anything?'

'Don't worry! Things have cut down on me. I had planned to take . . . oh well, you know, mustn't take a lady's name in vain and all that rot but she's given me the boot. Gone off with that Jew, Harry Goldstein, and he old enough to be her father.'

Edward was not sure he wanted to hear all this but he had obviously come upon Larmore at a moment of crisis.

'So what now?'

'Oh God, I don't know—end it all, I suppose. Baldwin might have offered me a cabinet post—do you believe it?—but the whips have heard of my money troubles and it's all up.'

'Surely there is someone you can go to?'

'I have been to everyone already. It looks as though I will have to go down to Winchester and beg an audience of Celia's brute of a father, but he hates my guts. Still, he may help me just for Celia's sake. More likely he'll say to her, hang the scandal, get rid of him.'

'Divorce, you mean?'

'Dirty word, isn't it? But maybe better than living with me.'

'I say, old chap,' said Edward uncomfortably, 'brace up. If there is going to be a smash then maybe it won't be as bad as you think. Have you had a chat with Lord Weaver? He might do

223

something for you though he's got his own troubles. You've heard about his stepdaughter?'

'Hermione? Yes, poor girl. God, is no one happy on this earth! Anyway, Corinth, since you are being good enough to let me wallow in self-pity, I may as well tell you there is something else, even worse.'

'What, for goodness' sake?'

'I've been such a bloody fool and now it's all going to come out. Your friend Weaver's got hold of it for one.'

'Got hold of what?'

'Oh, I can't really tell you. You know that blighter Friedberg who was at dinner with us when Craig was killed or killed himself, whichever it was?'

'Yes.'

'Well, I had fallen into a stupid trap he set me. I was in Germany about a year ago and I met Friedberg. He was very friendly—I can see why now. The long and short of it was I agreed to keep him informed about events in England—you know, not secret stuff or anything—in return for a . . . for a consideration. Anyway, I got drawn in. He pressed me; said if I didn't deliver better stuff he would tell the world I was a spy or something. I was frightened and tried to do what he asked, but—oh God, why am I telling you all this!' Larmore put his head in his hands. 'But it wasn't enough and Friedberg said he would expect something good when we met at Mersham or . . . or something nasty. Anyway, I had got something to give him— something I ought not to give him—but before I could betray my country the General died and Friedberg scurried off. Now I'm waiting for something awful to happen.'

Edward took a deep breath. 'Golly, you are in the wars, old man,' he said inadequately and contemplated putting an arm round his shoulders but decided against. 'Still,' Edward said, 'look at the bright side: you didn't do anything unforgivable.'

'No, but I have done enough for it to look pretty bad in one of Weaver's rags. I'll have to resign my seat, of course, but that's all right. I couldn't have hung on to it anyway with my debts.'

'Hey, wait a minute,' said Edward as the two sweating youths came off the court. 'Don't give way yet. Let me think. I know, let's both go and see Weaver. He's not a bad man and he knows what it is for things to go wrong with a fellow. He might be able to keep the hounds at bay. Anyway, it's worth a try.'

'Do you think so?' said Larmore, taking his head out of his towel.

'Yes, I do,' said Edward firmly, 'but before that, let's forget everything and bash a ball about—work up a sweat. What do you say, Larmore?'

Larmore stared at Edward. 'You know, Corinth, I never much liked you: stuck-up prig, I used to think—more money than sense—but I was wrong. You're all right. Yes, let's play squash and damn all the rest of it!'

*   *   *

Verity had been rather put out by Edward's behaviour the previous evening. She liked him and, considering he was a useless scion of the decadent aristocracy, he seemed to share to a remarkable degree her own values and her reluctance to let

225

sleeping dogs lie. It was all the more annoying that he should let her down, and himself for that matter, by fawning over an American girl with not a brain in her head. Furthermore, they had made no progress in discovering how General Craig had come to die, except that she was now convinced that he *had* been murdered. All the 'respectable' figures around the Duke of Mersham's table, not excluding the Duke himself it had to be said, had some reason to dislike or fear the old man. Verity abhorred everything the dead man had stood for but her natural instinct was to see justice done—a point of view her friend David Griffiths-Jones would have regarded as dangerous self-indulgence in bourgeois morality.

She regarded herself as a committed Communist—committed to bringing down the capitalist system and stringing up people like Lord Edward Corinth from lamp-posts—and she made no attempt to square her convictions with her personal regard for Edward as a man—at least, when he was not irritating her. She had been at first amused and then concerned to see the animosity between David and Edward. In an English way, their dislike of each other had been subsumed in good manners but she had been aware of how thin that carapace was. She could not admit it even to herself, but beyond their political differences she had sensed a 'locking of horns' over her which might have given pleasure to a less sensible girl.

She felt guilty in David's presence. His implied criticism of her for consorting with the class enemy she felt to have some justification. There was also the knowledge that David regarded her obsession with General Craig's death to be irrelevant in the fight to which she should be devoting all her energies. The only aspect of her investigation of which he seemed to approve was her interest in the German, Helmut von Friedberg. He had more or less directed her to do a Mata Hari on him and insinuate herself into his affections. She disliked the idea of prostituting herself—that was an exaggeration of course—but as a fundamentally honest person, pretending to like someone she loathed was not easy. She guessed that David would think her reservations on this score to be 'bourgeois' and she had to confess that, however hard she tried to throw off the conventions of her class and upbringing, she was irredeemably bourgeois. There was something hard, almost sinister beneath David's wholesome good looks and frank behaviour which she found both frightening and yet attractive. He was dangerous— not for anything he had done but because of what he *might* do. He was dangerous not like a half-tamed animal but like a sword. It is hard, cold and without feeling but it will not cut if you do not embrace it.

Gritting her teeth, she telephoned the German embassy and asked to speak to Baron von Friedberg. She hoped he would not be there or, if he were, he would not wish to speak to her. Maybe he would not even remember who she was. But no, he was there and he would be delighted to speak to her.

'Miss Browne,' he said in his almost perfect English, 'how happy I am that you have telephoned me. It was my desire that you should show me your London. Here at the embassy I attend official receptions, dinners, and talk to politicians—so boring and I never meet any real English people.' He went on in the same vein for several minutes, claiming to be despondent that his busy schedule prevented him from playing the tourist but in fact taking pleasure in making Verity aware of how important he was.

'Yes,' said Verity, 'I knew how busy you must be but since you had been so kind as to—'

'Of course, but I am desolated. I have to return to Berlin tomorrow and I do not know when I shall be back. Mein Führer,' he said importantly, and Verity could imagine him standing to attention and clicking his heels together, 'mein Führer requires that I make my report to him personally. I fly first to Berlin and then to Berchtesgaden, but tonight—there is a reception here at the embassy and after that there will be a small dinner-party, just a few friends. I would be honoured if you would join us.'

Verity said she would be delighted. There was some relief to her in the idea that there would be other people present. She admitted to herself that she had not liked the idea of fending off Friedberg at some intimate dinner for two. There were limits to what she would do for the Party. She wondered if he knew she was a Communist and did not care or whether he was ignorant of her political allegiances. She suddenly felt rather scared and reached out a hand to dial Edward's number but then thought better of it. She was still annoyed with him and she would enjoy proving to him that she was capable of putting her head in the lion's mouth and getting away unscathed.

She spent the afternoon in pleasurable self-indulgence which, since she was acting upon a direction from the Party, was not self-indulgence at all. If she were going to vamp she would go the whole hog. She began by having a long luxurious bath, washed her hair and considered make-up. Usually she scorned to use any and with the God-given clear skin of youth and large expressive eyes which she could if she wished employ to devastating effect, she normally saw no need for 'powder and paste' as she put it. Tonight was different, however. She opened her wardrobe. Her father was too busy to offer much in the way of moral support but he made up for it in part by giving her a more than generous allowance. This was a secret, of course, except that everyone suspected it. As a member of the Party she could never admit to existing on her father's handouts even though it was his money which made it possible for her to devote so much unpaid time to Party affairs. It was also a comfort to Verity to know that the money came not from some capitalist exploiter of the proletariat but a man famous for being a defender of the poor and the outcast.

Because he was such a good lawyer his services were also in demand by the rich and famous. An ascetic himself, except in his love of beautiful motor cars and his ancient and noble house near Reading, he spent his money on his daughter and on supporting the *Daily Worker*. Since his wife had died—of tuberculosis when Verity was nine—he had given up entertaining except where it was necessary for business, seldom ate in restaurants or went to the theatre, but spent long hours at his desk in his chambers in the Temple. He was universally respected by his fellow lawyers though he had no intimate friends among them. He had refused to be made a King's Counsel in case that compromised his freedom to act for political outsiders such as Gus Ramsbotham, the union leader and CP member who had been accused of inciting illegal strikes in the coal industry. It was a lonely life in many ways because no one else in his profession seemed to share his political views or would at least admit to it in public, and he deliberately held himself apart from his fellow lawyers for this reason. Among the younger members of the Bar he had fervent admirers and they might be seen at his coat-tails as he strode through the law courts on his way to do battle with the many-headed Hydra, capitalism. Verity was proud of him, loved him, but there was something lacking—he was too bound up with his crusade to spare a shoulder for his daughter to cry on. He was proud of her—her intelligence, her love of life— and above all they shared a devotion to the idea of justice even in a world which increasingly denied it. Had Verity been a man she would, no doubt, have followed her father into the law but for a woman this was impossible and, curiously, it never occurred to either father or daughter that this was unjust. It had been a disappointment to him— never declared of course—that he had no sons, just this one daughter. He wanted her to succeed as a journalist if this could be done without betraying her principles. Verity's father was not a Party member. Had he been, it was certain that he would have been prevented from practising at the Bar but in many respects he was more extreme in his views than his pragmatic daughter. Verity gave him hope that the world could change for the better, but as the political situation in Europe grew more desperate month by month he could see that even if a small light of freedom still burned in England it must soon be extinguished.

At Verity's last birthday—her twentieth—her father had given her a sum of money—a huge sum it seemed to Verity—to spend on clothes. He had an idea that girls ought to have fun and look pretty even if the world was coming to an end or perhaps because of it. It occurred to him that if Verity had had a mother instead of two faded elderly aunts to bring her up, she would have enjoyed treats and delights he could not begin to imagine. It was unthinkable of course that a daughter of his should 'come out' and be presented at Court. The whole 'debutante' cattle market filled him with horror. Along with public schools—he had been at Winchester—'the season' symbolized the class distinctions which he abhorred. But that did not mean Verity was not to go to parties and enjoy herself. 'Buy a dress, my dear, something to make an old man's eyes sparkle.'

'Oh Father, you are not an old man,' she had said. 'You are a gladiator. I was in court, remember, when you were defending that poor woman who had killed her husband—a man who had brutalized her and done terrible things to their children. You were amazing. I was bursting with pride, in fact I almost exploded.'

'A gladiator, eh, darling?' he said, pulling her on to his knee. 'An accurate comparison perhaps—"we who are about to die salute you", the future.'

It was this dress—her father's gift—Verity now took reverentially out of the wardrobe where it had hung undisturbed for almost a year. It was a

231

Schiaparelli, not one of Elsa's 'shocking pink' creations but a deceptively simple white gown which to be effective needed to be worn by a girl of flawless complexion and raven black hair. On many girls it would have looked absurd but on Verity it was a powerful statement of her strong personality which could dispense with showiness. Her normal self-confidence ebbed away as she prepared herself for what might prove a difficult evening. She looked despairingly at her small collection of jewellery, finally deciding to wear a pearl choker which had belonged to her mother. She wondered if her father would have approved of her using this dress and her mother's choker to seduce a Nazi. She decided he would certainly *not* approve and she was not sure she did but orders were orders. What she needed was a friend to bolster her confidence and tell her she looked stunning, but since leaving school she had never had any close girl friends. She had friends in the Party, of course, and she still saw one or two of the girls who had been at boarding school with her but she had never shared a flat with any of them and built a friendship on the shared intimacies which come from living with someone. Her world, the world in which she wanted to be successful, was a man's world and she had deliberately distanced herself from contemporaries who were already preparing to subjugate themselves to a man, bear his children, bask in his successes and tolerate his arrogance, infidelity and contempt. It was one of the things which had particularly attracted her to the Communist Party: the emphasis on equality between the sexes and shared responsibility even if, in practice, the women were always left doing the washing-up while the men talked, smoked, conspired and occasionally fought. And now she was going to have dinner with a Nazi, dressed as though she was expecting to dance with the Prince of Wales, in a Schiaparelli dress, a mink stole she had never had occasion to wear before tonight draped over her naked shoulders.

It was a source of embarrassment to Verity that her flat was in Hans Crescent, only a comrade's stone's throw from Harrods and Harvey Nichols, temples of bourgeois life, rather than in the Old Kent Road or Deptford High Street. However, it was certainly convenient for the German embassy in Carlton House Terrace. She got a taxi easily—so easily in fact, she had to ask the driver to circle Trafalgar Square a couple of times so that she wasn't embarrassingly early. When she did at last enter the portico of the German embassy, the fount of all evil as far as she and her political friends were concerned, her heart was beating fast and she was aware of a film of moisture on her upper lip which, as she was wearing white evening gloves, she was unable to wipe away without doing more harm than good.

The first thing which struck her was the effort which had been put into making visitors to the embassy aware they were entering another country. Two massive swastikas embraced an oversized portrait of the Führer, the work of a painter so in awe of his subject as to have reduced what talent he might have had to slavish sycophancy. But once past this reminder of what modern Germany was all about, Verity was surprised by how normal everything seemed. She observed two men in uniform, military attachés on their way out to some function, but the rest of those she saw going about their business were dressed in suits and wore sober ties and were indistinguishable from their counterparts in other embassies or in Whitehall. It was almost a disappointment to Verity. If you enter the devil's domain you want to be impressed—even a little frightened—but if the enemy proves to be no different in outward appearance to yourself and your friends it is subtly disturbing.

A lackey showed her into a large drawing-room noisy with people having a good time. Von Friedberg saw her immediately and, muttering some words of apology to the couple he had been talking to, he strode across the room, bowed, almost clicked his heels together, and kissed her hand. When he raised his eyes to her face they were brilliant with sexual hunger and, much as it might embarrass her, there was something exciting about recognizing—how could she not?—the man's undisguised admiration. The conversation all around them hushed and many eyes were turned to see who had made so dramatic an entrance. Von Friedberg introduced her to the Ambassador, a meek, worn-down-looking man, and then to other officials. There were many more men than women and what women there were had the look of seasoned cosmopolitans. Their faces were heavily made-up and their dresses, from Paris fashion houses, managed to look like suits of armour. Verity seemed to be by far the youngest present and she was soon surrounded by a crowd of young men of various nationalities, all speaking very good English. It so happened that Verity had spent three months at a workers' summer camp near Munich where the German Communist Party sent its young to relax and imbibe the spirit of the movement and meet representatives of the Party in other countries. With the help of a young man who fell hopelessly in love with her she learnt to speak fluent if not accentless German, but she had decided before she set out for the embassy to pretend to have no German in the hope she might pick up information when her hosts talked among themselves. If she was to be a spy there was no point in not thinking like one.

Gradually, the room emptied until at about nine thirty only those were left who had been invited to Friedberg's dinner-party—it was clearly his party not the Ambassador's. She had almost to pinch herself to remember that the men she had been talking to as normally and pleasantly as if she had been with like-minded friends in Bayswater or Islington were, some of them at least, representatives of a regime which was imprisoning political opponents—people with political convictions similar to her own—and making life for Jews and other declared enemies of the Nazi Party almost impossible.

Von Friedberg himself took her into dinner in a small dining-room off the big room in which they had been drinking champagne. The table was set for twenty but there were only six ladies including the Ambassador's wife, a big brassy woman who understandably seemed to see Verity as an interloper. Friedberg sat at the head of the table with the Ambassador at the other end. He sat Verity on his left and the Ambassador's wife, Carlotta, on his right. For the most part the men spoke English in deference to their guest and it suddenly occurred to Verity that she was the only non-German present. In a way this was a relief as she had not relished the idea of having to explain her presence to another English person whom she might come across outside the embassy. On the other hand, she wondered if she should be there at all and she said as much to Friedberg, but he smiled and kissed her hand again and said her presence delighted him. On his own territory he was more relaxed than dining at Mersham, when he had been nervous and unhappy even before the General died. He had been pleased to be invited to the Duke's table but, when there, he had felt himself to be an outsider and the other guests hostile to him and to the Führer, with the exception of Larmore whom he despised.

Before the first course was served there was a moment's silence and the Führer's health was drunk. For some reason it had never occurred to Verity that this might happen. Perhaps it was fortunate that it had not, as she found herself standing to drink the toast before she fully realized what was happening. Presumably, she comforted herself by thinking, David Griffiths-Jones would have expected her to go the full distance in her subterfuge, but she shuddered when she considered what some of her friends in the Party would make of it, friends who had friends in prison camps in Germany. Then she shuddered again as she considered what her host might do if and when he discovered he was entertaining a hated Communist. There was no reason why he should not find out since she had never made any secret of her Party membership. And all the time she shuddered, she talked and laughed as if this was just a normal dinner-party in a normal London house.

Fortunately, Verity was not called upon to dissemble to any great extent. As far as Friedberg was aware, she was a journalist working for *Country Life* and she did not disillusion him. When asked, she divulged that her father was a barrister, that she had no mother and lived in Knightsbridge, all of which seemed to satisfy her interlocutor. In order to forestall more probing questions, she asked him what was happening in Germany and why so many people were declared enemies of the state. Von Friedberg told her that in any great social revolution there were victims and that Germany had risen like the phoenix to take her historic place in Europe. 'We have to be ruthless, my child,' he said, horribly playful, taking her hand. 'Our enemies are not gentle people, not like the people you know, so when we find them we have to destroy them before they destroy us. It is as simple as that.'

She asked him about the Duke's dinner-party. 'The old man'—he meant the Duke—'is aware of what I have been telling you about our resurgence—that is the word, is it not?—but he and the people like him are too hesitant. They should welcome the new Germany. In Aryan partnership Germany and the British Empire will rule the world. The Latin nations are finished.' He clicked his fingers dismissively.

'What about Benito Mussolini's Italy?' asked Verity, interested as to how her host would introduce Fascist Italy into his pantheon. He did not even try. 'Pouff!' he expostulated, blowing between two fingers as if he was dispersing dandelion seeds. 'So much for Italy.' The contempt in his voice was palpable.

'There were others at the Duke's table. What did you think of General Craig, for instance?'

'Germany's inveterate enemy,' he pronounced. 'He died as he had lived—ugly.'

Verity was impressed by Friedberg's decisiveness, at least in his judgments. She continued: 'Peter Larmore? The Bishop?'

'Larmore has been useful to me but that is finished. He is finished.' Von Friedberg seemed to think he had made a joke.

'And the Bishop?'

'The Church of England—it is weak but the Bishop, maybe he is not so weak. I saw him kill your General Craig. That was a good deed.'

Verity gasped. Fortunately, she had a moment to collect herself as Friedberg's attention was taken by Carlotta, who evidently resented Verity's hold over her neighbour. Verity was addressed by a well-mannered young man, a Major Stille, whose acuity she feared. As she parried his innocent-sounding questions, her mind tried to deal with Friedberg's accusation. Made with the German's characteristic firmness, here for the first time was one of the Duke's guests prepared to say categorically that he had seen the General murdered. She must ask him to elaborate. Did he mean that he had seen the Bishop put poison in the General's glass? If he had, why had no one else seen it? And what possible motive could the Bishop of all people have for murdering the General? It was absurd. Ironically, she had her first witness and could only disbelieve him. Who then, she asked herself, would she have accepted as a murderer? If the German had said he had seen Lord Weaver or Peter Larmore doctor the General's port, would she have found it easier to accept?

She ate her dinner—caviar on blinis, turbot, roast pork, some sort of rum baba, hardly knowing what it was she consumed. It was only as she struggled with the rum baba that, seeing Carlotta engaged in conversation with the unpleasant-looking man on her right, she could edge the conversation back to the murder. 'I am intrigued, Helmut,'—he had earlier begged her to use his first name—'by what you said about the Bishop. Did you really see him put poison in the General's port?'

'No, my dear, not quite that but I saw him push the glass across the table when you and Lord Edward arrived and when we all settled down again at the table the General drank from the glass and died.'

Von Friedberg seemed quite unmoved by what he had witnessed, even took pleasure in the memory. She remembered how quickly he had made his escape after the General's death, before the police arrived, but presumably if he had panicked then, it was not because of the death but because he feared being caught up in a police investigation and the publicity which would inevitably ensue.

When dinner was over she suddenly felt exhausted. She summoned up the energy to make her goodbyes and declined her host's offer to send her home in an embassy car. Instead, a taxi was hailed and she sank back on the tarnished leather thankful to be out of a place so normal on the surface but so sinister in all that it denied and disguised. Von Friedberg had been courteous to

239

the last and she had weakly agreed to meet him when he returned from Berlin but she knew she would never see him again. In twenty-four hours Friedberg would have found out all there was to know about her and no one, certainly not a Nazi diplomat, likes to find they have been bamboozled. She shivered even though the night was warm and clutched the fur cloak which Friedberg had himself placed over her shoulders.

When she got home she rescued Max from the care of the elderly woman in the flat below hers. He gave little excited barks, licked her face and wagged his tail so energetically she found herself weeping with relief to have something honest and innocent to love and be loved by. She decided she would ring Edward in the morning. Whatever his failings he was a pillar of decency and normality in comparison with the man who had kissed her hand that evening and looked into her eyes like a wolf in white tie and tails.

CHAPTER TWELVE

WEDNESDAY

Edward was awakened at twenty-five past seven the following morning by Fenton bearing a cup of lapsang souchong.

'What's the matter, Fenton?' he said sharply, glancing at the clock on the bedside table. He knew Fenton would never have woken him half an hour earlier than was customary without a very good reason.

240

'Inspector Pride is on the telephone, my lord, asking to speak to you urgently.'

Edward got out of bed, took the tea from Fenton and sipped it and then, pulling on his dressing-gown and slippers, went out into the hall. He picked up the receiver: 'Pride, is that you?'

'Lord Edward? I apologize for telephoning so early but I wanted to reach you before you went out and before you read the morning papers.'

'Why? Whatever has happened?'

'I'm afraid it is Mr Larmore. I understand you played a game of squash with him yesterday?'

'Yes, but how the devil did you . . . ?'

'I am afraid you were one of the last people to see him alive. He shot himself in the head late last night. He was found by his man who was awakened by the shot.'

'Good God!' exclaimed Edward horrified. 'Larmore has shot himself? I can hardly believe it. When I saw him yesterday morning he was depressed, but after we had talked and played a game of squash he seemed much more cheerful. This is dreadful news.'

'Mr Larmore left three letters: one for the police, one for his wife and one for yourself.'

'He left a letter for me?' Edward was amazed. 'What does it say?'

'It is addressed to you, Lord Edward, so of course we have not opened it,' Inspector Pride rebuked him gently.

'Right, of course. When may I have it?'

'I wondered if you would mind coming down to the Yard, say at ten o'clock?'

'I'll be there, Inspector,' Edward said and rang off.

'Fenton,' he called. 'The Inspector says that Mr Larmore has shot himself.'

'I am very sorry to hear that,' said Fenton, appearing from the kitchen.

'Yes, and what's more he has apparently left me a letter along with one to his poor wife and one to the police. I played squash with him yesterday—I can hardly believe it.' Edward rubbed his forehead as, without knowing it, he always did when he was taken by surprise. He was shocked that someone who had been so very much alive a few hours before was dead. It did not seem real somehow. He bathed, shaved and dressed more rapidly than usual and, refusing Fenton's offer of eggs, distractedly chewed a piece of toast and drank his coffee. The papers arrived as he was eating and he glanced quickly at the *New Gazette*. There it was; just a brief announcement. 'Well-known politician commits suicide'. Obviously the news had only reached the paper just as the presses were about to roll because there was little but the basic facts. Apparently, Larmore's valet had heard the sound of a shot shortly after midnight. He had knocked at his master's bedroom door and, getting no reply and concerned by what he thought he had heard, he had opened the door and found Larmore lying across his bed—a gun still in his hand—having put a bullet through his brain. None of the other papers had anything to add and indeed the news had come too late to be in either *The Times* or the *Morning Post*.

Just as he was about to set out for the Yard, he decided he should ring Verity. In his shock he had forgotten that there existed a coolness between them and when she answered the telephone he

242

launched into his story. Verity was only too glad that they were back again on usual terms and agreed to meet him at Scotland Yard. 'I don't expect Pride will keep me long and then we can talk it over and see if it affects our investigation at all.'

'Yes,' said Verity, grateful that he was still assuming they were partners. 'I am due to see Lord Weaver at midday and I would like to talk to you before I see him.'

'Why are you going to see Weaver?'

'He wants me to tell him if I will accept his offer to write for the *New Gazette*.'

'And are you going to say yes?'

'I'm still not sure. I would like your advice,' she added, uncharacteristically uncertain of herself. 'On the one hand it is flattering to be asked and would do my career no end of good but on the other hand it may be against my principles to work for an archetypal capitalist. I really can't decide.'

'It might not do you much good with the comrades,' said Edward unkindly.

'No, well anyway . . .'

'Sorry,' said Edward, immediately contrite, 'I didn't mean to make a cheap jibe. Let's talk it through when we meet. I might try and oil in to see Weaver with you, if you didn't mind. There are a few things I would like to ask him and I had a message at the club that he had been trying to get hold of me.'

'Oh, Edward,' Verity suddenly burst out, 'have you talked to your brother yet? He ought not to read about Larmore in the newspapers. And that poor woman—was she called Celia?'

'Larmore's wife, yes. I'm afraid he led her quite

243

a dance but even so she will be devastated, but I don't think there is anything we can do. After all, I hardly knew him and I never met her except that once at that fateful dinner at Mersham.'

'Yes,' said Verity soberly. 'Fateful is the word.'

*   *   *

When Edward arrived at Scotland Yard he was shown up to the Inspector's office. 'We seem to meet all too frequently,' Pride said grimly, shaking Edward's hand.

As usual, Edward was irritated by the Inspector's manner which seemed to carry a hint of threat or at least complaint, as though this new death was Edward's fault.

'Before I give you the letter to read, would you oblige me by telling me what you discussed when you saw Mr Larmore yesterday? Did you meet by appointment?'

'No,' said Edward. 'We both use the club for squash and to swim. I have seen him there before and we always exchange a few words but this time he was looking so miserable I stopped to talk to him. In any case I was looking for someone to play a game of squash with.'

'And what did he say?'

'He said it was all up with him. He owed a good deal of money and . . . I assume this does not have to get back to his wife?'

'It depends, but if it is about his women I shouldn't think it need be mentioned at the inquest.'

'Oh, you know about that?'

'Yes, Lord Edward.'

244

'So, well, he said his mistress—he did not mention her name—had left him because he could not afford to keep her as she demanded.'

'That would be Mam'selle Carnot. We have already talked to that lady.'

'I see,' said Edward. 'Well then, you know everything, Inspector.'

'He said nothing else then?'

'What do you mean?'

'I mean, although Mr Lannore had debts, a gentleman of his station in life and with his friends might have borrowed without too much difficulty, I would have imagined.'

'I gathered he was deeply in debt, Inspector, and I got the impression that he was also concerned that his debts would preclude his being offered a position in the government. That coupled with his muddled love life must have tipped him over the edge.'

For some reason, although Edward had not liked Larmore, he thought he owed it to him not to give the Inspector any hint of his relationship with Friedberg. If it got out that he had been contemplating selling secret information to the Germans his name would be excoriated and that would be an added burden for his widow and children to bear. If it did get out, it would not be through him, Edward decided.

'So there was nothing else?' the Inspector persisted.

'No, that was enough I should think, wouldn't you?'

'Would you say that the balance of the poor gentleman's mind was disturbed then?'

'He was certainly very depressed but I thought

after our game of squash he was in better spirits. I suggested he and I might go and see Lord Weaver who, I thought, might possibly have helped him with a loan.'

'I see, Lord Edward. Well, I think you did everything you could for Mr Larmore. We can only assume that later that night, brooding on his troubles, he decided it was not worth going on. You have nothing to reproach yourself with.'

Again there was the implication that he *might* have something to reproach himself with, but Edward checked himself from making some sharp response. He thought the Inspector might suspect he had not told him the whole truth and was needling him in the hope that he would blurt something out which he might later regret.

'May I see the letter now, Inspector?' he said coldly.

Inspector Pride took an envelope off his desk and handed it to him. Edward looked at it, turning it over in his hand. It was a perfectly ordinary white envelope with the words 'Lord Edward Corinth' scrawled in blue ink on the front and underlined rather heavily. The Inspector passed him a paper knife and he slit open the envelope. The single sheet of writing paper he drew out had Larmore's address printed at the top. It was undated. It read: 'My dear Lord Edward. You were very good to me when we met earlier today. I know you don't much like me but you are a good fellow. I feel I owe you something for trying to help me. Your idea of going to see Weaver—thinking about it, I just can't be bothered. As I said, it is all up with me and I don't think I can struggle any more. The only thing I really wanted was to be in the cabinet and whatever happens'—Larmore had underlined 'whatever happens'—I won't get that now.

'What I wanted to say was this: I know you think someone killed Craig at that awful dinner at Mersham. You might like to know that you were right. Someone did murder him—not me, but the Bishop, Cecil Haycraft. I don't know why but I definitely saw him push the glass of wine—port I mean—across the table while we were all disturbed by your arrival on the scene with that girl. He must have put poison in it because when the General drank from the glass he went into convulsions as you saw.

'I don't know whether this helps at all. Bishop Haycraft is a ghastly man—a leftie and a pacifist. I really would not have thought he had it in him to kill someone but I saw what I saw.

'Well, there we are then. Goodbye and thank you, Lord Edward.'

Larmore had signed himself 'Peter Larmore'. Edward, who was not normally susceptible, blinked back a tear. It was as though he had held out his hand to a drowning man but had not held on tight enough and he had slipped from his grasp into the sea.

The Inspector was looking at him quizzically. 'May I see the letter?' he asked, holding out his hand, when he saw Edward begin to fold it back into the envelope. Edward hesitated. He would have liked to keep from the Inspector what Larmore said he had seen Bishop Haycraft do but he realized that would be impossible. He handed Pride the letter without comment and the Inspector read it through without saying anything. When he had finished he returned it to Edward. 'I would be grateful, Lord Edward, if you would keep this letter carefully. It may need to be presented in evidence at the inquest.'

'But surely you would not want to make public Larmore's unsubstantiated allegation about the Bishop murdering General Craig?'

'No, but it is evidence that Mr Larmore's mind was disturbed just before he committed suicide and we might need to let the coroner read it or part of it. It would not be necessary to mention the Bishop by name.'

'I suppose so,' Edward acknowledged. At this moment the Inspector's telephone rang. He picked up the receiver angrily and shouted, 'What is it? Didn't I say I wasn't to be interrupted?' He listened for a few moments and then said to Edward, 'Miss Verity Browne is downstairs.'

'Oh yes, I'm sorry, Inspector, I hope you don't mind, I asked her to meet me here. We have finished, haven't we?'

The Inspector grudgingly agreed they had. 'Nothing more on Lomax's death and who attacked Miss Weaver, I suppose?' Edward inquired.

'No. We are still trying to trace Captain Gordon. We think he may have something to tell us. That's another inquest you will have to attend, Lord Edward.'

'Yes, I don't seem to be bringing people much luck, do I?' he replied with studied innocence. 'Oh, another thing, Inspector—may I know what Larmore said in his letter to the police?'

'He said he was killing himself because he had nothing to live for, but for his wife and children's sake he hoped it could be kept quiet.'

'I am so sorry for that poor woman,' said

248

Edward. 'She was at the seaside with the children, wasn't she?'

'Yes, sir, but she is back in London now, staying with friends. She asked me to ask you to telephone her. I think she wanted to hear from your own lips what her husband said to you.' Pride handed him a telephone number on a slip of paper.

'Oh golly,' said Edward.

'Yes, it won't be easy,' said Pride with satisfaction, showing him out.

* * *

Verity, Edward considered, was looking as fresh as May in a smart blue and white suit with huge lapels which might have seemed mannish on someone less feminine. Her small black hat was lightened by a white feather. Her lips were scarlet and he had a feeling this amounted to a challenge. If he disapproved, she would see it in his face. In fact, he wanted to kiss her but that would undermine their business relationship, he thought, and probably earn him a slap, so he contented himself with complimenting her.

'Oh yes,' she said casually. 'This is the outfit I usually wear to impress old men. Not you,' she added hastily, seeing the look of hurt in his eyes, 'I mean Lord Weaver.'

'I see,' said Edward smiling broadly. 'Look, I've got lots to tell you. Where can we go to talk?'

'It's such a lovely day,' said Verity, 'why don't we sit on a bench in those little gardens by the House of Commons? You know, where there is that new statue of Mrs Pankhurst. Max needs a walk in any case.'

'And how is Max?' said Edward genially, putting out his hand to stroke the dog's head. He withdrew it quickly as Max snapped at his fingers.

'Stop it, Max,' said Verity firmly. 'The trouble is I have taught Max to distrust aristocrats. You can't say I was wrong.'

It was indeed a day to be outside and instead of sitting they walked through the gardens, paying brief homage to Emmeline Pankhurst, to the river which in the sunlight looked deceptively clean and sparkling. They talked earnestly to one another, exchanging information and speculating on the two eyewitness reports of the Bishop having passed General Craig the poisoned port. Once or twice, passers-by glanced at them, wondering if they were lovers but deciding their faces were too serious for that unless their dalliance was illicit.

'I hate the idea of you going to the German embassy like that, Verity,' Edward was saying. 'They may seem like buffoons with their strutting up and down and their railway porter uniforms but they are dangerous, you know. A friend of mine who has been living in Berlin says that we don't know half of what is going on over there. People disappear and are never heard of again and they are threatening to kill all the Jews. Well, of course, they won't do that, but it is still pretty unpleasant.'

'I know,' Verity said sombrely, 'David was saying very much the same thing.'

David! The name spoiled Edward's mood. Verity noticed him scowl and asked innocently what was the matter.

'Oh, nothing,' Edward lied, 'but isn't it time we got a cab to Fleet Street?'

'Not a cab,' said Verity, 'I feel like a bus. I'm a

250

woman of the people, don't forget, not an effete aristocrat like you.'

'With a flat in Hans Crescent and a father who drives a Rolls Royce,' Edward returned unpleasantly.

'You know my secret,' Verity said lightly. She was abashed but also rather relieved Edward knew where she lived.

'I didn't really spy, but after all you did give me your telephone number which is a Knightsbridge exchange so . . .'

'Don't worry. I'm not ashamed of being rich— well, comparatively rich. It means I am better able to help the cause. Communists, you know, don't believe everyone should be poor. They believe everyone ought to be rich.'

'I thought you believed in redistributing wealth?'

'I do and so does Father, but we are not idiots. We live in a capitalist world where wealth is power. One day that will all be gone but, since it exists, we have to work with it and it would be stupid to throw away power when we need power to overthrow the system.'

'That sounds like David talking,' said Edward meanly, and immediately regretted saying it as he saw Verity colour. 'I'm sorry. All I meant was—and I was thinking of Nazis—if you touch pitch you can easily be defiled. I expect David would say the ends justify the means but I always think the means determine the ends. Look, there's a bus! Run!'

*   *   *

'Verity! Lord Edward! I had no idea you were coming, Lord Edward, but I am delighted to see

251

you.' Lord Weaver, taking the cigar out of his mouth, levered himself out of his chair and came out from behind his huge desk to greet them. 'I have been leaving messages for you all over the place.'

'How is Hermione?'

'Hermione, I am glad to say, is much better—sitting up in bed and asking to see you. Her mother wants to see you also and thank you for what you did, as do I. But what sad news about Peter Larmore!'

'Yes. In fact I was going to bring him to see you today.'

'See me?'

'Yes, you see I bumped into him at my squash club and he was in a bad way. Apparently he owed a lot of money and . . . well, may I tell you something in complete confidence?'

'Of course, but if it's the story going round Fleet Street that he had sold some secret papers to the Germans—that fellow Friedberg in particular—you are too late. I'm afraid all the world knows it—by that I mean a dozen influential editors and of course his political masters. Nothing could have stopped it being in the gutter press today except his death, and we would have had to follow suit.'

'And now?'

'Now it's in no one's interest to publish it. It might damage the government's negotiations with Chancellor Hitler if we are seen to smear his personal envoy, Friedberg. We wouldn't want that. Let's hope the *Daily Worker* doesn't get hold of it,' Weaver added meaningfully. 'They are outside the pale and have their own axes to grind.'

'If you mean, will I write about it, the answer is

no,' said Verity. 'We don't persecute dead men and their living families.'

'I was sure that was the case,' said Lord Weaver smoothly. 'But you said you were going to bring him to see me, Lord Edward?'

'Yes, I was sure you would do what you could to help him.'

'I am touched by your faith in me but I fear there was nothing anyone could do for Larmore. I will see if there is anything I can do for Celia and the children. I think you'll find people will rally round. But as I began to say, I wanted to talk to you about something much more important, at least to me: what you did for Hermione. You saved her life—it was nothing less—and Blanche and I owe you a great deal, Lord Edward.'

'I only did what Lady Weaver asked me to do.'

'Oh, don't be modest, Lord Edward. We are both greatly in your debt. You found her just in time. She was almost in a coma and in another two or three hours she would have been dead. There's no doubt about it: she owes you her life.'

Edward was now thoroughly embarrassed and to change the subject asked Lord Weaver if he had heard anything of Captain Gordon.

'No,' he said gravely. 'I have not. The police will trace him soon, I am sure. I feel very much to blame that the Cocoanut Grove, which I think you know I own, should have been used to disseminate drugs.'

'I guessed as much,' said Edward.

'Yes, the police are quite sure of it.'

'And how is Miss Pageant?' said Edward, deciding that this was a good moment to try and clear up one mystery. 'She is a most talented

253

singer.'

'Why, I am glad you think so, Lord Edward,' said Weaver, waving his hand. 'I must admit I am—what do you call it—*parti pris*? She is just in the next room.'

Edward started to get up from his chair, unable to disguise his astonishment. He had never expected Lord Weaver to be so candid about his relationship with the girl. Weaver went over to a door disguised as a bookcase. He opened it and called, 'Amy, come and say hello to Lord Edward and to Verity Browne.'

Amy Pageant came in looking cool and beautiful, her large eyes bright with anticipation and a smile on her wide mouth which made Edward's heart turn over. 'Amy, you know Lord Edward and Miss Browne, don't you?'

'Yes, of course,' she said coming over to shake hands. 'Isn't that good news about Hermione, Lord Edward?'

'It certainly is,' he replied. Her American accent made him think of jazz, black coffee and Manhattan cocktails. Suddenly, seeing Amy beside Lord Weaver, Edward noticed something. Before he could stop himself he said, 'You must be related!'

Lord Weaver smiled and said, 'How very perceptive of you, Lord Edward. Yes, Amy is my daughter but how you recognized it I do not know—me with a face like a turnip and she being the most beautiful girl in the world. I'm sorry, Miss Browne, but you must let an old man have his fancies.'

Verity said, 'No, you are quite correct, Lord Weaver, Amy is very beautiful. Lord Edward has

254

admired her very much since he first saw her perform at the club. But tell us, there has to be a story here.'

'Well yes, there is as a matter of fact,' said Lord Weaver, uncharacteristically shy but nevertheless putting his arm protectively around his daughter's waist. 'I can see the investigative journalist coming out in you. My first wife died in childbirth and to my enduring shame I left Amy to be brought up by two unmarried aunts of mine in Corner Brook. Now I guess that was very wrong of me and must sound heartless, unfeeling. All I can say in mitigation is that I was truly distraught when my poor wife died and in my madness I kind of blamed the innocent little baby for it. Crazy I know, but I was crazy.'

Weaver glanced at Amy who returned his gaze fondly. 'Oh, Pa,' she said softly, 'don't blame yourself.'

'But I do,' Weaver said energetically, 'and of course I paid for it by losing out on seeing my baby grow up. I guess I thought, as a pushy young man out to make a million dollars, that I could not cope with having a baby girl to look after, but I see now I was wrong—very wrong.'

'And why "Pageant"?' inquired Edward.

'That was my mother's maiden name,' Amy replied.

'So how . . .' Verity began.

'So how come we got reunited?' Weaver said, grinning broadly. 'I'll tell you how. One of the old aunts died and the other got kind of feeble and so she wrote me asking what she should do. At first I didn't know what to do. For one thing, I didn't know if Blanche would wear it. I mean, I never got

255

on so well with Hermione and I guess I thought if I suddenly produced a long-lost daughter then Hermione might get to hate me and then Blanche . . . To tell the truth, I asked the Duke what he advised.'

'You asked Gerald?' said Edward amazed.

'Why yes, sir, I did. The Duke is a very wise man in my estimation and so is the Duchess—wise, I mean. I told them that when I first had the letter I thought I was being blackmailed but the more I thought of it the more I wanted to see how my baby had turned out. And now I know,' he said, gazing fondly on his daughter who smiled back.

'You paid for everything anyway, Pa, so how could there be blackmail? I would not want you to think, Lord Edward, that my father had left me to fend for myself. I was as well educated and well looked after as I possibly could have been.'

'I don't mean money blackmail, sweetheart. I was terrified about Blanche. I am so fortunate to have found such a wonderful woman, Lord Edward, I really dreaded something coming between us but as it turned out I need not have worried. As I told the Duke at Mersham, before dinner—before poor Craig died—I had taken his and the Duchess's advice and told Blanche everything. She was just wonderful and was only cross with me for not having told her about Amy years ago.'

'Since you are being so frank with us, Lord Weaver,' Edward said, 'might I ask how your stepdaughter took the news?'

'Hermione? Hmf! That wasn't so easy—she said some pretty terrible things to both her mother and me. However, I guess she'll get over it.'

'You don't think—forgive me if I am being impertinent—you don't think taking drugs was her way of hurting you both—taking her revenge for plucking another daughter out of the hat, so to speak?' Edward had deliberately spoken crudely but Lord Weaver seemed unruffled by his words.

'I don't think so—I pray that it is not the case. I'm afraid she had been taking dope for some time. We had—her mother and I—tried everything to stop her.'

'What had you tried?'

'Well, Blanche kept her with her as much as possible and tried to distract her. I told her I would not increase her allowance unless she promised not to spend the money on dope, but it was no good.'

'Did you take her to a doctor?' Verity asked.

'No, she refused—said she was not ill, just bored.' He shrugged his massive shoulders. 'But what do I know? I feel such a fool, but then men are fools, are they not, Miss Browne?'

'Well, yes, they mostly are, I suppose,' Verity agreed, smiling. 'And I'm going to be a fool too and turn down your kind offer to work for the *New Gazette.* As you know, I am a member of the Communist Party—not a very good member and not typical, I suppose, as Lord Edward has been telling me, but I do have principles and I want to be true to them.'

'But Miss Browne—Verity—we would give you your own by-line and let you declare your political point of view.'

'That's very good of you, Lord Weaver, and you are destroying all my prejudices against newspaper tycoons, whom I have to believe to be ruthless capitalists with no regard for anything but money,

257

and that's not fair of you, but seriously I think your readers would feel, quite correctly, that I was airing my views in the wrong pulpit.'

'Well,' said Weaver, shrugging his shoulders, 'it is my loss. I have never said this to anyone before but if you change your mind there will be a job waiting. Mostly, if someone says no to me, I say goodbye for ever but you're special, Miss Browne.'

CHAPTER THIRTEEN

WEDNESDAY EVENING

While Verity had been making her goodbyes to Lord Weaver, Edward had taken the opportunity of inviting Amy to dinner before her show at the Cocoanut Grove. She had accepted and Edward had felt delight, excitement and guilt. He had not, he told himself, deliberately made his invitation to Amy when he knew Verity was otherwise engaged but, truth to tell, he did not want her to know what he had done. It was ridiculous really, he reassured himself. His relationship with Verity, as she would be the first to admit, was an uneasy friendship based on the desire they shared to get to the bottom of a mysterious death—nothing more. He was not her lover—he strongly suspected that David Griffiths-Jones enjoyed that position—so he would take out to dinner any girl he pleased. In any case, he wanted to ask Amy what she knew about Captain Gordon's activities. So why did he feel guilty?

That evening, before going back to the Albany

to change, he called in at King Edward VII, the private hospital in Beaumont Street where Hermione Weaver was recovering. He knocked at the door of her room and was bidden to come in by Lady Weaver who was sitting by her daughter's bed flicking over the pages of *Vogue*.

'Lord Edward!' she said with evident pleasure. 'This is so kind of you.'

Edward shook hands as well as he was able from behind a dozen roses he had bought in Marylebone Lane. 'Gosh, I needn't have bought these,' he exclaimed ruefully, looking at the array of vases filled with flowers on every shelf and ledge. 'How are you, Hermione?' he said gently. 'You must still be feeling rotten but really, you know, you are almost looking your old self.'

'Oh dear, Lord Edward, I hope not,' she answered, her voice weak and rather growly. 'I think I must have lost a stone in weight.' She tried to smile but the smile turned into a cough. When she recovered, she said, 'Please forgive my voice but by the time they had finished putting tubes down me they left my throat sorer than the worst sore throat you ever had.'

'That will soon pass, I'm sure,' Edward said, sitting down beside her on the seat vacated by Blanche who said she was going to stretch her legs. He took her hand gently in his and said, 'I hope the police haven't been harassing you. I gather from Inspector Pride that you didn't see who it was who attacked you but perhaps you don't want to talk about any of that.'

'No, Lord Edward,' said Hermione weakly. 'I would like to talk to you about it, but first I have to thank you for saving my life.'

'Oh, don't mention it,' said Edward, embarrassed. 'It was really your mother. She was desperately worried when you disappeared and she *ordered* me to find you. You know, your mother can be very difficult to resist when she wants you to do something for her.'

'Yes,' said Hermione, 'I know. I have caused her so much unhappiness. I don't know why, I just couldn't seem to help myself—being awful to her, I mean. I think it was the drugs. I just couldn't think of anything else. I was a typical bored little rich girl, I suppose, selfish and horrible, so when Charlie Lomax introduced me to dope—cocaine mostly—it was terribly exciting. I did not realize, fool that I was, that you couldn't just give up when you wanted. I was soon spending twenty or thirty pounds a week on the stuff and suddenly it wasn't fun any more. If I couldn't get my supply I was really upset.'

Hermione stopped and gestured to Edward to pass her the glass of water on the bedside table. As she sipped, Edward said, 'Look, this is tiring you. Why don't I come back in a day or two when you are a little better?'

'No,' she said urgently, reaching out for his hand. 'I want to tell you now. I want to get it off my chest. You do understand, don't you?'

Hermione suddenly looked very pathetic—ugly almost, but free of that hard, angry look which he had been used to.

'Yes, I understand,' Edward said softly. 'Go on with what you were telling me.'

'Well, by the time of that dinner-party at Mersham I was getting desperate. I owed Mr Lomax quite a lot of money. He had said he would

260

not supply me with anything else until I had paid him, so we agreed that I would get him invited to Mersham where I would give him the money and he would give me my dope. He seemed pathetically eager to be invited to dinner with the Duke and the other bigwigs. I sold some jewellery because I couldn't go to Mummy or my stepfather for more money without having to explain why I needed it. Then, when I got to Mersham, I was told that he wasn't coming after all. My mother and my stepfather thought I was in love with him. Love!' she said scornfully. 'I hated him.

'I was injecting my last shot of heroin into my arm when my mother came into my room and saw me. She did not understand what I was doing so, God forgive me, I told her. She begged me to give it up. I was horrible to her and said . . . and said . . . Hermione could hardly bear to continue but Edward did not interrupt her except to give her a little more water. He felt she needed to make her confession and he owed it to her to listen.

'I said I loved it—the drug—more than I loved her. I said awful things about my stepfather—how he had never loved me and . . . and so on. I said I did not believe this girl Amy was his daughter, whatever he said. You know all about her, don't you? Everyone does,' she said bitterly. Her voice shook with pain and Edward stroked her hand, saying nothing. 'I was very jealous and I think I really hated my stepfather for taking my mother away from me. I hated him for not being my father, I suppose, and I hated my father for being dead.' She shivered and made an effort to pull herself together. 'Anyway, as soon as I got back to London I made you take me to the Cocoanut Grove. I

261

desperately wanted to see Lomax as well as hoping almost as desperately that I would not. As you know, I did see him and at first he did not want to have anything more to do with me. He said he had been warned off me—by my stepfather, I guess. He was frightened but in the end he agreed to take me back home with him. I said I would tell the police everything I knew about his dope-dealing if he didn't. I was really desperate, you see. When we got to his horrible little house we . . . we both took a shot of . . . that stuff and I went off to lie on a bed and rest for the first time for ages. My nerves had been torn to shreds by not having anything to take but I guess I must have taken too much or else it was bad stuff—you often get sold bad stuff, you know,' she said, looking appealingly into Edward's face. 'I went into a kind of coma, I think, because I don't remember much more until I woke up here.'

'You don't remember *much*?' said Edward. 'Does that mean you do remember something?'

'I remember seeing your face all big and swollen, like the moon, looking at me and saying things I could not understand.'

'But nothing before that?'

'I think I heard some banging downstairs but I can't really remember,' she said sadly.

'You know they killed Mr Lomax, don't you?' said Edward brutally. He felt it was important Hermione faced up to everything that had happened if she was ever to recover from her ordeal.

'Yes,' she murmured. 'Inspector Pride told me.'

'Who do you think it was who killed him then?'

'I suppose it must have been Captain Gordon, but I don't know.'

'Why would he have wanted to do that?'

'Oh, Gordon had found out that Lomax was cheating him—selling stuff on his own account, you know, and keeping the profits.'

At that moment Blanche reappeared and Hermione, as though Edward had served his purpose, pushed his hand away in a petulant gesture and cried, 'Mummy!'

Blanche went to her daughter and took her hand. As Edward slipped out of the room he saw that both women were weeping.

*   *   *

Verity had been summoned to a meeting with David Griffiths-Jones. Verity had been in love with David, or at least they had had a love affair, and she was still not sure whether it was all in the past. It was very difficult to know with David what he was feeling, even what he was thinking. He was always affable but it was hard to get close to him. When she had first gone to work for the *Daily Worker* she was treated with some suspicion by others on the paper including the editor, Morris Block, a grizzled survivor of the Party's earliest days. Block had been in Russia during the October Revolution of 1917, having got to know Lenin in Switzerland before the war. He had written a book about the Revolution which had been a best-seller in both England and America and was therefore regarded with some awe by younger comrades. He had disliked Verity from the first. Her father had got her the job and he, as one of the main financial supports of the paper, could not be gainsaid, but Morris Block saw it with some justification as typical bourgeois string-pulling. He was suspicious of Verity's father and his connections with the English legal system which he regarded as wholly corrupt.

Young comrades took their line from the editor and treated Verity with barely concealed distaste. For example, if there was any sort of celebration— a birthday, say—she would only hear about it after the event. Verity understood why there should be this suspicion and reacted by working extremely hard both on the paper and helping organize marches and conferences, taking on the boring administrative work which most comrades did their best to duck. There was an added annoyance for Block: though Verity did not wear much make-up, she attracted all male eyes and there seemed too many extra male visitors to the office when Verity was ensconced there. She made no effort to soften her clipped upper-class accent which was much parodied by her colleagues. She refused to dress down and join the dowdy women in shapeless cardigans and woollen skirts, preferring to arrive in crisp little dresses which showed off her figure or white linen two-piece suits, and she insisted on bringing Max into work with her. Though the little dog was quite happy lying peacefully at his mistress's feet, Morris Block saw it as unserious and sentimental to bring pets into the office.

When David came into the *Daily Worker* to deliver an article on the Mosley marches in the East End of London—this was about three months after Verity had started work on the paper—he astonished and infuriated everyone, including Morris Block, by immediately taking Verity under his wing. He invited her to accompany him to

264

several Party meetings and it was assumed that they were lovers. However, it was some weeks before they actually did begin what turned out to be a brief but very physical affair. In fact, there was a period of a month or so when Verity, who was a virgin, graduated from being terrified that he would jump on her, to the moment when she wondered what was wrong with her that he did not.

David never explained himself, never said what he was thinking, and Verity never asked him. One evening, after a particularly tiring and fruitless meeting at which comrades refused to toe the Party line, David took Verity back to his tiny flat in Notting Hill. As soon as she was inside and without so much as offering her a drink he said, 'I think we ought to go to bed, don't you?'

It was the first time she had seen the inside of his flat, and no one else had ever been invited back as far as she knew. She had assumed that going back with David to his eyrie was an invitation to become his lover and she suspected that if she refused to sleep with him he would never forgive her. She did not intend to refuse him. She was, after all, almost twenty and she considered it was time she lost her virginity. She admired him and was rather in awe of him. He was a glamorous figure in the Party and it was something to have been chosen by him. All this was true but it was still a shock to have sex treated as if it was as much a matter of course as going to the pictures. Despite herself, Verity was rather put out by the unromantic way in which David had at last made the proposition she had been waiting for, but she tried not to show it. She went over to the fireplace, which had been blocked in but still boasted a mantelpiece. There was nothing on it but a thick layer of dust and a small mirror. Glancing into it she saw that David was undressing. She turned and said, 'Is this what is expected of us?'

'I don't care what is expected of us. I want you and you want me. Isn't that enough? Surely you don't expect me to go through all that bourgeois stuff—flowers, chocolates, me telling you how pretty you look in pink?'

'No, of course not! I knew what you meant when you invited me back here.'

'That's all right then.'

David went on undressing but Verity still stood doodling in the dust with her finger. David was much taller than she was and as he marched over to her, naked except for a pair of socks which somehow made him seem even more naked, she grasped the mantelpiece in what David took for alarm. Though she would die rather than admit it, this was the first time she had seen a man without any clothes on and she found her eyes focusing on his groin where there nestled among thin hair as golden as that on his head an absurd piece of flesh she identified as his penis. It looked too small to do what she had been told by her schoolfellows it was supposed to do. Was he deficient in some way, she wondered?

'I say, you do want to be my lover, don't you?' he said. It was the first time she had seen him even remotely unsure of himself and it made her feel better. This tiny doubt made him seem more human and therefore lovable.

'Yes, David,' she said and almost laughed, 'but you will have to be patient with me. You see, I have never done this before.'

'Oh, I see,' he said, his face clearing. 'Well, don't be nervous, I've got one of these.' He flourished a little packet at Verity containing, she supposed, a French letter. She knew about these but had never understood how they worked so she smiled weakly. 'That's good.'

They had seldom even kissed before and never like lovers so it was another surprise when he took her face in his large callused hands and kissed her on the lips. Suddenly, Verity was overcome with a swimmy sensation which made her feel she wanted to lie down.

David proved to be an efficient lover in no way lacking in what was necessary and that was a great relief. She had endured the fumblings of inexperienced youths before and had no wish to lose her virginity in some messy scramble. He had no embarrassment and seemed to approach love-making as it it were just another task the Party had set him. No, that was not fair, she considered as she helped him take off her brassiere and then her drawers. He was passionate in his way. It was just that there was something a touch clinical about how he avoided saying anything in the least romantic while he made love to her or, in fact, saying anything at all beyond the occasional grunted instruction. She did not want him to slobber over her and whisper lies in her ear but . . . he seemed unaware that she might like to hear that he at least *lusted* after her. Then there came a moment when she stopped analysing her feelings and began to relax.

When it was all over Verity was filled with gratitude. He had aroused her to a new understanding of the pleasure her body could give her. He had been gentle with her but masterful. He had made her understand why sex was so important to people and, for ever after, would be to her. She did not love him and she was quite sure he did not love her, but there was a respect and even, at least on her part, affection.

They made love many times over the next four months and Verity got to look forward to it so obviously that all her friends and certainly those she worked with noticed she was a different person—glowing with a knowledge of herself and suffused by a feeling of good will to all. Where she had been abrupt before, she was now patient. Where she had been—without meaning to be— supercilious, she was now friendly. The comrades warmed to her, and the others on the paper—with the noticeable exception of Morris Block—treated her as one of themselves. Then David disappeared without saying anything to Verity about where he was going or for how long. There was the briefest note left on her desk that she should not worry about him, which she wondered if she should interpret as meaning she should not wait for him. He did not reappear until she met him with Edward Corinth, five months later in the Parton Street bookshop.

David had appointed a Lyons Corner House in which to meet Verity and he was there sitting at a small table surrounded with tea and cakes when she arrived. It was really an absurd place to have chosen if his idea had been to be inconspicuous. Among all the ladies in their pearls and twinsets and the few men in suits and bowler hats, David stood out like a lighthouse on the Essex marshes. He was gold while they were base metal. In his grey flannels and white open-necked shirt he might have just strolled off the cricket pitch after scoring a century. Rather self-consciously, Verity took off her coat and sat herself down, noticing that David made no effort to stand up and greet her, like a gentleman. Max did not like David and growled before Verity hushed him and put him under the table. She was not quite certain if animals were allowed in a Lyons Corner House. 'Yes, madam?' said one of the Nippies, stopping for a moment beside their table.

'Oh, just a cup of tea, please,' she said, looking up at the girl, prim in her black uniform and smart little hat.

David looked at her sleepily. 'You're late,' he said. 'I suppose you have been with that boneless wonder, Corinth.'

'I have as a matter of fact,' said Verity defensively. 'And Lord Weaver.'

'That's interesting,' he said, sitting up in his chair. 'What did he want?'

'He offered me a job but I refused.'

'You little fool,' he exclaimed. 'You had the opportunity of penetrating that organization and you threw it away!'

One of the reasons David so fascinated Verity was that he was always shocking her. She presumed he regarded himself as entirely logical but just as she was congratulating herself on at last understanding how his mind worked, she discovered she had got him entirely wrong.

'Yes, I did. I've got principles, you know, David. I don't know how you could expect me to work for a rag like the *New Gazette*. Anyway, what do you mean, "penetrate"? I'm not a spy.'

269

'Look,' he said, as angry as she had ever seen him, 'you are of value to the Party only in so far as your social background and upbringing allow you to mix with people like Corinth and Weaver. The Party needs to know what is happening in the enemy's camp. In war, information is more valuable than a regiment of soldiers. You must see that, surely!'

'What do you mean, "war"?' said Verity. At that moment the waitress arrived with her tea so David had to keep silent. When the girl had gone he spoke more calmly, as if he now held himself in check.

'Verity, you have to understand that we *are* at war. In a year or five years or ten years we will be fighting with guns but for the moment this is an undeclared war, though none the less deadly for that. Fascism is the extreme and inevitable consequence of unbridled capitalism. History tells us that the time is approaching when world revolution will overturn capitalism, but the revolution will demand sacrifice and the Party, which is the tool of revolution, demands total commitment, total loyalty and total obedience. You do what you are told to do and it is not your job to question your instructions. Do you understand me?'

Verity was white with fury. Who was this man who hissed threats of violence at her? He was certainly not the David who had been her lover—who had stroked and caressed her and made her limp with longing for him. While he had been away he had changed, or someone had changed him.

'Was this what they taught you in Moscow?' she said suddenly, knowing the moment she uttered the

270

words she had hit on the truth.

David looked at her for a long moment and then his expression relaxed and he smiled. 'I'm sorry, Verity,' he said. 'I've been under rather a lot of strain recently. I shouldn't have said what I did.'

'No,' said Verity coldly, 'I'm glad you did. I understand what you want of me, David, but I don't think I can be what you say the Party says I should be. It's not in my nature. I shall think of myself as a loyal member of the Party still but don't ask me to spy on my friends for you.'

'No, of course not,' he said, backing down. 'I didn't mean that. I wanted to meet to ask you how you got on at the German embassy.'

'Oh, all right, I think. Friedberg seemed to like me but then he doesn't know that I am a Communist. I have a nasty feeling though that some of his henchmen do. There was a Major Stille there who looked straight through me.'

'Stille, eh?' said David and he seemed to be reaching back in his memory to identify him. 'What did he look like?'

'He was about thirty, I should imagine, spoke very good English—oh, and he had one of those duelling scars like the officers used to get at their military academies, or that was what I was told. He had blue eyes but black hair: I remember that well because it was so strange and because he stared at me so hard.'

'Good, that's very good, Verity,' he said, and she was pleased that he was pleased, but thinking of Stille made her shiver.

'I don't want ever to go back there, David,' she said, putting her hand on his.

'No, there is no need. They will know who you

are by now so you wouldn't be admitted anyway. Verity, I think I should warn you to be a bit careful.'

'How do you mean?' she said, withdrawing her hand.

'Oh, I don't mean they would hurt you or anything but they will be annoyed that you made a fool of them. Don't open your door unless you are expecting someone—that sort of thing. At least you have Max,' he said smiling. The little dog, hearing his name, growled softly. Changing the subject, he inquired, 'And have you found out who killed the General yet?'

'No, not yet but . . .' She was going to say, 'but Friedberg says it was Bishop Haycraft,' but decided not to confide in him. He wasn't her lover, he wasn't even her friend now. He was a stranger and a stranger who frightened her. David had told her that information was power so she would keep this information to herself, at least for the time being.

'But what?' he said. 'How much do you know about Craig? My hunch is that if you want to know who killed the man you ought to look back at his life—women, enemies, that sort of thing—though why anyone should care who killed him I cannot think. Every day hundreds of good men are killed—killed by people like him.'

'Oh, don't exaggerate, David.'

'I'm not exaggerating. I don't mean killed here in England—not yet, at least—but in Europe, in Germany in particular, quite innocent people are being killed every day. But then, they are foreigners so I suppose it doesn't matter.'

'Don't sneer at me, David. I expect innocent people are being killed in Russia too, am I right?'

'I don't think so,' he replied, oddly subdued by her question.

'But you should know. Isn't that where you have been?'

'I have, yes, and it is wonderful there, you have no idea, Verity.' His eyes shone and Verity thought, David, what has happened to you, but she said only, 'I have to go now.'

'Yes', he said, looking at his watch, 'so do I. See you about, Verity.'

'I expect so,' she said and put some coins on the table. 'Come on, Max,' she said, waking the dog who had a knack of falling asleep whenever his mistress informed him she wanted him to stay quiet. Max growled gently at David and Verity smiled. She kissed him on the cheek and they parted, he quite unconscious of the looks of admiration he attracted as he strode out into the busy street.

CHAPTER FOURTEEN

WEDNESDAY EVENING

When Verity got back to the flat she felt exhausted, as though she had been grappling with a monster— a sea monster, she thought, with innumerable legs and no discernible face. She longed to see somebody normal, somebody clean who was not hiding some secret loyalty, so she telephoned Edward. It would be comforting, she thought, to hear his nasal voice with its glassy, upper-class accent, so confident and reassuring. Fenton

273

answered the telephone and informed her, disapprovingly, that his master had just gone out.

'Where's he gone?' she asked innocently.

There was a pause and then Fenton said, 'I'm afraid I am not at liberty to say, miss.'

Verity was put out. She had clearly got on Fenton's wrong side and he was now determined to keep her at bay. He no doubt considered she was a bad influence and impertinent to boot.

'Please, Fenton, I need to talk to Lord Edward urgently.'

Fenton was again silent, perhaps remembering an earlier instruction from his master to give Verity Browne every assistance. 'He told me, miss, that he was taking Miss Pageant out to dinner and then accompanying her to the Cocoanut Grove where, I understand, she performs.'

Verity was knocked sideways. When had he made this rendezvous and why had he kept it from her? 'Oh yes, of course, I had forgotten, he did tell me,' she managed to say. Was Edward as devious as David? What a fool she was to believe in any man's veracity. She felt as if she was going to be sick. Was she jealous? Of course not! You couldn't be jealous of someone who meant nothing to you even if they did prove to be dishonest. Why was Edward taking Amy Pageant out to dinner and going on to the club with her? Well, she could guess why: because he admired her. She knew that already. But why tonight? He had not invited Amy when they had met her with her stepfather that afternoon, or had he? Damn it! Damn him!

'Do you know where they are dining, Fenton?'

'No, miss,' he said firmly, making it plain that he had divulged as much information as he thought

274

she deserved.

'Thank you, Fenton. Will you tell Lord Edward I rang?'

'Certainly, miss, I am glad to be have been of service. Good evening, miss.'

*   *   *

It was doubtless fortunate that Verity could not see how well Amy and Edward got on. No girl enjoys seeing a man she has come to consider a partner— a business partner or at least a partner in crime— drool all over the daughter of one of the chief suspects. Where Verity was down to earth, pushy, bubbling with ideas and determined to untangle any knot which might be puzzling her, Amy was soft, soothing and deliciously vulnerable. In reality she was tough, intelligent and highly ambitious. She liked Edward but, more to the point, she thought he might be useful in furthering her career. She knew she was good and had no intention of remaining a night-club singer for very much longer. Even when speaking, her voice had a husky, almost masculine timbre which Edward found fascinating, and when she looked at him with her large, brown eyes he found her irresistible. Amy was rather short-sighted but refused to wear spectacles so she liked to get close to the person to whom she was talking to see the expression on their face. The intimacy this engendered, even in the highly respectable surroundings of the Savoy Hotel, was beginning to have its effect on Edward. By the time she had told him of her lonely childhood with her maiden aunts in Corner Brook and how it felt to be deprived of a mother and abandoned by a father, he was close to declaring his undying love but, fortunately or not, before he made any rash declarations, Amy glanced at her watch and gave a scream. She was due on stage in twenty minutes. They rushed out of the hotel, Edward scattering largesse to waiters, captured a taxi from a fat gentleman almost apoplectic with good food and bad temper, and arrived at the Cocoanut Grove with just minutes to spare.

Edward, seated at a small table with a bottle of champagne open in front of him, marvelled that when Amy appeared on the tiny stage she seemed as relaxed and unflurried as if she had been waiting in her dressing-room—if that was what the tiny damp room she changed in could be called—for half an hour exercising her vocal chords instead of feeding him lobster on the end of her fork at the Savoy. He was swept away by the colour in her voice, the naked sexuality as she sang of love and treachery, parting and pain. The club was almost full—perhaps because news of Amy's talent was spreading or perhaps because rumours of the police investigation had given the Cocoanut Grove a spurious glamour—but Amy silenced the chatter and stilled the clink of glasses as she poured forth her emotion like strong, black, liquid chocolate. Verity would have been nauseated to see the effect on Edward, but even she would hardly have been able to deny that one day soon Amy Pageant was going to be a star.

Ten minutes into Amy's set, Edward was annoyed to feel someone at his shoulder demanding attention. He was just about to tell whoever it was to go to hell when he saw in the darkness the face of Captain Gordon, the dapper host of the Cocoanut Grove whom Inspector Pride was so anxious to interview. Edward slipped out of his seat and accompanied Gordon to the little office behind the dance room. In the brutal neon light Edward was shocked to see that he was a shadow of the supercilious man-about-town who had insulted him just over a week before when Hermione had run off with Charlie Lomax. White-faced, red-eyed, his hair no longer oiled to his head but ruffled and dirty, he was clearly a man on the run. He was frightened—Edward could almost smell the fear filtered through sweat, and stale cigarettes.

'Please forgive me, Lord Edward,' the man began—he seemed to be shivering with fear or at least anticipation. 'I was hoping to see you. I tried to get to see you at your rooms but they said you were not there.'

'For God's sake, man, what's the matter? What's happened? Here, have a cigarette.'

Edward proffered Gordon his cigarette case but the man's hands were shaking too much to open it. 'Here, let me,' said Edward, opening the gold case. He extracted two De Reszke Virginians and lit one for the Captain and one for himself. Gordon took a long drag and it seemed to help him. He was wearing what might once have been evening-dress but by now he had no jacket or tie and the shirt was grubby and stained with what looked like blood. He had a gash on his cheek as if he had cut himself or been cut, which possibly accounted for the blood on his shirt.

'Calm down, Gordon,' said Edward and the authority in his voice seemed to have a steadying effect on the bedraggled figure before him. 'Sit

277

down and tell me all about it. Is it the police you are afraid of? Much better make a clean breast of it.'

Gordon slumped into the manager's chair where for so many months he had dispensed threats and favours and Edward leaned against a filing cabinet, studying the man who sat in front of him smoking furiously.

'So tell me, is it the police you are running from?' Edward repeated at last. 'You're a bloody fool if you think they won't catch up with you in the end.'

'God no,' said Gordon, 'not the police. It's them . . .' His voice shook.

'Who's "them"?'

'They call themselves Triads—ever heard of them?'

'I don't think so.'

'They are Chinese gangsters—Hong Kong, really. They have been in London now for a year or more and they are engaged in trying to take over the dope trade.'

'Is that very profitable?' said Edward naïvely.

For a moment Gordon was his old contemptuous self again. 'For Christ's sake, Corinth, what are you—some sort of idiot? Profitable! The dope trade in London alone is worth several million pounds a year. People are looking for kicks that alcohol just can't provide. Heroin and cocaine are very fashionable and very expensive. I used to think it was ironic that this place was called the Cocoanut Grove, see?'

'So what happens then?' said Edward. 'How does the dope get distributed? Through places like this?'

'Yes, and through people like me, of course. The stuff comes into Liverpool on boats from the Far East but the Chinese need "respectable" people like me to get it around. Charlie Lomax was one of my runners.'

'Runners?' queried Edward.

'There are a lot of young men in so-called society who have to live expensively on nothing at all. I don't suppose,' he sneered, 'you can imagine what it means not to have a five pound note in the world and be expected to escort some neighing girl to a dance in Belgrave Square.'

'Why do it then?'

'Because that's all he knows—for God's sake, I'm not Sigmund Freud. What do I care? All I need to know is that Lomax and his like take dope into the heart of "society". Christ! If the old dowagers knew what a sewer their tittle girls were swimming in—the sharks and the rats biting at their little angels' heels . . . Anyway,' and his anger seemed to leave him, 'that's what happens.'

'But something went wrong, presumably?'

'Yes, that bloody idiot Lomax got hooked on the stuff himself. Instead of selling it, he was using it and you just can't get away with that.'

'So who killed him and almost killed Hermione Weaver?'

'Yes, that was bad,' said Gordon, lowering his head on to his chest. 'I had to give them the information—they forced me . . .' Gordon shuddered as though he was reliving an experience he wanted very much to forget. 'I had to tell them why I was short of what I owed.'

'The Triads?'

'Yes.'

'They went off after Lomax?'

'I guess so—yes, Lomax was a marked man.'

'And Hermione Weaver?'

'I suppose she was there when they came to call. Maybe they thought she was his girlfriend—I don't know. Anyway, they wouldn't have wanted to leave witnesses.'

'Why didn't you go to the police?'

'Are you mad? They'd have killed me straight off.'

'The police would have given you protection.'

'For Christ's sake, Corinth! Haven't you been listening? These men are not like us. They don't let things like "police protection" stand in their way if they want to kill someone. They laugh at the police. Bobbies on the beat with no guns! They think it's hysterical.'

'So why did you go on the run?'

'Well, however hard I tried to say I had told the police nothing they didn't believe me and they wanted their money. Then one of their thugs came after me. I saw him, thank God, just before I went into my flat, so I fled. I made an old girlfriend take me in, but yesterday I thought I saw . . .' He shuddered. 'I thought I saw his oriental face when I peered out of the window so today I have been running around London waiting till it was dark.'

'Has Lord Weaver got anything to do with this?' said Edward sharply.

'The dope? No, I don't think so. It's private enterprise, don't you know,' he said, curling his lips into what might have been a smile.

'But why did you think I would be here tonight?'

'If you hadn't been here I would have tried again at those rooms of yours, but I was afraid they

280

wouldn't let me in—looking like this, I mean.' He gestured with his hand and Edward had to agree that the Albany porters would have been highly suspicious.

'But I still don't understand what you think I can do,' Edward said.

'I want you to take me to the police and convince them I'm not making all this up about the Triads and how dangerous they are.'

'I really don't know if I believe you myself,' said Edward thinly. 'I mean, it all sounds so melodramatic.'

'Oh God, I thought I could convince you.' He suddenly slumped back in his seat as if he were ready to give up.

'Look here, Gordon, brace up. I don't doubt that you are genuinely at the end of your tether. I can see too that you are badly frightened. You've got yourself in one hell of a hole but I think you are rather exaggerating what these Triad people can do.'

'Oh Christ, Corinth. You've got to believe me. These aren't your normal East End gangsters. I've dealt with them before. These are . . . animals. I went through the war, Corinth, and I tell you I was never once as scared in the trenches as I am now.'

'See here,' said Edward, suddenly decisive, 'I'll ring Inspector Pride now and say we are going round to the Yard. Can you get that fat boy of yours at the door to get us a cab while I make the call?'

'Yes, and thanks, old man, I mean it: thanks a lot.'

Edward rang Pride, who was not at the Yard but at home in bed. Edward had a job getting the sergeant on duty to wake him up and he had to come over very aristocratic to make the man brave Inspector Pride's justifiable wrath at being bothered so late at night—it was after eleven. He heard the sergeant on the other line obviously being abused by the Inspector before Pride was made to understand that Lord Edward Corinth wanted to convey into his hands the elusive Captain Gordon. The sergeant, when he had put down the telephone, came back to Edward to tell him that Inspector Pride would meet him at Scotland Yard in forty-five minutes—the time it would take him to dress and drive over from leafy Wimbledon where he lived in suburban comfort. When Edward had put down the telephone receiver he went to look for Gordon, who had gone upstairs to see about the taxi, and bumped into Amy.

'I saw you leave the table and I guessed something had happened,' she said breathlessly.

'Don't worry,' he reassured her. 'Captain Cordon is here and he wants me to go with him to Scotland Yard. By the way, he says there are some very nasty people in this dope business and even though you are not involved, someone may have seen you with me. So please, I want you to be very careful. In fact it might be better if you came with me to Scotland Yard, and then we can decide if it is safe for you to be at home by yourself. If we are to believe the good Captain there are some violent Chinese gentlemen creating mayhem around here and I don't want to get you mixed up in it.'

Edward's big fear was that she already was mixed up in it by association with the Cocoanut Grove but he didn't want to frighten her. By this

282

time they had reached the door of the club. It was a warm night and the sky was very clear. It was getting on for midnight—the city was silent except for the occasional squawk of a taxi in Regent Street. The noise of the traffic had eased. There was no sign of Caspar, the club 'bouncer', but Gordon was waving down a taxi. The cab, which had begun to slow, suddenly picked up speed. Gordon stood in the middle of the street like a rabbit hypnotized by the cab's headlights. Edward, with a cry of alarm, sprinted toward him, a black, stationary figure outlined in the yellow glow of the headlamps. He launched himself at the man and the two of them rolled into the gutter. The cab swept past them, its mudguard grazing Edward's shins. Captain Gordon's story had been substantiated in the most convincing way. At least this time, Edward thought as he hugged the man to him like a mother with her baby, I have been able to prevent a death.

As he gathered his wits he heard a very shaken Amy Pageant saying, 'For God's sake, Edward. Are you all right?' Then she was there helping him to his feet. Before turning to see to Gordon, who still lay where he had fallen, he gathered her into his arms and kissed her, her scent filling him with a determination never to release her.

CHAPTER FIFTEEN

THURSDAY MORNING

Verity telephoned Edward at a frighteningly early hour to berate him for going off to the Cocoanut Grove the previous evening without her. She would have liked to accuse him of . . . of something . . . she wasn't sure what exactly, for taking Amy out to dinner but, on reflection, she did not think she dared tell him whom he could and could not entertain. When she heard how he had been knocked down and almost killed by a taxi and ended up in a peculiarly noisome gutter, her wrath left her and she felt positively cheerful. Despite Edward begging her to leave him alone to lick his wounds, she jumped in a taxi and came straight round to his rooms. Fenton's haughty demeanour as he opened the door of the apartment to Verity showed what he thought of his master permitting an unmarried girl to minister to his hurts while he was still in his dressing-gown and silk pyjamas.

'Very nice,' said Verity, giving his nightwear a steady stare. She poked him in the ribs and he groaned noisily. 'That will teach you to "pursue your inquiries" without a chaperone,' she said, smugly.

Edward groaned again even more piteously. He was a mass of bruises and he wanted to be cherished, not told his discomfort was all his own fault. In fact, he thought Verity might congratulate him or at least commiserate with him but she seemed intent on riling him. He had no idea why.

However, by the time Fenton appeared with his breakfast on a silver tray he was beginning to feel less like tenderized steak and was able to talk.

'You can imagine what Inspector Pride said when I presented myself at Scotland Yard looking as if I had been in a particularly nasty brawl—and Captain Gordon was, if anything, looking rather worse. Here, do you want to see my bruises?'

'No, thank you,' said Verity with a theatrical shudder, 'it might put me off your breakfast.' She buttered a piece of toast from the plate on his tray and drowned it in Oxford marmalade. 'It must be so nice to be cared for by someone like Fenton who will bring you china tea and soft-boiled eggs in bed.' She sighed theatrically. 'Why can't women have valets?'

'Ladies may have ladies' maids, I suppose,' Edward replied, seizing his cup of coffee before Verity could drink it.

'Am I a lady?' Verity mused. 'I wonder . . . I've gone to a great deal of trouble to turn myself into a woman comrade but I may have failed. I shall ask Fenton.'

'No, please don't,' said Edward hastily.

'But seriously, how could you go off detecting without me—or was it just spooning over Amy? I expect it was, dash it. Fenton was very evasive when I gave him the third degree yesterday. Anyway, what did you discover?'

'Ah, well, nothing, I suppose . . . nothing we did not know before, I mean.'

'You spent the evening "meditating on the very great pleasure which a pair of fine eyes in the face of a pretty woman can bestow",' said Verity, who had read *Pride and Prejudice* at school and had immediately identified with Elizabeth Bennet.

Edward blushed. 'Ah, I see Lord Edward "is not to be laughed at",' Verity added, getting up from her perch on the bed and going over to the window. She wished she did not feel interested in Amy Pageant.

'Gordon was in a pretty bad way when we got him to the Yard,' Edward repeated, hoping thereby to draw attention to his life-saving activities and choosing to ignore Verity's jibes.

'I don't feel sorry for Gordon,' said Verity scornfully. 'Why feel sorry for a dope-pedlar?'

'Oh, I don't know,' said Edward weakly. 'I just feel he may have been put in a difficult position, that's all.'

'For pity's sake, stop being saintlike and wish someone ill for once,' said Verity crossly. All this feeling sorry for people who ought to be in gaol is getting on my nerves. The inquest is tomorrow, isn't it?'

'General Craig's? Yes, tomorrow. I don't know when the inquest will be on Larmore—or Lomax for that matter. Never having attended an inquest in my life, it seems my diary is now to have "inquest" written on every page. Perhaps I won't have to appear at Larmore's. Pride couldn't tell me. I did say though that I would talk to Celia Larmore. Pride seemed to think I ought.'

'Well,' said Verity, 'we've still got a few more hours to try and come up with something.'

'Prove he was murdered, you mean? I think it's all too late. We've talked to everyone who might have killed him and it's hardly surprising that none of them confessed.'

'No, but two of them said the Bishop did it,' said

286

Verity triumphantly, taking the last slice of toast off Edward's plate and covering it thickly with butter.

'Yes,' agreed Edward, 'but I don't seriously think that a bishop of the Church of England would murder a distinguished general at a duke's dinner-party.'

'Well, someone did,' said Verity stubbornly, spearing a slice of peach with a fork.

'Sorry,' said Edward. 'I thought you said you didn't want any breakfast.'

'I don't,' said Verity, grinning as well as she could with her mouth full. 'There is one thing though—actually, it was David who suggested it.' Edward's face fell. 'He said that if Craig was murdered, the reason probably lay in his past.'

'I think David is right,' Edward admitted. 'I have been thinking along the same lines. I suggest, as soon as you have finished my breakfast,' and he looked meaningfully at Verity as she shoved the last of the peach into her surprisingly large mouth, 'we toddle along and have a word with Jeffries.'

'General Craig's valet?'

'Yes, as far as I know he is still staying at the General's house. He's going to go and live with his mother in Brighton or somewhere but I am sure he would not go before the funeral.'

'Who's organizing all that side of things?'

'There's this distant cousin—a lawyer, I think.' He read Verity's mind. 'He's the General's only living relative and will inherit what there is to inherit but he hardly knew the General and wasn't at the dinner so he's not a suspect, at least I don't see how he can be.'

'No, you are right, of course,' said Verity, looking round his breakfast tray to make sure she

287

had not missed anything.

'Still, I think we should speak to Jeffries. He's rather a depressed-looking cove, don't you know, but no fool. We probably ought to have thought of him before.'

'Will it be all right for me to come?' said Verity, unusually meekly. 'I don't seem to make a very good impression on valets. The Communist comes out in me, I am afraid.'

'What? Oh, you mean Fenton! Don't worry about him. His bark's worse than his whatnot. He'll love you one day.'

'If I live so long,' muttered Verity to herself.

'Of course you must come, and we won't telephone and make an appointment either. Let's take him unawares, "sleeping in his orchard".'

'What orchard?' said Verity, who had not taken to Shakespeare with the same enthusiasm she had for Miss Austen.

In the taxi to Cadogan Square Edward said, a little shyly, 'Will you come down with me tonight and stay at the castle? The inquest is at ten so it would be a bit of rush if you were going to come down by train in the morning.'

'Oh, that's very sweet of you,' said Verity, genuinely touched, 'but I don't think I could. After . . . well, you know . . . getting into your brother's house under false pretences and then writing that piece in the *Daily Worker* . . . I just couldn't.'

'No, I mean it. I've talked it over with Connie on the telephone and she insists. I won't pretend Gerald looks on you as his favourite person but he's not a fool and Connie says he realizes that you only did what any journalist would have done. You made no promises and therefore broke none.'

288

Verity was about to butt in but he raised his hand. 'Before you say anything else I think it might be important that you are there for another reason. Bishop Haycraft and Lord Weaver are also going to make statements at the inquest and they are staying at the castle tonight. I thought it might be our last chance of straightening things out.'

Verity was pleased that Edward should have included her in the 'we' who were going to get things 'straightened out' so on impulse she leant across and kissed him on the cheek. 'If you think it's all right, then I will be glad to come,' she said. 'It's just the Bishop and Weaver—no one else?'

'No. Obviously Mrs Larmore is not coming, and I believe Blanche is probably going to stay with Hermione. Apparently she is not at all well. Haycraft is leaving his wife behind, quite sensibly. I'm afraid the inquest is going to be a grisly if brief affair. There will be lots of you around, I expect.'

Verity was puzzled for a moment as to what he meant, then she understood: 'Oh, journalists?'

'Yes, vultures at the feast.'

'But why do you say it will be brief—the inquest?'

'Well, unless we come up with something very dramatic the verdict will be accidental death.'

'I see, and you don't think we will come up with anything dramatic?'

'I doubt it and, of course, you might argue that it is kinder to the General just to leave it at that. After all, if we were to prove he was murdered, what would it achieve? Nastiness all round and the General would be remembered not for what he did but for how he died.'

Verity, remembering her Commnnist principles,

wanted to say she did not feel a warmongering imperialist had much to be proud of anyway, but the words stuck in her gullet. It seemed wrong, whatever David might say, to besmirch the old man's memory.

'You don't mean that?' she said instead. 'Of course we must see justice done if we can. Everyone deserves justice even if most people don't get it.'

' "Revenge his foul and most unnatural murder"?'

'You are quoting again,' Verity accused him.

'Sorry! You started it. I don't know why but Hamlet has been rather on my mind.' He stroked his chin and repeated, 'Don't know why.'

At that moment the cab drew up outside 22 Cadogan Square and they got out. Edward paid the driver and then rang the bell. Nothing happened so he rang the bell again. He was just about to hammer on the door, thinking that the electric bell might not be working, when he heard a shuffling sound followed by a pulling of bolts. Then Jeffries' head appeared round the door.

'Lord Edward!' exclaimed the man, opening the door wider. 'I thought it might be newspaper people,' he said gloomily. 'They have tried everything to get in, even offered me money. As if I would ever . . .' He paused. 'And you, miss, are . . . ?'

'Oh, I am sorry, Jeffries, how rude of me. This is Miss Verity Browne. She was there when the General died. I don't know whether you saw her then?'

They were still standing on the doorstep and it looked as though that was where they would remain unless Edward produced something to persuade the suspicious old retainer that they were allies not the enemy. 'Excuse me, miss,' Jeffries went on, 'but weren't it you who wrote about the General's death in the . . . in the *Daily Worker*?'

It had taken Jeffries some moments to remember that journal's name and Verity got the feeling that the *Daily Worker* was not often seen in Cadogan Square. Why was it, she wondered, that gentlemen's personal gentlemen, as she had heard Edward describe valets, were so unwilling to throw off their chains and join the revolution? Could David and all the rest of them be wrong, and were the working classes satisfied with their lot? If so it was a poor outlook for the revolution. The Communist Party couldn't be solely a middle-class movement. If anything was to be achieved, the Party had to capture the hearts and minds of the workers, and the workers Verity had met recently did not seem likely to rise and cut their masters' throats or cry '*A la lanterne* as the tumbrels rolled by.

'Yes, Jeffries,' said Edward firmly, 'but Miss Browne is a friend of mine and you can trust her absolutely.'

Verity was gratified. Edward continued: 'She and I believe that the General may not have died by his own hand, as it is said. I mean—he did die by his own hand but he did not intend to do so.'

Still casting suspicious glances at Verity, Jeffries opened the door and she and Edward stepped into the narrow, gloomy little hall. It was odd, Edward thought, for such a handsome house to be so dark. Then he saw that it was a house in mourning: every shutter was closed, every curtain drawn to block out the sunlight. The occasional shaft of light which penetrated the gloom made rainbows on spiders' webs. Verity shivered and wondered whimsically if they would bump into Miss Havisham on their way to the pantry in the basement. The basement was clearly Jeffries' domain, his home, and hadn't the musty smell which pervaded the rest of the house. There was even a window unshuttered through which a weak and watery light shone. They were at the front of the house below street level and Jeffries' view of the world outside was the small 'area' with steep stone steps leading up to the street.

The melancholy manservant offered his guests no refreshment and brought out no chairs, so they perched against the knife cupboard as well as they could. 'We may be quite wrong, Jeffries, but it is our belief that the General did not die accidentally. We wondered if you had any thoughts about it?'

'How do you mean, my lord?' said Jeffries unhelpfully.

'Well, for instance, is it true he carried a cyanide pill around with him?' Edward ploughed on.

'Yes, sir, I told Inspector Pride he did.'

'Was it a pill he had from during the war?' Edward asked.

'Yes, my lord,' said Jeffries in mild surprise. 'How did you know that?'

'I have read that some officers carried cyanide in case they were captured and did not want to undergo questioning.'

'Yes, my lord, that was it. The General used to joke about it sometimes.'

'Joke about it? How, man?'

'He used to say he was afraid of nothing and that death had no dominion over him. I am not sure what he meant exactly, my lord, but especially when his wife died—God rest her soul—and later when he became very ill, I think it gave him comfort to know he could end it all.'

'But suicide—didn't he consider that cowardice?' said Edward unwisely.

'General Craig was the bravest man I ever knew, my lord,' said Jeffries indignantly.

'I don't doubt it,' Edward said.

'But you don't understand. No one can who did not know him like I knew him.' The little man screwed up his eyes and Edward saw that he was remembering something. 'I was his servant during the war, his batman. Once, about seven o'clock in the evening but very dark, we were in his car near the front line inspecting the battalion before an attack. I should tell you, he wasn't one of those generals who never came near his men—not at all. I was driving. He was asleep in the back—he had been awake for two days and two nights but he had a knack of being able to catnap whenever he could. He used to say to me, "Jeffries—Napoleon, Wellington, all the great generals, they had the knack of sleeping when and where they could, even in the midst of battle if need be. I'm not saying I'm any sort of Napoleon but at least I have that in common with those great soldiers."

'Anyhow, on this occasion, with the guns pounding away on all sides and the flashes—well, I have no very good sense of direction at the best of times—I turned right instead of left and we suddenly found ourselves in the middle of soldiers speaking a foreign language. I thought at first they might be French because they were holding the next part of the line but then I realized they were talking German. I can't speak German, you understand, but I could recognize it. I stopped the car and very gently woke up the General and told him what had happened. He was wonderful, sir.' Jeffries' eyes were shining as he remembered those far-away events as if they were yesterday. 'We started to turn the motor car around but we were challenged. Cool as a cucumber the General pretended he was a German officer. In the dark they could not see his uniform and it was too dangerous for anyone to shine a torch. He made the soldiers help turn the car around—it was a very narrow path we had come along and they had to manhandle the old girl. Then, just as we had thanked them and I was starting the engine, a flare lit up the sky and the soldiers saw who we were. "Drive like hell, Jeffries," he said and I did. When we got back to our lines we found that the General had taken a bullet in his shoulder but he never made a sound, just said, "Good work, Jeffries, but next time wake me if you don't know the way!"'

Jeffries seemed exhausted after telling his story and slumped in the wooden armchair which was the room's only seat. 'He was not a coward, my lord,' he mumbled.

'No, of course not. I never meant to suggest it. I just meant that I cannot believe a man like the one you describe would have killed himself.'

'Maybe not, my lord, maybe not, but,' said the man, shrugging his shoulders, 'he was very weary of this world. He thought it had all gone to the dogs. He thought there was going to be another war and that all he had been through had gone for nothing.'

'He hated Germans?'

'He did, sir, he hated the Hun as he would call

294

them—the Hun or the Boche—never Germans, he would never say Germans. I asked him once how he spoke such good Boche and he said he had been at a university over there as a very young man. Would it be Heidelberg, my lord? I think that was what he said.'

'Yes, Heidelberg.' Edward thought for a moment and then asked, 'Did he have any special enemies?'

'No, my lord,' said Jeffries firmly.

'No one, no one at all? No German for instance?' Edward pressed.

'Not that I know of, my lord. He did not like a lot of people—people he read about in the newspapers—but as far as I know he had no special enemies.'

Verity, who had been silent up to now, said, 'Jeffries, forgive me for seeming to pry, but how did the General's wife—Dolly, was that her name? How did she die? It must have hit him very hard.'

Jeffries looked at Verity suspiciously but seemed reassured by what he saw. 'Lady Dorothy, that was what I called her, miss. "Lady Craig" I suppose I should have said. She was a wonderful woman. There cannot have been another woman in the world who would have made the General happy. If you see what I mean, miss, he was a man's man. He had no truck with women as a rule. He hated chatter, hated dinner-parties. I was surprised when he told me he was going to that one, in fact. He said, "Jeffries, I've got to do my duty and that's why I'm going. To tell you true I would rather I was charging the fuzzies on board old Diamond"—that was his horse when he was out in the desert with Lord Kitchener, my lord, long before my time, of course. "I'd rather be in a cavalry charge than go,

295

my friend," he called me that sometimes,' said the valet proudly, ' "but I've got something I must do before I die." '

'What was that, do you think?' said Edward sharply. Somehow he felt that here might be the key to the whole mystery.

'I don't know, my lord,' said Jeffries disappointingly.

'But you were going to tell us how Lady Craig died,' Verity persisted.

'Yes, miss, that was very sad.' Jeffries shook his head gloomily. 'I think she had been ill for some months before either the General or I noticed anything was wrong. You know how it is, sir,' he said, looking at Edward as though asking for forgiveness, 'when you see someone every day you don't notice things. I thought she was looking thin and tired but I thought that was because she was worrying about the General. You see, I knew he had already been to the doctor, and though he wouldn't tell me what the doctor had said, from things I overheard him say to Lady Dorothy, I think the doctor must have told him then he had the cancer.'

'When was that?' asked Verity.

'That was about two years ago.'

'And Lady Craig died a year ago?'

'A year ago, miss. She collapsed one day on the stairs and I ran for the doctor while the General stayed beside her. When the doctor came he looked solemn and between us we got her into bed. He told the General that she needed an operation immediately.'

'That must have been a terrible shock for the General.'

'It was, miss. He almost went out of his mind. He blamed himself, you see. He thought that he should have seen *she* was ill but he had been too bound up with his own illness to see anything. Anyway, my lord, she had an operation that very week and died on the operating table. That was when I feared my poor master might kill himself, but then he heard something or saw something which made him change his mind although he was certainly never the same again.'

'Have you any idea what he saw or heard?' inquired Edward gently.

'No, my lord.'

'It wasn't the invitation to have dinner at Mersham Castle?'

'Oh no, my lord, it was long before that. I think it might have been something the doctor said to him after his wife died, but I am not sure why I think so except that, apart from the doctor, he hardly saw anyone at all.'

'I see. Well, thank you, Jeffries, you have been most helpful. I promise you if we discover that the General died because . . . because of someone else, we will tell you. Are you coming to the inquest?'

'Yes, my lord, Inspector pride has given me a train ticket.'

'Well then, we'll see you there. Oh, by the way, a last question: could the General have got confused and taken the cyanide pill by mistake for one of his painkillers?'

'No, my lord,' said Jeffries stoutly, 'he could not. The pills he took for his pain were small whitey-brown things he kept in a silver box in his pocket.'

'The cyanide capsule—did you ever see that?'

'Yes, sir. He showed it to me once, my lord,

when we were talking about the war, and I saw it after.'

'And that was different?'

'Yes, my lord, quite different. It wasn't round— more like a lozenge and made of a sort of glass, only not quite glass, to break between the teeth, he told me. Also it was much larger than his other pills.'

'And he kept the cyanide pill where?'

'He used to keep it in an envelope in the safe, I believe, my lord, but since Lady Dorothy died he carried it in his fob—the pocket in his waistcoat where in the old days he kept his watch on the end of his chain.'

'It couldn't have fallen out into his drink by accident?'

'No, my lord.'

'You are very sure.'

'I am sure, my lord.'

'But it's odd, isn't it, that he should have taken the trouble to transfer the cyanide pill to the waistcoat pocket of his dress suit? I mean, even if he carried it around for some sort of comfort it gave him to know it was there, it was surely taking things a bit far to take it into dinner with him?'

'I expect he thought it would be dangerous to leave it lying around his room, my lord, in case a curious servant found it and did themselves an injury.'

'Yes, perhaps so,' said Edward soothingly. 'You have been very helpful, Jeffries, and I hope talking about it—the General's death, I mean—hasn't distressed you.'

'No, my lord. To tell you the truth, I spend all the time thinking about the General. I feel my life

298

has ended with his, my lord. Without wishing to sound presumptuous, my lord, I was closer to General Craig than many wives are to their husbands and that is no disrespect to Lady Dorothy, and the world seems an empty place without him.'

Afterwards, when they were walking away from the dark, sad house, Edward said, 'You know, Verity, I'm beginning to think we have got this all wrong. I think we have made an assumption that has made us blind to the truth of the situation.'

'I think I know what you're going to say, Edward,' Verity interjected. 'What if it was General Craig who was out to do murder and by some chance drank the poison he intended for someone else?'

'Only, he would have seen it as his duty—as an execution,' exclaimed Edward, banging his hand into his fist. 'But who of that company would he have wanted to murder?'

'Any of them—most of them—I should think,' said Verity soberly. 'I mean, we know the Bishop was a convinced pacifist. Craig wouldn't have liked that, and we have two eyewitnesses who say they actually saw him pass the old man the port with the poison in it.'

'Yes,' said Edward, 'but don't forget Larmore. Maybe he knew Larmore was selling secrets to the Germans.'

'Von Friedberg, as a representative of all that he hated in the new Germany, would have been an obvious target if he had wanted to have his revenge on his old enemy.'

'Mustn't forget old Gerald,' said Edward firmly. 'Maybe he felt guilty because our older brother,

299

you know, would have been duke if he had not been killed in the early days of the war—fighting under whose direct command? General Craig's, that's whose. And he may have thought Gerald was making it too easy for the Germans. I mean, all these dinner-parties trying to treat the Nazis as though they were reasonable people. That would have upset him.'

Seeing the distress on Edward's face, Verity said hurriedly, 'Weaver has to be the General's most likely victim though. He was about to reveal an unpleasant story about his shooting German prisoners, wasn't he? By the way, why didn't you ask Jeffries about that?'

'Do you know, Verity, I just couldn't bear to. Sounds pathetic, I know, but after what he told us of his admiration—no, that's too weak a word—his hero-worship of the old boy, I couldn't face his unhappiness if we got on to discussing that. Am I mad?'

'No,' said Verity taking his arm, 'not mad, but I don't think you are ruthless enough to make a great detective.'

'No, I suppose not,' Edward agreed glumly. 'I certainly have it at the back of my mind that I forgot to ask Jeffries one vital question. If only I could think what it was, I would go back and ask him now but for the life of me I can't.'

'Hey there, don't look like that. The fact that you aren't ruthless—it makes you a nice man,' she said, pressing his arm against her, 'and I never thought I'd say that about a despised enemy of the working classes.'

He laughed. 'Look,' he said, 'you will stay at the castle tonight, won't you?'

'If you wish it and if you promise to protect me, I will,' said Verity.

'That's splendid! Hey! taxi!' he shouted, walking into the road at risk to life and limb. 'I'll drop you off in Hans Crescent and then I'll go back to the Albany, wire Connie we're coming, and then I'll come back about five with Fenton and the Lagonda and we can be down in time for dinner. Will that suit you?'

'Yes,' agreed Verity, pleased that her saying she would stay at the castle after all had lifted his mood so dramatically. 'There's something I have got to do at lunch time but it won't take long.'

It was only after he had dropped her off at her flat that she realized they still had not reduced the list of suspects. Weaver, Larmore, Friedberg, Haycraft, even the Duke himself had reasons to bump off General Craig, and he had an equal reason for wanting to dispose of any of them. As she held Max in her arms and kissed his furry head she thought, Edward and I are like two dogs chasing each other's tails. There was a scent—the sweet scent of poisoned wine—but to whom did the scent lead? She put these thoughts aside with a sigh. Before she went to Mersham there was the little matter of a trial she had to attend and it was she who was in the dock.

CHAPTER SIXTEEN

THURSDAY AFTERNOON

David Griffiths-Jones grinned at Verity amiably but
the other two—a thin-lipped woman of about fifty
with iron grey hair tied at the back in a bun and a
haggard, depressed-looking man in his thirties, but
with the paper-white skin and dull eyes of someone
much older—looked at her with something close to
malevolence. What did they see, she wondered?
She had made an effort to dress sensibly, like a
good comrade, but she was aware now that she had
failed. She must look irredeemably bourgeois,
which of course was what she was. She wore no
make-up. She had put on a double-breasted brown
tweed coat with a large collar, wide lapels and
padded shoulders which she had bought a year ago
and never worn. When she had selected it to wear
to this 'kangaroo court' she thought the outfit had
an almost military feel but now she was not so sure.
The brown suede shoes were restrained enough
and the brown felt hat was serious but she saw now
that she ought to have resisted the feather. All in
all, she looked less like a soldier of the proletarian
struggle than a county lady who hunted three times
a week and owned several large dogs. Neither
image reflected the reality, as anyone with half an
eye could see. She was, in fact, a pretty, lively girl
blessed with intelligence and a strong sense of the
ridiculous.

'Verity, this is Comrade Lake,' David said,
indicating the thin-lipped woman. Verity smiled but

this was obviously the wrong thing to do: Comrade Lake pursed her lips even more tightly, if that were possible, but otherwise made no sign of being aware of the introduction. 'And this is Comrade Peterson. He has to catch the night train to Glasgow so he doesn't have very much time— indeed, neither do any of us,' he added, seeing Comrade Lake bristle.

'Is this some sort of court?' demanded Verity, suddenly angry. 'I thought, David, that you just wanted to have a talk about my future with the Party.'

'This is not a court, Verity,' said David soothingly, 'but we are a little concerned about your . . . your commitment to the Party. You have been absent from several meetings in the last few days and your participation was required in the Hoxton protest but you were absent. Why was that?'

'I have been busy,' said Verity guiltily. She could see where this line of questioning was leading and she did not like it.

'Busy?' echoed David.

'Yes, you instructed me to infiltrate the German embassy, if you remember.' She was rather pleased with the word 'infiltrate'.

'Don't answer Comrade Griffiths-Jones in that tone of voice,' said the woman, who reminded Verity of the headmistress of one of the four boarding schools she had briefly attended before being asked to leave. 'As a Party worker you must obey the instructions of comrades senior to you in the Party and not absent yourself from Party meetings without permission.'

'You are spending a great deal of time with

303

Edward Corinth, are you not?' said David.

'Yes,' said Verity, 'and before you ask, I do not approve of him and he is not my lover or anything like that. We are trying to discover who murdered General Craig—that is all.'

She could not quite think why but she felt when she said this as though she was not being entirely honest and that made her crosser than ever.

'But why should you wish to know who murdered General Craig, if indeed anyone did? He is of no importance—dead or alive. He was an imperialist warmonger and now he is dead,' demanded Comrade Peterson in a smoker's wheeze.

'There is such a thing as justice,' said Verity unwisely.

'Aye, there is,' said Comrade Peterson. 'These people you have been involved with—what do they understand by justice, these dukes and lords? Do they believe in economic justice?' he said bitterly. 'Do they not believe they have the right to exploit other people for profit? Is that justice, comrade?'

'No,' said Verity, abashed at the man's passion. Comrade Peterson was, she knew instinctively, talking from personal experience of poverty, starvation and despair which she could only guess at. She felt humbled. Maybe they were right; perhaps trying to discover who had killed General Craig was an irrelevance, and yet, surely, once one man's death ceased to be important then no man's death was significant.

David said, 'You see, comrade, the people you are mixing with are charming, even well meaning, and that is what makes them so dangerous. They are born to be enemies of the working class. It is important that you go among these people, as you must do, as their enemy. Your one reason for being with Lord Edward Corinth and his kind is to defeat them. Do you understand?'

Without waiting for an answer, he continued: 'I don't suppose for one moment that the Duke of Mersham is other than a kindly old fellow who would be distraught if he thought one child was hungry on his account, but the fact is, the wealth of this country—you must have heard your father say this often enough—is owned by a tiny percentage of the population and it is this wealth we in the Party are determined to redistribute. That is what we mean by justice. To put it crudely: the stock exchange must be pulled down and the country houses must be turned into holiday camps for the children of the working class.'

He held up his hand to stop her speaking. 'The greatest danger is that these good-natured drones—men like your friend Lord Edward Corinth, who have no social purpose—these people are giving the Fascists the power and confidence to delay our victory. Men like your duke are not bad in themselves but they are self-deceived; they think they can negotiate with the Fascists, talk to them as though they were reasonable people, but they are not. That, at least, is something General Craig understood. Even Weaver—with all his money and his newspapers—may not be totally corrupt but that makes him all the more dangerous. He tries to make deals with Hitler's cronies, men like your friend Baron von Friedberg, and he persuades politicians and the poor fools who read his newspapers that it is possible to talk to these men.'

'He offered you a job, did he not, comrade?' said

305

Comrade Lake, turning from philosophy to the particular.

'Yes,' said Verity, 'but I turned him down.'

'That was foolish of you,' the woman said. 'Why did you not consult Comrade Griffiths-Jones or another comrade before taking that decision?'

'You would have wanted me to work for the bourgeois press?' exclaimed Verity.

'Of course! We must use every means we can to bring about the revolution. The *Daily Worker* is an excellent organ and we are all grateful to your father for supporting it, but we are realists, comrade. The *Daily Worker* reaches Party members and, I regret to say, there are far too few of us. We have to tell the masses what is happening and why they should join us.'

This had been David's line, Verity recalled, and she still found it cynical. 'You want me to tell Lord Weaver I have changed my mind and that I will write for the *New Gazette*?'

'That is correct,' David said. 'Tell him you are going to Spain and you wish to report on the political situation there.'

'But I have no intention of going to Spain!' Verity said.

'Yes, you will accompany me to Madrid and Barcelona on Saturday. I have your ticket. If you let me have your passport I will get the necessary visas. There is much of interest happening in that country and we must do what we can to support the struggle. You will find it educational.'

*   *   *

When Verity left the shabby little room in East

London—the Party headquarters—she was still in a state of shock. She recognized that she had been chastised and brought to heel. She had been given an opportunity of recovering her position in the Party through unquestioning obedience. She understood that she had met three senior members of the Party on an official footing, so they must think she might be useful; that did something for her self-esteem. However, she had now to part from Edward Corinth—that was one of the reasons she was being ordered abroad—and she found this surprisingly hard to accept. Maybe they were right—the comrades—maybe she was being seduced by the easy charm of the aristocracy. Life for a comrade should not be easy and her life had been easy, she knew that. She had a talent for investigation, for getting to the truth, and she was being invited—no, ordered—to put this at the service of the Party. She could not bear duplicity but what if the Party demanded it—for the sake of the Party? What if the truth, as she saw it, was not palatable to the Party? All her upbringing, all her father's teaching, all her own natural sympathy, lay with socialist ideals and surely David was right: the ends justify the means—victory for socialism was inevitable and her task was to help see it was not delayed.

It was a subdued Verity who accompanied Edward down to Mersham that afternoon. How simple life had once seemed to her. A few hours before she had been quite certain who were good and who were bad; she had thought she knew it was wrong to lie and to cheat. A simple eagerness for truth and justice had seemed to be a more than adequate personal philosophy. Now she was confused and irresolute. She had been conscripted into an army to serve under a flag—a red flag—which demanded absolute obedience and justified duplicity and subterfuge when they served the greater good. She had been told, if not in so many words, that she was a humble foot-soldier in a great cause and that the struggle for social justice involved giving up personal liberty. She wanted to discuss her understanding of this new, harsh reality with her father but, as had so often been the case in the past, he was not to be found. He was abroad, in Greece perhaps; the clerk of his chambers was not sure and had no idea when he would return.

'It's a funny thing,' she said to Edward as they swung down the Great West Road in the newly repaired Lagonda, 'but I used to think it was the most wonderful thing in the world having a father who so many people admired and relied on but I now see it has its disadvantages.'

'You mean, with so many at the well-mouth, when you come with your little bucket you cannot get near the water,' said Edward acutely.

'How did you know?' she said.

'I had the same sort of feeling with my father. I was very much the youngest in the family, the afterthought, don't you know.' He took a gloved hand from the steering-wheel and touched his hair, uncertain why he was drawn to confess something so painful to this girl he hardly knew. 'My father lived for my eldest brother who was to be duke after he died. It never occurred to him that he might die first. It is a terrible thing for a father to have his son die before him, particularly in a world where passing down from generation to generation a title and a great house is all-important.'

'Your brother died in the war, didn't he? Surely, that made your father proud? Isn't patriotism what all the hereditary thing boils down to?'

Edward shot her a look to be certain she was not mocking him but she seemed to be deadly serious. 'Of course, but the pain is real enough, otherwise where would be the sacrifice?' he said. 'My father was destroyed by my brother's death and like your father, if for different reasons, showed little interest in me or even Frank thereafter. You know, I've been thinking: I believe one cannot understand the modern world unless one accepts the overwhelming power of patriotism. Christianity, your socialism, they are as nothing compared with patriotism, and aristocrats, in the last resort, have always been prepared to sacrifice their sons for their country. It's one of the reasons that there will never be a French-type revolution in this country, because the working class have always accepted that however foolish and incompetent—even corrupt—their rulers are, they are patriotic. It is the one thing which unites the classes. Did you see the sincere warmth with which the whole nation joined together to celebrate the King's jubilee? The confusion for people such as us now is that dictators like Hitler and Mussolini are clever enough to know the power of patriotism and use it for their own evil ends.'

'So people like your brother, the Duke, have sympathy for Nazi Germany because the Fascists claim to be patriots, is that right?'

'No, but people like my brother think Germany has had a bad deal, particularly from France which, don't forget, until 1914 was England's traditional enemy. They're just confused and they think if they

309

play by the rules and give Germany everything it can legitimately claim as a nation, then it will be satisfied. Unfortunately, men like our friend Friedberg don't play by any rules.'

Verity thought how grim he looked. Gone was the cheerful, lightweight sprig of nobility and in its place was a man of considerable intellectual quality, as determined in his own way as David Griffiths-Jones.

'I'm sorry,' he said, smiling. 'How did we get on to this? I must sound incredibly pompous.'

'No, not at all. I'm interested. I suppose I was thinking of General Craig. Was he a patriot or a warmonger? Does he deserve justice?'

'I think he deserves the truth,' Edward answered. 'Justice may not be ours to give but he deserves to have his death taken seriously and not just pushed out of sight and out of mind.'

This was so different from David's view that Verity found herself smiling.

'That's better, I have made you laugh,' said Edward, smiling himself.

'No, I mean I wasn't smiling at what you said: just how two people can see the truth so differently.'

'Me and Griffiths-Jones?'

Again, Verity was taken aback by his acuity. 'Yes—David. I'm afraid he would think you were sentimental.'

'Sentimental?'

'Yes. What is the death of one man, and a militarist at that, when there is a battle for socialism to be fought and won?'

'I have always thought it was the weakness of your movement that the individual is so despised. It

310

is not English. We believe in the liberty and significance of the individual. It has got nothing to do with the freedom of one class to exploit another for profit, as your friend David would have it. The English believe everyone has the right to their own home and the right to do what they want in their spare time. That doesn't sound like much but it means the right to be in a pigeon loft or on a cricket field rather than get into uniform after work and march off to a parade ground and shout "all heil" in front of some demagogue. No party rallies, no youth movements—well, the scouts of course, but you know what I mean. We English don't like coloured shirts, hymns of hate and "spontaneous demonstrations". That's why Mr Griffiths-Jones will never live to see his revolution in England. I hope you don't mind.'

No punctures or engagements with farm wagons delayed their journey and they turned on to the Mersham drive in good time for dinner. Verity shrunk back into her seat, for a minute unable to summon up her usual sang-froid. She knew that, with Edward by her side, she would not be insulted or probably even reproached but there would be something in the Duke's eyes which would shrivel her up, she was sure. She decided that she would not wait for the stricken-deer looks and would come straight out with the 'manly' apology, but it was not to be. As the Duke shook her by the hand at the castle's front door he said, 'Welcome, Miss Browne. I want you to know that on our part'—he looked across at Connie who was standing smiling, one arm in Edward's—'we do not in any way criticize you for writing in the . . . in the newspaper'—the Duke could not quite bring

311

himself to name it—as you did. As a newspaper reporter you only did your job and you betrayed no secrets.'

'Thank you, Duke,' she said with a warm smile which made the Duke smile too. 'I do owe an apology to the Duchess for pretending to be what I was not.'

Connie kissed Verity on both cheeks and said, 'It is enough for me to know that Edward counts you as a friend.'

Awkwardness removed, a greater warmth was generated between hosts and guests than if there had been no obstacles to overcome. The Duke said, 'You know, of course, that Cecil Haycraft and Weaver are also here tonight. I had invited General Craig's heir, the distant cousin, but Craig's solicitor, through whom I extended the invitation, has informed me that the man—I can't even remember his name, can you, Connie?'

'Wilson, Henry Wilson.'

'Yes, well, Wilson is too busy to stay a night and is going to drive to Mersham and back in the day. Most extraordinary, I call it.'

The Duke was obviously a little put out to have had his invitation refused but also relieved. He had no wish to discuss the General's death at length with a man who might legitimately argue that the Duke, by allowing his guest to die of cyanide poisoning in his house, had failed in his feudal duty as a host.

'Is Blanche coming, Connie?' Edward inquired.

'No. Apparently Hermione is not very well and she wants to spend most of her day at the hospital.'

Edward said, 'Oh, I am sorry about that. I hoped she might be on the mend.'

312

'So did the doctors, Blanche told me,' Connie said. 'However, she seems unable to shake off the effects of the drugs. She was given a massive overdose, you know. Apparently, her kidneys—or is it her liver? I don't know—are unable to cope. If you hadn't found her when you did, Edward, she would certainly be dead.'

'And the Bishop's wife—Honoria?' said Edward, wanting to change the subject.

'She has a host of duties in the diocese this weekend so she begged to be excused. The Bishop has to go straight back home after the inquest, but I do hope you both won't rush away.'

'I'm afraid I will have to go after the inquest,' said Verity, taking a deep breath. She was about to be rather cowardly and make an announcement which Edward might not like in front of his brother and sister-in-law so he could not make too much of a fuss. She had meant to tell him in the car but somehow there had not been time. 'I am going to Spain on Saturday and I have to pack and so on.'

'How exciting,' Connie exclaimed. 'On holiday?'

'Not quite, though as I have never been before I certainly intend doing some sight-seeing.'

'So why are you going?' demanded Edward, trying not to sound annoyed.

'Well,' Verity swallowed, 'you remember Lord Weaver offered me that job on the *New Gazette*?'

'Yes, which you had no hesitation in turning down.'

'Quite, but I had second thoughts.'

'Second thoughts!'

'Yes. I spoke to Lord Weaver on the telephone today and asked him if I could report from Spain. There are some very interesting political

313

developments going on there,' she gabbled. 'There is a real chance of a socialist government being elected and—'

'Is David Griffiths-Jones anything to do with this?' interjected Edward icily.

'Not really—well, I mean he is coming too, but we will be quite separate.'

Connie, seeing that Edward was about to upbraid Verity, hurriedly said, 'Well, that sounds most exciting, Verity. I do congratulate you. Will your name be on the reports or will they be—what is it?—"from a correspondent"?'

'No, Lord Weaver has been very kind and has offered me a by-line.'

'A by-line?' said the Duke, puzzled.

'She means she will be credited as the author, which is a great compliment,' Connie explained.

'It is, and there is also going to be a note attached that I am a member of the Communist Party. I don't want to pretend I am something I am not again,' she said, looking at Connie. 'There will be other reports from Spain from other reporters. I am not going to try and be neutral as if I were on the wireless.'

'I see,' said Edward, who had now calmed down. 'Why didn't you tell me before? Why this rush?'

'I'm telling you now,' Verity came back strongly. 'It has only just been decided.'

'Decided by whom?' Edward demanded.

'Ned, don't be a bully,' Connie said. 'Why should she tell you? Anyway, Verity says it has only just been arranged.'

'Yes, Duchess—'

'Oh Verity, please call me Connie, everyone does!'

314

'Thank you, Connie. Yes, it has only just been arranged. In fact I am hoping, if you don't mind, Duke, to have a word about it with Lord Weaver to confirm details—that sort of thing.'

'Of course,' said the Duke, who was almost as surprised as Edward. He did not quite feel he wanted Verity to call him by his first name yet but he wanted to be friendly. He liked most young people and he thought this pretty, enterprising girl was delightful if only . . . if only she were not a Communist. It all seemed a lot of rot to him; she would make the perfect wife for Edward, he thought longingly. He wanted an intelligent, active girl who would stand up to him—not one of those milk-and-water creatures he saw in the *Tatler* draped in their mother's pearls.

'What about the *Daily Worker*?' said Edward nastily. Are you dropping your old employer?'

'No,' said Verity, 'Lord Weaver said I can still send my stuff to them—a different market, he says.'

'I should say it is,' guffawed the Duke. 'Anyway, don't let's stand around in the hall. Come into the garden and have some tea. You must be thirsty.' The Duke always considered the journey from London to Mersham as being comparable with Livingstone's most perilous African explorations.

Sitting under the great copper beech in deck chairs, sipping tea from Crown Derby porcelain so delicate as to be almost translucent seemed to Verity as near heaven as was possible on this earth. True, the lawn was browning after a month without rain and the river beside her chair ran thin and shallow, but the feeling of being outside the real world, afloat on a sea of tranquillity, left her feeling uncharacteristically lethargic. She had got it off her

315

chest that she was going away with David Griffiths-Jones and though, she told herself, it had nothing to do with Edward, she had been nervous about what he would say. Now the tension had gone and though she realised he was hurt, she felt there was nothing else she could do. She had made some sort of choice—the nature of which she was unable to define but she sensed it was more significant than merely deciding to go to Spain on an adventurous holiday.

Looking round her, it seemed sad that all this had to go. The socialist revolution was inevitable and, more to the point, it was desirable, but even so . . . She stirred herself as a swan paddled past looking cross to find the level of the water so low. She wanted to be lying in a punt trailing her fingers in the cool water, and who was the shadow above her with the pole in his strong, manly arms? Edward or David—it was hard to see . . .

Edward gazed at Verity half asleep on the canvas chair. She looked so cool in her white linen suit. She had taken off her jacket which had fallen unheeded on to the grass and had even kicked off her blue and white shoes to Connie's evident amusement. Her long white arm hung beside her so that her fingers touched the grass and her eyes were closed. He was able to stare at her in repose for the first time and he followed the long curve of her neck down to her small, neat breasts and then onwards along slim legs visible below her pleated skirt.

'You like her,' Connie said in his ear and Edward suddenly realized his brother and sister-in-law had been observing him with amusement. He blushed despite himself.

316

'Oh, I don't know, Connie. She's certainly not interested in me. She's in love with Comrade David,' he said with heavy sarcasm.

'Not one of your favourite people, I would guess,' said Connie smiling.

'No. He looks like one of those young men in West End plays who come in through the French windows and say "Who's for tennis?", but his sole *raison d'être* is the "socialist revolution" which, from what I can make out, means stringing up people like me on lamp-posts and turning places like this'—he waved towards the castle—'into the Communist equivalent of YMCAs.'

Verity woke up with a start, apologized for dropping off to sleep and started to struggle to her feet. 'It's so restful here,' she said.

'Well, sit there a bit longer and enjoy the last of the sun,' said Connie. 'I have noticed, now we are into September, when the sun goes it gets cold quite quickly. I think both you and Ned are very tired. You've been rushing around London finding dead bodies and goodness knows what. You need to take it easy for a bit, Ned, and it will probably do Verity a lot of good to see the back of you for a bit. A change of scene, as Mother used to say, is better than a tonic.'

'And have you found out anything about the General's death, Ned?' asked the Duke.

'Not really,' said Edward, raising his hands in apology. 'We've got a few theories but I thought we might wait until later on, after dinner perhaps, before we air them. Somehow it all seems too peaceful here to talk about death and all that sort of thing, don't you know.'

Connie saw that he was trying to appear light-

317

hearted but that he was actually quite depressed.

'Yes, that's a good idea,' she said. 'What time is it now?' She looked at her husband who put on his glasses and consulted his hunter with considerable ceremony.

'Six o'clock, m'dear.'

'Lord Weaver and Cecil Haycraft will be here any minute and I must think about dressing. Dinner at eight, Verity—you're in the same room as you were before. Would you like to borrow my maid?'

'Oh, no, thank you, Connie,' she said. 'I'm afraid I haven't brought anything very smart to wear. I hope that doesn't matter.'

'No, my dear,' said the Duke, 'Ned, I am coming down in a smoking jacket. I told Weaver and the Bishop that it was all going to be informal. It doesn't seem right somehow to dress up as if this was some ordinary dinner-party instead of . . . well, you know what I mean—with the inquest tomorrow.'

Lying in her bath later, Verity heard tyres crunching on the gravel and guessed that the Bishop and her future employer, Lord Weaver, had arrived. In the short time that had passed since the fatal dinner at which the old man had been poisoned, a lot seemed to have happened. She had grown up, she considered. When she had taken Edward off his haywain and used him as a passport into Mersham Castle, she had been a girl—her political convictions, sincerely enough held, had not been a burden to her as they were now but as natural as the air she breathed. Now, everything was much more complicated. The aristocracy she was pledged to do away with were not the superannuated dinosaurs she had imagined them to be. Her comrades in the Party were more ruthless and their judgments less straightforward than she had assumed. In short, the world was an altogether more dangerous place than she had thought in her innocence. She was by no means daunted; she felt herself to be on the edge of her real life. As the Bible said, she had until now thought and understood as a child; henceforth she would see the world clearly, as it really was, even if she did not like what she saw. She was going to be a good journalist—she knew that—and it looked as though there was going to be a lot to report in Spain and elsewhere in Europe during the next few years.

CHAPTER SEVENTEEN

THURSDAY EVENING AND FRIDAY

Dinner was over and the servants had left the Duke and his guests to their coffee and brandy. Everyone was relieved that the Duke refrained from offering port. Connie and Verity were not asked to leave the table, which they would certainly have refused to do. Lord Weaver raised the topic which had been studiously avoided while they ate dinner: 'Edward, what have you discovered about General Craig's death? I know you have been sleuthing. You obviously don't have much faith in our good Inspector Pride.'

'I have spoken to Pride,' the Duke interjected, 'and I can tell you that, short of Ned or someone else coming up with new information, the verdict will be accidental death.'

Lord Weaver dragged on his cigar and growled, 'He took the cyanide mistaking it for one of his morphine pills?'

'Yes,' said the Duke. 'Do you have any evidence that might persuade a jury to a different verdict, Ned?'

'No, no evidence, but Verity and I have a few ideas about what might have happened.'

'I know what you are going to say,' said the Bishop unexpectedly. 'You think I killed the General, and you would be right: I did.'

There was an audible gasp from Connie, and the Duke said, 'Oh look, I say—' before he was cut off by the Bishop.

'I don't say I meant to kill him—as a Christian and a pacifist, I could never knowingly kill someone however much I disapproved of them and I certainly disapproved of the General. He was a warmonger of the old school. He spent his life fighting. He hated Germans and he told us he did not believe talking to them would do any good. He told me that the only thing a German understood was a bayonet. I have to say, I was horrified. If we don't believe that discussion can replace war as a way of settling disputes then we are all doomed.'

'How do you mean, Bishop, that you killed the General accidentally?' said Edward coolly.

'It's simple! When we returned from having greeted you in the hall and settled ourselves down again, I noticed that the General's port glass was standing in front of Weaver's place. So, without thinking, I pushed it back to where the General was seated. A few moments later he lifted the glass and

320

drank from it and was immediately convulsed. I was struck dumb, but I assumed that the General must have decided to commit suicide and by some accident Lord Weaver had almost drunk the wine he had poisoned.'

'I'm most grateful, Cecil,' said Weaver calmly, taking the cigar out of his mouth and bowing his head in the Bishop's direction. 'I have to confess, I don't feel like dying yet. I have a wife whom I love very much. I have just found a daughter I had lost and I believe I have a lot to offer this country—which I am now proud to call my own—in the dangerous years ahead.'

Edward said, 'Two people I talked to told me they had seen you pass the poisoned glass over to the General, so I thought it unlikely you knew what you were doing.'

'Otherwise I would have been more surreptitious?'

'Yes . . . by the way, how did you know it was the General's glass?'

'Because it was not quite one of the set. It was larger than any of the others,' said the Bishop.

'How very observant of you. I noticed that too and for a moment I wondered if someone had introduced a special glass on to the table but my sister-in-law tells me it is one of hers. I wondered also, Bishop—purely as an academic exercise, you understand—what possible motive you might have for killing the old soldier.'

'I have told you that I did have a motive,' the Bishop said: 'my dislike, no, my abhorrence of the General's bloodthirstiness. He had still some influence in high places, I understand, and it would have been a tragedy in my view if his aggressive

Germanophobic views had been listened to where decisions on policy are made.'

'Ironically,' said Edward, 'the General had the same motive for wanting to get rid of you, Bishop.'

'What on earth do you mean?'

'Well, it occurred to me that just as each of the men drinking port round my brother's table had a motive for murdering the General—'

'For God's sake, Ned, what nonsense is this?' broke in the Duke.

'Let him finish, Duke,' drawled Weaver, 'he's just getting interesting.'

'I was saying, just as you all had a motive for killing General Craig, he had the same motives, in reverse one might say, for killing any of you. For instance, he believed the Bishop's pacifism would lead to war by giving the Germans the idea that Britain would not fight for its own or its allies' rights.'

'He was right. I hope that we will never go to war so that France can continue to extort Germany's wealth in the name of reparations,' said the Bishop firmly.

'And you, Lord Weaver,' Edward went on as if the Bishop had not spoken, 'he knew you had a damaging story about his having killed, in the last war, German soldiers after they had surrendered and been disarmed. That was a tale he did not want airing. To be branded a murderer in public when he knew he had only been doing his duty . . . well, you can imagine what he might have done to avoid it. His reputation would have been tarnished whatever was said in his defence, and therefore his influence at what he regarded as a crucial moment in the history of Britain and her Empire would have been weakened or destroyed. Added to which, he thought the political viewpoint of your paper would, like the Bishop's views, hasten war because it would send Hitler a message that we would not stand up to him.'

'But people don't murder for such impersonal reasons, do they?' said Connie. 'I thought murders were done for greed, jealousy, revenge—that sort of thing—not for politics.'

'I wish murders weren't committed for political reasons but I am afraid they are, at least in the shabby age we live in. Besides, Craig was seeking revenge. Don't forget the General was a man in a hurry. He knew he was dying of cancer. At best he had only a few months to live, and what was his motive force throughout his life? Duty. He might have regarded it as his last duty to do what he could to prevent his country, as he would see it, going along the path to perdition.'

'And what might my motive have been for killing the General?' asked Weaver in an interested, uninvolved tone of voice.

'I'm only guessing here,' said Edward, 'from something Gerald mentioned in passing. I think the General might have come to know about the daughter by your first wife whom you had abandoned in Canada. You might not have cared to have had that revealed in a rival newspaper.'

'You're quite right, of course,' said Weaver. 'Craig had a friend back in New Brunswick where I lived as a young man—a man named Packer, a nasty piece of work—dead now, I'm glad to say. He and I crossed swords once or twice when I was making my first fortune. He always seemed to get the worst of it and, of course, didn't like me much.

323

Matter of fact he tried to shoot me but he missed, which was typical of the man. Anyway, he told Craig about my first wife and the baby—how I had left her to be brought up by . . . well, I had nothing to be proud of. Thanks to Packer, Craig had the whole story. He kept quiet about it until . . . the long and short of it is, he thought I would not want the story to get into the press—I mean, of course, the yellow press, not my own fine, upstanding publications.' He drew on his cigar and puffed out a cloud of smoke which he examined closely before going on. 'Craig believed I would agree to publish anti-German stories in my newspapers if he kept silent.'

'Blackmail!' exclaimed Haycraft.

'Hardly that, but I don't pretend I wasn't a little put out. However, it had the happy result of hastening my decision to tell Blanche of Amy's existence and that I intended to do what I should have done years ago and bring her over to England. I consulted the Duke here, as about the wisest man I knew, and it was he who urged me to do what I thought was right regardless of how it might hurt Blanche and Hermione. So you can see, I have a lot to be grateful to the General for.' He stubbed out his cigar and took another from the box on the table, nodding to his host for permission.

'Yes,' said the Duke, 'and when we talked just before the dinner I was delighted to hear that you had decided to make a clean breast of it all. It was one of the reasons I wanted to bring you and Craig together at Mersham so you could resolve your differences on neutral ground. I was horrified that my old friend could have brought himself to attempt . . . to try—well, you used the word,

Cecil—blackmail—even if he considered his motives to be honourable. Did you say anything to him, Joe, about what you proposed to do?'

'I intended to but I never got the chance.'

This was the first time anyone had heard the Duke call Lord Weaver by his Christian name, and Connie and Edward both looked at him curiously. The Duke was not one to make any man an intimate he had not known in childhood, but clearly Lord Weaver was an exception.

'Yes, I decided, whatever the pain might be for Blanche or Hermione, I should do what I ought to have done years before and bring Amy to live with me. Amy joining the family where she belongs has been a great joy to me. She has never said one word of complaint about the way I abandoned her though, before God, she had every right to do so.'

'And Blanche, Hermione? Were they as pleased?'

'Blanche was angry with me for not telling her before about Amy and welcomed her as warmly as—'

'But Hermione was less pleased?'

'It's a private matter, Lord Edward, but if you must know, Hermione was not pleased. She used some harsh words to me, but then she is an ill person.'

'So,' said Edward, 'you had no motive to kill the General, but I still believe he might have wanted to kill you. Did that poisoned glass of port end up in front of you, Weaver, by accident or on purpose? We may never know for sure.'

'But,' said Connie, very shocked, 'how could he—the General, I mean—have been sure that we would all sit down where we had been sitting before?'

'He could not,' Verity said, 'but he might not have minded if anyone else had taken the poison by mistake—after all, Friedberg and poor Mr Larmore were in his eyes tarred with the same brush. He Suspected Larmore was passing secrets to the Nazis—as indeed he was—and, of course, Friedberg was the devil incarnate.'

'But,' said Connie again, 'was his hatred of Germany so . . . so deep?'

'Edward discovered from Jeffries, General Craig's valet, that it was very deep, didn't you?' Verity said solemnly.

'Yes,' Edward agreed, 'and to top it all, I discovered that the surgeon who had operated on his wife—the only person I think he truly loved— and who failed to save her—the cancer was far too advanced—was a German: Hans Hollweg. He is naturalized British and one of the best surgeons in the country. I don't doubt for a minute he did everything for the poor woman he could, but she died anyway.'

'Oh God,' said Connie, 'that poor lonely old man.'

'But you said we all had motives when it came to killing the General, Ned. I didn't have a motive.'

'Yes you did, Gerald. Had you forgotten that Craig was in command of Frank's battalion at the beginning of the war? You might have held him responsible for his death,' he said soberly.

'But that's ridiculous,' spluttered the Duke.

'I know it is,' Edward said, putting his hand on Connie's to reassure her. 'In fact, I know, the General respected you—he was one of your oldest friends. On the other hand—I'm only guessing—he

326

thought you were wrong to hold these dinners. He respected you and what you stand for and he had no intention of harming you personally, but he might have thought it was his duty to disrupt your efforts to bring German and British top brass together.'

'But how could he have been sure of not hurting Gerald?' demanded Connie in a voice that trembled however hard she tried to control it.

'He could be certain that when Gerald got back from greeting Verity and me, he if no other would sit in his former seat, at the head of the table, and would therefore be very unlikely to take the poisoned glass.'

'Golly,' said the Bishop, 'you really think, Lord Edward, that the General was indulging in some mad Russian roulette?'

'I can't be sure but I think it is possible. He knew he was dying. He may have been depressed and lonely with his wife dead and a new war with Germany on the cards. By the way, Haycraft, I beg to disagree with you on one thing: I don't think the General was a warmonger. I think he hated war and like all of us could not bear the idea of a new, even more terrible war coming to kill a new generation of young men, but he saw the way to avoid it as being resolute refusal to surrender to what he considered unjustifiable demands from the new Germany, and for what it is worth, which isn't much, I agree with him.'

The Bishop gave a little moue of disapproval. 'How does this affect the inquest?' he said after a pause.

'It doesn't,' said Lord Weaver firmly. 'As Lord Edward has said, there is not an atom of proof for any of this, and even if there was, how would it help anyone to have it aired in the gutter press? If the General was a murderer he got his just reward— what more could any potential victim of his malice ask? Let him go to his rest in Westminster Abbey the revered soldier—no doubt he earned it on many a battlefield. In old age we may all end up embittered and disillusioned and in that light, if I were his intended victim, I forgive him.'

'Well said, Joe,' the Duke exclaimed. 'Just what I would have expected you to say, though. You are a true gentleman.'

Lord Weaver sucked at his cigar with evident pleasure and embarrassment at the Duke's encomium.

*   *   *

The following morning, after the inquest, Lord Weaver offered to take Verity back to London in his Phantom III, a new Rolls-Royce of which he was inordinately proud, but Edward said he would drive her back to town in the Lagonda. Verity might have found it useful to have had a couple of hours private conversation with the press lord but she knew Edward would be mortally offended if she said as much.

The inquest had gone smoothly enough. The little black-suited coroner, whom they all agreed resembled Dr Crippen, had conducted the proceedings quickly and efficiently. Dr Best gave his evidence of finding the General dead from cyanide poisoning and confirmed that the post-mortem had revealed that the cancer from which he was suffering would have killed him in a few weeks. Jeffries had been called next and confirmed that the General had a cyanide capsule from when he had been in France during the war and that he also had morphine tablets. He said he did not believe the General could have confused the two but this opinion was speedily put to one side by the General's doctor, Dr Cradel, who confirmed that when he had had to tell the General that he was dying and there was nothing to be done about it, he had been depressed and bitter—as anyone else would have been in the circumstances. The doctor reminded the coroner that the General's beloved wife had also died of cancer and this might have added to the General's depression. He had no close relatives or friends to look after him as far as the doctor could discover, but when he had suggested the General take on nursing help he had refused grumpily, insisting that Jeffries could do everything necessary.

The Duke, Weaver and Bishop Haycraft all gave evidence of how the company had got up from table in some disarray to greet Edward and Verity when they arrived unexpectedly while the port was being drunk. The coroner, as he was supposed to do, took the view that the General might have become confused and taken a pill he thought was one of his painkillers to discover too late that it was his cyanide capsule.

Neither Verity nor Edward were called and the coroner summed up to the effect that this was a tragic accident. The General would never have committed suicide at the Duke's dinner-table—that was patently absurd—so this could be the only conclusion any reasonable man could come to, and the jury agreed. The scribblers representing the popular press were disappointed that there was no society scandal to report and decided they had to make the best of what they had: a great imperial soldier dying at one of England's most picturesque castles at dinner with several distinguished figures. The coroner had been able to avoid saying anything about Larmore being at the dinner—his was a name not to be mentioned in polite society— and Friedberg's name seemed not to mean much to the journalists present who regarded all foreigners as little more than jokes.

So it was with relief they all gathered in the drive to see Lord Weaver off. Verity took the chance of discussing the terms of her assignment for the *New Gazette* with him. Edward walked off to inspect the Rolls. Its V12 engine excited Edward. Hudson, Lord Weaver's chauffeur, was delighted to find someone almost as knowledgeable as himself about motor cars and gave Edward a guided tour of the Rolls's intestines while Verity and Lord Weaver stood a few yards off talking earnestly.

'Yes, my lord, it's a beautiful car. Lady Weaver has insisted on keeping her Phantom—the Mark I—even though I have pointed out to her all the improvements they have made. Her ladyship says she finds her car extremely comfortable and quiet and since she has no wish to travel over sixty miles an hour she has no interest in a more powerful engine.'

'Oh, Lady Weaver has the Phantom I, has she?' said Edward. 'I must admit I have some sympathy with her, Hudson. It's a magnificent vehicle. Am I right in saying it has a 7.6-litre six-cylinder engine?'

'Yes, my lord,' said Hudson enthusiastically, 'but look at the line of this.' He stroked the bonnet of the gleaming Rolls as if it were a big cat.

Seeing that Verity was still deep in conversation with its owner, Edward tactfully continued to admire the great machine. He cocked his head on one side. 'I can see what you mean, Hudson. You might think it was sitting back on its haunches as though it was going to spring on some antelope.'

Hudson looked doubtful. 'That would be more your Lagonda you will be thinking about, my lord.'

'Perhaps, perhaps,' said Edward abstractedly, still watching Verity out of the corner of his eye. 'How fast does it go? I don't suppose Lord Weaver has allowed you to stretch it, has he?'

'No,' said the chauffeur regretfully, 'but it moves so strong at sixty-five I don't doubt it could do seventy-five if pushed.'

'I like the body style, Hudson. Did Lord Weaver consult you at all on the choice of coach builder?'

'Yes, my lord, his lordship was good enough to ask me to advise him. We had it built in Crewe, of course,' said the chauffeur, becoming proprietorial, 'and we chose the teak . . .'

At that moment Weaver and Verity came up, having finished their confabulation and Hudson touched his cap. Weaver took the cigar out of his mouth and said to Edward, 'I see you admire my automobile, Lord Edward.'

'Indeed, I do, Weaver,' said the other. 'It is quite magnificent but I shall wait a few years before I go that way. For the present I shall stick with my Lagonda.'

'It has recovered from the—'

'Oh yes,' said Edward hurriedly, 'it has been completely repaired—good as new.' He glanced at Verity. He did not want her to have any excuse for not letting him drive her to London. 'I thought I would telephone Amy when I get back home. There's a show on at the Palace she might enjoy. I suppose she could manage a matinée? Where is she staying? With you and Lady Weaver?'

'Oh no, Lord Edward, did she not tell you? She's in New York.'

'New York! But I only saw her a few days ago.'

'Well, not New York yet. I guess she must still be on the *Queen Mary*. A theatrical agent, Mort Gagenau, a friend of mine as a matter of fact, was over here from the States and I took him to see Amy at the Cocoanut Grove. He liked her so much—he was "nuts about her", he said—he got her an audition for a new Gershwin show coming on Broadway in the fall. I'm surprised she didn't tell you, but then I guess you were all over the place and maybe she wasn't able to reach you.'

Edward, slightly dazed by the news that Amy had put the Atlantic Ocean between them, caught sight of Verity, who was having difficulty keeping her face straight.

'Well, goodbye, Lord Edward. I hope to see you soon. You must come and lunch with me at my club' He turned to the Duke: 'Goodbye, Duke. And thank you, Connie, for all your kindness. Next time I hope we will meet on a happier occasion.'

John the footman, under Hudson's watchful eye, put the last of the luggage in the Rolls. 'Goodbye, Joe,' said the Duke, pressing the tycoon's hand warmly. He had admitted to himself that over the past fortnight his feelings for the man had changed from respect to affection. They had known each other for three years; they had in fact been introduced by no less a personage than the Prince

332

of Wales at a dinner at Fort Belvedere and they had immediately taken a liking to one another. Although the Duke had refused to believe that the General was anything but a man of honour, he had been shocked by what Weaver had told him about his old friend's attempt to pressure him—he would not call it blackmail—and he admired Weaver for the dignified way he had dealt with the matter. The Duke had hoped to bring the two men together at Mersham but he now realized Craig was too embittered ever to have recognized in Weaver a man of honour and a potential ally. The Duke considered that his old friend's mortal illness, the pain and loneliness he had suffered since his wife's death, had disturbed the balance of his mind. He had admired the General ever since he had first met him before the war when he had been his brother's superior officer. His courage and patriotism had impressed the Duke even then, long before the disaster of 1914 and his brother's death. He had never for one moment held the General to blame for that. It was just one of the many tragedies of that appalling conflict and why he had dedicated himself to preventing another war which could only be more savage than its predecessor.

The Bishop had taken an early train as he needed to be in Worthing by midday, and now Edward and Verity, despite Connie's urging to stay a little while longer, prepared to take their departure. The Duke shook his brother by the hand and asked him to come and see them again soon. When he came to Verity, Edward thought for one minute he was going to kiss her on the cheek but in the end decorum prevailed and he shook her hand too. Connie did kiss Verity, even though she had not fully forgiven her for the subterfuge which had brought her to the castle. She now feared that this girl was going to make her brother-in-law unhappy, but she felt she owed it to Edward to try to like her. She did admire Verity: she represented modern woman determined to make her mark in a man's world. She admired her enterprise even if she did not altogether approve of her methods of getting what she wanted. She instinctively believed in the girl's basic honesty. Despite the trick she had played on her, Connie was prepared to accept that Verity was well named. As for her politics, she and the Duke had discussed them and come to the conclusion that they were a young girl's way of showing her independence and would soon change. In this belief they were quite wrong but it allowed them to make sense of the fact that someone as 'normal' as Verity—patently 'one of us' as the Duke had said, who dressed and spoke like any of the girls they met in society—was devoting herself to bringing about a revolution which would destroy everything they valued and which Verity seemed to have no hesitation in enjoying. It was a paradox but then, as Connie said to the Duke as they lay in bed that night with the lights off waiting for sleep, 'I feel a generation older than that girl even though I'm only a few years her senior. I just don't understand what makes her tick.'

'Nor do I,' said the Duke sleepily, 'but she's a damn fine filly all the same and Ned's a lucky man.'

'Don't count his chickens for him,' said Connie, but the Duke was already asleep.

On the way back in the car Edward could not talk to Verity about her plans—how long would she be in Spain, was she going to be with Griffiths-

Jones, did she like David better than him? In fact, he doubted whether he could ever ask the latter question and he knew that if he needed to ask her, he already had his answer. So they talked of the inquest.

'How did you think it all went, Verity?'

'All right, I suppose. It wasn't the truth but what is the truth?'

'You're bally right it wasn't the truth. After the inquest I had a word with Jeffries. The General was murdered by someone at that dinner-party, and all my ideas and theories are complete balderdash. I am a fool, a damn fool, a very damn fool.'

'For goodness' sake, Edward, what did Jeffries tell you?'

'There was a simple question I didn't ask which I should have asked. Pride didn't ask it either. There was an important fact Jeffries hid from us. He only vouchsafed this information when I talked to him after the inquest.'

'Was this after you talked to Dr Best?'

'Yes, and then I had a few words with that frightful fellow, Pride. He was his usual patronizing self but I got the feeling he did not really believe the General's death was an accident. He said, with what I considered tasteless jocularity, "I trust you have not stumbled over any more dead bodies?" "No, Inspector," I said, "and may I ask *you* if you have made any arrests? Have you penetrated the Triads yet and broken up their drugs network?" It was a silly cheap thing to say, I know, but I was riled. He said, "We are working on it. Captain Gordon has given us some useful information." I asked if he would be charged with drug dealing.

Pride said there wasn't enough evidence.'

'But he confessed, didn't he?' said Verity scandalized.

'Yes, but Pride said he doubted that the confession would stand up in court. It had been made before he was cautioned. Anyway, I suspect they have done a deal with him. If he helps them track down the top men they won't charge him. Not that they ever will catch the heads of the dope ring if Gordon is right, and I expect he is, that the Triads run London's drug world. The British policeman will never penetrate their organization. How would they ever get anyone to testify against them? No chance.'

'But you said you thought Pride did not believe the verdict was right?'

'Yes, he was gnomic—I think that's the word. He said, "Sufficient unto the day is the evil thereof." Then, he asked me what my theory was. I said I agreed with the coroner's verdict and then we were interrupted by the coroner himself, who wanted to speak to Pride.'

'So you think we are all part of a conspiracy to keep the ugly truth out of the press?' said Verity. 'We are all happy to have a verdict of accidental death in order that there should be no dirt flung about?'

'Yes, a typical conspiracy among the upper classes to keep the people ignorant of the real truth about the goings-on of their superiors,' Edward agreed sarcastically.

'What did Dr Best say to you?' said Verity, taking no notice.

'Oh, he's such a nice man. I think he suspects something. He asked after my knee and then he

336

said, "A terrible business! Did you know, I am retiring next month? Seeing that poor man after the agony of his death shook me more than I can say and it made me aware that I am not fit to practise medicine in this brutal modern world." He said that when he bought the practice immediately after the war Mersham was a quiet place—boring even—a typical rural community. The children had croup or measles, the old had arthritis and occasionally someone fell off their horse or had a baby—that was all. There were times, bless his heart, when I remember him complaining to us he was bored, but now look at it: death and destruction. That's what he said to me, Verity: "I see only death and destruction." '

'Then you spoke to Jeffries?'

'Yes, I saw him standing by himself looking miserable as usual so I went up to him and said, "I expect you are glad all that's over, aren't you, Jeffries?" "Yes, my lord," he said gloomily. I put on my hearty voice and said, "Cheer up, man! You're going to live with your sister and your mother, are you not?" "I was," he replied, "but we have had words, my lord." '

'Words?' Verity said.

'That's all he would say. I expect it was about money or maybe he just couldn't face living in a small house with two old women. He's a solitary soul. Anyway, I asked him if he was all right for money as tactfully as I could. "Yes, thank you, my lord," he said. "The General made generous provision for me." "Good!" I said as cheerfully as possible. "So you can find somewhere nice to live?" He supposed so, and then I asked him how long he could stay at Cadogan Square. He said the lawyers

337

had given him permission to stay until the house was sold, as caretaker.'

'So that was all right?'

'Yes, but it was then he dropped the bombshell under my feet. He was just turning away when he said, "I thought you said, my lord, that you were going to find who had killed the master." "What!" I said. "You heard the verdict, Jeffries: the General's death was an accident." "But what about the cyanide capsule then, my lord?" he said.'

'What did he mean, Edward?'

'That's what I asked him. Then he told me. He said he was packing up the General's clothes to take everything back to London when he found the cyanide capsule still in the pocket of his waistcoat, the fob.'

'He found the cyanide *after* the General was dead?'

'That's right. You see it all now, don't you, Verity? I am the biggest fool on earth. All the time I was working out my theories they were based on the wrong assumption. I am the most priceless ass, I really am. All that stuff I was telling everyone last night about the General wanting to murder someone was so much balderdash—pure bunkum. The poison belonged to someone else. The General *was* murdered and the killer is out there somewhere, probably laughing fit to burst.'

'Hang on,' said Verity, worrying they might have an accident if Edward did not calm down and stop hitting his head with a flailing hand. 'Why didn't he tell Inspector Pride or us when we went to see him?'

'He doesn't like Inspector Pride, apparently. He thinks he's "common".'

'But why not tell us then? I may be common but you aren't.'

'Don't be silly, Verity! He says we just didn't ask him. It's quite true; I knew there was a question I ought to ask him but I couldn't think what it was. I should have asked him if the General had two cyanide capsules—he didn't, as a matter of fact— and if Jeffries had found the capsule in his clothes after his death. I just took it for granted that the capsule had been the source of the poison, fool that I am.'

'So why did Jeffries *really* not tell us?'

'I don't think he trusted us.'

'Me, you mean,' said Verity. 'He would have trusted you, but he knew I had spilled the beans in the *Daily Worker* of all places! Why didn't I let you go alone? I knew I was hopeless with valets. Look at Fenton!'

'Oh, don't blame yourself. Jeffries is a confused man. He loved the General and would like his murder to be avenged. On the other hand, the accidental death verdict means he can go to his grave without any slur, any stain on his escutcheon.'

'Where is the capsule now?'

'He says he is keeping it safe.'

'Keeping it safe! What did you say?'

'I said I would come and talk to him in the next day or two.'

'Golly, what a turn-up for the books,' said Verity. 'So who did murder General Sir Alistair Craig VC?'

'I think . . .' said Edward slowly, 'I think Connie was quite right as usual and I have known it all along.'

'But you are not going to tell me?'

'Forgive me, Verity, but I have made such a bally pig's dinner of all this, I want to be sure this time before I sound off.'

'Well,' said Verity, a little huffily, 'don't forget I'm going to Spain tomorrow.'

'Yes, I know,' said Edward sombrely, 'but with any luck all this will be cleared up before you go— or not at all. Ah, here we are: Hans Crescent— home sweet home.'

CHAPTER EIGHTEEN

FRIDAY EVENING AND SATURDAY

Verity stopped outside the ground floor flat and rang the bell. 'This won't take a second, Edward,' she said. 'I'll just pick up Max. Mrs Parsons is a dear but I don't like her to have to look after my naughty dog a minute longer than she has to.'

There was a noise of shuffling and then bolts being drawn and the door opened on the chain. 'It's only me, Mrs Parsons,' said Verity brightly. 'I have just come to pick up Max.'

'Is that you?' said the old woman peering at Verity suspiciously. 'Oh yes, it *is* you.' As she struggled to open the door, Edward thought he saw that she was crying. When she finally appeared in carpet slippers and with an embroidered shawl pulled over what looked like her nightdress they could see that the old woman was in some distress.

'Whatever is it, Mrs Parsons?' Verity said in alarm.

'Miss Browne, I have such terrible news. I have

been trying to tell you but I lost the telephone number you gave me where you were going to be. I haven't slept a wink.'

'Please, Mrs Parsons, tell me what has happened,' said Verity, now thoroughly alarmed.

'It's Max.'

'Max?'

'Yes, you see I was just taking him out for a walk yesterday afternoon, it was about three I think, yes it was because I had just listened to that programme on the wireless about—'

'Please, Mrs Parsons, what has happened?'

'I'm trying to tell you, Miss Browne,' the old woman quavered.

'Yes, I'm sorry,' said Verity. 'I didn't mean to shout at you.'

'As I was going out of the front door I bumped into this nicely spoken young man. He was such a gentleman. He held open the door for me and he stroked Max and said what a nice dog he was, and of course he is, and he asked if he belonged to me and I said no, I was looking after him for Miss Browne who lived upstairs. And the man asked what his name was and I said Max. And then he said he was a great friend of yours, Miss Browne, and I said oh, but you were away for the night but you would be back tomorrow. And he said what a pity to have missed you but he would come back in the morning but in the mean time would I like it if he took the dog for a walk. And well, I said—and I know it was wrong of me but he seemed so nice and my leg was playing up—well I said 'Would you?', and he said he would take him round the gardens and knock on my door in half an hour and give him back. He seemed such a nice man so I . . .

341

oh I'm so sorry, Miss Browne . . .' Mrs Parsons began to cry in earnest. 'I said yes.'

'And he never came back?' said Edward. Mrs Parsons nodded miserably. 'Look, Verity,' he said, 'don't worry, I'm sure we can find Max. Let's take the bags upstairs and then we will plan our campaign. Did you tell the police, Mrs Parsons?'

'No, I thought he would come back before . . .'

'Never mind,' said Verity bravely. 'Don't get yourself too distressed, Mrs Parsons. We'll just take the luggage up to my flat and then come back and see what's the best thing to do.'

When they reached the flat Verity took out her key to unlock the front door but as she touched it, it swung open. 'Let me,' said Edward firmly, putting down the suitcases and gently moving Verity to one side. He went into the narrow hall and then pushed open the door of the living-room. There was nothing out of the ordinary to be seen. He opened another door and looked into the kitchen which again was undisturbed. Then, with Verity behind him, he opened the bedroom door. The sight that met his eyes made him cry out, and he immediately turned to try to prevent Verity from entering and seeing what he had seen, but he was too late. Verity gave a high-pitched scream and ran into the room. Someone had taken a kitchen knife and with it had hacked off the head of the little dog and then taken the trouble to lay the corpse against the pillows on the bed. The sight of the obscene arrangement parodying the teddy bear which might have been there on the counterpane was something he was never to forget. On the other side of the room, a swastika had been scrawled on the dressing-table looking-glass in what Edward

342

assumed was the dog's blood.

Verity screamed again and then turned and grabbed Edward, burying her face in his shoulder. 'Max!' she sobbed. 'Max, how could they . . . ?'

Edward half dragged Verity out of the room and insisted she take some brandy from a bottle on the sideboard in the living-room. Then he made her come down with him to Mrs Parsons' flat from which he called the police. He had no doubt that this was the Nazis' revenge for Verity's folly in going to the German embassy as Friedberg's guest. When they discovered she was a Communist activist they must have thought she had deliberately made a fool of the Führer's personal envoy, and this was their response. He felt physically sick. There could be no doubt that these were evil men and from that moment, whatever anyone told him to the contrary, he remained convinced that they would have to be fought and destroyed like vermin.

Verity's tears soon turned to ice-cold anger and she wanted to go straight round to the embassy and accuse them of the dog's murder. It was only with considerable difficulty that Edward managed to convince her of the futility of doing any such thing.

'There are other ways to fight them,' he said.

'Yes, there are,' said Verity with stern determination.

Edward had been going to try to convince her that she should not go to Spain with David Griffiths-Jones but he saw that there was now no point in even trying. Her commitment to the Communist Party had been sealed in Max's blood and, furthermore, Edward appreciated that she probably needed to get out of the country. In

London she would only do something which would attract the wrath of her enemies.

After the police had been—Edward had considered speaking to Pride but thought better of it—he insisted that Verity come to the Albany with him. There could be no question of her staying, let alone sleeping, in her flat. Verv gently, he placed the dog in one of the ruined pillowcases and then wrapped a sheet around it. The police had taken away the knife to test it for fingerprints but Edward had little doubt there would be no fingerprints on it; even if there were, what chance would there be of getting anyone in the embassy to agree to having their fingerprints taken?

He took Verity back with him to his apartment despite her protests and asked if she would mind staying in the spare bedroom for the night. 'Won't the landlords or whoever they are protest at you having a girl in your rooms?' She smiled a watery smile.

'No,' said Edward, even though he was not certain one way or the other. Fenton was surprisingly gentle with Verity when he understood what had upset her. He petted and pampered her, which in normal times she would not have tolerated and he would never have attempted.

The following day Verity was going to Spain so she did not ever again have to sleep in the flat desecrated by cold, calculated murder. She would have it cleaned out and sold. 'It's not suitable for a comrade anyway, is it?' she said to Edward. 'When I get back I'll buy some modest bed-sit in the East End.'

'No, you won't,' said Edward. 'That's not your style.'

In the morning, Verity telephoned David, explained briefly what had happened to make her take refuge with Edward in the Albany, and asked him to pick her up, go back to the flat with her and pack a few necessaries. They would then take the boat train from Victoria and be in Spain forty-eight hours later. It was evident to Edward as he stood at the doorway unwillingly overhearing her conversation that she could not wait to be away. Edward did not blame her but was a little hurt that David and not he had been selected to take her back to the flat and then on to Victoria.

'Don't be silly,' she said when he hinted at his feelings. 'You have already done enough, more than enough. Now it's David's turn to "do his bit" as they used to say in the war. He says he can find somewhere to garage the Morgan while I am away which is one problem solved. It's so sweet of you to say you'll keep an eye on my flat and . . . that you will bury Max for me.'

As they sipped coffee, strong and black, served by Fenton, who seemed almost light-hearted, whether at seeing his master with a woman or because this particular woman was getting out of his life, Edward could not say, he asked, 'What were you going to do with Max while you were in Spain?'

'I was going to ask you to look after him,' she said brightly.

'Me! And if I had refused?'

'I don't think you would have refused.' She smiled at him in that way she had and he knew she was right: he would not have refused, however inconvenient it might have been.

When the porters alerted them that Griffiths-

345

Jones had arrived, Verity put her arms round Edward's neck and kissed him on the lips. 'Don't look so mournful,' she said. 'I'll be back soon and perhaps we can detect another murder. I'm sorry we weren't very successful in putting General Craig's killer behind bars. Perhaps your theory was right though, and he was his own murderer. Still, I'm not altogether convinced but . . . but what does it matter.' Then, seeing that her high spirits were making him even more gloomy, she added, 'We've had fun, haven't we, Edward? I mean, not fun exactly but it was interesting, wasn't it?'

'Yes, of course,' he muttered. 'I think we make a good team. Here, let me come and see you off.'

'Oh no,' she said hurriedly. 'I'd rather you didn't. Let's say goodbye here.' She kissed him again as though now there was nothing to fear from being intimate. 'I must go. I'll send you a postcard from Barcelona.'

'I'll look for your name in the *New Gazette*,' he responded, trying to sound cheerful.

She made a little grimace as though she was going to say something but then, perhaps realizing there was nothing else to say, she raised her hand in a half-wave and disappeared down the corridor clutching a small valise.

Edward was left feeling curiously desolate. He sat in his leather armchair and stared at the ceiling until he guessed that Verity and David must have gone, then he strolled aimlessly down to the hall. He had nowhere to go. Amy was in America and he did not want to see any of his relatives. Then he remembered that he had promised Lord Weaver to visit Hermione. He said she had been asking about him. In any case, he had a few questions that he

346

wanted to put to her about . . . but Verity had said it did not matter any more. Perhaps she was right, but even so it was at least something to do.

* * *

Hermione was sitting up in her hospital bed looking pale and much thinner than when he had last seen her. Her hair was lank and her eyes feverish. Edward was quite alarmed at her appearance but she seemed delighted to see him.

'It is kind of you to have come, Lord Edward,' she said formally. 'Mummy's coming at lunch time but I get very bored.'

'When do they say you can go home?' Edward asked, sitting himself down on a metal chair beside the bed.

'I don't know—not for ages, perhaps not ever,' she said dramatically. 'Of course, they won't give me any straight answers but I get the feeling I may have damaged myself worse than . . . worse than they first thought.'

'Oh, I am sorry. You look much better,' he lied gallantly.

'Thanks,' she said, not pretending to believe him.

'I am afraid I didn't come here just to see how you were. You see, I have come to the conclusion that you killed General Craig but that you were really trying to kill someone else. Am I right?'

Hermione looked at him long and meditatively as if she were trying to decide something or as if she were judging him.

'Look,' she said at last, heaving a great sigh, 'I didn't think much of you at first. I thought you were a prig and you made me ashamed of myself. Then I suppose I got some sort of crush on you and you were nice to me even when I had treated you very shoddily, so I think I owe you the truth. I can't see it matters now,' she added, unknowingly echoing Verity's words. 'It has been a terrible burden and I would like to tell someone. I'm not religious else I could confess to a priest but if it won't be too much of a burden I would be just as happy to confess it all to you. Is that unfair of me?'

'No,' said Edward gently. 'Not unfair at all. I think I know what you are going to tell me but I would like to hear it from your own lips.'

'I don't know why,' she went on as though she had hardly heard him, 'but there are some things I really can't tell Mummy and I don't dare tell the police.'

'Of course,' said Edward. 'Fire away.'

'I gather,' she began, 'that the inquest came back with an accidental death verdict?'

'Yes, they seem to think Craig muddled up his pills.'

'But you don't think so?' She looked at him sharply.

'What does it matter what I think?' he said. 'But no, as it happens, I think it was an accident but of a different kind.'

'It matters to me what you think,' she said simply. 'I was pretty odious to you and yet you stood by me—saved my life even—and when you came to see me I lied to you. At least, I did not tell you the whole truth.'

Edward said, 'You don't have to tell me anything.'

'Well, as I say, I think I owe you something—I

348

think I owe you the truth. What do you think happened?'

'I thought at first that the General was murdered but I ended up thinking he might have been hoist by his thingamyjig.'

'What do you mean?'

'I thought he might have meant to kill your father but by accident killed himself.'

'Goodness me!' Hermione sounded amused. 'But why should he have wanted to kill my stepfather?'

There it was again, Edward thought, the careful definition of her relationship with her mother's husband.

'I think he was obsessed with the way the British press was, as he saw it, being over-sympathetic to Germany's territorial demands which he thought brought a new war closer.'

'But that's not a motive for murder!'

'It might be. Don't forget how much it means to your stepfather's generation to prevent another war with Germany. And there was something else,' he said reluctantly, seeing the disbelief in her eyes. 'Your stepfather was going to print a story about the General suggesting that he had been responsible for killing unarmed German prisoners during the war.'

'I see,' said Hermione meditatively. 'Perhaps, after all, then I ought to leave it at that.'

'It is whatever you want but, as you said, it might help you to tell someone exactly what happened and why. I promise I won't tell anyone. Why should I? What would be the point?'

'Oh, I don't mind about that so much, though I would not want to hurt my mother,' she added, and

349

Edward was pleased she was able to think of someone else beside herself.

'I was trying to kill my stepfather because I hated him, because he came between me and my mother, and because he wouldn't give me any more money to buy drugs even though he had oodles of it. In fact, it was all he was good for: money. Then, just a few weeks before we went to Mersham, he had dared to confess to us—my mother and me—that he had a daughter and that he was proposing to bring her into the family. I hated him even more then for the insult to my mother.'

'You were jealous of Amy Pageant?'

'Not jealous—I just could not bear the idea that there was someone he loved more than my mother, more than me. The next thing, he would cut me out of his will—he hated me, I know he did—and leave all his money to her.'

Edward shook his head. 'I think you are wrong; he does love you, or he wants to, if you will let him. I don't understand why, once you had decided to do this horrible thing, you settled on doing it at Mersham. Surely, that was an odd time and place to choose?'

'Well, I was desperate and anyway I did not see him much at home. We kept out of each other's way. And I thought no one would know it was me if I did it "in public", you might say—and I was right, wasn't I?'

'You are forgetting,' Edward said, 'you killed General Craig, not your stepfather, and they could hardly suspect you of killing a man with whom you had no connection.'

Again, it was as if Hermione did not hear him. She was reliving events in her own mind: 'You see, as I told you, the only reason I agreed to come to Mersham was that I needed to see Charlie Lomax. He was supplying me with dope and he was keeping me short. He wanted more money—much more money—money I did not have, and when I couldn't pay he said he would teach me a lesson.'

'Teach you a lesson?'

'Yes. He thought if I became desperate enough I would get the money somehow even if I had to steal it.'

'Wouldn't your stepfather have given you money if you had explained everything to him?'

'I had already tried that and he had refused me. He hated drugs and said under no circumstances was he going to pay for them. He wanted me to go into some sort of a clinic but I told him to go and boil his head. Anyway, when I got to Mersham I discovered Charlie Lomax had cried off. I had thought that if I got him invited to Mersham, as he begged me to, he would have had to come—he was the most frightful snob—but I was wrong. Obviously, at the last moment, the thought of meeting me there scared him off or maybe he was still torturing me. I was at my wit's end, really desperate. I plugged myself with the last of my heroin supply. Then, as I told you, my mother came into my room just as I was giving myself the injection. That made me even madder. I love my mother, in fact she's the only person I have ever loved and I never wanted to hurt her but I did . . . I have.

'When I knew you were coming instead of Lomax I thought I would at least make you suffer. You seemed to me to be just the sort of stuck-up prig I hated. I think I was wrong, but who cares—it's too late now. Then I remembered that it wasn't you I hated: it was my stepfather. It was he who had stolen my mother from me and it was he who was making me suffer now by not giving me money for the drugs I was desperate for. It was fortunate really, the Duchess took all us women out to drink coffee in the drawing-room. I hadn't had an opportunity to poison my stepfather's drink during the meal and now I thought I had lost my chance for good. But then you and Miss Browne arrived. In the fuss, while everyone crowded into the hall, I slipped out of the French windows in the drawing-room and round to the dining-room windows which I knew were open. Then I saw all the port glasses, mostly half-drunk, so I knew they would be finished when everyone settled down. The glasses were all in a muddle and I wasn't sure which was my stepfather's—however, I knew where he was sitting. So I took the glass nearest me which turned out to be General Craig's and broke the capsule of cyanide into it and then pushed it in front of my stepfather's place.'

'That was a very wicked thing to do,' said Edward, aghast. 'So what did you do next?'

'I ran back through the windows, then into the drawing-room and attached myself to the little crowd of ladies who were seeping into the hall to greet you. No one knew I had been missing, though maybe my mother did, I'm not sure. Anyway, then we all went into the dining-room. I made sure everyone could see where I was and what I was doing, which was nothing except showing interest in what had happened to your car and how you had been rescued by Miss Browne.'

'And then . . . ?'

'And then I saw the Bishop—silly old fool—push

the glass I had poisoned back to the General's place.'

'Why didn't you warn him?'

'How could I?'

'You could have knocked over his glass or something.'

'I don't know, it all happened so fast. The General drank and was making those terrible noises before . . . before I knew what was happening.'

'But you are sorry now?'

'I suppose I am sorry about General Craig though he seemed an old idiot to me and Mummy says he was going to die anyway. I'm not sorry I tried to kill my stepfather, just sorry I didn't succeed. I might be so rich now,' she said the last words dreamily, 'but it doesn't matter.'

'Of course it matters,' said Edward. 'It was a wicked thing you did. Don't you understand that, Hermione?'

'Maybe, but that wasn't the way I thought of it. I was high, don't forget, and this just seemed a suitable way of getting revenge and, I hoped, getting my hands on a great deal of money. I was feeling really strange. You don't know what it feels like being without dope—you will do anything . . . anything.'

Edward looked at her with horror and pity. Here was a girl who had what most people would say was everything but in fact she had nothing.

'But how had you got hold of the cyanide?' said Edward at last.

'Oh, Charlie had given it to me for a dare once. I had been saying I had nothing to live for and he said, "Well, end it then, you stupid cow. No one will care," something like that. I didn't use it then but I stored it up to use one day.'

'How did you end up in Lomax's house filled with drugs? I suppose what you told me last time was a pack of lies. Did you see who killed Lomax?'

'I killed him, stupid.' Hermione looked at him with such cold contempt it made him shudder. 'After the General died instead of my stepfather I was more desperate than ever. I had to get drugs so I had to get to Charlie Lomax and *make* him give me what I wanted. I knew the only place I could be sure of meeting him was the Cocoanut Grove so I made you take me there. As soon as I spotted him I made a beeline for him and he wasn't able to escape from me this time. I cornered him in Captain Gordon's office. I told them both I was desperate and I said if they didn't give me what I wanted I would go to the police. Captain Gordon said Charlie was to take me home and give me what I needed. I think he wanted me out of the way. He was having some trouble with his suppliers and he was afraid if I went to my stepfather or the police—not that I ever would, of course—he would be in even more trouble.

'I don't know what they intended to do with me but when we got to that place Lomax called home he started teasing me. He said I was a no good rich bitch and that I had promised to bring him new clients from among my friends and I had let him down. I said I didn't have any friends but he didn't believe me. Then he said I was so ugly and . . . well, he made all sorts of horrible remarks about me. He left me and went off to the lavatory where I knew he stored his dope. There was a carving knife on the table beside a mouldy loaf of bread and I picked it up and followed him. He hadn't closed the lavatory door and he had his back to me. I swear I didn't know what I was going to do but he heard me and turned around. I remember he lifted his hands in the air and smiled so I stabbed him. When I was sure he was dead I went looking for his drugs cache which I eventually found in the lavatory, taped to the top of the water pan thing. Then I pushed myself full of really good stuff.'

'Did you mean to kill yourself?'

'No . . . I don't know, I just wanted to be out of it all and I was.'

'So when I found you so near to death and called the police, it was natural that we should think Lomax had been killed by the dope ring he was involved with and that they had tried to kill you because you were there and saw what happened.'

'Yes, I suppose I was just lucky.'

'Lucky!' Edward exclaimed. Hermione lay back on her pillow ghastly pale and seemed not to want to say anything more.

At last Edward said gently, 'How did you start taking dope, anyway?'

Hermione opened her eyes. 'The usual thing.' She spoke in such a low voice Edward had to bend forward to catch her words. 'I was bored and I was ugly. No one seemed to like me except my poor mother. To go to all those dances and balls knowing everyone hates you and no one wants to dance with you is awful. I used to go with someone and as soon as we reached the party the man would disappear and I would see him dancing with some girl prettier and nicer than me. Sometimes I spent hours in the "powder-room" so people could not see I had no one to dance with and that was depressing. If I hadn't been so rich I wouldn't even

355

have been invited to most of them anyway. Maybe that would have been a good thing. I used to take Benzedrine before going out in the evening to make me feel more confident and then more of the stuff when I was sitting in the Ladies. You can get it—Benzedrine—in Harrods, you know, and morphine, lots of stuff like that sold in kits, like first aid, you know. Then Charlie Lomax was nice to me and he said he could fix me up with something better and there I went.'

'Did he have lots of customers?'

'Charlie? Oh yes, "society" is full of drugs. Everyone knows it but no one says anything. It's funny, I used to call it "my sweet poison". It made you feel so good, so warm, so content, but you always knew, in the back of your mind, that there was something better just round the corner.'

Shaken and at a loss for words, Edward said finally, 'The story you have told me is a frightful one, Hermione. I understand that you were a victim of unscrupulous, evil men but to try and kill your stepfather—'

'But don't you see,' she said, grabbing his hand, 'he killed me or tried to. He stole my mother and then he wouldn't give me the money to buy the dope sold in the club which he owns.'

Hermione's agitation was horrible to see, and as soon as he could release his hand he called for a nurse and asked for something to calm her. The nurse looked at him askance but he was beyond caring.

When he left the hospital Edward felt drained and unutterably weary. He wandered about the city streets trying to comprehend what he had been told. It was a ghastly story. His self-esteem was at rock bottom. He had thought he was so much cleverer than Inspector Pride but actually he was stupider, much stupider. He had worked out his own theories without any evidence and decided he had got at the truth when he was really nowhere near it. Sensible, clean, honest Connie had seen it: she had said murderers kill for revenge, love and hate, greed—not for politics.

He decided he would go and see Blanche. Perhaps he could understand more about Hermione if he talked to her. At least it would comfort him to talk to someone he liked and whose opinions he respected. He could not tell her that her daughter was a murderer, of course; he could tell no one.

When he reached Eaton Place he discovered the door of the Weavers' house was open and Lady Weaver was coming out, obviously in a state of great distress. She saw Edward and at first seemed not to know who he was.

'Lady Weaver, Blanche,' said Edward, 'is there something the matter?'

'Oh, Lord Edward, it is you. Yes, there is something wrong. I was just going to the hospital. It is Hermione—my daughter Hermione. They telephoned me to say she's dead.'

CHAPTER NINETEEN

SATURDAY AND AFTER

'Oh God, but I have only just come from there.'
'You were visiting Hermione?'

'I was very worried about her. She seemed feverish. I called the nurse.'

Blanche was looking at him oddly and, ridiculously, he did feel guilty—as though he had killed her. Perhaps he had; perhaps by easing her soul of its great burden he had killed her. If so, surely it was just—God taking her because she had caused so much misery. No, that was not the way it worked; she was a poor girl, deeply unhappy, maddened by drugs.

'Please,' he said, 'may I come to the hospital with you?'

Blanche made no objection—she seemed indifferent whether he came or not. In the taxi he said, 'Does Lord Weaver know?'

Blanche, who was staring blindly out of the taxi window, said she had telephoned him at his office and he was going straight to the hospital. When they arrived they found Weaver already there. He was smoking a cigar but when he saw his wife he threw it in an ashtray and took her in his arms and they held each other. When at last he released her he nodded to Edward but showed no curiosity as to why he was there to share this very private grief.

Edward followed them into the room where Hermione lay and beside whom Edward had so recently sat hearing her confession. Blanche, when she saw the body of her daughter, livid and mouth slightly agape, broke down into a savage fit of weeping. The nurse hurried to get her water but all Edward could do was to stand there unhappily, wishing he was a thousand miles away. At last, when the weeping had subsided, Blanche turned to him accusingly.

'What were you talking to Hermione about? Did

358

you upset her? She was better yesterday. Why did she die so suddenly? What did you do to her?'

'Please, Blanche, Lord Edward did nothing,' said her husband soothingly. 'The doctor says her liver was irreparably damaged.'

'No, no, he killed her. She was . . . Hermione was getting better . . .'

'I think you had better go, Lord Edward. Please don't take any notice of what Blanche says. We know you did everything you could for Hermione and we are very grateful. We just blame ourselves for not having been there when . . . when she needed us.'

Edward, with relief, left the room and the hospital. He knew he ought not to be upset at what the distressed mother had said to him but he was, of course. He had failed. Wherever he went there was death. He had come to England from Africa with a light heart determined to do something useful but all he had done was . . . Oh God! Suddenly it came to him that there might still be another death to lay on his conscience. He stepped out into the street and hailed a passing taxi and gave the address in Cadogan Square.

During the short journey, he tried to make sense of what Hermione had told him. Did he believe her story? She was such a liar, but yes, he did. There was something so matter-of-fact about her confession, so convincing in its detail, that he could not disbelieve her. He had been repulsed by her complete lack of remorse. She had killed an innocent man; never mind that he was dying of cancer, he had a right to live his life to the end. She had attempted to murder her stepfather who had tried to love her and whom she had rejected. She had murdered Charlie Lomax, a man responsible for much misery and perhaps even death among the young people he supplied with drugs: one could not regret his passing but it had been murder and, in killing Lomax, Hermione had almost certainly made it impossible for the police to assemble enough evidence to put Captain Gordon and his cronies behind bars.

Hermione had blamed all her troubles on drugs and no doubt she had exacerbated her psychological problems by taking heroin and cocaine, but when Edward considered the problems overcome by those who had been wounded or lost loved ones in the war her troubles seemed very small beer.

He had set out, casually enough, to discover how General Craig had died. He had approached the problem as though it were a simple academic exercise. He had, in his arrogance, believed he had worked out what had happened to make the old soldier drink poison, only to be confronted with the knowledge that he had totally failed to understand one single thing or recognize motive and evidence even when they stared him in the face. He was disgusted with himself.

In this mood of self-flagellation he paid off the taxi in Cadogan Square and knocked on the door of the General's house. There was no answer. He knocked again and then again. He had just decided that Jeffries was not in the house and was turning away when there was a shuffling and groaning as if he had woken the dead and the door opened a crack.

'It's you, is it?' said the valet. Edward was momentarily shocked out of his introspection. The veneer of respect a valet would normally show towards a visitor to the house, which he would have supposed in Jeffries' case to have been thicker than his own skin, had been jettisoned, and Edward's immediate thought was that the man was mentally disturbed.

'What do you want?' said Jeffries rudely.

'May I come in?' Edward was sure that if he did not act immediately the door would be shut in his face so, taking advantage of Jeffries' hesitation, he pushed his way into the house as though there was no question of his not being admitted. The house looked darker and dirtier than ever.

'How long are you stayin' here, Jeffries?' said Edward, trying to inject normality into the conversation.

'I can stay here until the house is sold,' said the old man, grudgingly.

'Then what? Where will you go to then?'

'I don't know. I will find somewhere,' Jeffries mumbled.

'Look here, man,' said Edward with forced energy, 'you mustn't go to pieces. It would have been the last thing the General would have wanted.'

'Why are you here?' said Jeffries fiercely, as though he resented being taken out of his misery and loneliness even for a moment.

'I thought you would like to hear what I have discovered about your master's death,' Edward replied.

'You don't know anything, otherwise you would have said at the inquest,' Jeffries said bitterly.

'I do know now,' he said. 'I haven't any proof but am afraid your master was killed by mistake. One of the guests at that dinner wanted Lord Weaver dead and killed the General instead.'

Edward was disconcerted to find that Jeffries displayed no interest in what he was saying. He was shifting his feet as if he could hardly bear to have Edward in his presence. The latter, if pressed, might have told Jeffries who the murderer was if it would have given the old servant peace of mind, but he asked no questions. As his eyes began to adjust to the gloom he was able to examine the man. He was shocked by what he saw: he was dirty and haggard and Edward could smell his rank body odour.

'Jeffries, are you eating properly?' he asked ingenuously.

The man seemed not to hear him. He stood there in the hall sunk in apathy, too depressed to move. Edward decided he must get help. Clearly the man should not be left on his own. He tried once more to rouse him.

'You miss the General, don't you?' he said gently. 'How long was it that you worked for him?'

'He was all the family I ever had,' Jeffries replied at last, as if answering in his sleep. 'He took me to be his batman as a young soldier in South Africa and I looked after him, along with Lady Dorothy when he married her, God bless her, until the day of his death. And now it is finished.'

'The General would not want you say that,' Edward chided him. 'He would want you to have a long and peaceful retirement.'

Jeffries did not even bother to answer him. It was as if he had never spoken. Edward was suddenly reminded of his father's grief when Frank had been killed. Here was the same abandonment to sorrow, the same surrender to depression which in his father's case his two living sons had seen as a rejection of themselves. When an object of such devotion is taken away, when the source of all hope is removed, the will to live is also destroyed.

Reluctantly, he at last left the house, promising to return. As he strolled disconsolately back towards Piccadilly brooding over Jeffries, he was aware of a nagging feeling that he had omitted to do something he ought to have done. It was not until he was actually walking up the steps into the Albany that he remembered: the other capsule. Hermione had not used General Craig's cyanide capsule; Jeffries had said he was keeping it 'safe'. He ought to have taken it from the man and destroyed it. His heart lurched and without a moment's further thought he turned on his heel, much to the porters' amazement, walked into Piccadilly and stopped a taxi. 'Cadogan Square!' he said to the driver. 'As fast as you can.'

The traffic was bad and finally, in his agitation, he threw some money at the taxi driver and took to his heels. In ten minutes, sweating and panting, he was back at the General's former house. He did not know why he was so certain that Jeffries was intending to end his own life. It wasn't so much his depression, it was perhaps more his having so deeply withdrawn into himself. Then—fool that he was—he had had to start talking about how the old soldier and the valet had met. He cursed himself for his idiocy, and knocked on the door so loudly a constable on his beat asked him what was the matter.

'Look here, constable, this is the house of General Craig who died two weeks ago.'

'I remember, sir—he was poisoned, wasn't he? Nasty business.'

'That's right, officer,' said Edward impatiently. 'I'm a friend of the General's and I have reason to believe that the General's valet, who is still living here, means to do away with himself. I know he is here because I saw him an hour ago and I was worried about him then, but now he is not answering the door.'

'Maybe he's out, sir,' said the policeman doubtfully.

'No, no, I tell you, he doesn't go out. Look, there's a window ajar down in the area—can you help me open it?'

'Well, I don't know, sir. That might be breaking and entering, sir.'

'Not if we have reason to believe something's amiss. Come on, officer, I don't think we have much time.'

The constable made up his mind and responded to the urgency and authority in Edward's voice. Together, they set about forcing the window open. It took longer than they had expected because it was stuck, either by dirt or just age, and was reluctant to budge, but at last it gave and the two men—Edward first, followed by the constable—clambered through. They were in the butler's pantry and Edward knew that Jeffries' sitting-room and bedroom were just the other side of the narrow passage. Edward thought he smelt it before he saw anything—a faint scent of burnt almonds. Jeffries was sitting in his armchair, his hands clasped in front of him, almost as though in prayer. His face was contorted with the agony of his death but there clearly had not been the same convulsions which had brought the General juddering to the floor. Looking at the dead man, Edward guessed that he had broken the cyanide capsule in his mouth. There was no glass or cup beside him or on the floor which might indicate that he had taken the cyanide in drink. Perhaps Jeffries had not wished to risk diluting the poison and not accomplishing his own death, or perhaps it had just never occurred to him to try and make his passing easier.

Edward turned to see the constable holding a silk handkerchief to his mouth, trying not to retch. 'We are too late,' Edward said sadly. 'There's a telephone in the hall, I'll go and ring up Inspector Pride at Scotland Yard.'

Pride, when he arrived at the house, once again treated Edward as an object of suspicion but he was forced to admit that even in the absence of any sort of suicide note, Jeffries' death could only have been self-destruction.

'Who was there to write a note to?' Edward said. 'The two people he loved, the General and his lady, were already where he was going.'

CHAPTER TWENTY

ENDINGS

The General might have been pleased that his funeral, while not as grand as Earl Haig's, was still solemn and memorable. Many of his former comrades in arms came out from retirement to see the old soldier interred in Westminster Abbey, in itself a signal honour, and his pall bearers were six

365

senior serving officers. In the address, reference was made to his patriotism, to his courage and to his achievements on and off the battlefield. Edward listened from half-way back and was relieved that no mention was made of the nature of his death or, of course, of killing prisoners of war. The General deserved this at least, Edward considered.

Jeffries was buried in a cemetery of especial ugliness and anonymity in west London. Edward, who had organized the funeral, went there with the dead man's sister, a cross-faced woman who seemed interested only in her brother's money. He refused to go back to town with the woman, of whose company he had already had quite enough, and instructed Fenton to drive her to Victoria in the Lagonda while he made his own way back. He walked for a mile or two before jumping on a bus which meandered slowly through parts of the city which he had never visited and hardly knew existed.

At home, Fenton brought him a whisky and soda, and he read once again a postcard which had come that morning from Spain. In her rather childish scrawl Verity had written: 'Barcelona is beautiful and I am learning Spanish. Hope all is well, see you, love V.'

Edward felt he had to get out of London, out of England. The air in his rooms suddenly felt tired and stale. When Fenton came to tell him his supper was ready he said, 'Fenton, I think it is time we had a change of scene. We shall depart these shores for foreign climes in search of spiritual refreshment and adventure. What say you?'

'I shall attend to the matter in the morning. Will it be Spain or the United States of America you intend to visit, my lord?'

'Good God, Fenton!' Edward expostulated. 'If you are not careful I shall suspect you of exhibiting a sense of humour and that would be one shock too many in my weakened state. Before we go anywhere I have one final funeral to attend to, have I not?'

'Yes, my lord. I am afraid the little dog is beginning to smell.'

' "If you find him not within this month, you shall nose him as you go up the stairs into the lobby"?'

'Yes, my lord.'

'Right, no time like the present. Give him to me and then fetch the Lagonda.'

Edward had, he knew, one other debt to pay: he had promised to go and see Celia Larmore and tell her of his last meeting with her husband. But that would have to wait. First he must fill his lungs with country air.

On the road, the wind in his face revivified him and the cares of the past two weeks slipped away. He put his foot on the accelerator and pushed it to the floor. He heard the sound of bells. At first he thought they were in his head. Then he looked in the mirror.

'Blast it!' It was a police car. He slowed and stopped by the side of the road. A large bovine policeman got slowly out of the car and came over to the Lagonda.

'Good afternoon, sir. And where might you be going in so much of a hurry?'

'I am going to a funeral,' said Edward haughtily.

'I see, sir. Well, it may be your own funeral if you drive at that speed. You must have been doing sixty-five at least.'

It was fortunate the policeman did not demand to look in the boot of the Lagonda where his suspicions might have been aroused by the spade and the corpse it contained.

'Yes, I am sorry, officer,' said Edward, suddenly contrite. 'It was foolish of me but then I am foolish. I shall go more slowly in the future.'

The police officer looked at him, trying to gauge whether the young man was drunk or just fey. Deciding on the latter, he chose to be generous.

'I have given you a warning, sir. Take heed of it. Next time you may not be so fortunate.'

'Thank you, officer. I promise I will be good.'

Edward drove on slowly for another hour until he reached a stretch of woodland he had always liked, on the downs near Hungerford. He found a place in a circle of ancient trees and dug a hole deep enough to keep out the foxes and buried Max. When he had finished, he rolled a stone above the grave and then, perspiring, went to sit in the Lagonda to rest before setting off back to London. He tried to think of a prayer to say but nothing appropriate came to him. Then, faintly, above the rustling of the trees in the wind, he heard the tumbling skylarks choiring and he knew that their cries were all the prayers Max needed.